Tales of the White Knight:

Tirant lo Blanc

Tales of the White Knight:

Tirant lo Blanc

JOANOT MARTORELL
&
MARTI JOHAN D'GALBA

Edited and Translated by

Robert S. Rudder

ABOUT THE TRANSLATOR

Robert S. Rudder holds a Ph.D. in Spanish from the University of Minnesota, where he was an instructor for a number of years. He has been a professor of Spanish literature at the University of California, Los Angeles, and at other universities in California. His translations of Spanish and Latin American works have been published in *Poet Lore, Ivory Tower, Greenfield Review* and *Drama & Theatre*. He is the editor and translator of over a dozen books, including the *Lazarillo de Tormes* and *The Celestina*. He is also the author of *The Literature of Spain in English Translation*, and *The Paradox of Saint Teresa of Avila*.

Cover illustration (Acuarela Tirant y Carmesina)
by Alicia Arlandis

Front illustration from the Spanish translation of 1511

Copyright © 2013 by SVENSON Publishers
Claremont, CA.

All rights reserved.

ISBN:-10:1491055049
ISBN-13:978-1491055045

For

José Rubia Barcia

Friend and colleague at UCLA

A true "caballero andante"

TALES OF THE WHITE KNIGHT

INTRODUCTION..ix
CHAPTER I - COUNT WILLIAM OF WARWICK 1
CHAPTER II - THE TOURNAMENT 24
CHAPTER III - SICILY 47
CHAPTER IV - CONSTANTINOPLE.....................................77
CHAPTER V - THE BATTLEFIELD.....................................103
CHAPTER VI - A TRUCE 154
CHAPTER VII - IN THE PRINCESS'S BED 176
CHAPTER VIII - THE BETROTHAL 199
CHAPTER IX - WIDOW REPOSE 235
CHAPTER X - THE BARBARY COAST...............................253
CHAPTER XI - PLAERDEMAVIDA 283
CHAPTER XII - CONQUEST..291
CHAPTER XIII - THE WEDDING 319
CHAPTER XIV - DEATH 331
CHAPTER XV - AFTERMATH 345
DEO GRATIAS..354

JOANOT MARTORELL

TALES OF THE WHITE KNIGHT

INTRODUCTION

"Tirant lo Blanc is the best European novel of the fifteenth century," says Dámaso Alonso in his excellent study.[1] Miguel de Cervantes, writing from the 17th century, affirms: "as far as style is concerned, this is the best book in the world."[2] If this is so, why has the novel all but disappeared from view?

Some place the blame on the language of the original: Catalan, whose literature is not widely read in the original tongue. Others say it is the fault of the erotic scenes -- too shameful for the polite society of earlier times. To my mind, a heavily contributing factor is its rhetoric. As Joseph Vaeth says: "Within this work may be found religious and philosophical discourses, speeches and disputations...; formal debates...; documents and papers...; formal challenges and replies...; dramatic lamentations; long and fervent prayers; and allusions to classical Latin authors, to biblical characters and to figures prominent in medieval literature." He goes on to say that if the novelist had omitted many of these elements, "his book would in that case have been reduced to approximately one-fourth of its present size, but quite probably it would now be considered a masterpiece of narration and dialogue."[3]

Such has been the aim of this translation: The story line has been slightly abridged, but the most dramatic change is that most of the rhetoric has been eliminated.[4]

Who was the author of this spicy, brutally realistic novel of kings and knights of the fifteenth century? We know that Joanot Martorell, son of the king's chamberlain, Francesc Martorell, was born in Valencia in about 1413. He lived in England during the years 1438 and 1439, and also traveled to Naples. Death came to him in 1468. During his life he wrote several letters of combat, and he began to write his novel Tirant lo Blanc in about 1460. Whether or not he actually finished the book is still a matter of debate, for it was not published during his lifetime.

Another writer, Marti Joan de Galba, adds his name as a second author, and says that he wrote the last one-fourth of the book. But he died six months before it was published, and his contribution, if any, is questionable.

And what was the success of this novel? Only 715 copies were printed in 1490. A second edition did not appear until 1497. An abridged translation into Spanish was finally produced in 1511, and no further Spanish editions appeared until the 20th century.[5] It was translated into Italian in the 16th century, into French in the 17th century, and finally into English late in the 20th century.

Of interest is the fact that soon after the appearance of Tirant lo Blanc, and throughout the 16th century, Spain was flooded with novels of chivalry. But these were of quite a different nature. Although the major characters are also knights highly instilled with the code of chivalry, they become involved in fantastic adventures filled with dragons, enchanters, and the like, following the lead of the French romances that were translated into Spanish beginning in the 13th century. These Spanish novels of chivalry were produced in such great numbers and read so widely that no less than Spain's great mystic, Saint Teresa of Avila, was for a time a voracious reader of them.

While Tirant lo Blanc had no literary followers until Cervantes more than one hundred years later, it does have the honor of being "the earliest existing romance of chivalry printed in the Peninsula."[6] This being so, from where did Joanot Martorell receive his inspiration? Although Professor Henry Thomas notes that "the tracing of sources... (may be only) one degree higher than the hunting of cats,"[7] we feel compelled to relate some of the more important discoveries of literary scholarship. The first section of the book is in imitation of an English romance, "Guy of Warwick", in which England fights off a Danish invasion. When Tirant lo Blanc appears for the first time, asleep on his horse, and stumbles upon the hermit who explains at great length the order of chivalry, the entire section (which this present translation omits) is taken from Ramon Lull's Libre del Orde d'Cauayleria.[8] Tirant himself may be an amalgamation of several historical figures: Roger de Flor, Richard Beauchamp, Louis IX, Peter II of Aragon, Joan Hunyadi lo Blanch of Hungary, etc. Tirant's adventures in Africa closely parallel many people, events and place names from Ramon Muntaner's Chronica.[9]

More important than any of these "sources", however, is this question: What did Martorell do with the material that came to him from books, from life, and from his imagination?

Cervantes, writing more than one hundred years after Tirant lo Blanc was published, was sufficiently impressed to talk about it in his Don Quixote not once, but on two separate occasions, in fairly glowing terms.[10] Furthermore, some readers have pointed out scenes that appear to be similar in both books: both Philippe and Don Quixote find holes in their stockings, which leads one into great searching for a lost needle, and the other into even deeper depression; there is a cat-howling episode in both books, etc. And there is one other way that Tirant lo Blanc points the way toward the Quixote: in the framework. Cervantes uses a device often found in the novels of chivalry that preceded his work, stating that his book is no more than a "translation" from another language. (While, in fact, the authors of those books are simply advertising the next novels they intend to write in the series, much as the "Hardy Boys" or "Nancy Drew" series advertise in the final pages of each novel.) But in the Quixote the device has a far deeper purpose: Cervantes informs us that Don Quixote is a flesh and blood figure whose real-life adventures appear in several Arabic histories, and one in particular, by a certain Cide Hamete Benengeli. With the aid of a translator, Cervantes says, he is now bringing the story of Don Quixote's life back into the Spanish tongue. What we have here is, of course, a ploy to make the characters seem more real, and Cervantes makes this assertion with a broad wink, for while we are "suspending our disbelief," we also know that it is nothing more than his artistry.

And what of Tirant lo Blanc? According to Martorell's dedication, his book is also a translation: from the English original, he is translating into Portuguese, and from the Portuguese into Catalan. But where is the English original from which this book is simply a translation? There is no character in English literature or history named Tirant lo Blanc, and discounting the beginning pages, taken from the "Guy of Warwick" romance, there is no book in English from which this one has been translated. As for the translation into Portuguese, there is no book about Tirant in that language. So why does Martorell tell us all this? (Although, as we have noted, other novels of chivalry speak of themselves as "translations", all were printed after the publication of Tirant lo Blanc.) Is this novel then, which Cervantes so admired, also presenting us with a "true history" which has been "translated" in a way similar to the Quixote? Within Tirant lo Blanc we also find allusions to historians who have "originally" set these words down. For example: "Here the book returns to the emperor..." "Hippolytus... performed singular acts of chivalry which this book does not relate, but defers to the books that were written about him." Is there any difference between this and the statements of Cervantes about his characters? ("Here Cide Hamete Benengeli leaves him for an instant and returns to Don Quixote..." "The history goes on to tell that when Sancho saw...") But we are given no broad wink from Martorell. It is all true, he tells us, and there is nothing more to be said. That Martorell died before the work was published, and that Marti Joan de Galba may have made some additions before it was finally published, does not clarify the matter. For De Galba also affirms that the book is no more than a translation from the English to the Portuguese, and from that language into the Valencian tongue, and that he is merely finishing what Martorell was unable to complete.

There are no broad winks. But the characters belie the "history": They come to life as no straight-forward, factual history can bring its subjects to life. As Dámaso Alonso so accurately puts it: this fifteenth century work "is precisely that whip that could excite Cervantes' imagination. Tirant was not yet the modern novel, but in it were many elements, and furthermore, essential elements of what would become the modern novel."[11]

Having read this novel, who could forget the characters that Martorell has brought to life? Who would not feel grief at the death of Tirant and the princess, no less united in soul than Calisto and Melibea in Spain (making their appearance a few short years later in Fernando de Rojas' masterpiece, La Celestina), than Romeo and Juliet in England, and no less tragic. And in remembering Tirant, who would not smile at the thought of him serving as a go-between for Prince Philippe and the infanta, Ricomana. Could anyone be more delightful than the forthright Plaerdemavida (whose name translates literally as "Pleasure-of-My-Life") — surely one of the best delineated characters in any literature. Or anyone more villainous than the odious Widow Repose — a figure stamped indelibly on our minds, wearing her ridiculous red stockings and hat in the bath.

 As Cervantes says: "In (Tirant lo Blanc) knights eat and drink, sleep and die in their own beds, and make their wills before they die…" And his praise for Tirant is also borne out by the characters in the Quixote. For in many of that book's most memorable episodes, they too eat and drink (and regurgitate), they sleep (when someone or something does not awaken them to a new adventure), Don Quixote makes out his will (to the contentment of some of the beneficiaries), and finally he dies in his bed (and Cervantes warns us that no one should try to revive him: "For me alone Don Quixote was born, and I for him… We two alone are as one." This identification of the author with his work was felt no less keenly by Martorell. As he says in his dedication: "And so that no one else may be blamed if errors are found in this work, I, Johanot Martorell, knight, alone wish to bear the responsibility, and no one else with me, for this work has been set down by myself alone…"

 If Don Quixote's Dulcinea did not exist until she took form in his (or in Cervantes') mind, or the windmill that was a giant, or the Cave of Montesinos, they have now come into existence in the mind of every reader of that novel. So may Tirant and his men, the princess, the emperor, Plaerdemavida, also come to life alongside the gentle and not so gentle folk of Cervantes, in every reader's imagination. Let me leave the reader with these words about Tirant lo Blanc by Cervantes: "Take him home and read him, and you will see that what I have said of him is true."[12]

 Finally, thanks are due to the many people who have supported me on this project and on others in the past: To Walter Pattison who awakened me to the excitement and beauty of Spanish literature; to my late friend, Arturo Serrano Plaja, who made a valiant attempt to refine my taste, and who guided me throughout the years; to my many colleagues and friends at the University of Minnesota; and also to good

JOANOT MARTORELL

TALES OF THE WHITE KNIGHT: TIRANT LO BLANC

CHAPTER I -COUNT WILLIAM OF WARWICK

In the fertile, rich and lovely island of England there lived a most valiant knight, noble by his lineage and much more for his courage. In his great wisdom and ingenuity he had served the profession of chivalry for many years and with a great deal of honor, and his fame was widely known throughout the world. His name was Count William of Warwick. This was a very strong knight who, in his virile youth, had practiced the use of arms, following wars on sea as well as land, and he had brought many battles to a successful conclusion.

The count found himself at the advanced age of fifty-five, and moved by divine inspiration he decided to withdraw from the practice of arms and make a pilgrimage to the holy land of Jerusalem. This virtuous count wanted to go, because he felt sorrow and contrition for the many deaths he had caused in his youth.

That evening he told the countess, his wife, about his plans, and although she was virtuous and discreet, she became very upset at the news because she loved him so much. In the morning the count had all his servants, both men and women, come to him, and he said:

"My children and most faithful servants, it is the will of His Divine Majesty that I should leave you, and the time of my return is uncertain. Since the journey will be very dangerous, I want to pay each of you now for all the good services you have rendered to me."

He had a large chest full of money brought out, and to each of his servants he gave much more than he owed, so that they were all very satisfied. Then he gave the countess all his land and all his rights. And he ordered that a ring of gold be made with his and the countess's coat of arms on it, and this ring was made in such a way that it was divided into two parts. Each part was a complete ring in itself, showing half the coat of arms of each of them, and when the two halves were joined together the entire coat of arms could be seen.

When all this had been done, he turned to the virtuous countess, and said kindly:

"I know that you will accept my departure with love and patience, and if it is God's will, my journey will soon be over. I am leaving in your charge everything I have. And here is half of the ring I had made. I beg you dearly to hold it in my stead, and to guard it until I return."

"Oh, dear!" cried the countess. "Then it's true, my lord, that you are leaving without me? At least allow me to go with you so that I can serve you. I would rather die than go on living without you. Just when I was thinking that all my misfortunes were over, I see that my unhappiness is only increasing. I'm left with only this poor son as a pledge from his father, and his sad mother must be consoled with him."

She seized her small son by the hair and pulled it, and then slapped his face, saying:

"Cry, my child, for your father's departure, and you will be good company to your mother."

The tiny infant, who had been born only three months before, burst out crying. The count, seeing both mother and child in tears, felt deeply grieved, and he could not hold back his own tears. And for some time he could not speak, while all three of them wept.

The count took his leave of her, kissing her again and again, tears running freely from his eyes. He said farewell to the other ladies, and when he left he took only one squire with him.

Leaving his city of Warwick, he boarded a ship, and sailed with a good wind, and as time passed he arrived safely at Alexandria. There he disembarked and made his way to Jerusalem. When he reached Jerusalem he confessed his sins, and with great devotion he received the precious body of Jesus Christ. Then he entered the holy sepulcher of Jesus Christ and prayed there fervently and tearfully, with great contrition for his sins.

After visiting all the other sanctuaries, he returned to Alexandria. Then he boarded a ship and went to Venice. When he was near Venice he gave all the money still in his possession to his squire who had served him well, and he arranged a marriage for him so that he would not want to return to England. Then he had his squire spread the news that he had died, and he arranged for merchants to write to England that Count William of Warwick had died while returning from the Holy Land of Jerusalem.

When the countess heard the news, she felt deeply grieved, and went into mourning, and she arranged for the funeral rites that such a virtuous knight deserved. With the passing of time, the count returned alone to his own land, having let his hair grow down to his shoulders, while his beard, completely white, reached to his waist. He was dressed in the habit of the glorious Saint Francis, and lived from charity, and he secretly entered a devout hermitage of Our Lady which was very close to his city of Warwick.

This hermitage was in a lovely spot on a high mountain, with a dense thicket of trees, and a clear running spring. The count retired to this solitary place, and lived alone to escape the materialistic world and to do penance for his sins. Living from charity, he went to his city of Warwick once a week to beg for alms. With his thick beard and long hair the people there did not recognize him, and he went to the countess, his wife, to beg. When she saw him asking for charity so humbly, she made them give him more than they gave any of the others. And he spent his poor, miserable life this way for some time.

Sometime later the great King of Canary was filled with anger because some pirate ships had plundered a village that belonged to him. He left his land with a large armada, and sailing with a favorable wind he reached the fertile, peaceful shores of England.

In the dark of night the entire fleet entered the port of Southampton and all the Moors went ashore very quietly. When they were on land, they put their troops in order and began to attack the island.

When the peace-loving king received the news, he gathered as many men as he could to put up a resistance, and went into battle with the Moors. The fighting was great, indeed: many men died, especially the Christians. Because the Moors were greater in number, the forces of the English king were destroyed. He had to retreat with his remaining men, and he took refuge in a city called Saint Thomas of Canterbury where that holy body now rests.

The King of England mustered more men, and he learned that the Moors were conquering the island, killing many Christian men and dishonoring the women and young girls, making captives of them all. When this Christian king discovered that the Moors held the pass near a watercourse, he placed his forces in a passage at the hour of midnight. But he did not do it very secretly, and the Moors heard of it, and held back until it was broad daylight. Then they pressed them in a very cruel battle where many Christians died, and those whose lives were spared fled with the unfortunate king, while the Moorish king remained in the camp.

Great was the misfortune of this Christian king who lost nine battles, one after another, and had to withdraw to the city of London. When the Moors learned of it they laid siege to the city. Every day there was heavy fighting until finally the poor king was forced to leave

London, and he went toward the mountains, passing through the city of Warwick.

When the countess heard that the king was fleeing to that city, she had food and everything necessary prepared for the night. The countess, who was a very prudent woman, began to think of how she could strengthen her city so that it would not be lost so quickly, and as soon as she saw the king she said to him:

"Virtuous king, I see that Your Grace, and all of us on this island, are in great danger. But Sire, if Your Highness would like to remain in this city, you will find it abundant in provisions and everything necessary for war. My lord and husband, William of Warwick, who was count in this land, provided this city and his castle with arms as well as bombards, cross-bows and culverins, and many other kinds of artillery. And divine Providence, in its mercy, has given us a great abundance of fruit from the land for the last four years. So Your Grace may be safe here."

"I am very happy", said the king, "to stay here, and I pray you, countess, to arrange things so that my army will have everything they need."

The countess and two of her ladies immediately left the king, and went with the magistrates of the city through the houses, making them bring wheat and barley and everything necessary. When the king and his men saw what a great abundance there was of everything, they were very pleased.

When the Moors discovered that the king had left the city of London, they pursued him until they learned that he had taken refuge in the city of Warwick. On the way the Moors attacked and took a castle called Killingworth, two leagues from where the king was. Since they had now conquered a great part of the kingdom, the Moorish king appeared with all his forces before the city of Warwick. The wretched Christian king, seeing that there was no hope, did not know what to do: he climbed to the top of a tower in the castle, and watched the huge body of Moors burning and destroying villas and castles, killing as many Christians as they could, both women and men. Those who were able to escape came running and shouting toward the city. Their terrible screams could be heard a good half league away, and it would have been better for them to die than to become captives of the infidels.

As the king watched the immense suffering and destruction, he thought he would die from all the grief he felt. Unable to look any longer at the desolation, he came down from the tower and went into a small chamber where he began to sigh deeply. Tears ran from his eyes, and he lamented more gravely than any man had ever done. The stewards were outside the chamber listening to the king's agony, and when he had cried and lamented at length, he said:

"Lord, Thy compassion and pity will not allow for this. Thy mercy will not allow Thy Christian people, great sinners though they may be, to be afflicted by the scourge of the Moors. Rather, defend and preserve them and let them be returned to Thy holy service so that they may serve Thee and praise Thee and return glory unto Thee."

While the poor king was lamenting, he put his head down on the bed, and it seemed to him that he saw a very beautiful lady coming through the doorway to his chamber, dressed in white damask, holding a small child in her arms. Following her were many other ladies, all singing the Magnificat. When he had finished his prayer, the lady walked toward the king, and placing her hand upon his head, she said:

"Oh, king, be doubtful of nothing. Be very confident that the Son and the Mother will help you in this great trial. The first man you see with a long beard who asks you for alms in the name of God, kiss him on the mouth as a sign of peace, and beg him graciously to put aside the habit, and make him captain over all the people."

The poor king awoke and saw nothing. He was astonished at the dream, and he thought about it a great while, remembering everything he had seen. Then he left the chamber, and there stood all the principal knights, who told the king:

"Your Grace, all the Moors have set up their tents in front of the city."

The king did everything possible to have the city well guarded that night.

The following morning the hermit-count climbed the high mountain to gather herbs for his sustenance, and he saw the great number of Moors teeming over all the land. He left his desert habitation and went into the city.

The poor old man, who had spent several days on a diet of nothing but herbs, saw that the city was in deep sorrow, and he went to the castle to beg alms from the countess. When he was inside the castle he saw the king coming from mass, and when he saw him so nearby, he sank to his knees and begged him in God's name to give him alms. The king remembered the dream and helped him up. Then he kissed him on the mouth, took hold of his hand and led him into a room. When they had sat down, the king said to him:

"I beg you to help and advise us in our time of need, for I see that you are a holy man and a friend of Jesus Christ. I beg you dearly, if you love God and if you have charity in your heart, cast off the clothing you are wearing for penance, and dress yourself in the clothes of charity, which are arms. For with God's help and your command we will have a glorious victory over our enemies."

When the king had finished these words, the hermit began to speak:

"My lord, I am astonished that Your Grace is asking me, a poor, weak man, for advice and help. As Your Excellency can see, my old, weak body is in a state of decrepitude because of its many years and the harsh life I've led so long on the mountain, eating only herbs and bread. I don't have the strength to bear arms. I beg Your Excellency to allow me to decline."

The king became very pained at this answer, and said:

"Reverend Father, I kneel at your feet and with these tears I again beg you, if you are a steadfast Christian, to have compassion on me, a miserable king, and on all Christians. All their hope and mine is in the mercy of God and in your great virtue. Don't refuse me this."

The painful tears of the king moved the hermit to pity, and his heart softened.

After a brief pause while the hermit made the king rise, he said:

"Out of love for you, my king, I will obey your commands and try to save you and your kingdom. And, if necessary, I will place myself in the thick of battle, old as I am, to defend Christianity and bring the haughty Mohammedan sect to its knees, with the understanding that Your Excellency will be guided by my advice."

The king answered: "Reverend Father, since you grant me so much grace, I promise you, on my word as king, that I will not go one step beyond your orders."

"Now, my lord," said the hermit, "when you are outside in the great hall, show a happy and very content face to the knights and all the people, and speak to them very complacently. And when you dine, eat well and enjoy yourself, and show much more happiness than you ordinarily do, so that all those who have lost hope will regain it. For a lord or a captain should never wear a sad face, no matter how great an adversity there may be, so that his people will not be discouraged. Have some Moorish garments brought to me, and you shall see what I am going to do. When I was on my way to the Holy Land of Jerusalem I stayed in Alexandria, and in Beirut they taught me the Moorish tongue, because I was there many days. In Beirut I learned to make explosives of certain materials that delay six hours before they ignite, but when they do, they could burn up the entire world, and all the water in the world would not be able to extinguish them, unless oil and pine resin is used."

"It is astonishing," said the king, "that they can only be extinguished with oil or pine resin. I thought water would put out any fire in the world."

"No, my lord," said the hermit. "If Your Grace will allow me to go to the castle gate, I will bring you a special substance, and with clear water or wine you will be able to light a torch."

"In faith," said the king, "I will take great pleasure in seeing it."

The hermit immediately went to the castle gate since, when he entered, he had seen quicklime there, and he picked up a little sod and came back to the king. Then he took some water, and throwing it on the quicklime he lighted it the way a straw lights a candle.

The king said: "I would never have been able to believe such a thing if I had not seen it with my own eyes. Now I am certain there is nothing that men cannot do. I beg you, Reverend Father, please tell me what we need to make the explosives."

"My lord," said the hermit, "I will go and buy it, because it is much better to know if the materials are good, and I have made them many times with my own hands. When they are made, Sire, I will go to the Moors' camp alone, and put the explosives near the king's tent. At the hour of midnight the explosives will ignite and all the Moors will run there to put out the fire, and Your Grace will be armed and waiting with all your men. When you see the huge fire, attack them with all your forces, and Your Lordship may be sure that ten thousand of your men will cause confusion among one hundred thousand of theirs."

The hermit's words pleased the king, and he gave deep thanks for his offer, and was very happy. He immediately gave orders that everything the hermit had commanded should be carried out.

The hermit, who had left the king, soon returned with the things they needed for the explosives, and he said to the king:

"My lord, there is only one element we lack, but I know that the countess has it. When her husband, William of Warwick, was alive, he had a great deal of it since it can be used for many things."

The king said: "Then I want both of us to go to the countess now to get it."

The king sent word to the countess that he wanted to speak with her. When the countess came out of her room she saw the king and the hermit.

"Countess," said the king, "by your grace and virtue, be so kind as to give me a little sulfur, the kind which causes heat and does not burn itself up, the kind that the count, your husband, put into the torches so that no matter how much the wind blew they would not go out."

The countess answered: "Who told Your Grace that my husband, William of Warwick, could make torches like that with that kind of flame?"

"Countess," said the king, "this hermit standing here."

And the countess quickly went to the weapons chamber, and she brought back so much of it that the king was highly pleased.

When the king had returned to the great hall where the meal was already prepared, he took the hermit by the hand and sat down at the table, making the hermit sit at his side, honoring him as he deserved. The king's courtiers were astonished at the great honor the king was bestowing upon the hermit, and the countess was even more astonished because she was accustomed to giving him alms. And she said to her ladies:

"Oh, how angry I am at my great ignorance! Why did I not honor this poor hermit much more? Now I see that he must be a man who has led a very holy life."

Rising from the table, the King of England gave the hermit permission to go and make the explosives. A few days later, when they were finished, the hermit went to the king and said to him:

"Sire, if Your Grace will give me leave, I will carry out our plan. Your Excellency should have all the men get ready.'"

The king said that he would. In the dark of night the hermit changed into the Moorish clothing that was prepared for him. He went out through a back door of the castle very secretly, and no one saw him. Then he went into the Moors' camp.

When he thought the time right, he threw the explosives into the camp, near the tent of a great captain who was a relative of the Moorish king. And when it was almost midnight the fire broke out, and it grew so great and so terrible that everyone was astonished at the enormous flames. The king and the other Moors, unarmed, hurried to where the fire was greatest in order to put it out. But instead of being extinguished, the more water they threw on it, the more brightly it burned.

When the King of England saw the huge fire, he went out of the city, armed, and with the few men he still had he attacked the Moors. And they brought such great destruction to them that it was fearful, and they spared no one.

When the Moorish king saw such a large fire and so many of his men dead, he mounted a horse and fled. He took shelter in a castle he had taken, named Killingworth, together with all those who had escaped the camp, and they recovered their resolve.

He and all the other Moors were astonished at how they had been defeated, and they could not understand what had caused such a great disaster, because their forces were fifty times greater than those of the Christians. When the Moors fled, the Christians pillaged their camp, and day was upon them when they entered the city victoriously.

After four days had passed, the Moorish king sent his emissaries with a letter challenging the King of England, and it said the following:

"To you, Christian king who rules the isle of England, I, Abraim, king and lord of Canary, say that if you wish the war between you and me to end, and the killing between your people and mine to cease, let us have a joust, king against king, under the following pacts and agreements: If I should defeat you, you will hold all England under my power and command, and you shall give me two hundred thousand pieces of gold in tribute each year. And if fortune decides that you are the conqueror, I shall return to my own land, and you will remain in yours in peace, and you and all your people will enjoy full peace and tranquility. And in addition I shall restore to you all the cities and castles that I have won and conquered by my own victorious hand.

"These words are not spoken for vainglory or out of disdain for the royal crown, but so that God Who is great may give to each that share which, by his merits, he will deserve."

Two great Moorish knights, whom the King of Canary was sending to the city of Warwick as envoys to the King of England, left the castle of Killingworth, and before they departed, they sent a messenger to the city to request safe conduct.

When the messenger came to the gates of the city the guards told him to wait a little while, and they would return with the reply. One of the guards quickly went to the king to tell him. After the king had held a brief counsel, he told the guard to let him in. When the messenger was inside the city, the Count of Salisbury spoke to him and said:

"Messenger, on behalf of His Majesty, the king, I can tell you that the envoys may come without danger and in safety, for they will not be harmed in any way."

And the count gave him a silk garment and one hundred pieces of gold. The messenger departed, very content, and before the envoys came, the hermit said to the king:

"My lord, let us put fear into the hearts of these Moors. Your Majesty should order two grandees to go out to the gate and receive the envoys. And let many men, very well armed, but without helmets, go with them. Have three hundred men at the gate to guard it, armed like the others. And let all the ladies and maidens who are able, old as well as young, hang banners in the windows and on the roofs, as tall as the women's chests, and each of these women should put armor on her head. When the envoys pass by they will see the coats of mail shining, and will think they are all warriors. Have the three hundred guarding the gate follow them by other streets, and let them appear in the square and on the corner. Then, after the envoys have passed by, let them do the same again and again until they reach Your Highness. And you may be sure that they will be frightened when they see so many soldiers after the battle they have lost. Seeing the great number of men, they will believe that many have come from Spain or France or Germany to help us."

The king and all his council thought very highly of the hermit's words. It was decided that the Duke of Lancaster and the Count of Salisbury should receive the envoys, and that four thousand men should go with them, each wearing a garland of flowers on his head. They went a good mile out of the city to receive the envoys.

Then the Duke of Bedford said:

"Tell us, Father, since there are so many ceremonies to be performed for the envoys, how should they find the king, clothed or naked, armed or unarmed?"

"That would be a good question," said the hermit, "if there were not so much anger behind your words. But I see the meaning of your words, and that they are intended more for malice than good. It is because I am old and a hermit that you are trying to besmear my advice and belittle me before my lord the king. Hold your tongue. If you do not, I shall put a bridle in your mouth that will make you stop at every turn."

At this, the duke rose to his feet, drew his sword, and said:

"If it were not because you are so old and you wear the habit of Saint Francis, I would take this sword and cut your skirts right up to the waist."

Then the king rose angrily to his feet, seized the duke and took the sword out of his hand, and had him imprisoned in the tower. All the other noble lords there calmed the hermit, telling him that because of his age and the habit he wore he should be forgiving, and he was content to forgive. But the king would not, in spite of all the pleas of the hermit and the other noble lords.

In the midst of these troubles, news was brought to the king that the Moorish envoys were approaching, and those who had been chosen went out quickly as they had arranged.

When the envoys stood before the king, they gave him the letter, and the king commanded that it be read in everyone's presence. The hermit drew near to the king and said to him:

"Your Highness, accept the challenge."

Then the king said:

"I agree to the battle, in accordance with the conditions your king sets down."

He begged the envoys to remain there until the following day when he would give them the formal reply. He showed them to very comfortable chambers and gave them everything they needed.

Then the king convoked a general council, and while it was being prepared, the hermit, along with the other lords, went to the king.

He knelt at the king's feet and kissed his hands and feet, and very humbly begged him to give him the keys to the tower so that he could release the duke. The hermit pleaded so much, as did the other lords, that the king was obliged to give them to him. Then the hermit went with the others to the tower where the duke was imprisoned, and there they found a friar hearing his confession, because he was certain he would be killed. When he heard the door open he was so startled that he felt he was losing his mind, for he thought they were coming to take him out to execute him.

When the hermit saw him he said:

"My lord, duke, if you and I have spoken harmful words to each other, I beg you to forgive me, for I most willingly pardon you."

When they had made their peace they all returned to the council where the king and all the dukes, counts and marquis were, and they read the letter from the Moorish king once more. Because the king and all the others loved and revered the hermit and they saw that he led a saintly life, and that he expressed himself well and was knowledgeable about arms, they all agreed that he should be the first to speak, and this led to the following discourse.

"I will tell you my opinion, although I realize that I am not worthy to speak of such things since I know little of the use of arms. Because of the weak disposition of my lord, the king, who is young and has a weak constitution and is sickly, although he has the courage of a virtuous knight, it would not be fitting or just for him to do battle with a man as robust as the Moorish king. Instead, let the Duke of Lancaster, who is the uncle of my lord king, undertake this battle, and let our king grant to him the scepter and the royal crown so that the Moorish king will not be deceived and so that he may combat a true king."

Scarcely had the hermit spoken these last words when three dukes sprang to their feet in great anger: the Duke of Gloucester, the Duke of Bedford, and the Duke of Exeter. And they began to cry loudly that they would not consent for the Duke of Lancaster to enter into battle and be made king, because each of them was more closely related to the king, and it was more just for them to do battle than the Duke of Lancaster.

The king would not permit any further discussion, and he said:

"It is not my pleasure that any of you should take my place in battle. Since I have accepted, I wish to carry it out alone."

A baron stood up and said the following:

"Sire, may Your Excellency forgive me for what I am about to say. We will never consent to what Your Highness has said. If our Heavenly Father has indeed given you the desire, he has taken from you the strength. We all know that Your Highness is not ready for such a formidable and arduous battle as this will be. Let Your Grace be ruled by our counsel and will. If we believed that Your Excellency were disposed for such an undertaking, we would very willingly have agreed to what Your Highness has commanded."

All the other barons and knights praised what this baron had said.

"My most faithful vassals and subjects," said the king, "since it is not to your liking, and you see that I am not fit to combat the Moorish king, I give you my thanks for the great love you have shown me, and I submit to your will. But it is my wish and my command that no one, under pain of death, shall be so bold as to say that he will take my place in battle, except the one I shall choose. Unto him I shall give the crown, the kingdom and the royal scepter."

Then the king said:

"Dukes, counts and marquis, and all the rest of my most faithful subjects, I am relinquishing my station, the scepter and the royal crown, and my title to my beloved father hermit."

He removed the garments, and said:

"As I relinquish these royal robes, and put them on the father hermit, in the same way I relinquish my throne and my station to him. I beg him to accept, and to do battle for me with the Moorish king."

When the hermit heard the king say these words, he arose quickly because he wished to speak, and all the great lords who were there also stood and gathered so closely to the hermit that they would not let him speak, but instead removed the habit he was clothed in and made him dress in the royal robes. As the king turned over all his power to the hermit, it was duly noted in the presence of all the council and with the consent of all the barons. When the hermit king heard the pleas of all those in the council, he accepted the kingdom and the battle, and quickly asked them to bring him armor that would fit him well. They brought him many suits of armor, but of all the ones they brought him there was none he was pleased with.

"In faith," said the hermit king, "nothing will stop this battle, even if I have to go dressed in only my shirt. I beg you, my lords," said the hermit king, "to be so good as to go to the countess and entreat her by her great virtue and kindness, to lend me the armor of her husband, Sir William of Warwick, which he wore when he went into battle."

When the countess saw so many dukes, counts and marquis, and the entire council of the king approaching, and she heard the reason they had come, the virtuous countess gave them a suit of armor of little value. When the king saw it, he said, "This is not the one I asked for. There is another that is much better."

All the barons returned once more to the countess and asked for the other armor, and the countess told them that there was no other. When the king heard the answer, he said:

"My lords and my brothers, let us all go, and we shall try our luck."

When they were all before the countess, the king said:

"Countess, out of your great kindness and gentility, I beg you to lend me the armor of your husband, Sir William of Warwick."

"Sire," said the countess, "may God take this child from me, for I have no other dear thing in the world: I have already sent the armor to you."

"That is true," said the king, "but this is not what I asked for. Lend me the armor that is in the small chamber in your bedroom, covered by green and white damask."

The countess knelt, and said:

"Sire, by your mercy and your grace, I beg Your Majesty to tell me your name and how you came to know my lord and husband, Count William of Warwick."

The king answered: "My lady, because you wish me to tell you, I will. I was in his company continually, for in the wars we were brothers in arms."

The countess immediately replied:

"I beg Your Lordship to forgive me for not doing all that I could have for Your Highness when you were a hermit. If I had known how close you were to my lord, William of Warwick, I would have honored you much more and given you more of my possessions than I did."

The king was very content with the words of the countess:

"Where there is no error there is no need to beg forgiveness. I only ask you, out of your great virtue and genteelness, to lend me the armor I have asked you for."

The countess immediately had other armor brought to him, covered with blue brocade. When the king saw it, he said:

"Countess, my lady, how well you have kept the arms of your husband! In spite of all the supplications that these lords and I have made to you, you have been unwilling to lend them to us. These are the ones which William of Warwick used in tournaments; the ones I want are hanging in the alcove, and are covered with white and green damask, with the emblem of a lion wearing a golden crown. And if my entering there would not anger you, countess, I am sure that I would find them."

"Oh, wretched me!" said the countess. "It's as though you had been raised in this house! Your Grace may indeed go in and look, and take everything you wish."

When the king saw her willingness he thanked her, and they all went into her chamber and saw them hanging there. The king had them brought to him, and he had them repaired.

The battle was arranged for the following day. In the evening the king went to the main church and stayed there all night, kneeling before the altar of the holy Mother of God, Our Lady, with all his armaments upon the altar. When it was full daylight, he very devoutly heard mass. After mass he had himself fitted with armor inside the church, and ate a partridge in order to fortify himself. Then he went out to the field.

When the hermit king was in the field he saw the Moorish king with all his foot soldiers and horsemen. All the Moors climbed to the top of a hill to view the battle, and the Christians remained near the city. The hermit king held a well sharpened lance and had a small shield on his arm, along with his sword and a dagger. The Moorish king had a bow and arrow, a sword, and on his head was a helmet wrapped with a turban.

When the two brave kings were in the field, they charged at each other. The Moorish king quickly shot an arrow which hit the center of the hermit king's shield, passing freely by him near his arm, and at once the Moorish king shot another which hit him in the thigh, but with the armor the hermit king was wearing the arrow could not penetrate it completely. The hermit king hurled the lance at him when they were near. The Moorish king was very skillful with his arms: when he saw the lance coming he deflected it with his bow. By this time the hermit king had drawn so near that the Moorish king could not shoot more arrows. When he was so close that he could almost touch him with his hand, the hermit king cried out in a loud voice:

"If You help me, Lord, it will not matter if all the Moors in the world attack me."

When the Moorish king saw him so near, and realized that he could not shoot any arrows, he felt that he had lost.

After the hermit king had thrown the lance, he quickly reached for his sword, and drawing as close to the Moorish king as he could, he gave him a mighty blow on the head. But he did him little harm because of the thick turban the Moorish king wore! Then the hermit king struck him a mighty blow with his sword, cutting off his arm, and as he plunged his sword fully into his side the Moorish king fell to the ground. As quickly as he could, the hermit king cut off his head. Then he picked up his lance and stuck the head on the end of it, and rode back into the city in triumph.

Imagine what rejoicing there was among the Christians, the women and the young girls, when they thought they were now released from their captivity! When the king was inside the city he had the doctors brought to him, and they ministered to his wounds.

On the morning of the following day the king held his council in the bed where he lay, and it was decided that two knights would be sent as envoys to the Moors, to tell them that they wished to observe the pacts they had all agreed to and sworn to, and that they could go to their own lands in safety, with all their ships and clothing and jewelry, and that no one in the kingdom would harm them.

The envoys departed, and when they were with the Moors they explained their mission to them. They were given lodging, and were asked to await the reply. The Moors told them this in order to do them great harm, for they were now very vengeful because of the death of their king.

Among them a great dispute arose over whom they would make king. Some wanted Cale-ben-Cale, others wanted Aduqueperec, cousin-german of the dead king. Cale-ben-Cale was chosen king, and he immediately ordered the envoys seized, along with all who had come with them, and he had them put to death. They cut off their heads, put them inside a packsaddle, and sent them to the city on a mule. The guards who were in the city towers saw two horsemen driving the mule on. When they were near the city they abandoned the mule and galloped away. The captain of the guards saw them and ordered ten men on horseback to go and see what it was all about. When they got there they wished they had not gone out to see such a terrible thing, and they immediately went to tell the king and his entire council. When the king heard the news he was very much taken aback, and he said:

"Oh, cruel infidels: you who have little faith, for you cannot give what you do not have! Now I make a solemn vow, wounded as I am, never to enter a covered building, except to hear mass at a church, until I have driven these Moors from the entire kingdom."

He quickly had his clothing brought to him, and he left his bed and had the trumpets sound. The first to leave the city was the king, and he had all the men who were more than eleven years old and less than seventy summoned, and under penalty of death they all had to follow him. That day his tents were raised on the very spot where the Moors had been defeated, and the king had a great deal of artillery for war brought out.

When the virtuous countess learned that the king had proclaimed such a summons, and that those who were more than eleven years old were to follow him, she was very upset, for she realized that her son was included. So she hurried to where the king was, and fell to her knees on the hard ground. Then, with a grieving voice, she began to say:

"Have pity on me. I have nothing of value except this son who is so young that he cannot help you. Grant me this favor in memory of your great friendship and love for my virtuous husband. And let me remind Your Grace of the alms that I used to give you when you were a hermit. Please hear my supplications, and leave my son with me. His father is dead, and the only thing I have to console me is this poor son."

The king saw the countess's error, and quickly replied:

"I would very much like to obey you, Countess, if your petition were honorable and just. But it is well known that men must learn to use arms, and they must know the practice of war, and the gentle ways of this blessed order of chivalry. It is customary for men of honor to begin to use arms when they are very young, for they learn better at that age than at any other. And because he is now at the best age in the world to see and understand the great honors that knights achieve, I wish to keep him in my company as my own son. He must come with me, and tomorrow I shall dub him a knight so that he may imitate the virtuous actions of his father, William of Warwick."

"I am called mother only by this son of mine," said the countess, "and if he dies in battle, what will become of me, for I shall have lost my husband and my son and all that I had in this miserable world?"

When the countess had finished, her son began to speak:

"Madam, I beg you, please do not cry for me. You know that I have now reached an age when I have to leave the protection of my mother's wings, and that I am worthy of bearing arms and going into battle to show the mettle I am made of, and who my father was. If it is God's will, He will keep me from harm and will allow me to carry out such actions that He will be pleased, and they will give consolation to my father's soul, and Your Grace will be made happy."

When her son had gone, the countess went into the city, weeping, and many virtuous women of the city went with her, consoling her as best they could.

That night the king had the camp well guarded, and he allowed no one to take off their armor. In the morning, when the sun came out, he had the trumpets sound, and they moved the camp to within half a league of where the Moors were. When the tents were set up he let the men rest. This happened after the noon hour.

When the Moors learned that the Christians had come out of the city, they were astonished, because a short time before they had not dared take a step outside the city, and now they came looking for them. Some captains said this was because of the great cruelty of their king, Cale-ben-Cale, who had killed the Christian ambassadors so cruelly, and they said that they might be recruiting men from Spain or France:

"That is why they are coming so near, and you can be sure that any of us they capture will be cut to shreds."

One of the ambassadors who had taken the letter to convene the joust, said:

"They paid us many honors, and as soon as we were in the city we saw great numbers of men in the towers, the squares, in the windows and on the rooftops. It was astonishing to see so many armed men. By Mohammed, I would guess there were two hundred thousand soldiers. And this wicked king killed their ambassadors without reason."

After all the captains had heard the words of this ambassador, they talked to the other Moors who had gone into the city with him, and when they knew the truth of the situation, they killed Cale-ben-Cale and chose a new king. Nonetheless, they armed themselves for battle and went in sight of the Christians.

The sun was nearly down, but they still decided to go up a nearby hill. When the hermit king saw them, he said:

"In faith, they're afraid of us. That's why they've gone up to such a high place. Let everyone do what I do, and with Divine help we will have vengeance on our enemies."

He took a basket in one hand, and a spade in the other, and went in front of them all. When the great lords saw the king do this, each of them did the same, and followed him.

Before leaving the city, the virtuous king had procured everything necessary for the war. Around the palisade he dug a deep ditch that led to a large water hole, and they left a great entryway in the middle, through which one hundred fifty men could pass at one time. On the other side they dug another ditch that led to a high cliff.

The king said:

"Since we've finished, and there are only two hours left till dawn, you, Duke of Gloucester, and you, Count of Salisbury, go quickly to the countess, and ask her to give me two large barrels that belong to William of Warwick. They are full of copper spikes, and she will find them upstairs, in the weapons room."

They went there quickly and begged and commanded her, on the king's behalf, so that she gave them to them, even though she was upset with the king because he had not given her son back to her. But she realized how great their needs were, and so she did it, although she could not help saying:

"Lord, have mercy on me! What's going on that this king knows so much about my house? There's nothing I have that has to do with weapons or war that he doesn't know about. I don't know if he is only guessing or if he's a wizard."

The barons had the barrels of spikes loaded onto carts, and took them to the camp. When they were before the king, they told him everything the countess had said, and the virtuous king burst out laughing, and he smiled and joked with them at length.

Afterward he had the spikes taken to the gate, and they placed them on the ground so that when the Moors came through, they would stick into their feet. He also had many holes, like wells, dug, so that if they escaped one danger they would fall into another. And the Christians worked at this all night long.

When daylight broke, the Moors began to beat drums, and they blew trumpets and pipes, and shouted their battle-cries, and with great joy they streamed down the mountain to attack the Christians. The hermit king ordered all the men to lie down on the ground, and pretend to be asleep. When they were almost within range of bombards they all got up, and gave signs of being unprepared for battle. When the Moors were inside the entryway, the king said:

"Gentlemen, do not dismay, I beg you. Let's turn our backs, and pretend to run away."

When the Moors saw them fleeing, they rushed forward as quickly as they could. They ran inside the entryway which, as we have mentioned, they could not pass through because the copper spikes stuck into their feet. When the virtuous hermit king saw the Moors inside the entryway he made his men slow down, like an expert in war and weaponry, and he saw the Moors stopping because of the wounds from the spikes, while others were falling into the wells that were covered by branches with dirt piled on top. Then the king began to shout with a loud voice:

"Oh knights of honor, take your eyes from the city, and turn your faces to the enemies of the Christian faith. Let us attack with great courage, for this day is ours. Give them a cruel battle, and grant mercy to no one!"

The king was the first to strike a blow; then the others followed. The Moors saw the Christians doing battle savagely while they were all unable to move because of their wounds, and so they were forced to die, and great destruction was wrought unto them. Those who were coming behind saw how the Christians were slaughtering the Moors, and they fled back to the castle they had come from, without offering resistance.

The king pursued them, killing and beheading as many as he could catch. When the king was worn out from his wounds, he stopped for a moment and they captured a very tall Moor of enormous proportions. After the king had knighted the countess's son, he wanted him to kill that Moor. And very bravely the boy stabbed him with his sword until he killed him. When the king saw that the Moor was dead he took the boy by the hair and threw him on top of the Moor, and rubbed him hard against the man, filling his eyes and face with blood, and he made him stick his hands into the wounds, and in that way he baptized him in the blood of the Moor. He grew up very bravely, and in his time in a large part of the world there could not be found so worthy a knight.

When the good king saw that the battle was won, he began to pursue the Moors, and he killed all those he caught. This was the greatest destruction and slaughter of men that took place in that time, for ninety-seven thousand Moors died in the space of ten days. Since the king could not walk well because of his wounds, they brought him a horse so he could ride.

"In truth, I shall not," said the king. "All the others are going on foot, and if I went on horseback it would be very unjust."

They went along slowly until they came to the castle where the Moors had barricaded themselves, and here they made camp and rested that night. In the morning, when it was broad daylight, the king ordered the trumpets blown, and all the men armed themselves. The king put on his royal tunic and went in front of all the rest, and they charged the castle. They were met by cross bows and spears and rocks that were thrown down on them from the top of the castle. And the king pressed on so hard that he went ahead alone, without anyone being able to help him. The countess's son shouted loudly:

"Run, knights of honor! Let us run and help our king and lord who has placed himself in great danger!"

And he took hold of a small shield that a page was carrying, and jumped into the moat to go to where the king was. The others, seeing the small boy going by, all rushed forward at the same time to get to the other side, and many knights died or were wounded. But the small boy, with the aid of Our Lord, suffered no harm.

When they had all crossed over they gathered a great deal of wood, and they set fire to the door of the castle. The boy began to shout as loudly as he could, and he said:

"Oh, English ladies! Come out, and regain your lost liberty: the day of your redemption has come."

Three hundred nine women were inside the castle. When they heard that voice they all ran to the back door of the castle, for there was a huge fire at the other one and all the women were welcomed by the Christians, and among them were many noblewomen.

When the Moors saw the great fire, and that the entire castle was burning, they wanted to surrender, but the valiant king would not permit it.

Instead, he wanted them all to die by fire and the sword. And those who came running out of the castle were either quickly killed, or the spears forced them back inside. In this way twenty-two thousand Moors were killed and burned that day.

The hermit king left the castle with all his men, and they went through all the kingdom to those places the Moors had taken. They did not find one Moor that they wanted to spare, and they went all the way to the port of Southampton where they found all the vessels and ships on which they had come. Afterward the king ordered that any Moor who came to the island of England, no matter what his business might be, should die without mercy.

When they had retaken the entire kingdom, the king's vow was fulfilled and all the people went into the city of Warwick. When the countess learned that the king was coming she went out to welcome him with all the ladies and maidens of the city, since not one man had stayed there except the sick and wounded. When the countess was near the king, she fell to her knees, and all the other women shouted with a loud voice:

"Welcome, victorious King!"

The virtuous gentleman embraced them all, one by one, and took the countess's hand, and they walked along, talking, until they were inside the city. The countess thanked him profusely for all the honor he had bestowed on her son, and then she thanked all the other great lords.

Having rested for a few days, the hermit king was in his chamber one day, thinking to himself. Since he had ended the war, and the entire kingdom was at peace, he decided to reveal who he was to his wife, the countess, and to all the others, so that he could return the royal scepter to the first king, and go back to his penance.

He called his chamberlain, and giving him the half-ring he had divided with the countess before going to Jerusalem, he told him to speak to her and give her the ring. The chamberlain quickly went to the countess, and kneeling before her, he said:

"My lady, one who has loved and continues to love you sends you this ring."

The countess took the ring, and when she looked at it she turned pale. She ran into her chamber and opened a box where she kept the other part of the ring. She put the two parts together, and saw that they were one piece, revealing the family arms. She understood that it belonged to her husband, the count, and she cried out:

"Tell me, sir, where is my husband, the Count of Warwick?"

And she tried to find the door to leave the chamber, but in her confusion she could not. Then she fell to the floor in a faint.

When the chamberlain saw what a state the countess was in, he ran to the king in fright. The king said:

"My friend, what's wrong? What news do you bring me?"

The chamberlain fell to his knees before him, and said:

"I dearly wish you had not sent me. I don't know what special power that ring has, or if it was made by sorcery and your worship took it from the Moors, because as soon as the countess placed it on her finger she fell to the floor, dead."

The king got up from his seat and quickly went to her chamber where he found her more dead than alive, with all the doctors at her side. As soon as the countess regained consciousness, and saw her husband and king, she quickly got up and knelt before him to kiss his feet and his hands. But he would not allow it, and instead he took her arm and lifted her from the floor, and embraced and kissed her many times. Then he revealed who he was to all the lords in the kingdom, and to the entire town. And all the lords and ladies came to honor the king and their new queen. When the son learned that the king was his father, he hurried to the chamber and knelt and kissed his hands and feet many times over.

There were great celebrations, and after nine days four hundred carts arrived, loaded with gold and silver, jewels, and very valuable items which they had found in the Moors' possession. The king ordered the jewels, the gold, and the silver to be given to four lords: the Duke of Gloucester, the Duke of Bedford, the Count of Salisbury, and the Count of Stafford.

After this had been done the king called a general council for the following day. When they were all present, the king came into the council chamber in his royal robes, the crown on his head and the scepter in his hand, and sitting down, he said:

"My lord and king, Your Highness must be content with the grace that almighty God has given you, for with the help of your vassals you have recovered the entire isle of England. And so, in the presence of all these worthy lords, I return to you the kingdom, the crown, the scepter and the royal robes."

He immediately removed the garments and dressed again in his habit.

The king and all the barons recognized his great virtue and gentility, and gave him many thanks. The king asked him to remain in his court, and offered to make him Prince of Wales, but he excused himself, saying that he would not leave God's service for the vanities of this world. Then he left the king and those in the court, and went to his village, about a league from the city, and there he rested for a few days.

When the countess learned that her husband had gone, she left the castle without saying a word to the king or to anyone, and went with her ladies and maidens to be with her husband.

Within a few days the king and his people were ready to leave. Then the hermit-count told his son to go with the king, and to serve him fully. And if disagreements arose in the kingdom, in no case should he turn against his king and lord.

After the king had left for London, the countess begged her husband:

"My lord, let me stay with you so that I may serve you. Let us make a hermitage separated into two parts, with a church in between."

So much did the countess implore him that the count was forced to obey her. The countess then wanted to go to another site that was lovely, with many trees and a beautiful, clear spring, and in the middle of that fine meadow was a pine tree of striking beauty. And every day all the wild beasts of the forest came to drink from that clear spring.

When the hermitage was finished, and the count and countess were about to go and live in it, the Count of Northumberland arrived, as an ambassador of the king, to ask them to go to London, for the king was to marry the daughter of the King of France. And if the count could not go, the countess was requested to go, for she was needed to teach the queen the customs of England.

The count-hermit answered:

"Ambassador, tell His Majesty, the king, that I would be very happy to serve His Excellency, but I cannot abandon the vow I have made to serve God. As for the countess, her presence there can take the place of both of us."

The countess would have preferred to remain behind and serve her husband, but when she saw her husband's wishes, and realized her duty to the king, she agreed to go. The count left them with many tears and went to the hermitage. And every day, after prayer, he went underneath the beautiful tree to see the animals drink from the clear spring.

JOANOT MARTORELL

CHAPTER II - THE TOURNAMENT

Day after day the English knights were languishing. Abandoning themselves to idleness, they spent many days in peace, tranquility, rest and enjoyment. So that they would not be completely idle and fall into languor, the King of England decided that as the wedding had been arranged he would invite everyone to his court and have a display of arms. The news of the great celebration that the king was preparing was spread throughout all the Christian kingdoms.

It happened that a gentleman of ancient lineage, a native of Brittany, was traveling in the company of many other gentlemen who were going to the celebration. He fell behind the others, and went to sleep on his horse, because he was so weary from the long journey he had made. His horse left the road and took a path that led him to the delightful spring of the hermit, who at this moment was finding pleasure in a book entitled *Tree of Battles*. As he read this book he constantly gave thanks to God, our Heavenly Father, for the singular favors he had won in this world by serving the order of chivalry.

While he was at this task he saw a man coming along the plain on horseback, asleep. He stopped reading, and decided not to wake him. When the horse was in front of the spring and saw the water, it drew closer, wanting to drink, but because the reins were tied to the saddle bow, it could not. And it struggled so much that it was inevitable that the gentleman should awaken. As he opened his eyes, he found himself confronted by a hermit with a very long and completely white beard, his clothing torn, revealing a thin body.

The gentleman was astonished at such a sight, but with his good sense he realized that it must be some man who led a saintly life, and who had withdrawn to that place to do penance and save his soul. He quickly dismounted and bowed deeply to him. The hermit received him cordially, and they sat down in the delightful, green meadow. The hermit began to speak:

"Gentle sir, I beg you upon your courtesy and gentility to tell me your name and upon what business you have come to this lonely spot."

The gentleman quickly answered:

"Reverend Father, since your holiness wants to know my name, I will be very happy to tell it to you: I am called Tirant lo Blanc. My father was lord of the March of Tirania, which faces England along the sea, and my mother was daughter of the Duke of Brittany, and her name is Blanca, and so they decided to name me Tirant lo Blanc. The news has spread among all the Christian kingdoms that the King of England has called for a court to be held in the city of London, and that he has arranged a marriage with the daughter of the King of France, who is the most beautiful maiden in all Christendom and has qualities that no one else possesses. I can give you an example: While I was in the court of the King of France, in the city of Paris, last Michaelmas, the king was holding a great celebration because that day the wedding had been agreed to. The king, the queen and the infanta were all eating at the same table, and I can tell you truly, sir, that as the infanta drank red wine, it could be seen as it passed down her throat because her skin is so very fair, and everyone there was astonished. Afterward it was said that the King of England wishes to become a knight, and that he will then make knights of everyone who wishes to enter the order of chivalry. I asked kings-of-arms and heralds why the king had not been made a knight during his wars with the Moors. And I was told that it was because he had been defeated in all the battles he undertook against the Moors until the appearance of that famous knight and conqueror, Count William of Warwick, who quickly defeated the Moors and put all his kingdom at peace. They say, moreover, that on Saint John's day the queen will be in the city of London and great celebrations will be held that will last a year and a day, and so we thirty gentlemen in name and in arms have left Brittany, prepared to enter the order of chivalry. And as I came along the road, fortune decided that I would fall somewhat behind because of my horse's weariness and because of the great hardships I have endured on the long journeys I have made—for I left after the others. As I was thinking to myself I fell asleep, and my horse left the main road and brought me before your reverence."

When the hermit heard the gentleman say that he was going in order to receive the order of chivalry, he heaved a deep sigh and began to think, remembering the great honor chivalry had bestowed upon him for so long.

"I tell Your Lordship," continued Tirant, "even if there were many more dangers in it than there are, that would not stop me from receiving the order of chivalry. No matter what happens to me, I will consider my death worthwhile if I die loving and defending the order of chivalry and serving it with all my strength so that I won't be reprimanded by good knights."

"My son," said the hermit, "because you so desire to receive the order, do it with renown and fame. On the day you receive it perform a show of arms so that all your relatives and friends will know that you are ready to maintain and serve the order of chivalry. Now because the hour is late and your company is going far ahead, I think you should leave: you are in a foreign land and do not know the roads, and you run the danger of becoming lost in the great forests hereabouts. I beg you to take this book and show it to my lord, the king, and to all the good knights so that they may know about the order of chivalry. And when you return, I pray you, my son, come by here and tell me who have been made new knights, and about all the celebrations and festivities that take place, so that I will know about them, and I will be very grateful to you."

And he gave him the book, taking his leave at the same time.

Tirant took the book with great joy, giving him many thanks and promising to return, and Tirant said, as he left:

"Tell me, my lord: if the king or the other knights ask me who is sending the book, what shall I say?"

The hermit answered:

"If you are asked such a question, say that it was someone who has always loved and honored the order of chivalry."

Tirant bowed deeply to him, mounted his horse, and went on his way.

Meanwhile his companions were wondering what could have become of him and why he was delayed. They were afraid that he might have become lost in the forest, and many of them turned back to look for him. They found him on the road, reading about the chivalresque acts written down in the book, and of all the order of chivalry.

When Tirant reached the town where his companions were staying, he told them about the beautiful adventure Our Lord had taken him on, and how the saintly hermit had given him that book. And they read all that night until morning when it was time to leave.

They traveled a day at a time until they reached the city of London, where the king was with many knights. Many had come, both from his own kingdom and from foreign lands, and no more than thirteen days remained before the celebration of Saint John's day.

When Tirant and his friends had gathered together they went to pay homage to the king, who received them very cordially. The infanta was two days journey from there in a city named Canterbury where the body of Saint Thomas of Canterbury lies. On Saint John's day the celebrations began, and that day the king was seen with the infanta, his bride. These celebrations lasted a year and a day.

When the celebrations were over the king was married to the infanta of France, and all the foreigners took their leave of the king and queen and returned to their own lands.

After Tirant left the city of London with his companions, he remembered the promise he had made to the hermit, and when they were near the place where he lived, he said to them:

"Gentlemen, my brothers, I must go to where the hermit is."

And everyone in his company begged him to let them go too, for they had a great desire to see the saintly hermit. Tirant was most content that they should, and they all set out on the road toward the hermit. At the time they arrived, the hermit was under the tree, in prayer.

When he saw so many people arriving he wondered who they could be. Tirant drew closer than the others, and when he was near he dismounted, and all the rest with him, and they approached the hermit with deep humility, kneeling and paying him the honor he deserved. Tirant wished to kiss his hand, as did all the others, but he would not permit it.

The hermit, very attentive and courteous, paid them great honor, embracing them all and begging them to sit on the grass near him. And they answered that he should sit down and they would all remain standing, but the valorous gentleman would not allow it and made them all sit next to him. When they were all seated, they waited for the hermit to speak. The hermit, understanding the honor they were paying him, said:

"I could not possibly tell you, magnificent gentlemen, how content I am at seeing so many good people. Please tell me if you are now coming from the court of my lord, the king. I would like to know who became new knights, and about the celebrations that have taken place. And I beg you, Tirant lo Blanc, tell me the names of all these gentlemen here."

And he paused. Tirant turned to his companions, for there were many of higher lineage and wealth, and he said to them:

"Oh, valiant knights! I pray you to answer the questions that the reverent hermit has asked us. I have told you many times of his wisdom and holiness; and he is a father of chivalry and deserves great honor, so I beg you to speak to him."

They all answered:

"You speak, Tirant. Speak for us all, for the holy father met you first."

"Then, since that is your pleasure," said Tirant, "and the father commands it, if I am wrong about anything, please correct me."

They all said they would.

Then the hermit said:

"I beg you, please tell me who was judged the best of the knights and who was given the honor of this festive occasion?"

"My lord," said Tirant, "many gentlemen of great authority and power came to these celebrations. There were kings, dukes, counts and marquis, nobles and knights and many gentlemen of ancient lineage; and almost all those who were not knights were given the order of chivalry. The Duke of Acquaviva put on a display of arms with great knightly spirit and many men were with him, and from among them more than sixty gentlemen were knighted. This duke jousted on foot and on horseback, and he was always victorious. The brother of the Duke of Burgundy went into battle with great courage like the virtuous knight that he is. Next the Duke of Cleve jousted, and he was highly praised. Many other gentlemen who came jousted like noble knights, and I can tell you, sir, in all truth, that more than one hundred fifty knights were killed.

"And I will tell Your Grace something astonishing: One day a boy (It looked to me like he was no more than fourteen or fifteen years old, and everyone honored him, including the king, and they called him the high constable of England) came to the lodging of these gentlemen here and asked for me. He did not know my name, but he recognized me, and he begged me very graciously to lend him my horse and arms because the king and the countess, his mother, did not want him to joust on foot or on horseback on account of the danger. He begged me so much and with such good grace, that I could not refuse him, and I told him that I would be very pleased to give them to him.

"I tell you, sir, of all the knights who took up arms, there was no one who performed as beautifully or as well as he did. The first time he went out he caught his adversary in the middle of the headpiece so that most of the lance went through him. When the knight was dead and the king heard that it was his constable who had jousted so well, he sent for him. And the constable was so frightened that he made excuses not to go, but finally he went to the king, and the king reprimanded him severely. His Excellency showed that he loved him very much, indeed, telling him that he had fought without his permission against a man of enormous strength, the Lord of Escala Rompuda. And furthermore, he told him not to dare to joust anymore without his permission."

When the constable saw how severely the king was reprimanding him, he angrily said: 'Well, my lord, is it true then that even though I've received the order of chivalry, I must be held as the least of all knights because Your Majesty will not let me joust for fear that I might die? Since I am a knight I must do the works of a knight, the same as all good knights. If Your Majesty doesn't want me to face the danger of weapons, order me to go around dressed like a woman with the queen's maidens. Doesn't Your Majesty know that when my father and lord, William, Count of Warwick, held the royal scepter he conquered the Moors? And he took me by the hair and made me kill a Moor even when I was young, because he wanted to make me a conqueror, soaked with blood, and leave me that for a legacy? My lord, if I want to imitate my father in chivalry, Your Highness should not stop me. I beg Your most serene Majesty to give me leave to combat a knight tomorrow, hand to hand, to the death.'

"Then the king said:

"'I truly believe that this will be the best knight in the world, or he will be the worst, because his life will not last long. And by the faith I owe to chivalry, I will not allow that to happen. Since fortune has allowed you to be victorious, you should content yourself with the battle prize.' And he would not hear another word."

Then the hermit said:

"Tell me, since you have spoken so much about this constable, who was honored above all the knights?"

Tirant was quiet, and would not reply.

"Tirant, my son," said the hermit, "why don't you answer my question?"

A knight named Diafebus stood up and said:

"Sir, I will tell you the truth: the one judged best of all the battles was Tirant lo Blanc. He was also the first to receive the order of chivalry from the king, and he was the first to joust. On that day he was taken to a hall and given a chair made entirely of silver. Then the Archbishop of England came before him, and with the king and all the others there, he said:

"'You, sir, who are receiving the order of chivalry, do you swear that you will defend ladies and maidens, widows, orphans, and even married women with all your power if they should ask your aid?'

"When he had sworn the oath, two great lords, the mightiest there, took hold of his arms and led him before the king. The king laid the sword on his head and said: 'May God and my lord, Saint George, make you a good knight' And he kissed him on the mouth.

"Then seven maidens came in, dressed in white, representing the seven joys of Virgin Mary, and they strapped his sword on him. Then came four knights, the most dignified to be found, representing the four evangelists, and they put spurs on him. Afterward the queen came, and she took him by one arm, and a duchess took the other, and they led him to a beautiful platform and seated him in the royal chair. Then the king sat on one side, and the queen on the other, and all the maidens and knights sat around them, below. Next a very abundant collation was brought. And this, sir, is the procedure that was held for all those who were made knights."

"Tell me, if you will, about the jousts Tirant participated in."

"My lord, on the eve of the appointed day, Tirant went to where the twenty-six knights were. When he was at their door he delivered a document stating that any knight who wanted to joust against him would have to battle until one of them had drawn blood twenty times, or until either of them capitulated. His conditions were immediately accepted, and we returned to our lodging. The next day all the maidens came for him and took him to the list, fully dressed in his armor. The king and queen were already on the catafalques when Tirant came in completely covered with armor, except for his head. In his hand he held a fan that had the crucifixion of Jesus Christ painted on one side, and the figure of Our Lady painted on the other.

"When Tirant was in the middle of the field he made a deep bow to the king and the queen, and then he went to each of the four corners of the list, and made the sign of the cross at each corner with the fan. He found the defender at the far end of the list, and Tirant went to the other end of the field. When everyone was quiet the king ordered them to begin. Quickly they dug in their spurs, lances in the sockets, and they clashed so fiercely that their lances flew to pieces. Afterward they turned and charged many times with many singular encounters. On their twentieth turn the defender struck the beaver of Tirant's helmet and bent it, wounding him in the neck, and if the lance had not broken our knight would be dead. He and the horse fell to the ground. Tirant quickly got up and another horse was brought to him that was better than the first, and he begged the judges to give him permission to get another lance. Tirant had a very thick lance brought to him, and the other man did the same, and they clashed with a mighty blow, and Tirant's lance passed completely through the other man so that he fell to the ground, dead. The maidens took Tirant's horse by the reins, and led him with honor back to his lodging. They removed his armor and looked at the wound on his neck, and they made the doctors come to care for him. The maidens tended to Tirant very well because they were very happy that the first knight to joust for a maiden had been the victor.

"The king and all the great lords went into the palisade where the dead knight lay, and with a great procession they carried him to the Church of Saint George where they had made a chapel for those who died jousting. And in this chapel only knights could be buried.

"My lord, when Tirant was well again, he gathered all his company once more, and we went to the twenty-five knights. He gave them a written document stating that he wished to fight a knight on foot and to the death, and they accepted. Tirant went into the list armed in the normal fashion, with an ax, a sword, and a dagger. When they were inside the pavilion everything necessary was prepared. The sunlight was divided so that it would not shine into one man's eyes any more than into the other's.

The king came with the other assistants and they went up to the catafalques, while each of the knights stood armed at the gate of his pavilion, their axes in their hands. When they saw the king, they knelt to the ground on one knee, paying deep reverence to the king and queen, which showed plainly that they were very worthy knights, and all the maidens knelt on the ground and begged our Lord to give victory to their knight.

"When the people were quiet, the trumpets sounded and the heralds cried out that no man or woman should dare speak, cough, or make any noise at all under penalty of losing their life.

"When the announcement had been made, the two men came at each other, using their weapons so valiantly that it was impossible to know who was winning. The battle lasted a long time, and because the defender was so hard pressed he grew short of breath. Finally he reached a point where he could no longer hold up his ax, and his face showed that he would prefer to make peace rather than do battle. When Tirant saw the condition his adversary was in, he took his ax with both hands, and gave him such a blow on the helmet that he stunned him and the man could not keep his footing. Then Tirant went up to him and gave him a mighty push that knocked him to the ground. When he saw him in such a pitiful state, he removed the helmet from his head, using his dagger to cut the cords it was tied with, and he said:

"'You can see, virtuous knight, that your life is in my hands, so you command me. Tell me if you want to live or die. I will have more consolation from good than from evil, so command my right hand to have mercy on you and forgive you, and not to harm you as much as it could."

"'I am more hurt,' said the knight, 'by your cruel words, full of vainglory, than I would be of losing my life. I would rather die than ask forgiveness from your haughty hand.'

"'My hand is accustomed to forgiving conquered men,' said Tirant, 'and not to harming them. If you wish, I will very willingly free you from all the harm I could cause you.'

"'Oh, what a wonder it is,' said the knight who was lying on the ground, 'when men are victorious because of luck, or someone else's misfortune. Then they're loose with all kinds of words. I am the knight of Muntalt, reproachless, loved and feared by many, and I have always had mercy on men.'

"'I want to use these things you've mentioned in your favor,' said Tirant, 'because of your great virtue and goodness. Let us go before the king, and on your knees, at my feet, you will have to ask me for mercy, and I will forgive you.'

"In a great rage the knight began to speak:

"'God forbid that I should commit an act that's so shameful to me or mine, or to that eminent lord of mine, Count William of Warwick, who gave me this bitter order of chivalry. Do whatever you please with me, because I would rather die well than live badly.'

"When Tirant saw his ill will, he said:

"'All knights who want to use arms to acquire renown and fame are cruel, and have their seat in the middle of hell.'

"He pulled out a dagger and stuck the point of it in his eye, and with his other hand he gave a mighty blow to the hilt of the dagger that made it come out the other side of his head. What a valorous knight this one was, preferring death to shame and the vituperation of the other knights!

"After some days it happened that their Majesties, the king and queen, were resting in a meadow near the river, dancing and enjoying themselves. A relative of the queen, named Fair Agnes, was there. She was the daughter of the Duke of Berri, and the most graceful maiden I have ever seen. My lord, on that day this Fair Agnes wore a very pretty bauble between her breasts. When the dances were over, in the presence of the king and queen and all the knights, Tirant went up to the genteel lady and kneeling, he said:

"'My lady, knowing of your great worth in lineage as well as beauty, grace and wisdom, and all the other virtues that can be found in a body more angelical than human, I would like to serve you. I would consider it a great favor if you gave me the bauble you're wearing between your breasts. If you give it to me, I will accept it and wear it in your honor and service. And I swear before the altar and on the order of chivalry, to combat a knight on foot or on horseback, to the death, armed or unarmed.'

"'Oh Holy Mary be with me!' said Fair Agnes. 'You want to joust to the death for such a small thing of so little value? So that you will not lose the prize of your good works and the order of chivalry, I shall willingly consent in the presence of the king and the queen. Take the bauble with your own hands.'

"Tirant was very happy with the reply of Fair Agnes. Since the bauble was tied on with her dress straps, it could not be removed without untying them, and when he did, his hands could not help touching her breasts. Tirant took the bauble in his hand and kissed it. Then he fell to his knees, and said:

"'I give you many thanks, my lady, for this great gift. I am happier with it than if you had given me the entire kingdom of France. And I swear to God that whoever takes the bauble from me will leave his life in my hands.'

"And he put it on the crest of the cap he wore.

"The next day, while the king was at mass, a French knight named Lord Vilesermes came. He was a very brave man and very experienced in weapons, and he said to Tirant:

"'Knight, wherever you are from, you have been far too daring in touching the glorified body of Fair Agnes, and no knight in the world ever made such a wicked request. You must return the bauble to me willingly or by force. It is my right to possess it because since infancy I've loved, served and venerated this lady. And if you will not give it to me, your life will not last long.'

"'To my way of thinking,' said Tirant, 'it would be a great offense if I gave away what was given to me freely, and what my own hands untied. In truth, I would be considered the most vile knight ever born if I did such a thing. And yet, knight, your evil tongue shows that you are far too haughty, and I will have to pull you down.'

"The knight attempted to take the bauble away from him, but Tirant was ready. He pulled out a dagger he carried, and all the others lay hold of their weapons. A fight broke out, and before they could be separated twelve of the knights and gentlemen were dead. The queen, who was nearest to them and heard the noise and the loud cries the people were making, placed herself between the men to separate them.

And I can give you a good account because I was wounded four times and many others were wounded too. When the king found out about it, everything had quieted down. But before three days had gone by, the French knight sent a page with a letter for Tirant, and it said the following:

"'To you, Tirant lo Blanc.

"'If you dare to confront the danger of weapons that are customary among knights, let us make an agreement: armed or unarmed, on foot or on horseback, dressed or naked, in whatever way you feel most comfortable, your sword and mine will fight to the death. — Written by my hand and sealed with the secret seal of my arms.

"'Lord Vilesermes.'

"After Tirant had read the letter, he took the page into a room, and giving him one thousand gold coins he made him promise not to tell anyone about this. When the page had gone, Tirant went alone to see a king-of-arms, and he took him three miles away and said to him:

"'King-of-arms, by the trust that has been given to you and by the oath you swore on the day you were given this office, you are bound to hold secret what I am going to tell you, and to advise me well and faithfully about the use of weapons.'

"The king-of-arms, whose name was Jerusalem, answered:

"'My lord, Tirant, I promise you by the office I hold and by the oath I have sworn, to keep everything you tell me secret.'

"Then Tirant showed him the letter, and made him read it. When he had finished, Tirant said to him:

"My good friend, Jerusalem, I will be very honored to satisfy the desire of that virtuous knight, Lord Vilesermes. But since I am young and I know nothing about the practice and custom of chivalry (for I've just turned twenty years old), and I trust your great discretion, I want your advice. And don't think that I've told you this out of cowardice or fear. I wouldn't want to be condemned by the king who has instituted certain laws about the jousts in his kingdom, or by good knights for being weak in this matter.'

"The king-of-arms answered:

"Oh, knight, virtuous young man, beloved by everyone! I will give you the advice you are asking me for. You, Tirant lo Blanc, can fight this knight without any reproach from the king, judges or knights, since you are the defender and he is the one who began this wickedness. Do you know when you would be at fault? If you had been the challenger. So perform like a good knight, and always show the bold spirit of a knight to the people. Go into battle quickly, and have no fear of death.'

"'I feel very comforted by your advice,' said Tirant. 'Now I want to beg you earnestly, Jerusalem, by the office you hold, to be judge of the battle between Lord Vilesermes and me, and to have jurisdiction over it all so that you will bear true witness about everything that happens between him and me.'

"Jerusalem said:

"'I will be very happy to arrange it. But according to the requirements of our office I could not be your judge, and I will tell you why: No knight, king-of-arms or herald who gives advice can be a judge. Not even my lord, the King of England, if he is the judge of a battle, should say favorable words about anyone. And if he did he could be called an unjust judge, and that battle should not take place. But so that neither you nor he will lose the battle prize, I will find you a competent judge who will be suspect in nothing. He is a member of our office, and his name is Claros of Clarence—a man who is very knowledgeable about arms.'

"'I know him well,' said Tirant, 'and I am satisfied with him if Lord Vilesermes agrees, because he is a good king-of-arms and he will give the honor to the one who earns it. I want him to be informed about everything because Lord Vilesermes sent a page to me with this letter, and if I sent him an answer in the same way it could be found out easily and the battle would not come to the conclusion that he and I want. So let us do this: let us go back to my lodgings, and I will give you a 'carte blanche' signed by my hand, and sealed with my coat of arms. And you will arrange the battle so that it's all to his advantage. Since he is the challenger and I am the defender, and he is giving me the choice of weapons, as he says in the letter, I willingly renounce the choice, and I will let him choose whatever pleases him most. I will do only what you say and order. And no matter how cruel the weapons he chooses, you will tell him that I agree: that way my glory will be even greater.'

"Tirant went back to his lodging with the king-of-arms, and he immediately drew up the 'carte blanche.' That is, it was signed by his hand and sealed with his arms; and he gave it to Jerusalem, the king-of-arms.

"The king-of-arms departed to arrange the battle, and he searched throughout all the king's and queen's estates. When he saw that he could not find Lord Vilesermes he went into the city and found him in a monastery of friars, where he was making confession. After he had confessed, Jerusalem called him aside and asked him to come outside the church so that they could talk, for in such a place it is not fitting to speak of criminal things. They left the church and the consecrated ground at once, and Jerusalem began to speak:

"'Lord Vilesermes, I would feel very honored if I could arrange peace and harmony between you and Tirant lo Blanc. But if you do not wish to come to an agreement, here is your letter and his answer, a 'carte blanche,' sealed and signed by his hand. He commanded me, as part of my office, to come to you to arrange the battle in this way: concerning the weapons, he says that you are to be given the power to choose whatever pleases you, provided they are equal and without trickery. And the battle should take place this evening, if possible.'

"'I am very satisfied,' said Lord Vilesermes, 'with Tirant. Nothing but complete virtue could be expected of him. I accept the power that you give me on his behalf to choose the weapons and the battle. It will be this way:

"'It is my decision that the battle will be on foot, in shirts made with cloth from France, both of us having paper shields, and on our heads a garland of flowers, with no other clothing at all on our bodies. The offensive weapons for both of us will be Genoese knives with a cutting edge on both sides, and very sharp points. In this way I will combat him to the death. And I am astonished at you, king-of-arms, when you try to make peace out of discord. Our minds are made up to go into battle, and you talk to me of peace.'

"'What I said,' said the king-of-arms, 'is part of my office: not to want the death of any honorable knight.'

"'Since we agree, I accept the battle with Tirant.'

"'I am happy that you are in agreement,' said the king-of-arms. 'Let us go get the weapons and everything you need before nightfall.'

"They both went immediately to buy the knives, and they had them well keened, with very sharp points. Then they found cloth from France, and they quickly had the shirts cut and sewn. They made them a little long, and the sleeves cut short—up to the elbow—so that their movements in battle would not be hindered. Then they took a sheet of paper, and cut it down the middle and with each half they made a shield. Imagine what sort of defense a half sheet of paper could make!

"When they had finished it all, the knight said to the king-of-arms:

"'You have arranged the battle, and you are here on Tirant's behalf. But I want no one to take my side except God alone, and my own hands which are used to bathing themselves in the noble blood of war. So you take some of the weapons, and I will take the ones you've left.'

"'Lord Vilesermes, I'm not here to take anyone's side. Even if you were to give me all that you have, I wouldn't defraud my honor or my office. Let's do what we have to do; otherwise, give me my leave and find someone else you trust.'

"'Upon my Lord and Creator, king-of-arms, my words didn't have the meaning you're giving them. I only wanted us to go to battle, because I see nighttime coming on. Since you're our judge, arrange things quickly.'

"'My lord, I'll tell you how it's going to be,' said the king-of-arms, 'I can't be a judge between you since I've advised you and Tirant, and I could be reprimanded as an unjust judge if I did. But I'll get another competent judge that both you and he can trust, whose name is Claros of Clarence. He's a king-of-arms, and he knows a great deal about war and arms. He came a short while ago with the Duke of Clarence, and he is a man who would rather die than do anything against his honor.'

"'I'm satisfied with everything,' said the knight, 'as long as the matter is equal and it is secret.'

"'I give you my word,' said the king-of-arms, 'not to tell this to anyone at all except to Claros of Clarence.'

"'Now,' said the knight, 'take the weapons and give them to Tirant, and let him choose the ones he likes best. I will wait for you in the hermitage of Saint Mary Magdalene. So that if anyone in my company should see me, I can pretend that I'm there to pray.'

"Jerusalem left and went looking everywhere for Claros of Clarence, king-of-arms. When he found him he told him everything, and the man said he was very willing to do it. But the sun had already gone down, and it was growing late now, and he did not want to endanger two knights in the dark night. Instead he would be willing to be judge the morning of the following day, when the king was at mass and everyone was resting.

"Jerusalem went back to Tirant and told him how the battle was to take place and about the weapons he had chosen, and he said that he was to take whichever of the two he liked better. And in the morning while the king was at mass, the battle would take place.

"'Since the battle will not take place this evening,' said Tirant, 'I don't want to have the weapons in my possession. If I should defeat or kill him I would not want people to say that I had performed some trickery on the weapons while I had them during the night, and that

that was the reason I defeated him. Give them back to Lord Vilesermes, and tomorrow when the battle takes place, have him bring them.'

"When Jerusalem heard Tirant speak that way, he looked into his face and said:

"'Oh, virtuous knight, versed in arms! You are worthy of wearing a royal crown: I cannot believe that you will not be victorious in this battle.'

"The king-of-arms left Tirant and went to the hermitage where the other knight was, and he told him that the hour was growing late, and the judge could not decide the battle well if it was not daytime, but that they had arranged it for the following day when the king would be at mass. Lord Vilesermes said that he was satisfied with that.

"Early in the morning the kings-of-arms got the two knights and took them to the middle of a forest where no one would be able to see them. When they saw that they were ready, Jerusalem said:

"'Knights of great virtue, this is your death, and your sepulcher. These are the weapons chosen by this knight and accepted by Tirant. Let each take whichever ones he pleases.'

"And he placed them on the lovely meadow grass.

"'Now,' said Claros of Clarence, 'gentlemen of great nobility and chivalry, you are in this isolated place. Expect no help from relatives or friends. You are at the point of death, so place your hope only in God and in your virtue. I want to know who you wish to serve as judge of this battle.'

"'What?' said Lord Vilesermes. 'Didn't we agree that it would be you?'

"'And you, Tirant, who do you want to be judge?'

"'I want it to be the one Lord Vilesermes wants.'

"'Since you want to have me as your judge, you must swear by the order of chivalry to obey all my commands.'

"They swore that they would. After the oath, the knight said to Tirant:

"'Take the weapons you like and I will go into battle with the ones you leave behind.'

"'No,' said Tirant. 'You have been holding them, and they were brought here in your name. You are the challenger, so you choose first, and then I will take mine.'

"And the knights stood there, arguing about ceremony; the judge picked up the weapons to put an end to the dispute. He put some of them on the right side and the others on the left. Then he picked up two straws, one of them long, and the other short. The judge said:

"'Whoever gets the longest one, take the weapons on the right; and whoever gets the short one, the weapons on the left.'

"When they had each picked up the weapons, they quickly took off all their clothes and put on the painful shirts that could well be called hair-cloths of sorrow. The judge made two lines on the field and he placed one of the men on one line and the other man on the other, and he ordered them not to move until he said to. They cut a tree's branches so that the judge could be on a sort of catafalque. When everything was ready the judge went to Lord Vilesermes and said:

"'I am judge by the authority you have given to me, and it is my duty to warn you and beseech you not to come to such a narrow strait as this. Remember God and don't die so desperately. As you know, the justice of our Lord does not pardon a man who brings on his own death, and he is condemned for all eternity.'

"'Let's stop all the talk now,' said the knight. 'Each of us knows his worth and what he can do, both in the temporal life and in the spiritual one. Have Tirant come here to me, and it might be possible for us to come to an understanding.'

"'I don't think that what you're asking is reasonable,' said the judge. 'You are equals: why should he come to you? But in any case, Jerusalem, go and ask Tirant if he wants to come and talk to this knight.'

"Jerusalem went to Tirant, and asked him if he wanted to go there. Tirant answered:

""'If the judge is commanding me to go, I will, but for that knight over there I wouldn't take a step backward or forward for everything he's worth.'

"Jerusalem told him how the judge was obligated to do everything possible to make peace between the knights. Then Tirant said:

"'Jerusalem, tell the knight that I see no reason why I should have to go to him. If he wants something from me, let him come here.'

"He took the answer to him, and then the judge said:

"'All right. It seems to me that Tirant is doing what he should do. But, knight, you can go to the middle of the field, and Tirant will come there.'

"So it was done that way. When they were facing each other, Lord Vilesermes said:

"'Tirant, if you want to have peace with me, and if you want me to forgive you because of your youth, I'll do it—on condition that you hand over the bauble of that illustrious lady, Dona Agnes of Berri, to me, along with the knife and the paper shield so that I can show it to the ladies. Because you know very well that you're not worthy of having anything at all from such a lofty and virtuous lady as she is. Your station, lineage and condition aren't good enough even to allow you to take off her left slipper. They're not even enough to raise you to my rank; in fact, it was out of kindness that I decided to do combat with you.'

"'Knight,' said Tirant, 'I'm not unaware of who you are, or what you can do. But this is not the time or place for us to discuss the merits of our lineages. I am Tirant lo Blanc: when a sword is in my hand, no king, duke, count, or marquis can deny me. That is known throughout the world. But anyone can easily find the seven capital sins in you. Let's go to battle and do what we came here for, and let's not go on with unnecessary and worthless words: if even one of my hairs fell to the ground, I wouldn't surrender it to you, much less allow you to pick it up.'

"'Since you don't want to reach an agreement,' said the judge, 'do you want life or death?'"

Lord Vilesermes said:

"'I am very sorry about the death of this haughty young man. Let's go to battle, and let each one go back to his place.'

"The judge got up on the catafalque that had been made with branches, and he shouted:

"'Go now, knights, and let each of you act like a valiant and good knight!'

"They went at each other in a fury. The French knight carried his knife high, in front of his head, and Tirant held his just above his chest. When they were close to each other, the French knight struck hard at the middle of Tirant's head. Tirant parried and struck back, and he dealt him a blow on top of his ear that almost dug into his brain. The other man struck Tirant in the middle of his thigh, and the wound gaped about a handsbreadth. He quickly stabbed him again in his left arm, and the knife sunk in as far as the bone. They both fought so hard that it was dreadful. And they were so close to each other that with every swing they took they drew blood. It was a pitiful sight for anyone who saw the wounds of the two men: their shirts had become completely red from all the blood they lost. Jerusalem repeatedly asked the judge if he wanted him to make them stop fighting, and the cruel judge answered:

"'Let them come to the end of their cruel days, since that's what they want.'

"'I am convinced that at that very moment both of them would rather have had peace than war. But since they were very brave and very courageous knights they fought ceaselessly, without mercy. Finally Tirant saw that he was near death because of all the blood he was losing, so he drew as close to the other man as he could, and stabbed him in the left breast, straight into his heart. The other man dealt him a mighty slash to his head, causing him to lose the sight of his eyes, and he fell to the ground before the other one. And if the Frenchman had been able to hold himself up when Tirant fell, he could easily have killed him if he had wanted. But he did not have enough strength, and he immediately fell dead on the ground.

"When the judge saw that the knights were lying there so still, he got down from the catafalque, and going up to them, he said:

"'Upon my word, you two have behaved like good and very honorable knights: no one could find fault with you.'

"And he made the sign of the cross twice over each of them, and taking two sticks he made a cross and laid it over the two bodies. Then he said:

"'I see that Tirant's eyes are still open a little, and if he isn't dead he's very near to it. Jerusalem, I charge you to stay here and guard these bodies, and I'll go to the court to give the news to the king.'

"He found the king leaving mass, and in everyone's presence, he said:

"'My lord, in truth, there were two most valiant knights in Your Majesty's court in the morning, and now they are so near death that there is no hope for them.'

"'Who are these knights?'

"'My lord,' said Claros of Clarence, 'one is Lord Vilesermes and the other is Tirant lo Blanc.'

"'I am very displeased,' said the king, 'by this news. Let us go out there before we eat to see if we can help them.'

"'In faith,' said Claros, 'one has already departed from this world, and I believe the other will soon join him—that is how badly they were wounded.'

"When the relatives and friends of the knights heard the news they gathered up their arms and rushed as quickly as they could, on foot and on horseback, and our Lord God gave us the grace to get there before the others. We found Tirant so covered with blood that he was unrecognizable, and he had his eyes slightly open.

"When the others saw their lord lying dead, they quickly ran toward our knight, wanting to take his life, and we defended him very well. We split our group into two parts, and, with our backs to each other, we kept his body between our lines. There were many more of them than of us, but every place they advanced they found their way blocked. At the same time they shot arrows and one of them struck poor Tirant, who was lying on the ground.

"The high constable arrived immediately, with many men, and he separated us. Soon afterward the king came with the tournament judges. When they saw the knights, one dead and the other seemingly in the throes of death, they ordered no one to move them until they had held counsel.

"While the king was in council, listening to the tale of Claros of Clarence and Jerusalem, the kings-of-arms, the queen arrived with all the ladies and maidens. When they saw them they wept for the deaths of two such singular knights. Fair Agnes turned to Tirant's relatives, and said:

"'Knights who love Tirant, are you doing so little for your good friend and relative that you let him leave life like this? That's the way he'll die, lying on the cold ground, his blood pouring out. A half hour more, and he won't have a drop of blood left in his body.'

"'My lady, what would you have us do?' said a knight. 'The king has commanded, under penalty of death, that no one should dare to touch them or move them from here.'

"'Oh, poor me!' said Fair Agnes. 'Our Lord does not want a sinner to die, and the king does? Have a bed brought, and put him on it until the king finishes his counsel: the wind is getting into his wounds and will make him worse.'

"The relatives immediately sent for a bed and a tent. While they were getting it, Tirant was continually nauseous because of the wounds and because of all the blood he was losing. When Agnes saw how much pain Tirant was in, she said:

"'In all conscience, I should not be blamed by father or mother, by brothers and sisters, or other relatives, or by our lords the king and queen, because I am doing this with pure intentions.'

"She removed the clothes she was wearing, which were of white velvet, and she put them on the ground, and had Tirant placed on top of the clothing. Then she begged many of her maidens to take off their clothes and lay them over Tirant. When Tirant felt the warmth of the clothes he opened his eyes wider than before. Fair Agnes sat down and took his head and put it in her lap, saying:

"'Oh, poor me, Tirant! What an unlucky bauble it was that I gave you. If I had known that something like this would happen, I wouldn't have given it to you for anything in the world. I beg you, knights, bring the body of Lord Vilesermes here, next to me. Even though I did not love him while he was alive, I do want to honor him in his death.'

"They quickly brought him to her, and putting his head on the left side of her lap, she said:

"'Lord Vilesermes spent seven years of his life trying to win me, and this is his reward. He performed extraordinary acts of chivalry out of love for me, and he wanted to marry me. But I am of greater lineage and wealth, and I refused to consent to something that was for his pleasure and satisfaction. And now the poor knight is dead because of jealousy.'

"The king came out of his council, having heard the complete story from the kings-of-arms, and he had the three archbishops, the bishops and all the clergy come in a solemn procession from the city, to honor the dead knight. Tirant's relatives had doctors and a bed and tent brought, and everything else that was needed. They found that he had eleven wounds in his body, and four of them were critical.

"After Tirant had been treated and all the clergy had arrived, the king and the judges ordered the dead knight placed in the box that the dead are carried in, covered with a beautiful gold cloth that was used for knights who die in battle. Tirant went behind him, carried on a large shield. Even though his hand was useless and he could not use it or hold it up, it was decided to tie it to a stick, with the bare sword that he had killed him with in his hand.

"In this fashion the clergy went first, and afterward came the dead knight with all the knights on foot. Then came the king with all the great titled lords. Then came Tirant the way I have described, with the queen following, and all the ladies and maidens. Then came the High Constable with three thousand armed men. They went to the Church of Saint George, and here they very solemnly held a requiem mass.

"When the king and queen left the church with all the others, they accompanied Tirant to his lodging, and every day the king went to see Tirant until he had completely recovered. That is what was done to all the wounded. And thirty maidens were given to Tirant to serve him continually.

"At the hour of vespers the king and the queen went to the Church of Saint George, and had Tirant brought there, and after vespers the king had the following proclamation read:

'As we, judges of the tournament, have been given license by the king to judge all the battles that will be held within the time established by His Majesty we state and declare:

'Lord Vilesermes died like a good knight and we declare that he is to be buried and admitted to the holy mother Church, and that the glory of the battle will be given to Tirant lo Blanc.'

"When the judgment was published, the clergy sang a very beautiful litany over the knight's sepulcher, and the honors given him lasted till nearly midnight.

"Afterward they took Tirant to his lodging, with the king and queen and all the others paying him great honor. And they also honored all the other victorious knights."

"May you have joy and consolation from what you most love," said the hermit. "For you have told me how Tirant has been the victor over three knights he defeated."

"My lord," said Diafebus, "he has done even more singular deeds that I have not yet told Your Grace."

"I would be very pleased," said the hermit, "if you would tell me about them."

"My lord, your holiness should know that two months after Tirant had gotten out of his bed and could bear arms again, something very strange happened to him.

"The Prince of Wales came to the celebration with a large retinue of noblemen. His lodgings were near the city wall, and as he is a great hunter he had many greyhounds. One day the king went to his lodging with three or four knights to greet him, because when they were children they had been great friends and they were very close relatives. The prince wanted to joust, and when he saw the king he begged him to have the tournament judges come to counsel him. Tirant was returning from the city, and when he was in front of the prince's lodgings a greyhound broke its chain and got out of its cage, and it was so fierce that no one dared to go near it.

"As Tirant was passing through the middle of the square he saw the greyhound running swiftly toward him to attack him. He quickly dismounted and pulled out his sword. When the greyhound saw the sword, it turned back and Tirant said:

"'I don't want to lose my life or my honor for an animal.'

"And he mounted his horse again. The king and the judges were standing where they could see him. The Prince of Wales said:

"'In faith, my lord, I recognize that evil tempered greyhound, and since he's loose, if the knight that just went by is brave, we'll see a pretty battle between them.'

"'I believe,' said the king, 'that that is Tirant lo Blanc, and since he's made it run away one time I don't think it will dare to go near him again.'

"When Tirant had gone twenty steps further, the greyhound again ran at him in a rage, so Tirant had to dismount again, and he said:

"'I don't know whether you're a devil or under a spell.'

"He took out his sword, and ran toward it, and the greyhound ran in circles around him, but it did not dare go near him for fear of the sword.

"Now, said Tirant, 'since I see that my weapons make you afraid, I don't want anyone to say that I fought you with superior arms.' "He threw his sword behind him. The greyhound made two or three leaps, and ran as swiftly as it could. It picked up the sword with its teeth and carried it off a distance. Then it came running back at Tirant.

"'Now,' said Tirant, 'I'll attack you with the same weapons you want to use against me.'

"They struggled together in a fury, and bit each other mortally.

"The greyhound was huge and sublime, and it made Tirant fall to the ground three times, and three times it nearly knocked him down. This struggle of theirs lasted half an hour, and the Prince of Wales commanded his men not to go near to separate them until one of them was defeated.

"Poor Tirant had many bites on his legs and on his arms. Finally Tirant grabbed it around the neck with his hands and squeezed as tightly as he could, sinking his teeth into its throat with such ferocity that it fell to the ground, dead.

"The king quickly came out with his judges and picked Tirant up and carried him to the prince's house, and there they had the doctors come to minister to him.

"When the queen and the maidens heard about Tirant, they quickly came to see him. When the queen saw how badly he was hurt, she told him:

"'Tirant, honors are won by danger and work. You get out of one bad situation, and you fall into another.'

"'Most serene lady, full of all human and angelic perfection, let Your Majesty be the judge of my sin,' said Tirant.' I was not intending to bring harm to anyone when a devil in the form of a dog appeared before me with his master's consent, and decided to satisfy my desire.'

"'You shouldn't be sad at all, no matter how many misfortunes befall you,' said the queen, 'for here you show your virtue all the more.'

"At this moment the king and the judges came out, and they told Tirant that as they had seen the battle between him and the greyhound, and since he had thrown away his sword and the two were equal in arms, the judges were giving him the honor and the prize in battle, as if he had defeated a knight. And they commanded the kings-of-arms, heralds, and messengers to announce throughout the city the honor that was bestowed on Tirant that day. And when they took him to his lodging they gave him those honors that are given in other battles."

"I am very content with everything you have told me," said the hermit. "As long as I have lived in this miserable world I have never heard of such great celebrations."

When they thought it was time to go, they all took their leave of the father-hermit, each thanking the other.

And from this time forward the hermit is never mentioned again.

CHAPTER III - SICILY

Tirant and his companions journeyed until they reached the city of Nantes. When the Duke of Brittany heard that Tirant was coming with his relatives, he went out to welcome him with all the city magistrates and many knights, and they paid him the highest honor they could, for he had been the best knight of all those who had been at the festivities in England. The duke feted him, and Tirant was held in high esteem by all the people in the land.

One day while Tirant was with the duke and many other knights, relaxing and talking, two knights came from the King of France. The duke asked if there was any news from the court, and they told him that the Genoese had invaded the island of Rhodes, and that the Christians there were in need of help.

The news had reached the King of France, and he had lamented loudly, but did very little. Then the knights left the court of the King of France, and came to the Duke of Brittany. The duke showed compassion for the Grand Master and the religious at Rhodes, and he told everyone there that he would send ambassadors to the King of France. Then, if the king wanted to send assistance to the Grand Master of Rhodes, and if he wanted him to go as captain, he would do it very willingly and he would spend two hundred thousand crowns of his own money on it.

The morning of the following day they chose four to be ambassadors: an archbishop, a bishop, a viscount, and Tirant lo Blanc. When the ambassadors were before the King of France, they explained their mission, and he told them that in four days he would give them an answer. A month went by and they still did not know what he intended to do. Finally he told them that at the moment he could not intervene in these things because he was occupied with other matters that were more important to him. The ambassadors returned with the reply.

When Tirant saw that so many Moors were on Rhodes and that no one was sending help, he talked to many sailors, asking if he could do something. They told him that if he would go, he could help them very much, and that he would not have to enter the castle of Rhodes from the dock, but would be able to go in another way.

Tirant bought a large ship, and had it well stocked and armed. It happened that Tirant had become a good friend of the five sons of the King of France. The youngest of them all, whose name was Philippe, was somewhat unlearned, and was considered gauche, so the king thought very little of him, and no one ever spoke about him. A gentleman who served him, knowing that Tirant had a ship and was going to Rhodes and then to Jerusalem, wanted to go there very much. So he told Philippe:

"My lord, knights who want honor should not stay in their parents' home while they're young and able, especially if they are younger than their brothers, and their father ignores them. Think of that famous knight, Tirant lo Blanc: After the great honor he received in the battles he won in England, he is now preparing a large ship to go to Rhodes and to the holy land of Jerusalem. Oh, what glory it would be for you if you and I would leave here secretly, without saying a word to anyone until we were on the ship, one hundred miles out to sea! And Tirant is such a virtuous knight that he will obey you and honor you as someone from your house deserves."

"My good friend, Tenebroso, I know that the advice you are giving me is good," said Philippe, "and I will be very happy if we can do it."

"It seems to me," said the gentleman, "that I should go to Brittany first, to where Tirant is preparing the ship. We are such good friends that I will ask him to let me go along to the holy land of Jerusalem, and I'll ask him what things will be needed for me and two squires. After we have his decision we'll put everything we need on the ship."

Philippe was very satisfied with this, and he said:

"Tenebroso, while you go talk to Tirant I'll get all the money I can, and clothing and jewels."

The following day the gentleman left with two squires, and Tenebroso journeyed until he came to where Tirant was. They were very happy to see each other, and Tenebroso told him the reason for his visit. Tirant was highly pleased, for he knew that Tenebroso was a very valiant gentleman and very discreet, and he valued his company. He answered him:

"My lord and brother, Tenebroso, my worldly goods, myself, the ship, and everything I have are at your service."

When Tenebroso heard Tirant say this, he was the happiest man in the world, and he gave many thanks to Tirant for his great gentility.

He left one of his servants there to prepare a room inside the ship where they could eat and sleep, and where Philippe could stay secretly. Tenebroso set out again, riding until he was back with Philippe who was waiting for him in great anticipation. Philippe was very pleased with Tirant's answer. Tenebroso told him to get ready to leave, and Philippe said that he already had everything he needed to take.

The following day Philippe went to his father, the king, and in the queen's presence he begged him to allow him to go to Paris to see the fair, which was two days' journey from there. The king told him coolly:

"Do whatever you like."

He kissed his hand, and then the queen's hand. They set out on their journey very early in the morning, and finally they reached the sea port. Philippe slipped into a room on the ship without letting anyone see him. When the ship had weighed anchor and they were two hundred miles out to sea, Philippe revealed his presence to Tirant. Tirant was very surprised at this, but because they were so far out to sea, they had to continue on their course toward Portugal, and they arrived at the city of Lisbon. When the King of Portugal learned that Philippe, son of the King of France, was on the ship, he sent a knight who graciously begged him to come ashore to rest from the long sea voyage. Tirant and Philippe dressed in their finery, and accompanied by many knights and gentlemen who had come with Tirant, they left the ship and went to the palace. When the king saw Philippe he embraced him and paid him great honor, and did the same to the others. They remained in the king's court ten days.

When they decided to leave, the king had them fill the ship with everything they needed. From there Tirant sent a gentleman to the King of France with letters explaining what had happened to his son. When the King of France learned that his son was in such good company he was very pleased, and the queen was especially happy, because so much time had passed with them knowing nothing that they thought he was either dead or had entered some monastery.

Philippe took his leave of the King of Portugal, and the ship set sail, reaching the Cape of Saint Vincent to pass through the Straits of Gibraltar. There they encountered many Moorish vessels, and when they saw the ship, all the vessels went into formation. They attacked it fiercely, and the combat lasted half a day, with many men from both sides dying. After Tirant's men had rested, they renewed the battle, and it was very fierce. Now Tirant's ship was much larger and lighter than any of those of the Moors, but it was alone, while there were fifteen of the others, large and small, and all of them carried weapons.

One very able sailor on the ship, named Cataquefaras, had sailed a great deal, and he was very clever and valiant. When he saw that the situation was taking a turn for the worse, he took many ropes from the ship and made a net. He placed those ropes from stern to prow and around the mast, and he put them up so high that the men did not find their weapons hindered in any way; instead it kept them from being taken prisoner. For the missiles that the Moors launched were so many and so thick that it was a great marvel to see, and if the ship had not been covered by that net of ropes, it would have been completely filled with stones and iron bars. In that way it was protected so that no stone could pass through it; instead, when a stone hit against the ropes, it bounced into the sea. What else did this sailor do? He took up all the mattresses that he found on the ship, and he covered the forecastles and the sides of the ship, and as the missiles fell on top of the mats they could not damage the ship. And he did still more. He took boiling oil and tar, and when the ships drew alongside, they threw the oil and boiling tar with ladles, causing grave injuries to the Moors, who had to draw apart from the ship. But still they passed through the entire Straits of Gibraltar, fighting night and day. There were so many missiles, darts and spikes that the sails were pinned to the ship's mast when the Moors left them. They were very near land, and certain that the ship would run aground, stern first, near the city of Gibraltar. But the sailors were so capable that they quickly put the ship around and raised the sails. Then they passed out of the Straits and entered the great sea.

Philippe, Tirant and many others were wounded in these battles. They went to a deserted island near the land of the Moors, and there they tended to their wounds and repaired the ship as well as they could. Then they sailed along the Barbary Coast where they fought many battles with Genoese and Moorish vessels until they were close to Tunis. There they decided to go to the island of Sicily to take on wheat. They went to the port of Palermo where the king and queen were, with their two sons and a very beautiful daughter named Ricomana, a very intelligent maiden of many virtues. When the ship was in port, they made a scribe disembark along with five or six men, with orders to tell no one about Philippe or Tirant, but rather to say that their ship had come from the west and was on its way to Alexandria with some pilgrims who were going to the Holy Sepulcher.

When the king learned that they had come from the west he had the scribe from the ship and all the others called before His Majesty so he could have news of those lands. Before the king, they told about the great battles they had had with the Moors and Genoese in the Straits of Gibraltar, and forgetting at that moment Tirant's words, they mentioned that Philippe, son of the King of France, was there, in the company of Tirant lo Blanc. When the king heard that Philippe was on that ship, he had a great wooden bridge, covered with cloth and satin, constructed from land to the ship. And to pay him honor, the king went on board the ship with his two sons, and implored Philippe and Tirant to come on land and rest a few days from the great hardships they had endured at sea, and from their battles with the Moors. Philippe and Tirant thanked him and told him that, to please him, they would go with His Majesty.

The king brought them to the city, furnished them with very nice quarters, and had them served excellent dishes and other things men need who have been at sea.

Philippe, following Tirant's counsel, told the king that they would not stay in their room until they had seen the queen. And the king was very pleased. When they were upstairs in the palace, the queen, along with her daughter, the princess, received them very graciously. And when they returned to their lodgings they decided that she was everything a king's daughter should be.

Afterward, every day at mass or after eating, they were with the king and especially with the infanta, who was so pleasant to the foreigners who came and went, that everyone spoke of her great virtue. And by speaking with the infanta everyday at the king's court, Philippe grew very enamored of her, as she did of him. But Philippe was so shy when he was in her presence that he scarcely dared speak, and when she asked him questions, he did not know how to respond to some of them. Tirant quickly answered for him and said to the infanta:

"Oh, my lady, what a thing love is! That Philippe! When we are in our lodgings or away from here his lips never tire of praising Your Majesty, and when you are present he is overcome with love, and finds it difficult to speak. In truth, I tell you, if I were a woman and I found someone with his genteel quality, and I knew he was of a long and good lineage, I would forget everyone else and would love only him."

"Oh, Tirant," said the infanta. "Your words sound nice, but if it turns out that he is vulgar by nature, what pleasure would it be for a maiden to have everyone laugh at him? For love's sake, don't tell me such things; I would prefer a man who was prudent and discreet, rather than for him to be vulgar and avaricious."

"My lady," said Tirant, "you are right, but he doesn't fit that description. He's young and of tender years, but he's old in the best sense, generous, more valiant than anyone, and very amiable and gracious. During the night he gets up and doesn't let me rest the way I would like. If I want to give him pleasure I have only to speak of Your Majesty. If this isn't love, tell me, what could it be? My lady, love someone who loves you. He is the son of a king, like you, and he loves you more than his life. If he does not talk as much as Your Grace would like, that is a virtue. Guard yourself, my lady, from those men who boldly dare to court a maiden. That kind of love is not good love: it comes and goes. And men like those are called corsairs, because they make booty of everything. My lady, give me a man who appears before his lady with great fear and shame, with his hands trembling, and who can scarcely utter a word."

"Tirant," said the infanta, "because of your great friendship with Philippe, you are right to honor him so much. With your noble order of chivalry, you can do nothing but what is expected of you, and that's why I think highly of you. But don't imagine that I'm a woman who is easily convinced. I have to put my hands in up to the elbows in the sense of knowing his manners, his station and condition, and if he could bring me happiness. Although I'm happy when I see him, experience tells me that he seems vulgar and avaricious, and both of those vices are incurable."

"I beg Your Highness to give me an audience, and not to be angry at what I say to you. I see ambassadors from the Pope coming to the court to arrange a marriage between Your Highness and his nephew (and some wonder if he isn't his son). And I also see ambassadors from the King of Naples, the King of Hungary, and the King of Cyprus. Although I may not have the power of the most Christian King of France, I would like to talk to your father and Your Highness about the wedding. I see that you are wise and discreet, my lady. But because of your perfection you deserve to be on the imperial throne and subject to the crown of France: it is of greater height than the Roman Empire."

At this time the queen arrived and interrupted their delightful conversation. After a few moments the queen said to Tirant:

"Virtuous knight, scarcely an hour ago the king and I were speaking of you and your chivalrous deeds, and the king wishes to place an undertaking in your charge that is very important to him and to me.

And I regard you so highly that if you attempt it you will surely come out of it with honor. But to avoid all doubts I will put forth all the obstacles there that I can."

"My lady," said Tirant, "Your Excellency speaks in such a covert manner that I don't know what to reply, unless Your Highness can give me a clearer explanation. But whatever I can do for Your Excellency, with the consent of the king, I'll do it most willingly, even if it should be to carry the cross on my back."

The queen gave him many thanks. Tirant took leave of the queen and the infanta, and when he was at his lodgings he was sorry that the ship was not repaired so that he could depart immediately.

Tirant saw a ship on the high seas. He wanted to have news before going to dine, and he sent an armed brigantine that left very swiftly and then returned. They told him that this ship came from Alexandria and Beirut, and that it had touched on the island of Cyprus, but that it had not been able to land at Rhodes, because there were so many Moors that held it besieged on land and sea. Many Genoese vessels were guarding the port, and the city of Rhodes was in such straits that they had no bread to eat. It had been three months now since the Grand Master or anyone in the castle or the city had eaten. They ate nothing but horse meat, and the day they could find even that was a fortunate one. They truly believed that in a few short days they would have to surrender to the Moors.

When Tirant heard this news, he reflected at length. And he decided to load the ship entirely with wheat and other victuals, and embark to give aid to Rhodes. He quickly sent for merchants, and he gave them so much money that they loaded the ship with wheat, wine and salted meat.

When the king learned of this he sent for Tirant, and said:

"The glory of your undertaking puts all the princes of Christianity to shame who have refused to aid the master of Rhodes. I would like to go with you to Jerusalem (in disguise so that no one would recognize me). That would please me more than if you gave me a kingdom, and I would be in your debt for the rest of my life. So I beg you with great love, don't refuse this to me."

When the king had finished, Tirant said:

"If it should become necessary, I will treat Your Highness as my own lord, as though I had served you all my life. As for going on my ship, my lord, the ship, my possessions, and myself all belong to Your Excellency, and you may command and order everything as if it were your own."

And so they agreed. When the king had seen the ship, he asked for his room to be prepared near the mast, because a ship is safer there when disaster strikes.

Every day the king and Tirant discussed many things, and finally they spoke about Philippe. Tirant wanted to arrange a marriage between him and the infanta, and for him to have the dowry the king had mentioned. The king favored a union with the house of France, but he said:

"Tirant, I won't make a decision about any of these things until I know what my daughter thinks. If she agrees, then I will consent to the marriage. I will be very happy to talk to the queen and to my daughter, and if they agree, the wedding will be held before we leave."

The king had the queen and his daughter brought to his chambers, and he said to them:

"The reason that I had you come here, my queen and my daughter, was to tell you about a journey I will be making soon. I have decided to go with Tirant to Jerusalem, and so that no one will know me I am taking along only one gentleman to serve me. And because my life and death are in the hands of God, our Heavenly Father, I would like to see you well married, my daughter. If you like the king's son who is here, and who would unite us with the greatest king in Christianity, I am certain that with Tirant's aid and counsel and Philippe's willingness, everything can be arranged satisfactorily."

"It seems to me," said the infanta, "that Your Majesty knows it will be two weeks before the ship's cargo is loaded and it's ready to weigh anchor. In that time, Your Highness, with the counsel of my uncle and your brother, the Duke of Messina, you can take care of the matter, because the duke is expected here tonight or tomorrow."

"You speak well, my daughter," said the king, "and what you say is reasonable."

"Pardon me, Your Highness," said the infanta, "but since Your Excellency has decided to go on this saintly journey, you should hold a great celebration so that Tirant and all the men with him will be more willing to serve you when you are at sea, and besides if it reaches the ears of the King of France, he will know that Your Highness is showing consideration to his son, Philippe. Next Sunday a celebration could be held that would last three days; the tables could he set night and day, and there would always be enough food on them for everyone who wanted to attend.'

"In faith, my child," said the king, "you've thought it out better than I could have, and I am very happy to do it, But I'm very busy planning my journey, and I want to leave the kingdom in such a good state that no one will note my departure, and besides there could be many problems when we are in the land of the Moors. So I would like you, my child, to plan this and be in complete charge of it ."

The king immediately had the steward and the purchasers brought in, and he told them to do everything his daughter, Ricomana, commanded, and they said they would be happy to.

The infanta planned everything very well, and many different dishes were chosen. Now the infanta held this celebration solely to see how Philippe would conduct himself at the table.

The infanta gave instructions that on the day of the great feast the king, the queen, Philippe and she would eat together at a table above the others, and that the Duke of Messina, Tirant, and all the counts and barons and others would eat at a table below the king's. The evening before the celebration the king sent two knights to Philippe and Tirant, asking them to go with him to mass and to dinner the following day. And they humbly accepted the invitation.

In the morning they dressed in their finest clothing, and all their men did the same, and then they went to the palace and paid homage to the king. The king received them very kindly, and he took Philippe's hand, as did the Duke of Messina to Tirant, and they went to the church. When the king was at his chapel, they asked his permission to accompany the queen and his daughter, and the king gave his consent. As they walked with the ladies, Philippe took the infanta's arm so that he could be closer to her, and Tirant never left Philippe's side for fear that he would do or say something foolish that would annoy the infanta.

When the mass was finished and the king and all the others had gone back to the palace, the dinner was ready. The king sat in the center of the table with the queen at his side. To honor Philippe, the king had him sit at the head of the table, with the infanta facing him. Tirant wanted to remain standing in order to be near Philippe, but the king said to him:

"Tirant, my brother, the Duke of Messina is waiting for you, and he doesn't want to sit down without you."

"My lord," said Tirant, "if you please, tell him to take a seat, because at a feast like this it's fitting that I should serve the king's son."

The infanta was impatient, and with a rather cross look on her face she said to him:

"Don't bother yourself about being at Philippe's skirts all the time, Tirant. In my father, the king's house, there are enough knights to serve him so that you don't have to do it."

When Tirant heard the infanta speaking so heatedly and saw that he had to leave, he put his mouth to Philippe's ear and said to him:

"When water is brought to the king, and you see the infanta getting up and then kneeling and holding the vessel for him, you do what she does, and be careful not to do anything gauche."

He said that he would, and Tirant left him. When they were all seated, the king's water bowel was brought, and the infanta knelt and held the laver. Philippe tried to do the same, but the king would not allow it. And the same happened with the queen. When it was the infanta's time to wash, she took Philippe's hand so that they could wash together, and Philippe courteously and with gentility, said that it was not seemly. Then he knelt and attempted to hold the dish for her, but she refused to wash until they both washed together. Then the bread was brought and placed before the king and the others, and no one touched it as they waited for the dinner to be brought. When Philippe saw the bread before him he quickly took a knife, and picking up a loaf of bread he cut through it and made twelve large pieces. When the infanta saw such a sight she could not contain her laughter. The king and everyone there, including the serving boys, made great sport of Philippe, and since the infanta was laughing too, it was inevitable that it should come to Tirant's attention, because he did not take his eyes from Philippe for a moment. Standing up, he ran from the table and said:

"By heaven, Philippe must have stained his honor with some great foolishness."

He went to his side at the king's table, and saw the slices of bread that Philippe had cut. When he saw that neither the king nor anyone else had touched their bread, he immediately understood the reason for the outbursts of laughter. Tirant quickly picked up the slices of bread; then he reached into his pocket, took out twelve gold ducats and put one ducat on each slice, and he had them given to the poor. When the king and the infanta saw what Tirant had done, they all stopped laughing. The king asked Tirant the meaning of what he had done.

"My lord," said Tirant, "when I have finished what I must do I will tell Your Highness."

Tirant gave out all the bread slices, each one with its ducat, and he put the last one to his mouth, said an Ave Maria over it, and gave it away. The queen said:

"I would like very much to know about this ceremony."

Tirant answered:

"My lord, Your Excellency and all the others are astonished at what Philippe began and I have finished, and you've all mocked him. The reason for it, since Your Highness wants to know, is that the most Christian kings of France, because of all the blessings they've received from the immense goodness of Christ our Lord, began this tradition: Before any of their children entered the order of chivalry, they were not allowed to eat the first loaf of bread that was put in front of them at dinner until they had cut it into twelve slices, and placed a silver "real" on each one, and had given it to the poor in memory of the twelve apostles. Then, after the order of chivalry had been bestowed on them they would put a piece of gold on each slice. And even down to today everyone in the house of France continues the custom. And, my lord, that's why Philippe cut the bread and made twelve slices, one for each apostle."

"Praise God," said the king, "that sort of charity is the most beautiful I've ever heard of. I'm a crowned king and I don't give as much in alms in a month."

Dinner came, and the infanta told Tirant to go back and eat. Philippe saw what he had done wrong and how discreetly Tirant had remedied it, and he was very careful with the meal, and ate only as the infanta did.

When they left the table, the infanta began to talk to one of her ladies whom she deeply trusted, and with a little anger mixed with love, she began to lament:

"Look at what a sad state I'm in, to have this Tirant as the enemy of my desires: I can't talk alone to Philippe for even an hour. Tell me, Tirant, why do you make me so mad? You must know how nice it is to be alone with the person you love. Now, poor me, when I want to sleep I cannot, night is longer than I would like it to be, nothing that I eat tastes sweet to me—instead it's as bitter as gall. If this is life, what can death be?"

And the love-struck maiden lamented, tears flowing from those eyes that had sparked many flames in Philippe's heart. While the infanta had this sad face, the king and his brother, the Duke of Messina, came into her chambers.

When they were in the room the king, seeing such grief in her face, said to her:

"What's wrong, my daughter? Why are you crying?"

"And don't I have reason to, Sire? Your Grace is about to leave. What am I to do all alone? Who will be here to console me? How will my soul find peace?"

The king tenderly consoled his daughter as best he could. Then they went to the queen. The four held counsel, and the king said:

"I beg you, Duke, tell me what you think of this marriage with Philippe."

"Sire," said the duke, "since Your Highness and Philippe are going on this holy pilgrimage, I feel that this marriage should take place only with the consent of his father and mother."

Tirant was then put in charge of writing letters to the King of France, and he explained all the details of the marriage pact, if the king would agree. The King of Sicily then prepared a brigantine to go to the mainland with the letters.

At the same time, Tirant's ship was loaded with wheat and other provisions. When the brigantine was ready to depart, the king pretended he was going on it, and he had the news spread that he was going to Rome to talk to the Pope. That night Tirant had the king and Philippe brought on his ship, and when all the men were on board, Tirant went to take his leave of the princess and everyone in the court. Tirant then set sail at night, and in four days he was within sight of Rhodes.

When the Genoese saw the ship coming, they thought it was one of the two they had sent to bring provisions to their camp. They could not imagine that any other ship would dare to come into the midst of as many ships as were in the port. The ship approached, and as it drew near it unfurled all its sails. This, and the shape of the ship, made the Genoese realize that it was not one of theirs, and they hurried to prepare to attack. But the ship was so close that none of their ships had time to raise their sails, and this ship swiftly sailed through all of them at full mast. However, they used lances, spikes and bombards, and all the weapons used at sea. Then Tirant ordered the helmsman and the pilot not to turn the ship, but to head the prow straight into land. And they did, at full speed.

When the people in the city saw the ship beach itself, they thought it was the Genoese coming to take the city. All the men ran there and bravely attacked it. They were also being attacked by the ships at sea, and they were in dire straits until a sailor quickly took one of Tirant's flags and raised it. When the people from the city saw the flag they stopped fighting. Then one of the men told them that the ship had come to help them. Hearing that the captain of the ship was

French, and that the ship was loaded with wheat for them, the people on land went to tell the Grand Master.

When the Grand Master discovered that it was Tirant, he was very anxious to see him, because he had heard of his fame. He sent two knights of the Order to the ship, to ask Tirant to come on land. Tirant told them to tell the Grand Master confidentially that the King of Sicily and Philippe, son of the King of France, were on his ship and that they were going on a holy pilgrimage to Jerusalem, and to ask if they would be safe on his land. The Grand Master promised to keep their presence secret. Then the king and Philippe disembarked, in disguise, and went to the rooms that were prepared for them. Tirant then went on land, well-outfitted. When Tirant was with the Grand Master they talked at length. The Grand Master told him how the sultan was besieging them on land, day and night, and that the Genoese were doing the same by sea; that they were at the point of surrendering because of their great hunger, and they could not last much longer. They had eaten all the horses and other animals, including the cats, and it would be a wonder to find one still alive.

Tirant then had many barrels of wheat brought from the ship, and he asked the Grand Master to have it distributed among all the people, and he said there was still more for the castle. They also gave them the oils and the vegetables and meat, and all the other supplies.

That night Tirant and his men stood watch over the port. The Genoese ships—especially the captain's ship—were very close to land. It was nearly midnight when a sailor approached Tirant and said:

"Sir, what would Your Grace give to someone who, tomorrow night, set fire to the ship that's so close to shore, and that they say belongs to the Genoese captain?"

"If anyone could do that," said Tirant, "I would gladly give him three thousand gold crowns."

"Sir," said the sailor, "if you promise me, on your word as a knight, to give them to me, I will do everything I can. And if I'm not able to do it I will become your slave."

"My friend," said Tirant, "I don't want you to put any obligations on yourself: the shame you will bring if you don't do it, will be punishment enough for you. As for me, I promise you on my order of chivalry, that if you set it on fire tomorrow, I will give you everything I said I would, and more."

The sailor was very satisfied because he knew he could do it, with all the skill he had both on sea and land. In the morning he prepared everything he needed.

When the Grand Master had heard mass, he went to see the king, Philippe and Tirant, and they spoke at length about the war and about many things regarding the city which I will not go into so as not to be tiresome. A very old knight of the Order, who had come with the Grand Master, said:

"It seems to me, gentlemen, since you have brought enough supplies to last the city several days, that my lord, the Grand Master, should make a gift for the sultan of many different kinds of foods, in order to make him lose any hope he has of taking us by hunger."

All the great lords praised the old knight's advice, and the order was immediately given to send him four hundred hot loaves of bread straight from the oven, wine, honey and sugar sweetmeats, three turkeys, chickens and capons, honey, oil, and all the other things they had brought.

When the sultan saw the present, he said to his men:

"Damn this present and the traitor who sent it! This will bring the perdition of my honor, and will be my ruin."

When it was nearly midnight, and very dark, the sailor had everything ready to set the captain's ship on fire, and he did it this way:

The sailor had fixed a very strong capstan into the ground near the sea. Then he put a thick rope in a boat along with a hemp cord as thick as a man's finger. He got into the boat, and two men rowed for him. When they were so near the ship that they could hear the men on the sterncastle talking, they stopped rowing. He took off all his clothes and tied the cord around his waist. Then he took a very sharp knife so that he could cut any cords he needed to, and he tied it in back of him so that it wouldn't hinder him when he swam. He attached one end of the cord to the knife sheath, and he told the men in the boat to keep feeding him line. When everything was ready he slipped into the water, and swam until he was so close to the ship that he could hear the men on watch talking. Then he swam underwater so that no one would see him, and he reached the rudder. He looped the cord through an iron ring under the rudder, and swam back to his boat. He took the end of the cord and tied it to one end of the thick rope and he held it up and greased it thoroughly. Then he took a chunk of grease for the bar, to let it slide through easily and noiselessly.

Finally he gave orders to the men, and swam back to the ship and greased the ring. The men on the boat stuck an iron pin through the cord and pulled until the pin caught on the ring. And the sailor knew that the other end of the rope was in the boat. When he thought it was time, they rowed back to land. He tied one end of the rope to the capstan, and the other end was tied to a large boat, a type of whaling boat, that had been filled with firewood and candlewood, all soaked with oil so it would burn well.

They set it afire, and let it catch well. Then one hundred men were set at the capstan, and they began to turn it with all their strength. And with the power from the capstan it all happened so quickly that the large boat had barely started to move when suddenly it was flush against the side of the ship. With the huge fire on it sending out enormous tongues of flame, it quickly set fire to the ship with such a fury that nothing in the world could have put it out. The men on the ship thought only of getting away in small boats. Others threw themselves into the sea to swim to the other ships, while many were burned to death because they did not have time enough to get off, and the fire caught many others sleeping.

When it was daylight Tirant took three thousand crowns and gave them to the sailor, along with a silk garment lined with martens and a brocade doublet. The sailor thanked him very much and was very pleased.

Then the sultan summoned his captains, both on sea and land. He told them what had happened, and also about the present the Grand Master had sent him to show how well supplied the city was with everything it needed and more. And as winter was setting in, the cold weather and rain were beginning to bother them. So they decided to raise camp and go back, but with the intention of returning another year.

He quickly ordered the camp trumpets and pipes to play, and the ships to raise their sails and come near the island, because he would be there to get all the men.

When Tirant saw the Moors raising camp, he armed himself, and with all his men he left the city and went to the camp. He set fire to the palisades and huts so that if they came back they would have to build them again.

Then the sultan set sail and returned to his land. The lords there were well informed about the reason he was returning, and they went together to see him. They took him prisoner, and put him in a lion's den where he died horribly. Then they chose another sultan. The new sultan ordered all the Genoese ships to form a large armada with all the men who had come from Rhodes, along with many more, and he had them advance on Greece. And so it was done. And the Grand Turk was also invited, and he came with many soldiers on horseback and on foot. In the two armies were seventeen thousand Moors.

And as soon as they set foot in Greece, they took over many villas and castles, and seized sixteen thousand small children, and sent them all to Turkey, to the land of the sultan, to be raised in the Mohammedan sect. And they sent many ladies and maidens into perpetual captivity.

And the Island of Rhodes was freed from the power of the infidel.

When the people at Cyprus knew that the sultan's armada had left the city of Famagusta, they quickly loaded many ships with wheat, oxen, sheep and other victuals, and they took it all to Rhodes because of the great hunger there. Many other places also sent supplies. And in a short time the city and the island had so much that all the elders said they had never seen or heard their ancestors tell of so great an abundance on the Island of Rhodes.

A few days after the sultan had gone, two galleys arrived from Venice, loaded with wheat, and carrying pilgrims to the holy land of Jerusalem. When Tirant learned about it he went to tell the king and Philippe, and they were very happy to hear it.

That night the king and Philippe and Tirant said farewell to the Grand Master and boarded the Venetian galleys with the few people who came with them, for all the others stayed at Rhodes. Diafebus, Tirant's relative, did not want to stay behind; nor did Tenebroso, so he could serve Philippe.

They made such good time that in a few days they reached the port of Jaffa, and leaving there, as the weather was fair and the sea was calm, they reached Beirut with no trouble. All the pilgrims disembarked there and found good guides: there was a guide for every ten people. When they were in Jerusalem together, they stayed two weeks to visit all the holy places. Then they boarded the galleys again and raised the sails, and they had such good weather that they reached the island of Sicily in only a few days.

There was great rejoicing among the Sicilians at the return of their lord, and a courier was sent to the queen to tell her of the king's arrival. The king asked about the queen's health, and about his daughter and two sons, and his brother, the duke. They answered that they were all very well, and they told him how the King of France had sent forty knights as ambassadors, with a company of gentlemen.

They rested there a few days because they were very tired from the sea voyage. After they had rested, the king and all the company set off for Palermo where the queen was staying.

On the day that he was to arrive, his brother, the duke, came out first, accompanied by very fine people. Then came the archbishop, with all the clergy. Then came the queen, accompanied by all the ladies of honor in the city; then, after a moment, the infanta Ricomana came with all her maidens and those of the city, very well dressed, and they were a wonderful sight to behold; then came the forty ambassadors of the King of France, wearing gold chains and dressed in garments of crimson velvet which reached to their feet.

When the king had greeted the queen, and his daughter had paid him reverence, Philippe and Tirant bowed to the queen. Philippe took the infanta's arm, and they went to the palace. On the way the forty ambassadors came to pay their respects to Philippe before they did to the king, and Tirant said to Philippe:

"My Lord, tell the ambassadors to go and pay reverence to the king before they speak with you."

Philippe told them, and the ambassadors replied that they had been instructed by their lord, the King of France, his father, to go to the king and give him the letters they were bringing after they had paid obeisance to him. And Philippe again told them that above all they should go to the king before speaking with him.

"Since Philippe wishes it," said the ambassadors, "we will do as he commands."

When the king reached the palace with all the people, the ambassadors from the King of France went to pay him reverence, and they gave him the letters. The king received them very warmly, and paid them great honor. Then they went to Philippe and honored him, as was their duty, because he was the son of their own ruler. Philippe regaled them, and there was great rejoicing.

After the celebration for the king's arrival was over, the ambassadors explained their mission, which had three parts. First, that the King of France was very pleased to have his son Philippe marry the infanta Ricomana, as Tirant had arranged. Second, that if the King of Sicily had a son, he would give a daughter of his to him as his wife, together with one hundred thousand crowns as a dowry. Third, that he had asked the pope, the emperor, and all the princes of Christianity to send him aid, because he had decided to march against the infidel, and all those to whom he had sent word had offered to help him. And on behalf of their lord, the King of France, they were asking him to give assistance, and if his lordship decided to send an armada he should make Philippe captain and send him too.

The king's reply was that as far as the marriage was concerned he was very pleased, but as to the rest he would hold counsel.

When the infanta learned that her father had consented to her marriage with Philippe, she said to herself:

"If I can find some defect in Philippe that shows that he's gauche or avaricious, he will never be my husband. From now on I intend to devote every moment to discovering the truth."

And while the infanta was deep in thought, a maiden in whom she had complete confidence came into her chambers, and said to her:

"Tell me, my lady, what is Your Highness thinking about that makes you look so disturbed?"

The infanta answered her:

"I'll tell you. My father, the king, has given his consent to the ambassadors from France for the wedding, and I have a deep suspicion that Philippe is gauche, and that he may even be avaricious. And if he is, in the slightest, I wouldn't be able to stay in the same bed with him for an hour; instead I would become a nun or go into a convent. I've done everything I could to get to know him, but because of that traitor, Tirant, fortune hasn't been with me. Yes; I Pray God that I'll see him boiled and fried because that day when the bread was cut I would really have known Philippe if it hadn't been for him."

When Philippe received the money his father had sent, he dressed in elegant clothing, and he wore many jewels and gold chains and other valuable jewelry.

On the day of Our Lady, in August, the king invited Philippe and all the ambassadors, and everyone who held a title in his land to dine. When the king was sitting at the table it began to rain very hard. The infanta was very pleased, and she said:

"Now I can find out what I want to know."

When the tables were cleared the minstrels came, and they danced a while before the king and queen. Then came the collation. The king went into his chambers to rest, but the infanta would not stop dancing for fear that Philippe would leave.

When it was nearly time for vespers the skies cleared and the sun came out, and then the infanta said:

"It's such a nice day, wouldn't it be a fine idea for us to go riding through the city?"

Philippe quickly answered:

"My lady, why would you want to ride through the city in this terrible weather? If it starts to rain again you'll get drenched."

Tirant saw through the infanta's wiles, and he tugged at Philippe's coattails to make him be quiet. The infanta caught a glimpse of the signal Tirant was making, and she became very angry. She ordered the horses brought out, and they all sent for the animals. When the infanta was mounted she almost turned her back on Philippe, but kept sight of him out of the corner of her eye. And Philippe said to Tirant:

"Send for another suit of clothes so that this one won't be ruined!"

"Oh," said Tirant, "the clothes be damned! Don't worry about your clothing. If this suit gets dirty, there will be another one."

"At least," said Philippe, "see if there aren't two pages who will carry my coattails so they won't drag along the ground."

"For the son of a king," said Tirant, "you're very stingy! Hurry along now, the infanta is waiting."

Then Philippe, very troubled, started out. While the infanta, who had been watching them talk, wasn't able to make out their words.

So they rode through the city, and the infanta enjoyed herself immensely, seeing how the clothes of that miserly Philippe were getting wet, and how he was always looking at them. The infanta, to have more pleasure, told them to bring the falcons and they would go a little way out to the outskirts and hunt some quail.

"Don't you see, my lady?" said Philippe. "This is no time for hunting. There's nothing but mud and water everywhere."

"Oh, you niggardly fellow!" said the infanta. "This oaf still won't do anything that I want.'

But she paid no attention to him, and went out of the city and found a peasant. She took him aside and asked him if some river or canal was not close by. The peasant answered:

"My lady, straight ahead, not far from here, you'll find a large canal that will come up to a mule's groin."

"That's just what I'm looking for."

The infanta went ahead, and they all followed her. When they came to the water, the infanta rode through it, and Philippe stayed behind and asked Tirant if there were any servants who would hold up the tails of his clothing.

"I'm tired of your prattle. Don't worry: I'll give you mine. The infanta has gone through and she's riding ahead. Hurry, and go to her side."

And Tirant laughed out loud so that it would look as though Philippe had been telling him a joke. When they had gone through the water, the infanta asked Tirant what he was laughing at.

"In faith, my lady," said Tirant, "I was laughing at a question Philippe has been asking me all day long, before we left Your Highness's chambers, then when we were riding, and now as we went through the water. He asked me what love is and where it comes from. The second thing he said to me is: Where does love abide? I tell you, on my word, that I don't know what love is or where it comes from, but, my lady, the true and loyal love that Philippe feels for you does not retreat from anything."

"Let's go back to the city," said the infanta.

As they went through the water, she watched to see if the two men were talking together again. Philippe, seeing that his clothes were already soaked, was unconcerned as they rode through the water. And the infanta was very much relieved, and believed everything Tirant had said to her. But her soul was still not entirely at ease, and she went to Tirant and said to him:

"I'm in a situation where fortune holds me in its hands. I would rather renounce my life and possessions than take a husband who is gauche, vile and avaricious. And I want to tell you in all truth, Tirant, that my fortune has always been adverse. Now if I take this man for a husband, and he turns out not to please me, I would find myself having to do very desperate things, because it is my opinion that it's better to live alone than to live with a bad companion."

Tirant quickly replied:

"Philippe is one of the best knights in the world today. He is young, more genteel than any other man, courageous, generous and more wise than gauche. That's been his reputation wherever we've gone, among knights, duennas and maidens. Even the Moorish women who saw him, loved him and wanted to serve him. If you doubt it, look at his face, his hands, his feet, and his entire body. And if you would like to see him completely naked, I can arrange that too, my lady. I know that Your Highness loves him deeply, for he is loved by all people. You are to blame, my lady, if you don't have him by your side in a bed perfumed with benjamin, civet, and pure musk, and on the following day if you complain to me about him I will suffer whatever torment Your Highness decides."

"Oh, Tirant," said the princess. "I would be very happy if I could have someone who would please me. But what use would it be if I had a statue at my side who could only give me pain and desperation?"

At this moment they reached the palace and found the king in the hall, speaking with the ambassadors from France. When he saw his daughter he took her by the hand and asked where she had been. Dinner was ready, and Philippe and the ambassadors took their leave of the king and the infanta, and went to their chambers.

After dinner they began to dance, and the infanta purposefully caused the dancing to continue until late at night. The king saw that it was past midnight, and he left without a word so that he would not disturb his daughter's pleasure. And as it began to rain the infanta sent word to the king, asking him to permit Philippe to remain that night, and to sleep in the palace with her brother, the infante. The king answered that that was agreeable to him.

After the king had left, the dancing ended and the infante begged Philippe to stay there that night to sleep because most of the night was already past. Philippe answered that he was deeply grateful, but that he would go to his lodgings.

The infanta took hold of his clothes and said:

"Since it is my brother, the infante's, wish for you to stay here, this will be your lodging tonight."

Tirant said:

"Since they are so fond of you, stay here to give them pleasure, and I'll stay with you so that I can serve you."

"That won't be necessary, Tirant," said the infanta, "because in the house of my father, my brother, the infante, and myself, there will be no lack of people to serve him."

Seeing how angrily she spoke, Tirant realized that they did not want him, and he left with the others for his lodging. When they had gone, two pages came with torches and asked Philippe if it was his desire to go to sleep. And he answered that he would do whatever his lady, the infanta, and her brother commanded. They said that it was time now. Philippe bowed to the infanta and followed the pages, who led him to a room where there were two beds.

The king had ordered a very special canopy made entirely of brocade, to be given to his daughter on her wedding day, and he had another placed in a room to serve as its model. When the brocade canopy was finished, the two beds were placed next to each other, and the coverlet was of the same brocade. And on it they put the sheets for the wedding, with embroidered pillows, so that it was an exceptional bed. The other bed in the same room was entirely white, and there was a great difference between the two.

When Philippe saw such a luxurious bed he was astonished, and he thought it better to lie down on the other one. That evening, while dancing, he had slightly torn his stocking, and he thought that his servants would not come as soon as he would get up in the morning. The pages had been well instructed by the infanta, who was in a place where she could see very well what Philippe would do. Philippe said to one of the pages:

"Please go bring me a needle and a little bit of white thread."

The infanta had seen him give orders to the page but she did not know what he was asking for. Then the page went to the infanta, and she had them give him a needle with a little thread. The page took it to him, and found him pacing from one end of the room to the other, and he did not say one word to the second page who was there.

When Philippe had the needle he went to a torch and opened a blister that was on his hand. The infanta immediately thought he had asked for the needle because of the blister. He put it on the bed where he had decided to sleep. Philippe then took off his clothing and sat on the bed. After the pages had removed his stockings, Philippe told them to go to sleep and to leave a torch lit for him.

They did so, closing the door. Philippe got up from where he was sitting in order to get the needle and sew his stocking, and he began to look for it from one end of the bed to another. He gloomily lifted the coverlet, and he twisted and turned it so much that it fell on the floor. Then he lifted up the sheets and tore the entire bed apart without finding the needle. He thought about making up the bed again and sleeping in it; but when he saw it all undone, he said to himself:

"Oh well. Won't it be better for me to sleep in the other one instead of making this one up again?"

A very singular needle was that for Philippe. He lay down in the bed of rich covers. The infanta, who had seen the entire display, said to her maidens:

"Upon your life, look how great the knowledge of foreigners is, especially Philippe. It was my intention to test him, as I have done other times, with these two beds. I thought that if Philippe were gauche and avaricious he would not dare sleep in a bed like this one, but instead would lie down in the other which is more plain. He has done something quite different: he has torn apart the plainest one and has thrown its covers on the floor, and he has gone to bed in the best one to show that he is the son of a king. Now I can see that Tirant is a loyal knight who has always told me the truth."

And with this thought, she left to go to bed.

Very early in the morning Tenebroso came to Philippe's chambers with his pages, and brought him more clothing so that he could change. When the infanta was dressed and still fastening her skirt, she sent for Tirant and with a show of great happiness she told him:

"I have come to realize how special Philippe is. I have seen with my own eyes his speech and royal manners, and that he is very generous. Until now I felt very hesitant about giving my consent to this marriage, but from now on I will do everything His royal Majesty, my father, commands me."

Tirant heard the infanta's words, and he was the happiest man in the world. He quickly answered:

"I am very happy that Your Excellency has come to know the truth. I am going to speak with my lord, the king, immediately in order to bring the matter to a swift conclusion."

Tirant took his leave of the infanta and went to the king and told him:

"I see the ambassadors from France in great anguish about this wedding so I have come to Your Majesty to beg you to either have it take place, or give the ambassadors your leave so that they can return to their king. And if it will not make Your Majesty angry to have me speak with my lady, the infanta, on Your Highness' behalf, I believe that she will be inclined to do whatever Your Majesty commands."

"If God gives health to my soul and my body," said the king, "that will please me. I beg you to go to her and make the request on my behalf and your own."

Tirant left the king and went back to the infanta. He found her combing her hair, and he told her about the conversation he had had with the king. Then the infanta said:

"My lord Tirant, I have complete confidence in your nobility and virtue, so I am putting this entire matter in your hands, and I will agree to everything. If you want it done now, I will do it."

Tirant saw how willing she was, and he saw Philippe at the door, waiting to accompany the infanta to mass. He asked the infanta to have the maidens leave because he wanted to tell her other things in Philippe's presence. The infanta ordered the maidens to go, and they were very surprised to see the infanta speaking so docilely to Tirant.

When all the maidens were gone, Tirant opened the door to the chamber and had Philippe enter.

"My lady," said Tirant, "here is Philippe who has a greater desire to serve your ladyship than all the princesses in the world, and so I beg Your Grace, here on my knees, to kiss him as a sign of good faith."

"Oh, Tirant!" said the infanta. "These are the words you wanted to tell me? Your face reveals what you bear in your heart. When my king and my father commands it of me, then I will do it."

Tirant motioned to Philippe, who quickly took her up in his arms, and carried her to a lounge that was there, and kissed her five or six times. The infanta said:

"Tirant, I placed no little trust in you. What have you made me do? I thought of you as a brother and you have put me in the hands of someone I am still unsure of—I do not know whether he will turn out to be my friend or my enemy."

"Your words are cruel, my lady. How can Philippe be an enemy to Your Excellency if he loves you more than his own life, and desires to hold you in that bed where he slept this evening, completely nude, or in your chemise? You can be certain that this would be the greatest blessing in the world. So, my lady," continued Tirant, "allow Philippe, who is dying of love for you, to enjoy part of the glory that he has desired so much."

"May God not permit it," said the infanta, "and may He keep me from an error like that. I would think of myself as vile if I gave my consent to such a thing."

"My lady," said Tirant, "Philippe and I are here only to serve you. Let your benign grace have a little patience."

And Tirant caught her hands while Philippe attempted to make use of his own resources. The infanta cried out, and the maidens came and calmed them down.

When the infanta had laced up her garments, she dressed very elegantly, and Philippe and Tirant accompanied her and the queen to mass. And there, before mass, they were engaged. The following Sunday the wedding was held with great ceremony, and celebrations took place which lasted a week, with jousts, tournaments, dances, and buffoonery, night and day.

In this way the infanta was entertained, and she was very pleased with Tirant, and much more with Philippe whose work was so wonderful that she never forgot it.

When the wedding celebrations were over, the King of Sicily decided to lend his assistance to the King of France, and he had ten galleys and four large ships armed, and gave the men six months' wages. Tirant bought a galley, but he refused to accept wages or to associate with anyone, because he intended to act on his own. When the galleys were armed and well stocked with food, they received word that the King of France was in Aigues-Mortes with all the vessels of the King of Castile, of Aragon, Navarre and Portugal.

Philippe was chosen captain, and the infante of Sicily went with him, and they found themselves in the port of Savona with ships from the pope, the emperor, and everyone who had offered their aid. They all left together and sailed until they came to the island of Corsica where they found the King of France. There they took on water, and they approached the great city of Tripoli in Libya before dawn, and no one in the entire armada knew where they were going with the exception of the king. But when they saw the king's ship turning and everyone taking up arms, they realized that that was their destination. Then Tirant, who was on his galley, went to the king's ship on a skiff. He climbed aboard with many others, and they found the king arming himself and preparing for mass.

During the reading of the Gospel, Tirant knelt before the king and begged him to let him make a vow, and the king gave his consent. Tirant placed himself at the feet of the priest who was saying mass, and knelt down, and the priest took up the missal and turned it toward the king. Tirant, while kneeling, put his hands on the book and said:

"By the grace of Almighty God, I belong to the order of chivalry. As a knight who wants to attain honor, I make my vow to God and all the saints in paradise, and to my lord, the Duke of Brittany, captain-general of this armada, that I will be the first to touch land and the last to return."

Afterward Diafebus vowed to write his name on the gates to the city of Tripoli.

Then another knight made a vow that he would go so near the wall that he would put an arrow inside the city.

Another knight stood up and vowed that he would enter the city and take a Moorish maiden from her mother's side, that he would put her on the ship and give her to Philippa, the daughter of the King of France.

Another knight vowed that he would place a flag on the highest tower in the city.

On the king's ship there were many knights—more than four hundred fifty. And where there are many, envy and ill will are engendered, for the sin of envy has many branches. Many were moved by the desire to make Tirant break his vow, and they made preparations with boats and vessels and small galleys to be the first to reach land.

There were so many Moors that when they saw such a great armada they positioned themselves near the sea to stop the Christians from reaching land. All the galleys pressed forward toward land, and they were so close that their sides nearly touched.

When they were so near to land that they could throw down the ladders, all the ships turned about so the men could disembark. But Tirant ordered his galley to head in to land, prow first. When he felt the ship touch land, Tirant, who was standing, armed, on the prow, jumped into the water. The Moors saw him and ran toward him to kill him; but Diafebus and others defended him. Many armed men and many sailors leapt after him in order to go to his aid.

As soon as the king's galley and the others had turned about, they lowered their ladders. But who dared disembark when they saw so many Moors? The greatest fight was where Tirant stood. Virtue, goodness, strength and wisdom were in the king and his men who, as valiant knights, climbed down the ladders, and their haste to attack the Moors was so great that many fell into the sea. When all the men were on land, they gave the Moors great battle, and many men from both sides died.

As soon as the Moors attempted to take refuge in the city, many good knights went in and took five streets of the city, but they were unable to take more. All the knights fulfilled their vows on those five streets that they took, and they loaded the ships and the galleys with the great booty that they had taken. But so great was the aid that the Moors received that they could not push on.

When they had to withdraw, therein lay the great danger, and many of them died.

When they were all on board, Tirant remained behind, because he had not yet fulfilled his vow. His galley had now debeached, and its ladder was on land, waiting for Tirant to board. A knight who was searching for honor, and who well deserved it for his virtues, was named Ricart lo Venturos, and he remained behind with Tirant. Ricart said to Tirant:

"All the men are on board or are dead. Only you and I are still here. You had the glory of being the first of the conquerors, because your feet were the first to touch this cursed land. But don't forget how I defended you many times from danger. You go on board the galley first, so that we can be equals in honor and fame and brotherhood, for at times a person who wants all worldly glory loses everything."

"There is no time to waste on words," said Tirant. "Life or death is in your hands. I will be considered victorious if both of us die at the hand of these infidels, and I'm sure that our souls will be saved if we die with our faith firm, like good Christians, defending ourselves. So give me your hand, Ricart, and let us die like knights."

The two knights were in the sea up to their chests because of the lances, darts, spears and stones that were being hurled at them. When Ricart saw that Tirant was going up to the shore to attack the Moors, he caught him by the coat and brought him back into the water, and said:

"I know of no knight in the world as fearless as you are. And since I see how great your courage is, do this: Put your foot on the ladder first, and then I will be first to climb up."

The king was in great anguish, afraid that those two knights would be lost. Tirant wanted to give him part of the honor, so he put his right foot on the ladder. Then Ricart went up first, and Tirant was the last of all, and so he fulfilled his vow.

There was much discussion about these two knights: some said that Tirant had fulfilled his vow, and the king and many others paid him high honor. When Ricart saw that they all were honoring Tirant, he said:

"If the matter is duly judged by the code of chivalry, who should the honor and glory be given to, if not to me? Tirant was a coward in battle even when fortune aided him, so the prize for this act should be given to no one but me. I am barefoot, and I will never again put shoes on my feet until His Majesty, the king, and the noble knights make a decision about this. It is well known that after all the men had retreated, Tirant and I stayed behind alone on the shore. He and I argued at length about who would be the first to go on board. When he saw that I did not want to, he put his foot on the ladder before I did. And so, my lord, may it please Your Highness to summon your sacred council, and let Your Majesty give the honor to the one it belongs to, as it rightfully and justly belongs to me. And if Your Highness does not want to judge this case, I say in the presence of everyone that I am a better knight than Tirant, and I will fight him, man to man, to the death.'"

The king answered:

"Ricart, no good judge can decide anything if he does not listen to all sides first, and this cannot be done without Tirant here."

This conversation came to Tirant's attention, and he brought his galley alongside the king's ship. When he came aboard, the king was in his chambers, sleeping. When Ricart heard that Tirant had come, he went up to him and said:

"Tirant, if you dare to say that I'm not a better knight than you are, I offer to do battle with you to the death." And he threw his gloves at him as a challenge.

When Tirant saw that he wanted to fight him with so little provocation, he raised his hand and dealt him a hard blow. The noise they raised was so loud that the king had to come up with his sword in hand. When Tirant saw the king, he went up to the forecastle, and from there he defended himself, and he said to the king:

"Sire, Your Majesty should punish this shameless knight who is the instigator of all evil. He has never found himself in a joust, much less seen the flash of an angry sword before his eyes, and now he wants to fight me to the death over nothing. If he defeats me he will have defeated all the chivalresque acts I have accomplished to my glory and honor. And if I am the victor I will have conquered a man who has never borne arms."

After he had said these words he swung safely down to his galley on a rope. If the king had been able to put his hands on him at that moment, because he committed such an outrageous act on his ship, it would not have been surprising if he'd had his head removed from his shoulders.

The king departed with the entire armada from Tripoli in Libya, and went toward Cyprus, sacking the Turkish coast and setting it red with blood and flames, and they loaded all the ships with the many riches they had taken. When they reached Cyprus they went to the city of Famagusta, took provisions of food and turned toward Tunis. There the king disembarked and they pressed the city hard in combat. Tirant and his men attacked a tower which had a deep moat at its foot, and Tirant fell into it. Ricart was heavily armed to see if he could take revenge on Tirant. When he reached the tower he saw Tirant lying in the moat. Ricart leapt into the moat, wearing all his armor, and helped Tirant get up. Then he said:

"Tirant, here stands your mortal enemy who can give you death or life. God forbid that I should let you die at the hands of the Moors, when I can give you aid."

And he pulled him out, for they would surely have killed him if they had found him there. When he was out, Ricart said to him:

"Now you are free, Tirant. Protect yourself from death as well as you can, because you can be sure that I will do everything in my power to kill you."

"Virtuous knight," said Tirant, "I have seen your great goodness and courtesy, and I know that you saved me from a cruel death. I kneel to the ground and beg your forgiveness for the way I offended you. I give you my sword so that you can take whatever vengeance you like on me."

When the knight heard such humble words, he forgave him and was happy to be his friend, and from that time on they were good friends, and were inseparable in life, until death.

After the king had taken and sacked the city of Tunis, Ricart would not go onto the king's ship, but went on Tirant's galley instead. When the king and the knights heard what had happened, they praised both of them because each had shown great gentility,

After the King of France left the city of Tunis, they turned toward Sicily to see his daughter-in-law and to disembark in Palermo. When the King of Sicily learned of his arrival, he had a great celebration prepared for the King of France. The King of Sicily went on board his ship, and when they met they were both delighted. They went on land where the daughter-in-law was waiting, and the father-in-law and daughter-in-law met joyfully. The king gave her many presents and held her hand all day long and would not let her leave his side. And as long as the King of France remained there, each day, before the infanta arose, he would send her some expensive gift: one day brocades, another silks, gold chains, trinkets, and other jewels of great value. The King of Sicily presented the King of France with one hundred very beautiful and unique horses, which the King of France made a great show of appreciation over. And the King of Sicily had his daughter go on board the ships personally and inspect them to see how well they were stocked with food, and to supply them with everything they needed. The King of France thought highly of what his daughter-in-law was doing, and he was very pleased to see that she was a very discreet and diligent woman who was on board the ships from morning to night, and that she did not eat until they had been supplied.

When the ships were filled and the horses were put on board, the King of France took his leave of the King of Sicily, the queen and the infanta, and departed, taking the Prince of Sicily with him, and when they were in France he gave him one of his daughters for a wife.

The armada left the port of Palermo and turned toward Barbary, and moving along the shore line they came to Malaga, Oran and Tlemcen. They passed through the Strait of Gibraltar, then went to Ceuta, Alcazar Segur, and Tangier. As they turned along the other coast of Cadiz, Tarifa and Gibraltar, they went by Cartagena, for in those days the entire coast was in the hands of the Moors. From there they went by the islands of Ibiza and Majorca, and then they went to the port of

Marseilles to disembark. The king gave liberty to all the ships except the ones belonging to his son, Philippe; he wanted him to go along and see his mother, the queen. Tirant went with them, and from there he went to Brittany to see his father and mother and his relatives.

After a few days, while the King of France held the wedding for his daughter and the prince of Sicily, he wanted Philippe to return to his wife. Philippe received word that the King of Sicily's other son had renounced the world, and become a friar. Philippe begged his father, the King of France, to send for Tirant to accompany him to Sicily. The king wrote letters to the Duke of Brittany and to Tirant, asking him to go with Philippe to Sicily, and asking the duke to plead with him earnestly. When Tirant saw the petitions of two such great lords, he was obliged to obey their commands, so he left Brittany and went to the court of the king. The king and queen begged him earnestly to go with Philippe; and he very graciously gave his consent.

Philippe and Tirant left the court and went to Marseilles where they found the galleys well stocked. They boarded them, and had such a good voyage that in a few days they reached Sicily. The king, the queen and the infanta were very happy to see them.

CHAPTER IV - CONSTANTINOPLE

After a week, while the king was in council, he remembered a letter the Emperor of Constantinople had sent him, telling about certain troubles. He summoned Tirant, and had it read in his presence, and it said the following:

"We, Frederick, Emperor of the Empire of Greece by the immense and divine majesty of the sovereign and eternal God, extend health and honor to you, King of the great and abundant island of Sicily. By the pact made by our ancestors, sealed, signed and sworn by you and by me through our ambassadors: We do notify your royal personage that the sultan, the Moorish renegade, is inside our empire with a great army, and in his company is the Grand Turk. They have overpowered a large part of our realm, and we have been unable to lend assistance, for because of my old age I cannot bear arms. After the great loss we have suffered of cities, towns and castles, the dearest possession I had in this world was killed — my first born son who was my consolation, and a guardian of the holy Catholic faith — doing battle against the infidel, to his great honor and glory and to mine, And as a greater misfortune, he was killed by his own men. That sad, painful day was the perdition of the imperial house and of my honor. It is known to me and is common knowledge that in your court you have a valiant knight, whose name is Tirant lo Blanc; he belongs to the brotherhood of that singular order of chivalry said to be founded on that glorious saint, the father of chivalry, Saint George, on the island of England. Many singular acts worthy of great honor are told about this knight and are celebrated throughout the world, and they are the reason we ask you to beg him on your behalf and mine to come to my service, for I shall give him all my possessions he may desire. And if he will not come I pray Divine Justice to make him suffer my pain. Oh, blessed King of Sicily! As you are a crowned king, have pity on my pain so that the immense goodness of God will keep you from a similar situation, for we are all subject to the wheel of fortune, and there is no one who can detain it."

When the emperor's letter was finished, and Tirant had heard it, the king said:

"You should thank Almighty God, Tirant, my brother, for He has given you such perfection that your name reigns throughout the world. I place my trust in your generosity, and so I dare to beg you on behalf of the Emperor of Constantinople and myself. And if my pleas have no effect on you, at least have pity on that unfortunate emperor so that he will not lose his imperial throne."

When the king had said this, Tirant replied:

"If Your Majesty commands me to go serve that prosperous emperor who reigns in Greece, I will do it because of the great love I hold for Your Highness. But, Sire, I can only do as much as a man can do; that is plain to God and to the whole world. And I am even more astonished at that great emperor—who has passed over all the excellent kings, dukes, counts, and marquis in the world who are more knowledgeable and more valiant than I am in the art of chivalry—that he should pass over them for me."

"Tirant," said the king, "I know very well that there are good knights in the world, and you should not be forgotten among them. If, by chance, their honor should be examined, among the emperors, kings, and expert knights, the prize, honor and glory would be given to you as the best of them all. So I beg you as a knight to go and serve the imperial state, and I advise you to do so as if you were my son."

"Since Your Majesty commands and advises me to do this," said Tirant, "I will go."

The king ordered all the galleys to be stocked with everything they would need. And when the king told the emperor's ambassadors that Tirant was willing to go, they were the happiest men in the world, and they heartily thanked the king.

As soon as the ambassadors had reached Sicily they were ready to offer a salary to the men. They gave half a ducat each day to the crossbowmen, and a ducat to the soldiers. And since there were not enough men in Sicily, they went on to Rome and Naples, and there they found many men who accepted wages very willingly, and they also bought many horses.

Tirant took his leave of the king and queen, and of Philippe and the infanta. And with all the men on board, they let a favorable wind fill the sails, and they sailed quickly over a calm sea until one morning they found themselves before the city of Constantinople.

When the emperor heard that Tirant had arrived, he was happier than he had ever been, and he said that he felt as if his son had come back to life. As the eleven galleys neared shore, all the cries of happiness made the entire city resound. The emperor went up on a great catafalque to watch the galleys come in. When Tirant learned where the emperor was, he had two large flags of the King of Sicily brought out, and one of his own. He had three knights come out in armor, each of them with a flag in his hand, and every time they passed in front of the emperor they lowered the flags until they nearly touched the water, while Tirant's touched it each time.

This was a sign of greeting, and because of the emperor's dignity they humbled themselves so lowly before him. When the emperor saw this, which was something that he had never seen before, he was very pleased.

When Tirant was on land he found the Count of Africa waiting for him on shore with many men, and he welcomed him with great honor. They then made their way to the platform where the emperor was. As soon as Tirant saw him he knelt to the ground, along with all his men, and when they reached the middle of the platform they bowed again. When he was six feet away he knelt and tried to kiss his foot, and the worthy lord would not permit it. He kissed his hand, and the emperor kissed him on the mouth.

When they had all bowed to him, Tirant gave him the letter from the King of Sicily. After the emperor had read it in everyone's presence, he spoke to Tirant:

"This is no small happiness I feel at your arrival, virtuous knight. So that everyone will know how grateful I am to you, I am bestowing on you the imperial and general captaincy over the soldiers and over justice."

He offered him a rod made of solid gold, and on its enamel head was painted the coat of arms of the empire. When Tirant saw that it was the emperor's will he accepted the rod and the captaincy, and kissed his hand. The trumpets and minstrels began to play by order of the emperor, and they announced throughout the city by imperial proclamation how Tirant lo Blanc had been chosen captain by command of their lord, the emperor.

After all this the emperor came down from the catafalque to go back to the palace, and they passed by a very beautiful lodging that had been prepared for Tirant and his men. The emperor said:

"Captain, since we are here, go into your chambers so that you can rest a few days from the hardships you have endured at sea."

"What, my lord! Do you imagine that I would be so ill mannered as to leave you? My consolation is to accompany Your Majesty—to Hell itself, and even better, to the palace."

The emperor had to laugh at what Tirant had said. And Tirant continued:

"My lord, if it please Your Majesty, when we are in the palace, allow me to go and pay my respects to the empress and to your beloved daughter, the infanta."

The emperor gave his consent. When they were in the palace the emperor took him by the hand and led him to the empress's chamber. They found her in the following condition: the chamber was very dark, for there was no light at all, and the emperor said:

"My lady, here is our captain who has come to pay you his respects."

She replied in a very weak voice:

"Very well. He is welcome."

Tirant said:

"My lady, it is by faith that I must believe that the one speaking to me is the empress."

"Captain," said the emperor, "whoever holds the captaincy of the Greek Empire has the power to open windows, and to look everyone in the face, to remove the mourning they bear for a husband, father, son or brother."

Tirant asked for a lighted torch to be brought, and it was done immediately. When the light was cast on the room the captain discovered a pavilion entirely in black. He went up to it, opened it, and saw a woman dressed in coarse cloth with a large black veil over her head that covered her entirely, down to her feet. Tirant removed the veil from her head so that her face was uncovered, and when he saw her face he knelt to the ground and kissed her foot and then her hand. She held a rosary in her hand, made of gold and enamel; she kissed it and then had the captain kiss it. Then he saw a bed with black curtains. The infanta was reclining on the bed, dressed in a black satin skirt and covered with a velvet garment of the same color. A woman and a maiden were sitting at her feet on the bed. The maiden was the daughter of the Duke of Macedonia, and the woman was called Widow Repose, and she had nursed the infanta with her own milk. In the back of the room he saw one hundred seventy women and maidens, all with the empress and the infanta Carmesina.

Tirant approached the bed, made a deep bow to the infanta, and kissed her hand. Then he opened the windows. And it seemed as though all the women were coming out of a long period of captivity: they had been plunged into darkness a long while because of the death of the emperor's son. Tirant said:

"My lord, speaking by your leave I will tell Your Highness and the empress my idea. I see that the people in this notable city are very sad and troubled for two reasons. The first is because of the loss of the prince, your son. Your Majesty should not be troubled, for he died in the service of God, upholding the holy Catholic faith. Instead you should praise and give thanks to the immense goodness of God, our Lord, because He gave him to you and it was His wish to take him from you for His own good, and He has placed him in the glory of paradise. The second reason they are sad is because all the Moors are so nearby that they are afraid of losing their possessions and their lives, and as a lesser evil that they will become captives of the infidel. That is why Your Highness and the empress must show smiling faces to everyone who sees you: to console them in their grief so that they will gather courage to fight against the enemy."

"The captain's advice is good," said the emperor. "It is my wish and my command that men as well as women shed their mourning immediately."

While the emperor was talking, Tirant's ears were attentive to what he was saying, but his eyes were contemplating the great beauty of Carmesina. As the windows had been closed it was very warm, so her blouse was partly open, exposing her breasts like two apples from the garden of Eden.

They were like crystal and allowed Tirant's eyes to gain entrance, and they remained prisoners of this free person forever, until death separated them. The emperor took his daughter Carmesina by the hand and led her from the room. The captain took the empress's arm, and they went into the other room which was very nicely decorated and completely covered with works of art depicting the following love-stories: Florice and Blanchfleur, Thisbe and Pyramus, Aeneas and Dido, Tristram and Isolde, Queen Guinevere and Lancelot, and many more whose loves were displayed in very subtle and artistic paintings. And Tirant said to Ricart:

"I never thought there could be as many wondrous things on this earth as I am seeing."

By this he meant, more than anything, the great beauty of the princess. But Ricart did not understand him.

Tirant took his leave of the others and went to his chambers. He entered a bedroom and put his head on a pillow at one end of the bed. It was not long before someone came to ask him if he wished to dine. Tirant said he did not, and that he had a headache. He was wounded by that passion that traps many. Diafebus, seeing that he was not coming out, went into the room and said:

"Captain, please, tell me what's the matter. I'll be glad to help you if I can."

"My cousin," said Tirant, "the only thing wrong is that the sea air has left me with ardor."

"Oh, captain! Are you going to keep things hidden from me? I have been the archive of all your good and bad fortune, and now are you keeping secrets from me? Tell me, I beg you. Don't hide anything from me."

"Don't torment me even more," said Tirant. "I have never felt a worse illness than I do now."

He turned over from shame, not daring to look Diafebus in the face, and no other words could come out of his mouth except:

"I am in love."

As he said this, tears flowed from his eyes. When Diafebus saw how ashamed Tirant was he understood why, because Tirant had always reprimanded all of his kinsmen and all his friends on the subject of love. And as Diafebus thought of the remedies for this illness, he said:

"Although you may think that it is difficult and strange to be subjugated by the yoke of love, you may be sure that no one can resist it. And so, my captain, the more intelligent a man is, the more he should hide his thoughts, and not reveal the pain and anguish that are attacking his mind."

When Tirant saw the good advice that Diafebus was giving him, he got up, feeling ashamed, and they went in to dinner, which was excellent, because the emperor had planned it. But Tirant could not eat. The others thought he was still feeling the ill effects of the sea. And because of his great passion, Tirant left the table and went into his room, sighing and ashamed of the confusion that was overcoming him.

Diafebus took another knight, and they went to the palace, not to see the emperor but to see the ladies. The emperor, who was sitting near a window, saw them passing by, and sent word for them to come up. Diafebus and the other knight went up to the emperor's rooms, and found him with all the ladies. The emperor asked what had become of their captain, and Diafebus told him that he felt a little ill. When he heard it he was very concerned, and told his doctors to go at once to see him.

When they returned, the doctors told the emperor that his illness had only been caused by the change of air. The magnanimous emperor begged Diafebus to tell him about all the celebrations that had taken place in England with the marriage of the king to the daughter of the King of France, and about all the knights who had jousted, and which ones had been victorious in the field.

"My lord," said Diafebus, "I would be very grateful if Your Majesty would excuse me from telling about these things. I wouldn't want Your Highness to think that because I'm a relative of Tirant I would favor him. I will tell you what truly happened. And as proof, I have all the acts signed by the king, and the judges of the camp, and by many dukes, counts and marquis, kings-of-arms, and heralds."

The emperor begged him to have them brought immediately. Diafebus sent for them and told the emperor extensively about all the celebrations, and he did the same about the jousts. Afterward they read the acts and they saw that Tirant had been the best of all the knights. The emperor was very pleased, and his daughter Carmesina even more so, as were all the ladies who were listening very attentively to all the magnificent chivalresque acts of Tirant. Afterward they wanted to know about the wedding of the princess of Sicily and the liberating of the Grand Master of Rhodes.

When everything had been explained the emperor held counsel, as he usually did for a half hour in the morning and one hour in the evening. Diafebus wanted to go with him, but the valiant lord would not permit it and told him:

"It is a well-known fact that young knights have a greater desire to be with the ladies."

He left, and Diafebus stayed behind, and they spoke of many things.

Princess Carmesina begged her mother, the empress, to let them go to another room where they could enjoy themselves, since they had been inside a long while in mourning for her brother. The empress said:

"My child, you may go wherever you please."

They all went to a marvelous hall built completely with brickwork, done artfully and with delicate craftsmanship. When the princess was in the hall, she drew apart from the others with Diafebus, and they began to talk about Tirant. When Diafebus saw that she was speaking of Tirant with such interest, he quickly said:

"Take everything that I say as a loyal servant, and keep it in the most secret part of your heart: It was only the fame of Your Highness that brought Tirant here to see you and serve you. Don't imagine, Your Highness, that we have come at the request of the valiant King of Sicily, or because of the letters your father, the emperor, sent to the King of Sicily. And Your Highness should not imagine that we have come to test ourselves in the exercise of arms, or because of the beauty of the land, or to see the imperial palaces. Your Highness, the reason for our coming was none other than the desire to see you and to serve Your Majesty. And if wars and battles take place, it will all be to win your love and admiration."

"Oh, wretched me," said the princess. "What are you saying to me? Shall I grow vain, thinking that all of you have come because of love of me, and not for the love of my father?"

"In faith," said Diafebus, "on that I could swear that Tirant, our brother and lord, begged us to come with him to this land to see the daughter of the emperor, whom he desired to see more than anything in the world. And the first time his eyes rested on Your Highness he was so overcome by the vision of Your Excellency that he took to his bed."

When Diafebus said these things to the princess she became withdrawn and remained deep in thought, and could not speak. She was half beside herself, her angelic face blushing, for feminine fragility had so overtaken her that she could not utter a word.

At that instant the emperor arrived and called Diafebus, and they spoke of many things until the emperor wished to dine. Diafebus excused himself, approached the princess, and asked Her Majesty if she would like to command him to do anything.

"Yes," she said, "take these embraces of mine and keep them for yourself, and give part of them to Tirant."

Diafebus drew near to her and did what she commanded.

When Tirant heard that Diafebus had gone to the palace and was talking to the princess, he wanted very much for him to come back so that he could have news of his lady. When he came into the room, Tirant got up from the bed and said:

"My good brother, what news do you bring me of the lady who has captured my heart?"

When Diafebus saw Tirant's great love, he embraced him on behalf of his lady, and told him their entire conversation. Then Tirant was happier than if he had been given a kingdom, and he recuperated so well that he ate well and was happy, and longed for morning to come so he could go and see her.

After Diafebus had left the princess, she remained lost in thought, and she had to leave her father's side and go into her chambers. The daughter of the Duke of Macedonia was named Stephanie. She was a young lady whom the princess loved deeply, because they had been raised together from the time they were very small, and they were both the same age. When she saw that the princess had gone into her chambers, she left the table and followed her. When they were together the princess told her everything Diafebus had said to her, and about the great passion she felt from Tirant's love.

"I tell you that I have been more pleased by the vision of this man than all the men I have ever seen in the whole world. He is tall, of excellent disposition, and he shows his great spirit by his manners, and the words that come out of his mouth are delightful. I think he is more courteous and agreeable than anyone I have ever known. Who wouldn't love a man like that? And to think that he came here more out of love for me than for my father's sake! Truly, my heart is inclined to obey all his commands, and the signs indicate that he will be my life and my salvation."

Stephanie said:

"My lady, from among those who are good, choose the best. Knowing his extraordinary feats of chivalry, there is no lady or maiden in the world who would not love him and obey his every wish."

While they were engaged in this delightful conversation, the other maidens came in, along with Widow Repose, who was very concerned with Carmesina since she had suckled her. She asked them what they were discussing, and the princess said:

"We were talking about what that knight was saying—about the great celebrations and honors that were given in England to all the foreigners who were there."

And they spent the night speaking of these and other things so that the princess slept neither a little nor a great deal.

The following day Tirant put on a cloak of gold braid, and in his hand he carried the gold captain's stick. All the rest of his countrymen dressed in brocades and silks, and they all went to the palace.

When the emperor heard that his captain had come, he told them to let him enter. As he came in the emperor was dressing and the princess was combing his hair. Then she brought him water to wash his hands, as she did every day. The princess was dressed in a skirt of gold thread.

When the emperor had finished dressing he said to Tirant:

"Tell me, captain, what was the illness you were suffering from yesterday?"

"Your Majesty, my affliction was brought about entirely by the ardor of the sea, for the winds of these lands are finer than are those of the west."

The princess replied before the emperor could speak:

"Sire, that ardor does no harm to foreigners if they behave as they should; instead it brings them health and a long life."

As she spoke these words she looked steadfastly at Tirant, smiling at him so that he could see she had understood him.

The emperor and the captain left the chamber together, talking as they went, and the princess took Diafebus' hand, and holding him back, she said:

"After what you told me yesterday I have not slept all night long."

"My lady, what can I tell you? We've had our share as well. But I am very happy that you understood Tirant."

"How could you think," said the princess, "that Greek women are of less worth than the French? In this land all women understand your Latin, no matter how obscurely you speak."

"That is why," said Diafebus, "we are more content having conversations with intelligent people."

"As far as conversations go," said the princess, "you will soon see the truth, and you'll see if we understand your wiles."

The princess ordered Stephanie to bring other maidens to keep Diafebus company, and many young ladies quickly appeared. When the princess saw him well engaged, she went back into her chamber to finish dressing. Meanwhile Tirant accompanied the emperor to the great church of Saint Sophia, and then left him there saying prayers, and returned to the palace to be with the empress and Carmesina. When he was in the great hall he found his cousin Diafebus there, surrounded by many maidens, and telling them about the love between Philippe and the daughter of the King of Sicily. Diafebus was so accustomed to being in the company of maidens, that it seemed as though he had been raised with them from birth.

When they saw Tirant come in they all stood up and welcomed him; then they made him sit with them, and they talked of many things. Then the empress came out, and she took Tirant aside and asked him about his illness. Tirant told her that he was much better now. It was not long before the princess came out.

Tirant took the empress's arm because, as captain, he held precedence over the others. There were many counts and marquis there, men of high position, and they went to the princess to take her arm, and she said:

"I want no one at my side except my brother Diafebus."

They all left her, and he took her arm. But God knows that Tirant would much rather have been near the princess than near the empress. As they went to the church, Diafebus told the princess:

"Look, Your Highness, how spirits attract."

The infanta said:

"Why do you say that?"

"My lady," said Diafebus, "because Your Excellency has on a sequined dress, embroidered with large pearls, and the sentimental heart of Tirant brings what it needs. Oh, how fortunate I would feel if I could place that cloak over this dress!"

As they were very near the empress, he pulled Tirant's cloak. When he felt his cloak being tugged, he stopped, and Diafebus placed the cloak over the princess's dress, and said:

'My lady, now the stone is in its place."

"Oh, wretched me!" said the princess. "Have you gone mad, or have you lost your senses?" Are you so shameless that you say these things in front of so many people?"

"No, my lady," said Diafebus. "No one hears or notices or sees anything, and I could say the Pater Noster backward and no one would understand me."

"You must," said the princess, "have learned about honor in school, where they read that famous poet, Ovid, who speaks of true love in all his books. If you knew what tree the fruits of love and honor are plucked from, and if you knew the customs of this land, you would be a very fortunate man."

As she was saying this they reached the church. The empress went behind the curtain, but the princess did not want to go in, saying that it was very hot. The truth was that she did not go in so that she could observe Tirant at her pleasure. He went near the altar where there were many dukes and counts, and they all gave him the honor of being first because of his station. He said mass on his knees, and when the princess saw him kneeling on the ground, she took one of the brocade pillows that had been placed there for her, and gave it to one of the maidens to give to Tirant. The emperor saw his daughter performing that courteous act, and he was very pleased. When Tirant saw the pillow that the maiden was giving him to kneel on, he stood up and then, with his cap in his hand, he bowed deeply on one knee to the princess.

Do not imagine that during the entire mass the princess could finish saying her Hours as she looked at Tirant and all his men dressed in the French fashion. When Tirant had gazed at the striking beauty of the princess, he let his mind play over all the ladies and maidens he could remember seeing, and he thought to himself that he had never seen or hoped to see anyone as well endowed by nature as she, for in lineage, in beauty, in grace, in wealth, along with infinite wisdom, she seemed more angelic than human.

When mass was finished they returned to the palace, and Tirant took his leave of the emperor and of the ladies, and went to his quarters with his men. As they reached their quarters he went into his chamber and fell upon the bed, thinking of the princess's great beauty. And her beautiful features only served to make him feel worse: so that while he had felt one pain before, he now felt one hundred. Diafebus went into the chamber, and when he saw him with such a sad face he said:

"My captain, you are the most extraordinary knight I have ever seen in my life. Anyone else would hold a great celebration for all the joy they had when they saw their lady. And the flattery and honor she paid you—more than to all the great lords there. And then she presented the brocade pillow to you with such grace and love in everyone's presence. Here, when you should feel like the most fortunate man in the world, you seem to have lost all reason."

When Tirant heard Diafebus' comforting words he said in a mournful voice:

"The reason my heart is grieving is that I am in love, and I don't know if my love will be returned. This is what torments me most, and makes my heart colder than ice. I have no hope of gaining my desire, because fortune always opposes those who are in love."

When Diafebus saw how tormented Tirant was, he would not let him continue, and he said:

"If you keep on behaving that way, infamy will follow you the rest of your life. And if this should reach the emperor's ears, God forbid, what would happen to you and the rest of us? He would say that you fell in love with his daughter the day you arrived in order to bring shame to his entire realm, the crown and the empire. So, my captain, use your discretion, and don't let anyone guess you're in love."

Tirant listened to the wise words of Diafebus, and he was very glad to have the advice of his good friend and relative. He thought for a moment, and then got out of bed and went to the hall to join his men who had been surprised at Tirant's discourteous behavior.

After they had eaten he begged Diafebus to go to the palace and give the infanta some very singular Hours he had, from Paris, which had solid gold covers and were very delicately decorated. They also had an ingenious lock so that when the key was removed no one could see where it opened. Diafebus wrapped the Hours and gave them to a page to carry. When Diafebus was in the palace he found the emperor in the ladies' chamber, and following Tirant's instructions, he told him:

"Your Majesty, your captain begs your permission to go see the Moorish camp within a few days. And he also sends Your Highness these Hours. If you don't care for them, he says they should be given to one of the infanta's maidens."

As soon as the emperor saw them he was astonished at their uniqueness. "This," said the emperor, "can only belong to a maiden of the royal family."

He gave them to his daughter, Carmesina. She was very happy because the Hours were so beautiful, and also because they were Tirant's, and she stood up and said:

"Sire, would Your Majesty approve if we sent for the captain and the minstrels, and had a small party? The mourning and this sadness have lasted such a long time."

"My dearest daughter, don't you know that I have no other consolation in this world except you and Isabel, the Queen of Hungary who, for my sins, is absent from my sight? And since my son died I have no other worldly good but you. All the happiness you can have will bring me peace in my old age."

The infanta quickly sent a page for Tirant and had Diafebus sit next to her. When Tirant received his lady's command he left his quarters and went to the emperor, who asked him to dance with his daughter, Carmesina. The dancing lasted nearly till evening when the emperor wanted to dine. Then Tirant returned to his lodging very happily, because he had danced continuously with the infanta and she had said many delightful things to him.

The following day the emperor held a great banquet for Tirant. All the dukes, counts and marquis ate at the table with him, the emperor and his daughter. The rest ate at other tables. When the meal was over there was dancing. After they had danced for a while came the collation. Then the emperor had them mount their horses so he could show Tirant the entire city.

Afterward the emperor called for a general council, and he told his daughter to be there because many times he had said to her:

"My daughter, why don't you come to the council often so that you will know how it is conducted? After I die you will need to know how to rule your land."

The princess went, both to see how the council was run and to hear Tirant talk. And when everyone was seated at the council, the emperor spoke to Tirant.

"I beg you, captain, to prepare for battle with our enemies, the Genoese. We have received news that Genoese ships, coming from Tuscany and Lombardy, have reached the port of Aulis, filled with soldiers, horses and provisions. Our own ships have reached the island of Euboea, and I believe they will soon be here."

Tirant took off his cap and said:

"Command me to go against the Genoese whenever you wish, Your Majesty. I am ready."

"I'll tell you what you must do for now," said the emperor. "Go to where my judgment seat is. I want you to sit on it, listen to the cases brought before you and judge them with mercy."

One of the members of the council named Montsalvat stood up and said:

"Sire, Your Majesty should take a closer look at these matters, for there are three obstacles. First, the Duke of Macedonia should not be deprived of his rights: he has the captaincy, and it is his privilege since he is closer to the throne. Second, it should not be given to a foreigner who has no official position in the empire. Third, before the soldiers leave here they should make a pilgrimage, bearing gifts to the island where Paris stole Helen, for that is how the Greeks were victorious over the Trojans in ancient times."

The emperor could not tolerate the knight's foolish words, and he said very angrily:

"If it were not for the respect I have for our Heavenly Father I would have you beheaded. It would fit all your merits, and it would be a sacrifice to God and an example to this world, because you are a wicked Christian. It is my command that Tirant, who is our captain now, be above all our captains: he deserves it because of his virtue and shining chivalry. The Duke of Macedonia, who is cowardly and inept at war, never knew how to win a battle. The person I designate will be captain, and anyone who contradicts him will receive my punishment in such a way that they will be remembered throughout the world."

The emperor stood up, and would not hear another word from anyone. He had a proclamation read throughout the city that anyone having a complaint against anyone else should go to the hall of justice the following day and from that day forward, and justice would be meted out.

The following day the captain sat on the imperial judgment seat, and heard everyone with a complaint, and made judgments on them all. For from the time the Grand Turk and the Moorish sultan had come into the empire no justice at all had been given.

Two weeks after Tirant came, all the emperor's ships arrived, carrying men, wheat and horses. Before the arrival of the ships the emperor presented the captain with eighty-three large and beautiful horses, and many suits of armor. Tirant had Diafebus come up first so he could choose from the weapons and horses. Then Ricart made his choice, and finally all the others, while Tirant took nothing for himself.

Tirant was deeply in love with the princess, and his suffering increased daily. His love was so great that when he was with her he did not dare talk to her about anything concerning love. And the day for his departure was drawing near, for they were waiting only for the horses to recover from the hardships they had endured at sea.

The discreet princess knew about Tirant's love. She sent a page to ask Tirant to be at the palace at noon because that was the time when all the others would be resting. When Tirant received his lady's command, he was the happiest man in the world. He immediately sent for Diafebus, to give him the news, and to tell him that she wanted only the two of them to go. Diafebus said:

"Captain, I am very pleased at this beginning, even though I don't know what the end will bring."

At the appointed hour the two knights went up to the palace and quietly entered the princess's chamber, hoping to have victory. When she saw them she was very happy. She stood up and took Tirant's hand, and made him sit next to her. Then Diafebus took Stephanie by one arm and Widow Repose by the other, and led them aside so they would not hear what the princess was saying to Tirant. The princess smiled and softly said:

"Since you are a foreigner I would not want you to come to any harm unknowingly. I know you came to this land at the bidding of the King of Sicily, because he had confidence in your merits. But he could not tell you of the danger that might befall you, because he did not know about it."

Tirant answered:

"So that you will not think me ungrateful for what you are telling me, I kiss your hands and feet, and I promise to do everything Your Highness commands me."

Tirant begged her to give him her hand so he could kiss it, but she would not. Then he insisted several times, and when he saw that she still would not, he called Widow Repose and Stephanie. To satisfy the captain they begged her to allow him to kiss her hand. She did it this way: not wanting to let him kiss the back of her hand, she opened it so he would kiss the palm. Because kissing the palm is a sign of love, and kissing the back of the hand is a sign of dominance. Then the princess said to him:

"Blessed knight, may merciful God keep you from the hands of that ravenous lion, the Duke of Macedonia: he is a cruel and envious man, and very knowledgeable about treachery. He is infamous for the fact that he has only killed people wickedly. It is well known that he killed that valiant knight, my brother. When my brother was fighting courageously against the enemy, he came up behind him and cut the straps of his helmet so that his head would be uncovered, and he was killed by the Moors. A great traitor like him should be feared. And so, virtuous knight, I advise you, when you are in battle, be wary of him. Don't trust him even while you are eating or sleeping."

It happened one day at dinner time that Tirant found the empress and the princess still at the table. He came into the hall and served the empress and her daughter as steward and cup-bearer, since this was his privilege as captain. When Tirant saw that the meal was nearly over, he asked the empress to clear up a matter he was uncertain about. The empress answered that if she could she would do it very gladly.

"Tell me, my lady," said Tirant, "for a knight, which is most honorable, to die well or to die badly, since he must die?"

And he said not a word more. The princess said:

"Holy Mother of God! What a question to ask my mother. Everyone knows it's better to die well than to die badly."

Then Tirant struck the table with his clenched fist and muttered, "So be it," so softly that they could barely hear him. Without another word he got up and went to his lodgings. And everyone was left astonished at Tirant's behavior.

The following day the princess was feeling very upset by what Tirant had said. In the morning, while the emperor was at mass with all the ladies, Tirant went into the church for prayer, and he told the emperor:

"Sire, the galleys are ready to go to Cyprus to bring back provisions. Does Your Majesty want them to leave?"

The emperor said:

"I wish they were one hundred miles out to sea right now!"

Tirant quickly went to the port to give the order for them to set sail. When the princess saw Tirant leaving, she called Diafebus and asked him to give Tirant the message that after he had eaten he should come to see her immediately, because she wanted very much to talk to him, and that later they would dance.

When Tirant heard the news he considered at once what it might mean. He had the most beautiful mirror bought that could be found, and put it inside his sleeve. When he thought it was about time, they went to the palace and found the emperor talking to his daughter. The emperor saw them coming and sent for his minstrels, and they danced for a good while. After watching them for a time the emperor withdrew to his chambers. The princess immediately stopped dancing, and taking Tirant by the hand they sat at a window. The princess said:

"Virtuous knight, I have great pity for you, seeing how disturbed you are. Tell me, I beg you, what is troubling you."

"My lady, since Your Highness is forcing me to tell you, I can only say that I am in love."

He said nothing more, and lowered his eyes.

"Tell me, Tirant," said the princess, "who is the lady that is causing you so much pain? If I can help you in any way, I will be very glad to."

Tirant put his hand in his sleeve, drew out the mirror, and said:

"My lady, the face you will see here can bring me life or death."

The princess quickly took the mirror, and with hurried steps she went into her chamber, thinking she would find a portrait of some woman in the mirror. But she saw only her own face. Then she was astonished that a lady could be courted in this way, without words.

While she was happily reflecting on what Tirant had done, Widow Repose and Stephanie came in. They found the princess sitting with the mirror in her hands, and they said to her: "My lady, where did you get such a pretty mirror?"

The princess told them about the way Tirant had declared his love for her, and she said she had never heard of it being done before:

"Not even in all the story books I've read have I ever found such a graceful declaration. How knowledgeable these foreigners are!"

Widow Repose answered:

"Tell me, my lady, should Your Highness be paying as much attention as you are to a servant your father has taken into his house nearly out of charity, and who was thrown out by that famous king of Sicily, along with other foreigners wearing gold and silk clothes they've borrowed? Do you want to lose your good reputation for a man like him?"

The princess was very upset by what the Widow had said, and she went into her chambers nearly crying. Stephanie went with her, telling her not to be so upset, and consoling her as best she could.

"Isn't it terrible?" said the princess. "Here I am, scolded by the very mistress who nursed me! What if she had seen me doing something really bad? I believe she would have sent out a crier to advertise it in the court and to the entire city. I trust God that her wicked, dishonest, cursing tongue will have the punishment it deserves."

"It's normal," said Stephanie, "for maidens in the court to be loved and courted, and for them to have three kinds of love: virtuous, profitable and vicious. The first one, which is virtuous, is when some grandee loves a maiden, and she feels very honored when others know that he dances, jousts, or goes into battle for her love. The second is profitable, and it is when some gentleman or knight of ancient and virtuous lineage loves a maiden and sways her to him with gifts. The third is vicious, when the maiden loves the gentleman or knight for her own pleasure, and he is generous in words that give her life for a year, but if they go too far they can end in a heavily curtained bed among perfumed sheets where she can spend an entire winter's night. This last kind of love seems much better to me than the others."

When the princess heard Stephanie say such witty things, she began to smile and most of her melancholy left her. While they were talking the empress asked where her daughter was, since she had not seen her for a long time. She went out into the hall and met the empress who asked her why her eyes were red.

"My lady," said the princess, "all day long today I've had a headache."

She made her sit on her knees, and kissed her at length.

The following day Tirant said to Diafebus:

"My brother, go to the palace, I beg you, and talk to the princess. See if you can find out how she felt about the mirror."

Diafebus went at once and met the emperor going to mass. When it was over Diafebus went up to the princess, and she asked him what had become of Tirant.

"My lady," said Diafebus, "he left his lodging to go sit in the judgment seat."

"If you only know," said the princess, "the trick he played on me! He declared his love for me with a mirror. Just let me see him and I'll tell him a few things he won't like "

"Oh my good lady!" said Diafebus. "Tirant brought a flaming log and found no wood to burn here."

"Yes," said the princess, "but the log has gotten wet. However, here in this palace you'll find a bigger and better one that gives much more warmth than the one you're talking about. It's a log called Loyalty, and it's very tender and dry, and it gives happiness to anyone who can warm themselves by it."

"My lady, let us do this," said Diafebus. "If it pleases Your Highness, let us take some of yours which is good and dry, and some of ours which is wet and moist, and let us make a shape in your likeness and Tirant's."

"No," said the princess, "it isn't a good idea to make two opposites into one."

And they joked in this way until they had returned to her chamber. Then Diafebus took his leave and went back to his lodgings where he told Tirant everything he and the princess had said.

After they had eaten Tirant knew that the emperor must be asleep, so he and Diafebus went to the palace. Through a window Stephanie saw them coming, and she quickly went to tell the princess:

"My lady, our knights are coming now."

The princess came out of the chamber. When Tirant saw his lady, he made a deep bow before her. The princess returned his greeting with a less pleasant expression than usual. Tirant was not very happy at the lady's expression, and in a low voice, he said:

"Lady, full of perfection, I beg Your Excellency to tell me what you are thinking. I don't believe I have seen Your Highness behave this way for many days."

"My behavior," said the princess, "cannot please God, and much less the world, but I will tell you the reason, and your lack of knowledge and goodness will be revealed. What will people say about you when they hear of this? That the emperor's daughter, who is in such a lofty position, has been courted by his captain whom he loved deeply and trusted. You have not kept the honor and reverence you are obligated to have for me. Instead you have acted with bad faith and dishonest love."

She got up to go back into her chambers. When Tirant saw that she was leaving he caught up to her, took hold of her shawl, and begged her to listen to him. Stephanie and Diafebus pleaded with her so much that she sat down again, and Tirant said:

"If there was any fault, you must forgive me, for love has absolute control over me. Doesn't Your Highness remember the day when the empress was present and I asked if it was better to die well or to die badly? And Your Majesty answered that it was better to die well than badly. I knew that if I did not let you know of my suffering, one night they would find me dead in the corner of my room, and if I did tell you, I would come to the point where I am now. And so, on my knees, I ask only that after my death your angelic hands dress me, and that you write letters on my tomb that say this: Here Lies Tirant lo Blanc Who Died of Great Love."

His eyes became a sea of tears, and sighing painfully he got up from the princess's feet, and left the chamber to go to his lodging. When the princess saw him leaving so disconsolately, she began to cry uncontrollably, and she sighed and sobbed so that none of her maidens could console her. Then she said:

"Come here, my faithful maiden, you know how to have pity on my torment. Poor me, what shall I do? I think he is going to kill himself. That's what he told me, and his heart is so lofty and noble that he will do it. Have pity on me, my Stephanie; go run to Tirant and beg him for me not to do anything, for I am very displeased at what he told me."

The princess was crying helplessly while she said this. To carry out her lady's wishes, Stephanie took a maiden with her and went to Tirant's lodging, which was very near the palace. She went to his room and found him taking off a brocade cloak, with Diafebus at his side, consoling him.

When Stephanie saw him in his doublet she thought he had taken off his clothes to place his body in the grave. Stephanie threw herself at Tirant's feet as if he were her real lord, and she said to him:

"My lord, Tirant, what are you trying to do to yourself? Her Majesty was saying all that just to tease you, I swear it."

She was silent and said no more. When Tirant saw Stephanie kneeling down, he at once knelt beside her. He did this because she was a maiden who served the emperor's daughter, and even more because she was the emperor's niece, daughter of the Duke of Macedonia, the greatest duke in all Greece.

Tirant replied:

"Death does not bother me when I think I'll be dying for such a lady. By dying I will come back to life in glorious fame, for people will say that Tirant lo Blanc died of love for the most beautiful and virtuous lady in the world. So, my lady, I beg you to go away and leave me with my pain."

The princess was in indescribable anguish when she saw that Stephanie was not coming back with news of Tirant. Not being able to endure it, she called one of her maidens, named Plaerdemavida. She took a veil and put it over her head so she would not be recognized, and went down the stairs to the garden. With the garden door open, she went to the house where Tirant was, without being seen by anyone. When she saw Tirant and Stephanie on their knees, talking, she knelt down too and said:

"I beg you, Tirant, if my tongue said things that offended you, do not keep them in your heart. I want you to forget everything I told you in anger, and I beg your forgiveness."

When Tirant saw his lady speaking with so much love, he was the happiest man in the world. Stephanie said:

"Since peace has been made, my lady, I promised him that Your Highness would let him kiss your hair."

"I will be very happy," said the princess, "to have him kiss my eyes and my forehead if he promises me, upon his word as a knight, not to do anything untoward."

Tirant promised very willingly, and swore it, and their sadness turned into great happiness and contentment. The princess, accompanied by Tirant and Diafebus, quickly went to the garden. The princess told Plaerdemavida to have all the other maidens come, and in a short time they were all in the garden, and Widow Repose with them. She had seen all the moves and suffered deeply because of the princess, and with her own involvement in the matter she had even more to think about. The emperor soon saw Tirant and his daughter in the garden. He went down to the garden and said to Tirant:

"Captain, I sent for you at your lodging, but they didn't find you there. I'm glad to see you here."

"My lord," said Tirant, "I asked for Your Majesty, but they told me Your Highness was sleeping. So that I wouldn't awaken you I came here with these knights to dance or practice some sport."

"What a black, evil sport we have!" said the emperor. "We must hold a council: it is very important."

He gave the order for the council bell to be rung. When everyone in the imperial council was together, the emperor had the emissary come forward, and said that everyone should know the bad news because it was not something that could be kept secret. Then he ordered the emissary to explain his mission. Making a humble bow he said:

"Most excellent lord, last Thursday night, fourteen thousand men came on foot and concealed themselves in a large meadow. Because of all the water there the grass grew very tall, and no one could see them. When the sun rose we saw horses and Turkish horsemen who must have numbered, in all, one thousand four hundred, more or less, together in a part of the water. The Duke of Macedonia, a very haughty man of little intelligence as his actions show, had the trumpets blow so that everyone would mount their horses. The constable and the others, who know more about war than he does, protested and told him not to leave. But no matter what they said he would not obey anyone. He went up to the river with all his men, and he ordered them to cross, both those on horseback and those on foot. The water came up to the horses' cinches and there were even places where they had to swim.

"Near the enemy's side there was a bank that the horses had great difficulty in climbing, and the enemy met them there. At the slightest advance that the soldiers or their horses made, they quickly fell into the water and were not able to get up, and they were all swept down river. If the duke had only gone one mile upstream all his men would have been able to get across without getting wet. The enemy drew back a little so that the men would come across, and they pretended to retreat to a small hill there, and the duke used all his forces to try to take them. When the men in ambush saw the Greeks fighting so boldly, they came out furiously and fell into the thick of the Christians, spilling their blood. The duke could not take the fierce battle any longer and he secretly fled without doing much harm to the enemy. And those who were able to escape went with him.

"After their victory the Moors laid siege to the city. The Grand Turk himself came, along with the Moorish sultan and all the kings that had come to aid them, and all the dukes, counts and marquis of Italy and Lombardy who were mercenaries. As soon as the sultan heard the news he gave himself the title of Emperor of Greece, and said he would not lift the siege until he had taken the duke and all those with him prisoner, and that he would then come here to attack this city. I can tell you, Sire, that the duke has provisions for only one month, a month and a half at most.

"So, my lord, Your Majesty must look into what we should do about all this."

Tirant said:

"Tell me, knight, upon your honor, how many men were lost in battle?"

The knight answered:

"Captain, it is known that of the men killed in battle, those who were drowned and those taken prisoner, we've lost eleven thousand seven hundred twenty-two men."

The emperor said:

"Captain, I beg you to do whatever has to be done, out of reverence for God and love of me, so that you can leave in fifteen or twenty days with all your men to help those miserable people."

"Oh, Sire!" said Tirant. "How can Your Majesty say that we won't have left in twenty days? In that time the enemy could attack the city, and they are so powerful that they could invade it."

Tirant again asked the emissary how many men there might be in the enemy's forces. The emissary answered:

"In faith, there are many Turks and they are very skillful in warfare, and are cruel, ferocious men. In our opinion and according to what some prisoners say, they number more than eight hundred thousand."

"My feeling," said Tirant, "is that a royal proclamation should be read throughout the city. All those who have hired themselves out, and those who want to, should go to the Imperial House to receive their payment, and they should all be ready to leave in six days."

The emperor thought that was good advice, and he thanked Tirant. As soon as the proclamation was read, all the grandees outside the city were notified and they were all soon there with their horses rested. And those who had come from Sicily were ready. The bad news of the losses that had been sustained ran throughout the city, and many of the townsfolk, both men and women, gathered in the market square. Some were crying for their brothers, others for their sons, some for their friends and relatives, and still others for the destruction of the empire. Most of the empire was lost, and the hope of the emperor and those around him was placed only in God. They were afraid there would be great starvation and thirst because of the enemy's victory, and that the city would be burned, and they could imagine themselves in captivity and miserable slavery. Two of the empire's barons told the emperor that he should send his daughter Carmesina to Hungary to be with her sister.

When Tirant heard these words, his face turned pale as death. All the maidens and even the emperor noticed, and he asked Tirant what had made his color change so much.

"Sire," said Tirant, "I've had a bad stomachache all day today."

The emperor had his doctors come immediately to give him some medicine. When the emperor saw that Tirant was all right, he turned to Carmesina and said to her:

"My daughter, what do you think of the things the council has said about you? In my opinion, it would be a good idea, because if the empire and all its people were lost, you would be safe."

The discreet lady answered her father, saying:

"Oh, merciful father! Your Highness should not allow me to be separated from you. I prefer to die near Your Majesty and in my own land than to be wealthy and living a life of pain and sorrow in a foreign land."

When the emperor heard such discreet and loving words from his daughter he was very pleased. On the morning of the following day the banners were blessed with a great procession and celebration. All the men armed themselves and mounted their horses to depart. First came the emperor's banner, carried by a knight named Fonseca, mounted on a grand and marvelous horse that was completely white. Next came the banner with the emperor's emblem, a blue field with the tower of Babylon all in silver, with a sword piercing this tower, held at the pommel by a gauntleted arm and with the inscription: "Fortune is Mine." Then came the squadron of the Duke of Pera with his banners and his family. This was followed by the Duke of Sinòpoli and the Duke of Desperses. Then came the Duke of Casàndria and the Duke of Montsant, each with their squadron that had come from Naples. These were followed by the Marquis of Sant Marcos from Venice, and the Marquis of Montferrat, the Marquis of Saint George, the Marquis of Peixcara, the Marquis of Guast and the Marquis of Arena. And then came the Marquis of Brandis, the Marquis of Prota, the Marquis of Montenegre and a bastard brother of the Prince of Taràntol, and many, many others, all with their squadrons. All in all, there were forty-eight squadrons, with one hundred eighty-three thousand men.

When the emperor saw all the men outside he called the captain from his window and told him not to leave. He wanted to talk to him, and he had some letters for him to give to the Duke of Macedonia and a few others. As soon as the foot soldiers and those on horseback were outside the city, Tirant returned and went upstairs to the emperor's chambers. He found him in his chamber with the secretary, writing, and did not want to disturb him.

When the princess saw Tirant, she called to him and said:

"Captain, I see that you are ready to leave. I pray that God will give you an honorable victory."

Tirant knelt before her and thanked her for her words. And he kissed her hand as a token of good luck. Then the princess said:

"Is there anything you would like from me, Tirant, before you leave? Tell me if there is, for I will grant you whatever you wish."

"My lady," said Tirant, "I would only like Your Highness to do me the favor of giving me this blouse you are wearing, because it is closest to your precious skin. And I would like to take it off with my own hands."

"Holy Mary, protect me!" said the princess. "What are you telling me? I'll be very happy to give you my blouse, my jewels, my clothes, and everything I have. But it would not be right for your hands to touch me where no one else has ever touched."

She quickly went to her room, and took off the blouse and put on another. She went out to the great hall where she found Tirant joking with the maidens. She took him aside and gave him the blouse, kissing it many times to make him more content. Tirant took it very happily and went to his lodging. And he told the maidens:

"If the emperor calls me, tell him I'll be right back, that I've gone to arm myself so that I can leave quickly."

When Tirant was at his lodging he finished arming himself, and he found Diafebus and Ricart there. They had come back to put on the coats of arms that had been made, of metal plates.

Then the three knights went to take their leave of the emperor and of all the ladies. When they went upstairs they found the emperor waiting for the captain to come, because he wanted to dine with him. When the emperor saw Tirant, he said:

"Captain, what coat of arms is this that you're wearing?"

"My lord," said Tirant, "if you knew what was in it, you would be astonished."

"I would like very much to know about it," said the emperor.

"Its force," said Tirant, "is to do well. When I left my land a maiden gave it to me, and she is the most beautiful maiden in the world. I'm not speaking in offense of the princess here, or of the other ladies of honor."

The emperor said:

"It is true that no good feat of arms was ever accomplished unless it was for love."

"I promise you," said Tirant, "on my word as a knight, that in my first battle I will make friends and enemies marvel at it."

The emperor sat down to eat, as did the empress and her daughter, and the captain sat beside her. And he had the two knights sit at another table with all the ladies and maidens. Then they all ate with great pleasure, and especially Tirant who shared a plate with his lady.

CHAPTER V - THE BATTLEFIELD

Tirant then took his leave of all the ladies and the others there. When the three knights were outside the city they gave their chargers to the pages and mounted other horses. Within a short time they reached the soldiers. Each knight went to his squadron, and Tirant went from one squadron to another, directing them constantly to stay in order.

That day they traveled five leagues. They set up their tents in a beautiful meadow where there was water. After they had eaten, Tirant had two thousand pikesmen keep watch until midnight, and he sent men along the road to see if they heard soldiers or anything else. Tirant kept watch over the camp, moving from place to place. At the hour of midnight he had two thousand other pikesmen take the place of those on watch, and he would not let them have pages, but made them all arm as if they were going into battle at any moment.

When Tirant was in a war he never took off his clothes except to change his shirt. Every morning, two hours before sunrise, he had the trumpets blow for the men to saddle their horses and to hold mass. Then the entire camp would arm themselves and quickly mount. At dawn they would all be ready to leave. They kept up this routine until they were a league and a half from the enemy, in a city named Pelidas, which was in danger daily of surrendering to the powerful Turks.

When they found out that soldiers were coming to their aid they were very happy, and they opened the gates to the city. The captain did not want to go in during the day so they would not be seen, but he did not do it secretly enough to avoid being heard. And the first to be notified that soldiers had gone into the city of Pelidas was the Grand Turk, but he did not know how many there were. The Grand Turk went at once to tell the Moorish sultan, who sent four men toward the city of Pelidas as spies to find out what they could about the men who had gone in.

The next day Tirant took a man with him who knew the countryside very well, and they rode out as secretly as they could, and drew near the camp by back roads. From a hill they could see both the city and the camp.

The Moorish sultan was at one end, and the Grand Turk at the other.

They recognized him by the large, painted tents they saw. When they had looked the situation over very carefully, they returned to the city. On the way back they saw the Moorish guards.

When they were back in the city and had dismounted, Tirant went to the square where he found most of the townspeople, and he told them:

"Come here, my brothers. We have just been spying on the enemy camp, and on our way back we saw four of the camp guards. For each guard you bring to me alive I'll give you five hundred ducats, and if you bring his head I'll give you three hundred. How many of you want to go?"

Seven men who knew the land well volunteered immediately. They left at night so no one would see them, and when they had traveled a good distance one of them said:

"Why don't we go to the spring near here, and cover ourselves with branches? The Moors are certain to come here to drink around noon with all this heat, and that way they'll fall into our hands."

They agreed to do that, and they kept a very close watch from their hiding place. When the sun came out they saw the Moors on top of the hill. As the sun grew hotter they became thirsty and went to the spring for water. When they arrived one of the Christians who was hidden said:

"Let's not move until they have drunk and are full of water: that way they won't be able to run very fast."

And that is what they did. When the Moors had drunk and eaten their fill the Christians fell upon them with loud cries, and immediately caught three of them. One tried to escape. When they saw that they could not catch him they shot at him with a crossbow. The arrow pierced his side, and he fell to the ground. They cut off his head and stuck it to the point of a lance. Then they tied the hands of the others and took them to their captain. When Tirant saw them he was very pleased, and he took the three Moors and had them closely guarded.

Tirant had ordered everyone to eat early that day, and to saddle the horses and arm themselves so they would be ready to leave. He had all the men go out of the city in order, both the foot soldiers and those riding horses. Behind them came three thousand men with the mares.

When they were near the Moors' camp he had all the soldiers go to one side so the mares could pass by without the other horses sensing them.

When the mares were at the entrance to the camp all the foot soldiers went in with them, and they divided into two groups: one went toward the Moorish sultan and the other toward the Grand Turk. Then the camp horses noticed the mares: some got loose, others broke their halters, and others tore out the stakes that held them fast. You should have seen the horses running loose through the camp: some here, some there, and all of them after the mares.

When this melee had gone on for a good while and the entire camp was in confusion because of the horses, Tirant came and fell on part of it with half his men. Then the Duke of Pera and his men attacked the other side, calling on that glorious knight, Saint George.

Finally the Moorish sultan and the Grand Turk and their men fled to the mountain while the others went to the plain. Tirant pursued them relentlessly, and he and his men killed everyone they caught, giving quarter to no one. All those who went to the mountain reached it safely, and those who went to the plain were either killed or taken prisoner.

They pursued them for three leagues, and those heading for the mountain (where the road was shorter) came to a river with a wooden bridge where they could cross safely. When the sultan and some of his men had crossed over and they saw the Christians close behind, they broke the bridge in the middle. Then those who had not yet crossed were lost while those who had already crossed the bridge were safe.

The Duke of Macedonia heard of Tirant's victory, and how none of the enemy were left except those who were badly wounded and could not flee. So he and his men went out and sacked the camp, and they found large amounts of gold and silver, clothing, weapons and many jewels. When they had taken everything, they put their booty in the town. The duke left soldiers to guard it, and he gave orders that if Tirant or any of his men came, they should not be allowed inside. When they had put away everything they had stolen, the duke took the route to the plain, and he and his men were astonished at all the dead bodies they saw.

The guards at the camp told the captain that armed men were approaching quickly. Tirant had all his soldiers mount their horses, and he prepared for battle, thinking that the enemy had regrouped in the villages that belonged to them. They went out to meet them, and when they were near they recognized each other. Tirant took the helmet off his head and gave it to a page, and all the other captains did the same. When they were close to the duke, Tirant dismounted and walked up to him, paying him great honor. The duke did not move at all except to put his hand on his head without saying a word. This made all the others very angry, and none of them would dismount for him. Tirant remounted his horse and tried many times to talk to him, but the duke scarcely uttered a word. But all the other knights and gentlemen paid great honor to the dukes and to Tirant. Then they rode together until they were near the tents.

Tirant said to the duke:

"Sir, if Your Lordship would like to stay in that meadow where there are very beautiful trees and you would be near the river, I'll have the men who are there move to another place."

The duke answered:

"I don't want to be near you. I prefer to go to a place farther away."

"You can do that," said Tirant, "but I said what I did out of kindness, thinking that you deserved it."

The duke would not listen to him, and turned his horse about without a word. He set up his tents a mile upriver.

After he dismounted Tirant sent three of his knights to the duke, and when they were there they said to him:

"Sir, our captain has sent us to Your Lordship to ask if you would like to eat with him. He knows that Your Lordship will have better food here, but you can have his more quickly, because all you have to do is wash your hands and sit down to eat."

"Oh, what a bother for nothing!" said the duke. "Tell him that I don't want to."

And he turned his back to them very haughtily. When the emissaries had mounted their horses to go, the duke told them:

"Tell Tirant that if he wants to come and eat with me, I would prefer that to eating with him."

"Sir," said Diafebus, "if there is no fire lit in your entire camp, what could you offer him? You couldn't give him anything but food for chickens and drink for oxen."

The duke answered angrily:

"I can give him chickens, capons, partridge and pheasant."

The knights refused to listen to him anymore, and they wheeled about.

After they had gone, a knight said to the duke:

"You didn't understand, sir, what that knight said to you. He told you that you would serve his captain food for chickens and drink for oxen. Do you know what he meant by that? Food for chickens is grain, and what oxen drink is water."

"On my father's grave!" said the duke. "You're right. I didn't understand. Those foreigners are very haughty. If I had understood him I would have made him leave with his hands on his head."

When Tirant heard what the reply was, he sat down to dine with the dukes, counts and marquis who were already there.

The morning of the following day the captain had a large and beautiful tent raised, with a bell on top. That tent was only for mass and council meetings, and he had it set up in a meadow between the duke's camp and his own. When the time came to say mass, Tirant courteously sent word to the duke to see if he would like to come to mass. The duke haughtily answered no, but the other grandees came very happily. After mass they held council, and it was decided that the Marquis of Saint George, the Count of Acquaviva, and two barons should go to the Duke of Macedonia as ambassadors. When they were with him the Marquis of Saint George said:

"Duke, you should not be surprised to see us: our captain and the illustrious dukes, counts and marquis have sent us here. We want you to give us a share of the treasure you took from the enemy camp."

And he said no more.

"How overjoyed I am," said the duke, "to hear idiotic words from such ignorant people! How could you think I would do such a thing when we have been battling day and night with sweat and blood against our enemy?"

The ambassadors got back on their horses, and in the camp they found the captain and the grandees holding a meeting in the council tent. Then the marquis told them about the duke's reply, and he said:

"Let us all mount our horses: an insult like this can't be forgotten!"

The marquis quickly left the tent and armed himself, as did all the others.

When the captain saw the disturbance in his camp, he was very upset and he immediately had a proclamation made that no one, under penalty of death, should mount their horses. Then he went up and down, seizing the knights, and he begged the dukes and marquis not to do this, because if they became involved in a quarrel, the Turks they had taken prisoner would fall upon them.

When the disturbance had subsided, Tirant ordered them to go to the battle site, and take the clothing from all the dead bodies they found and to keep it. Some of the knights asked why, and he told them that at some time they might be able to use it.

As the Moors were being defeated in battle and were fleeing, Diafebus thought about how to bring renown and fame to Tirant, in the present and the future. He went to him and asked him for the captain's ring. Tirant removed his glove, took off the ring and gave it to him. Diafebus halted for a moment even though the others were pressing forward, and he stopped one of his squires who was a good and faithful man, and gave him the ring. He instructed him about everything he was to say to the emperor and to Carmesina, and then to all the others.

To carry out his master's order, the squire wheeled his horse about, dug in his spurs and galloped away without stopping until he was in Constantinople.

When he stood before the emperor, he knelt and said:

"My lord, I have good news. Give me my reward."

After the emperor promised to do so, Pyramus gave him the ring, and told him all about the battle, and how they had conquered the Turks—which had been like a miracle.

The following day the sultan sent three ambassadors to Tirant. They put a sheet of paper on a stick and held it up as a signal for safe-conduct. When they were inside the tent the ambassadors were welcomed by the captain and all the others, and they gave the sultan's letter to Tirant. He had it read in everyone's presence, and it said the following:

"I, Armini, great sultan of Babylonia, and lord of three empires. Glorious Tirant lo Blanc, Captain of the Greeks and defender of the Christian faith, we salute you. And we declare to you, by counsel and deliberation of the Grand Turk and the five kings here under my power and command, with another ten who are in my own land, that if you ask me for a lasting peace or a treaty of six months, we will offer you our "white face" to show our honesty and the six months of peace, out of reverence for all powerful God, in the old manner. Written in our camp on the eastern shore on the second day of the moon and of the birth of our holy prophet Mohammed, etc."

After the letter had been read, Tirant told the ambassadors to explain their embassy. One of the ambassadors, Abdalla Salomon, stood up, bowed, and said:

"We have been sent to you, Tirant lo Blanc, captain of the Greek people, as representatives of the magnanimous and glorious lords, the Grand Turk and the sultan. After the great number of deaths you brought to our soldiers, you imprisoned a small child, the brother in law of our sovereign lord, the great sultan, his wife's brother, along with many other virtuous knights. We beg of you, on behalf of the thing you love most in this world, to give us the child. If you will not do this for love, ask a ransom for him, in silver or gold, and it will be granted."

Tirant replied:

"Since you hold up to me the thing I love most in the world, and you ask for a prisoner, I'll give him to you and forty more along with him. As for the other part of your embassy, I'll hold a meeting with my men, and then I will give you an answer."

Tirant summoned his constables and told them to go with the ambassadors to select forty-one prisoners for release.

Then Tirant addressed all the great lords there:

"Illustrious princes and lords. We've seen the request of the sultan and the Turk. Do you think we should grant them the truce they are asking for?"

First the Duke of Macedonia spoke:

"Most egregious and noble lords. This is more my business than it is the rest of yours because I am closer to the imperial crown. It's my advice and my demand that we grant them the six-month truce they're asking for, and even longer if they wish, and even peace if they want it, whether the emperor likes it or not."

The Duke of Pera couldn't stand to hear anything more from the Duke of Macedonia—for they were at odds with each other because each of them wanted to take the princess as his wife—and he said:

"Gentlemen, it seems to me that for His Majesty the emperor's benefit, and for the well-being of the entire empire and the republic, we shouldn't offer them peace or a truce."

Many felt they should accept a truce, but most agreed with the Duke of Pera.

Then Tirant said:

"Since His high Majesty, the emperor has given me the right to speak in his place, I tell Your Lordships that I don't think it would help anyone to have a truce with these evil people. All their blood that's been spilled is because of your might, and that's the reason they're asking for peace or for a six- month truce. Because during that time, gentlemen, you know that they'll be waiting for the Genoese ships to bring foot soldiers and cavalry. And in that time they would fill this land with such great numbers of men that afterward all the power of Christianity wouldn't be enough to throw them out."

The Duke of Macedonia spoke up and said:

"Tirant, if you don't want to have a truce, I do, and I'll make one. And I advise everyone to make it with me."

"Duke," said Tirant, "don't make disorder out of what the emperor has ordered. If you try to do that, I'll have you seized and taken to His Majesty, the emperor."

Then the duke stood up, his eyes moist, and he left the tent and went to his camp, and Tirant and his men went to their own.

Next to a spring of very fresh water that ran beside their camp, Tirant set up a canopy, with many tables placed around the crystalline spring.

Tirant had the ambassadors served at one table, and the prisoners that had been released to them at a lower table on the left; all the dukes and lords, low on the right. And they were served splendidly with chickens and capons, pheasant, rice and couscous, and many other dishes and very fine wines. The ambassadors were very pleased, seeing how Tirant had the dukes and himself served with such ceremony.

Then they all went to the council tent, and Tirant gave them the following reply:

"You tell the Moorish sultan and the Grand Turk that I will in no way give them peace now unless they face Mecca and swear in the presence of all the good knights that in six months they and all their men will leave the empire and will return the lands of the empire that they have occupied."

Then Ambassador Abdalla Salomon stood up and said: "Since you don't want to give us peace, wait for the fifteenth day of the moon. For on that day such a multitude of Moorish soldiers will come here that the earth will not be able to hold them up."

After they had departed Tirant ordered Diafebus to go to Constantinople that night with many soldiers, on foot and on horseback, and all the prisoners.

When Diafebus reached the city, the emperor and all the others acknowledged Tirant as the victor, and all the knights were praised, and the victory was celebrated with great joy. Diafebus delivered four thousand three hundred prisoners to the emperor on Tirant's behalf so that the Greeks would see his virtue and great generosity. The emperor had them taken and carefully guarded. The following day the emperor took fifteen ducats for each prisoner from his treasury, and delivered them to Diafebus to give to Tirant.

When the princess knew that Diafebus was free from his duties she sent word to him to come to her chambers. There was nothing Diafebus wanted more than to be able to talk to her and to Stephanie with whom he was very much in love. When the princess saw him she quickly said to him:

"My good brother, what news do you bring me from that virtuous knight who holds my heart captive? When will the time come that I can see him and have him near me without being afraid? You know that I want to see him more than anything in the world."

Diafebus answered:

"Your Excellency's loving words would have turned that famous knight's sadness to joy if he had heard them, and would lift his spirit to the highest heaven."

The princess was very pleased by what Diafebus said about Tirant. Then Stephanie said:

"You've spoken, and now it's my turn. Please listen to what I have to say. Tell me, my lady, who but Tirant is worthy of wearing the crown of an emperor? Who else but Tirant deserves to be your husband? Why didn't God make me the emperor's daughter? Why didn't he make you Stephanie and me Carmesina? I can assure you that I wouldn't refuse him anything. If he lifted up my skirt I would lift up my blouse for him, and I would satisfy him in every way I could. If Your Highness takes some foreign king, how do you know that he won't give you a life of pain? And if you want someone from this land, I'll talk against my father. Because with his rank he should be your husband, but when you want to play, he'll be snoring; and when you want to talk he'll be asleep. If you take the Duke of Pera, why he's not even your age. This is what Your Highness needs: Someone who knows how to keep you and your whole empire from danger. Who else can defend and increase it the way he is doing? He's the one who will make you run all around your bedroom, sometimes completely naked and other times in your nightshirt."

The princess laughed, delighted at what Stephanie was saying. Diafebus said:

"Lady Stephanie, by your nobility, tell me the truth: if it were Tirant's good fortune for the princess to take him as a husband, who would you take?"

"My lord Diafebus," said Stephanie, I can assure you that if fortune had the princess become Tirant's wife, I would take his nearest blood relative."

"If it were by blood line, it would have to be me, especially because I am as obedient to Your Grace as Tirant has been to the princess who, with her beauty and dignity, deserves to rule the world.

So please accept me as steward of your chamber, and kiss me as a token of faith."

"It would be neither honest or just," said Stephanie, "for me to grant you anything without the command of my lady who has raised me from an early age, especially in Her Majesty's presence."

Diafebus knelt on the floor, and with his hands pressed together begged the princess, devoutly and with humility, as if she were a saint in paradise, to permit him to kiss her. But for all his pleading, she would not give him permission. Stephanie said:

"Oh, hardened and cruel heart! Your Majesty never wants to lean toward mercy no matter how much you are begged. I will never be happy until I see Tirant with my own eyes."

"Oh, brother Diafebus!" said the princess. "Don't ask me for unjust things now."

While they were saying these pleasant words, the emperor sent for Diafebus to have him go quickly back to the camp.

The guards then came from their watch at sea and told the emperor that five large ships were coming from the east. The emperor, afraid that they were Genoese, stopped Diafebus from going that day, and had many men board their own ships and galleys in port. When the other ships approached, the emperor learned that they had been sent by the Grand Master of Rhodes, with soldiers on board.

The good prior leapt down to the land along with many knights of the white cross. Diafebus was at the port, near the sea, waiting for them. When they met they recognized each other, and Diafebus paid them great honor. Together they went to the great palace of the emperor, and found him seated on his throne. Bowing, the prior of Saint John said:

"Your Excellency, knowing that the greatest of all knights, Tirant lo Blanc, is in the service of Your Majesty as captain-general of all the empire, the Grand Master of Rhodes has sent two thousand paid soldiers, on foot and on horseback, to serve Your Highness for the space of fifteen months."

The emperor was very happy at their arrival. After they had rested for four days they left with Diafebus for the camp. When they were five leagues away, they learned that Tirant had gone forward to take a well-defended plaza, and they heard the loud pounding of bombards. When Tirant saw a part of the wall broken, he dismounted and gave battle on foot, and he went so near the wall that a large rock was thrown at his head, and he was felled. His men struggled to pull him out of the moat, and at this moment Diafebus and the prior came to the villa.

The Turks, inside, were terrified when they saw so many men coming, and they lost all hope. After Ricart had taken Tirant to safety, he again attacked the villa mightily, and they broke through by sheer force.

The Turks, far from any hope of victory, fell into a rage and prepared to die fighting. But as the Christians took the villa, they killed every Turk they saw without mercy, and so they were all given the terrible knife. The Prior of Saint John arrived in time for the attack on the villa, and his men shared in the booty, and this indicated to them that they would be victorious. They went to the cot where Tirant was lying, and explained to him everything the Master had commanded them.

Tirant thanked them and the Grand Master for the noble help they were bringing. But he said these words very wearily: he could barely speak because of the great pain he felt in his head. The doctors came, and they took sheep's heads and cooked them in wine, and applied this to Tirant's head with cloths. And the following morning he was well.

For a few days the men in the field rested. When the moon was in its fifteenth day, the Turks came just as the ambassador had said they would. They came up next to a bridge, with their encampment remaining on one side, and Tirant's camp on the other side, the bridge being broken in the middle. When all the men were together, they numbered two hundred seventy battalions.

When they were all ready, they had the bombards set in place. The following day their firing was so loud and came so often that Tirant found it necessary to shift his encampment to the top of a hill, very close to the river, where there were springs of pure water and large expanses of meadowland. At times all the bombards fired together. And although it was a very clear day, the sky grew dark, for they had more than six hundred bombards, both small and large, despite the fact that they had lost so many when they were defeated.

When Tirant's men so saw many of them, they were frightened at the large number of men on horseback and on foot. There were many who wished they were one hundred leagues from there.

When the sultan saw that he could not cross the river to engage the Christians in battle, he quickly had the bridge repaired. When Tirant saw them repairing the bridge, he took four of his men a league distant to a large stone bridge, and at each end of the bridge there was rocky ground and a castle. When the sultan had conquered all that land, he saw that bridge, but Lord Malvei, the gentleman who was lord of the two castles, would never make a pact with him, no matter how much he promised. For he never wanted to deny or be ungrateful to God or to his natural lord—the emperor. Instead, from those castles at the bridge, they often waged war against the villas and cities the Turks had taken. As a result, the sultan was forced to make a wooden bridge so that his men could cross over to carry out the conquest of the empire.

When Tirant reached the castle, he spoke with the knight whose name was Malvei and who had a very valiant son. The father occupied one castle, and his son the other. They each had thirty horsemen, and with the war they had become very wealthy. The son, whose name was Hippolytus, became a great friend of Tirant and almost never left his side. The father and son begged Tirant to grant him the honor of chivalry, and he did so.

Then Tirant had many trees in the woods cut down, the driest they could find. They measured the width of the river and they made beams, nailing them together with heavy spikes, and they made them so long that they reached across the river. And they put those beams underneath the stone bridge, and from one beam to another they nailed heavy joists, and over the joists they nailed wooden slabs. It was smooth from one end to the other, and it was well caulked with pitch. When this raft was finished, they put a chain at each end and attached it to the stone bridge. And they covered it well with green branches in order to hide it.

When the Turks had finished repairing their bridge, the men began to cross it on foot, little by little. But they readied the bombards so that, if the Christians came, they could defend the bridge and the soldiers who had already gone across. When Tirant saw the Turkish soldiers crossing, the men in his camp were very disheartened, but he encouraged them and raised their spirits. He had the trumpets blown so that everyone would mount their horses, and they shifted their camp near the stone bridge. When the Turks saw Tirant's camp being raised, they assumed that they were fleeing out of fear, and they went across more enthusiastically.

When the sultan and the Grand Turk had gone across with all their armies, their battalions in order, one after the other, they made their way toward the Christians. When Tirant saw that they were near, he crossed over the stone bridge and waited for them. The Moors, seeing them on the other side, quickly returned to their wooden bridge.

When they had crossed it, they made their way upriver to meet him and wage battle. And Tirant, when he saw them near, raised camp and went back to the other side.

This went on for three days.

The Turks held council, and the King of Egypt said:

"Give me one hundred thousand soldiers and I'll go to one side of the river, and all of you can stay on the other side, and at the same time that I engage them in battle, as quickly as you can, you must come to my aid. This way, we will be victorious."

All the captains and nobles praised the wise words of the King of Egypt, but the sultan answered:

"It's foolish to say that you will take them on with one hundred thousand men, even though they have even fewer. You take half our men, and I will take the other half. And whoever engages them first will do so, and if the other half will bravely help us, we will have true glory and honor."

And the discussion ended.

The kings took one half of the men, and the sultan took the other half and crossed the bridge. When Tirant saw how their forces were divided, with the river in between, he said:

"This is exactly what I wanted."

He raised his encampment that was on the side of the kings and had all the tents and carts placed inside the two castles with all the pages. And Tirant held his men back until nightfall. And before the sun had passed the columns of Hercules, Tirant crossed the bridge to the side where he had first been, and he had the foot soldiers climb a hill that was in line with the head of the bridge. When the foot soldiers were up, he had the men with weapons also go up, one squadron behind the other. The sultan, who was on that side, seeing that almost all the men had gone up the side of the hill to give battle, and that there were only four squadrons remaining, went swiftly toward them and attacked them, making them flee up the hill, and sixty Christians were killed. Tirant retreated, battling all the time, and night fell. The Turks came down to the foot of the hill and set up their tents.

When Tirant went up the hill, he found all the knights and nobles absolutely disconsolate. They were running here and there, crying and moaning, with sad, woeful countenances. When Tirant saw them acting that way, he called them all together and said:

"I only want to tell you that if you will put your effort into this, with the aid of Our Lord and His Holy Mother, Our Lady, I will make you victorious over your enemies within three hours."

Nearly all were consoled by the captain's words, except for the Duke of Macedonia who, before the battles were finished, sent a squire of his with instructions about what he should tell the emperor. When he reached the city, he dismounted and left his horse, indicating that he had fled the battle-site and that he had tears in his eyes. When he was in the palace, he found many people there, and he said:

"Where is that poor man they call the emperor?"

When he was informed that Albi, the Duke of Macedonia's squire, had arrived, the emperor quickly came out of his chambers. When Albi saw the emperor he fell to the ground, pulling his hair and lowering his eyes and face, and he said mournfully:

"It has been your will to degrade your captains and vassals, and to honor foreigners of ill repute, men who are known for no deeds, and who wear shoddy tunics. Oh, Emperor! You are lost and so are all your people, for it has been your wish to take away the succession of the empire from that famous and illustrious nobleman, the Duke of Macedonia, to give it to a vile foreigner who has led himself and all the men in the camp to their destruction, and has run away, and we don't know where he is. This is what the person who was the emperor deserved! For the Moors have them trapped on a small hill, and they have no bread or wine, or even water for the horses. By now they must all be dead. I am going to leave with my great pain, and you, who were the emperor, must remain with your own."

"Oh, woe is me!" cried the emperor. And he went into his chambers and fell upon his bed, lamenting.

The princess approached her father to comfort him, but there was no one to console the empress and the other maidens. Rumors of the bad news ran throughout the city, and everyone broke into loud wailing for the friends and relatives they believed had been killed. Let us leave them to their weeping and see what is happening to Tirant.

Having bolstered his men's spirits with his words, they were very optimistic, trusting the great judgment of the captain. Tirant left the encampment at the top well guarded, and took a man with him and went down the back side of the mountain without being seen. When he was at the bottom, he left his armor under a tree, and cautiously stole up to the castle of Lord Malvei. He picked up two stones, one in each hand, and just as they had agreed, he signaled by hitting them together. When Lord Malvei heard the signal, he opened the gates of the bridge. Tirant went in, and found everything that had been prepared. First he had a great deal of oil and tar poured into a wooden bucket, along with pitch and quicklime and other things that would help make a fire, and he gathered a good deal of dry wood, and he had it all spread on top of the wooden raft he had made, and tied two long ropes to each of the chains of the raft. The two men got into a small fishing boat, and each of them held one of the ropes. When the raft was untied, the current carried it downriver, and whenever it would become stuck on one side of the river one of the men would pull on a rope to free it. Tirant told them not to light the fire until they were near the bridge.

When the Turks saw such huge flames in the river, they believed they were lost, and the sultan and all his men abandoned their camp. Fleeing as quickly as they could, they ran toward the wooden bridge. As the sultan had a good horse, he first waited until the fire reached the bridge, and then he went across, and many men followed him. And if the two men had followed the captain's orders and waited to light the fire, all would have been killed or taken prisoner. In their rush to cross to the other side, many Moors and their horses fell into the water. The fire was so great that the entire bridge quickly burned down. And twenty-two thousand or more men were unable to cross the bridge.

When Tirant observed the fire going down the river, he cautiously worked his way back to his troops. He found nearly all of them mounted, wanting to get their enemies' booty. But Tirant would not allow it, telling them:

"We would gain no honor now. Tomorrow we will have the honor and the booty."

In spite of all that had happened, Tirant had a very tight watch set that night, saying:

"Not all of them could have gotten across. In their desperation, couldn't they fall on us?"

When the clear day broke and the sun appeared on our horizon, the captain had the trumpets blown, and everyone mounted. They had the carts and the pages brought out, and all the men went back down to their former camp, and from there they saw what was left of the enemy.

Diafebus, seeing the pitiful state of the Turks, took the ring from Tirant's hand, and Tirant said to him:

"Cousin, what are you doing?"

Diafebus said:

"I want to send Pyramus to the emperor. They haven't had word from us for so long!"

"I beg you, cousin," said Tirant, "send word to him that we need flour and supplies before we run out."

Pyramus left. When he reached the city of Constantinople, he saw everyone looking very said and oppressed, and all the women were crying. He went into the palace, and it was worse: their faces were scratched, their clothing torn. Of all those who saw him, no one said a word to him. When he spoke to anyone, they would not answer. He thought the emperor must have died, or the empress, or their daughter.

He went further inside, into a hall, and recognized the emperor's chamberlain, and he ran to him, laughing. The chamberlain said:

"With all your unbridled happiness, how dare you come to the emperor's chamber?"

"Friend," said Pyramus, "don't be angry with me: I don't know what is making everyone sad here. Let me talk to the emperor, and if he is sad, I will make him happy."

Without saying another word, the chamberlain went into the empress's chamber where he found the emperor with his daughter and the maidens, the windows closed and all of them in mourning. The chamberlain said:

"Sire, one of those reprobate traitors with that reprobate knight, Tirant lo Blanc, is at the door. His name is Pyramus, and I am certain he has fled the battle with his lord. He says he wants to talk to Your Majesty."

The emperor said:

"Tell him to get out of here, and to leave my lands. And if I find him or any of his master's men, I will have them thrown down from the highest tower in the palace."

And as the emperor spoke these words, imagine how the pain in the princess's heart grew twofold. For no matter how much harm Tirant might have done, she could not completely forget him.

After the chamberlain told Pyramus about the emperor's response, Pyramus said:

"In faith, I will not leave. For my lord Tirant has committed no treachery, nor have any of his men. If the emperor will not listen to me, tell the princess to come out here to the chamber door, and I will tell her things that will make her very happy."

The chamberlain told the emperor what Pyramus had said. Then the emperor told Carmesina to go out and talk to him, but that she was not to let him come inside the chamber. When the princess came out to the hall with such a sad face, Pyramus knelt and kissed her hand, and then he began to speak:

"My most excellent lady, I am startled by the great change I see in Your Majesty, in everyone in the palace and in the entire city. I'm very astonished because I don't know what has caused this, and no one I've asked has been willing to tell me. If His Majesty, the emperor, doesn't want that famous knight, Tirant lo Blanc, to be his captain, tell me, and we will quickly leave the empire."

When the distressed princess had listened to Pyramus words, with tears in her eyes she told him everything the duke's squire had said. When Pyramus heard such wickedness, he put his hands to his head and answered:

"My lady, have the ones who brought you such news, and caused the emperor so much pain, put into prison. And arrest me if the truth isn't that Tirant has been victorious and caused the sultan to flee, and burned down the bridge, and has more than twenty thousand of the enemy trapped near the river. If all this isn't true, let them cut me to pieces.

And as greater proof, here is the captain's seal that Tirant gave me."

When the princess heard such glorious news, she quickly ran into the chamber where her father was, and told him everything Pyramus had said. The poor emperor, with all the excessive happiness he felt, fainted and fell from his chair. The doctors were summoned, and they restored him to consciousness. He had Pyramus brought in, and as soon as he heard the news from his lips, he had all the bells in the city rung, and everyone went to the church, and there they gave praise and thanks to God, Our Lord, and to His Holy Mother, for the victory that had been achieved. When they returned to the palace, the emperor had the duke's squire imprisoned. Then Pyramus begged him to have the ships leave quickly with provisions for the encampment. The following day Pyramus left with many words of praise for Tirant and for many others. When this emissary returned with the news, Tirant was amazed at what the Duke of Macedonia had done.

The day Pyramus left, the Turks, having lost all hope, realized that they could not carry on the battle. So to choose the lesser of two evils, they decided to let themselves be taken prisoner.

Luckily, the wise Moor, Abdalla Salomon, was still with them, and they decided to send him as ambassador to Tirant once more. He put a rag on the end of a lance, and when Tirant saw it, he answered immediately. Abdalla Salomon went up to Tirant's camp, presented himself, and very humbly said:

"If Your Lordship, magnanimous captain, would do us the grace of sparing our lives, you would be regarded as glorious among your enemies. I beg you to act with all the virtue you have in you."

The captain had the Moor and all who were with him come into his tent, and he fed them. And they certainly needed it. Then the captain met with all the great lords, and they agreed with what Tirant said to them. He had Ambassador Abdalla summoned, and gave him the following reply:

"I don't think it will be very long before I'll give the sultan and all the others a fitting punishment, but so that they will see that I don't wish to harm them as much as I could, I'll be satisfied if they will bring all their offensive and defensive weapons to the middle of that meadow. And I don't want them all brought together, but one hundred at a time, and then they can bring the horses. That's the way I want it done."

The ambassador took his leave of the captain, and went back and did everything Tirant had ordered.

When all the weapons had been laid down, the captain had them all brought to the camp, and then all the horses were brought up. The Turks were very pleased that he didn't have them all killed, because they thought that even if they were held captive, they could be ransomed. Tirant had them come, unarmed, to the foot of the mountain, and there he gave them food in abundance while his men kept them guarded. Then Tirant went down to them and seized the Christian dukes, counts and knights, among them, and he had them come with him up to his camp. He made them go into a tent, and they were well-served with everything necessary for human sustenance. But many were not pleased that the captain was paying them so much honor when they did not deserve it, for they had come to help Moors against Christians. And when Tirant's men said so to their faces, they recognized their error, and stopped eating.

Tirant held the prisoners this way until the ships arrived.

Two days later the ships came loaded with provisions. After they had unloaded everything, the captain consulted with the others, and they decided to transfer all the prisoners to the ships and have them taken to the emperor. The High Constable was put in charge of them, and they set out. The constable had the sails raised, and with a favorable wind they reached the port of Constantinople in only a few days. The emperor and all the ladies were at the windows, watching the vessels as they approached. The constable had the prisoners disembark, and he took them to the palace. The constable went up to where the emperor was, and kissed his hands and feet. And delivering the good wishes of the captain, he presented the prisoners.

The magnanimous lord received them very happily, and indicated how pleased he was with the captain. And placing the prisoners under heavy guard, the emperor had the constable go into this chambers where the empress and the princess were. He asked him about everything at the encampment, and the constable told him, adding:

"Tonight or tomorrow, Diafebus will be here, with the noblemen that he is bringing as prisoner."

"What!" said the emperor. "Are there still more?" And his happiness grew greater than ever.

The following day Diafebus entered the center of the city with his prisoners, while his trumpets and tambourines played. The emperor and all the people were astonished at the great multitude of prisoners.

When they were at the square in front of the palace, the emperor was at a window. Diafebus bowed deeply to him, and quickly went up to his chambers to kiss his hand, and then did the same to the empress and the princess. After he had embraced all the ladies, he turned back to the emperor and gave him the good wishes Tirant had sent. When the emperor had spoken at length with Diafebus, he had the prisoners placed in the strongest towers they had.

When Diafebus had the opportunity, he went to the princess's chamber and found her with all the maidens. When the princess saw him, she got up to go to him. Diafebus hurried toward her, and knelt and kissed her hand, saying:

"This kiss is from someone whom Your Highness has condemned to a stronger prison than the one that the prisoners I have brought are in."

As the maidens approached, he could say nothing further for fear that they might hear him. But she took him by the hand and they went to a window-seat. Then the princess summoned Stephanie, and Diafebus said:

"Your Highness should not forget such a noble knight, and the lack of liberty he has had since the moment he saw you."

Smiling, the princess answered:

"Oh Diafebus, my brother! I receive your words as the vassal of your lord, and I return his wishes just as strongly, and even more so."

As they were speaking, the emperor came in and saw Diafebus deeply involved in conversation with his daughter, and he said:

"Upon my father's bones, what a wonderful sight to see how these maidens like to hear of the exploits of these good knights."

And he told his daughter to leave the room and go out to the main plaza in the market-place. Diafebus went with the emperor; then he came back to escort the empress and the princess. When they were in the market-place they saw a large catafalque that the emperor had made, entirely covered with cloth of gold and silk. When all the ladies had been seated, the emperor commanded that all the prisoners be brought out, and they were ordered to sit on the ground, Moors as well as Christians.

Then the people were silenced, and the following proclamation was read:

"We, Frederick, by divine grace Emperor of the Greek Empire of Constantinople. So that it may be known and made manifest to the whole world how these wicked knights and unfaithful Christians have accepted payment from the infidel, and taking up arms have united with them in waging war against Christianity. They are deserving of great punishment, and of being removed from the order of chivalry and disinherited by the nobility from which they are descended. So that it may be a punishment for them and an example for all others, we pronounce them traitors to all Christians here present. And we sentence them to be dealt with as all such traitors against God and the world."

When the sentence had been read, twelve knights came out dressed in long robes and hoods, and the emperor dressed in a similar fashion. Then they had the men rise from the ground, and they were brought up to the catafalque where they were assembled and then degraded as is done with evil knights, and then they were returned to prison. Then the emperor said:

"Let there be justice, and let us show mercy to no one."

The Duke of Macedonia's squire was brought out with a large chain around his neck. And he was condemned to die, hanging upside down, for all the anguish he had caused. When Diafebus saw the squire, he hurried to the emperor and knelt at his feet, begging him not to have the squire killed so that wicked people could not say that it was done because he had spoken badly about his captain. When the princess saw that Diafebus' words were futile, she too came and knelt at the emperor's feet to beg him. And when that proved futile, the empress and all the maidens came to plead for his life as well. The emperor said:

"Who has ever seen a death sentence revoked that has been handed down by the general council? I have never done it, nor will I do it now."

The princess caught his hands, pretending to kiss them, and she stealthily removed the ring from his finger without his noticing it, and said to him:

"It is not Your Majesty's custom to be so cruel as to sentence anyone to die with such pain."

The emperor said:

"My child, change his death sentence as you wish."

The princess handed the ring to Diafebus, and he rode swiftly to where they were holding the execution, and gave the ring to the constable. The squire was already on the ladder, about to be executed, and Diafebus grabbed him and took him to his lodging. When Diafebus left to go to the palace, the squire quickly ran to the monastery of San Francisco where he became a friar.

The next day, the emperor sent all the Turks who had not been ransomed to other places to be sold: Venice, Sicily, Rome and Italy. Those that could not be sold were traded for arms, horses or food.

When it came time for the constable and Diafebus to leave, the emperor took as much gold from his treasury as he had received from the ransom of the prisoners, and sent it along with them for the captain.

The day before they were to leave, Diafebus discovered that the emperor had retired, and he went to the princess's chamber. The first one he met there was Stephanie, and he bowed deeply on one knee and said:

"Gentle lady, I would consider myself the most fortunate man alive if you would accept me as your closest servant. I love you above all the ladies in the world."

At that moment the emperor's chamberlain came in and told him that the emperor wished to speak with him. Diafebus begged Stephanie to wait for him there, and said that he would return as quickly as he could.

When the emperor saw Diafebus, he told him that he and the constable were to leave before nightfall. Diafebus returned to the chamber and found his lady deep in thought and with tears in her eyes, because she knew that the emperor summoned him only to tell him that he must leave. Diafebus, seeing her so disconsolate, tried to show her that it was hurting him even more to leave.

While they were consoling each other this way, the princess came into the chamber from the treasure tower, wearing a blouse and a skirt of white damask, her hair falling down to her shoulders because it was so warm. When she saw Diafebus she tried to turn back, but Diafebus blocked her way.

"Shall I tell you something?" said the princess. "I don't care what happens in your presence. You are like a brother to me."

Plaerdemavida spoke up:

"My lady, can Your Highness see Stephanie's face? It looks like she's been blowing on a fire: her face is as red as a rose in May. I can't imagine that Diafebus' hands were idle while we were in the tower. We should have known he'd be here! She was here with the thing she loves most. I tell you, if I had a lover, I'd play with him too, the way both of you do. But I'm a barren woman, and I have no one to love. Lord Diafebus, do you know who I love with all my heart? Hippolytus—Tirant's page. And if he were a knight, I'd love him even more."

"I promise you," said Diafebus, "that in the next battle I take part in, he will be made a knight."

And they joked this way for a long while. Then the princess said:

"Do you know something, Diafebus? When I turn around and look everywhere in the palace and I don't see Tirant, I feel as though I'm dying. I want you to take him all my good wishes, and along with them—wrapped up so that no one will see them—half the load of gold a horse can carry so that he may spend it as he wishes. And when it is gone, I will give him even more. I don't want him or his men to lack for anything. Also, an aunt of mine left me a county called Sant Angel in her will. I want Tirant to have it, and for him to be named the Count of Sant Angel. So if it becomes known that I love Tirant, at least they will say that I am in love with a count."

Diafebus was astonished when he heard the princess uttering words filled with so much love, and he said:

"I don't feel capable of thanking you for the honor you are bestowing on Tirant. So I beg you, on behalf of that famous knight and then on behalf of all of us of his lineage, allow me to kiss your hands and feet."

Stephanie was so bursting with love that she could not contain herself any longer, and she said:

"I'm envious of what Your Excellency is doing for that glorious knight, Tirant. And since I must imitate Your Highness, allow me to give everything I have to Diafebus here."

And she got up and went into her chamber. There she wrote out a document that she placed in her bosom, and then she went back out to the princess.

Meanwhile, Diafebus had been pressing the princess to allow him to kiss her. But the princess would not give her consent. Then Diafebus said:

"Oh, how blind I've been! I would have given my life a hundred times to do some service for Your Majesty. And Your Highness will not allow me the pleasure of even a small part of the fruit! From now on, find yourself another brother and servant to be at your side. And don't imagine for a minute that I'll say anything to Tirant on your behalf, and even less that I'll take him the money. As soon as I reach camp, I'll take my leave of him and go back to my own country. But someday you'll be sorry I left."

Just then the emperor came into the chamber and told Diafebus that he should get ready to leave that same evening.

"Sire," said Diafebus, "I've just come from our lodging, and everyone is ready to leave."

The emperor then brought him out of the chamber and led him through the palace, reminding both him and the constable of what they were to do.

"Oh, poor me!" said the princess. "Look how angry Diafebus was! I don't think he'll want to do anything for me now. Stephanie, beg him for my love not to be angry."

"I certainly will," said Stephanie.

Plaerdemavida spoke up:

"Oh what a strange one you are, my lady. At a time when we're at war, you don't know how to hold the friendship of these knights. They put themselves in danger to defend Your Highness and the entire empire, and you raise a ruckus over a kiss! What's wrong with kissing? In France it doesn't mean anything more than a handshake. If he wanted to kiss you, you should have let him. And you should have done the same even if he had wanted to put his hand under your skirts, when there are times of great need like we have now. Later on, when we have peace, then you can make virtue out of vice. Good woman, good woman, how deceived you are!"

Stephanie had already left, so the princess went to her room and begged her to go and bring back Diafebus:

"Now I'm afraid he really will leave just the way he said he would. And if he goes away, it won't be surprising if Tirant leaves too.

And even if he doesn't, because of his love for me, many others will go too. And then, just when we thought we were winning, we would lose."

"Don't make things so hard," said Plaerdemavida. "Don't send anyone else, Your Highness. It would be better if you went yourself on the pretext of seeing the emperor. Then talk to him, and his anger will disappear quickly."

The princess hurried to her father and found him talking. When he had finished, she took Diafebus aside and pleaded with him not to be angry with her. Diafebus replied:

"Madam, it has to be one of two things: either kiss or leave. If you give me what I'm asking for, then you can command me to do anything, just or unjust, and I will do it."

"Since you won't wait for the one who holds my heart captive," said the princess, "kiss, kiss."

Diafebus knelt on the hard floor and kissed her hand. Then he went over to Stephanie and kissed her three times on the lips for the Holy Trinity.

Stephanie said:

"Since at your great insistence, and by command of my lady, I have kissed you, I give you my permission to take possession of me, but only from the waist up."

Diafebus was not slow to follow her request. He immediately put his hands on her breasts, touching her nipples and everything else that he could. His hands then found the document, and thinking it was a letter from a rival suitor, he stopped cold, almost losing his senses.

"Read what is written there," said Stephanie, "and lose your suspicions."

The princess took the document from Diafebus' hand and read it:

"I, Stephanie of Macedonia, daughter of the illustrious Prince Robert, Duke of Macedonia, promise you, Diafebus of Muntalt, to take you as my husband and lord. And looking toward our marriage, I bring you the duchy of Macedonia with all the rights belonging thereto. In testimony of which I sign and seal my name in my own blood.

"Stephanie of Macedonia."

This Stephanie was not the Duke's daughter. Her father was a glorious prince, and a very worthy and wealthy knight. He was the emperor's first cousin, and this was his only child. When he died, he left the duchy to her, stating in his will that it was to be given to her when she was thirteen years old. In order to have more children, her mother had then married the Count of Albi, and he had taken the title of Duke of Macedonia.

By now this maiden was fourteen years old.

When night fell and they were all ready to leave, Diafebus, happier than we can say, took his leave of the emperor and all the ladies, and especially of Stephanie, begging her to think of him while he was away. And she kissed him many times, in front of the princess and Plaerdemavida.

When they were back again with Tirant, he was very glad to see them. Diafebus and the constable gave him the money the emperor had sent.

By now the Turks were desperate, and they cursed the world and fortune that had brought them so much pain. By their calculations they had lost, between the dead and those taken prisoner, more than one hundred thousand men. In their anger they held counsel to decide how they might kill Tirant. It was decided that the King of Egypt should kill him, because he was more skilled at arms than any of the others.

The following day he called a council of all the great kings, dukes, counts, and all the Christians, and they gathered in the middle of a large meadow. When they were all there, the King of Egypt said:

"If you want me to challenge him to a battle to the death, he is a very spirited knight and he will not be able to refuse. Then, when he's here, we'll fight. If you see me getting the better of him, leave us alone, and I will kill him. But if he is beating me, shoot him down with an arrow. In either case, he will die and so will everyone who comes with him."

They were all pleased by what the king said. When the council was over, the King of Egypt went into his tent and prepared to write a letter.

Now the sultan had a servant who had been born a Christian in the city of Famagosta, and who had been taken prisoner at sea when he was very young. And with his youth and lack of discretion, they had made him become a Moor. When he grew older, he realized that the Christian law was better than the Mohammedan sect, and he decided to go back to the Christian faith. He did it the following way. He prepared his arms and a good horse, and set out for the bridge of stone where Lord Malvei was. When he was an arrow shot away, he put his headdress on the tip of his lance, asking for safety. When the men in the castle saw that it was only one man, they offered him safety. But when the Moor was near, an archer who knew nothing about the guarantee of safety, shot an arrow that wounded the horse.

Lord Malvei was very upset, and he promised the Moor that if the horse died they would give him a better one. The Moor told him how he had come there to become a Christian, and that he wanted to talk to the great captain. They agreed that he should return the following day and that Lord Malvei would advise Tirant. The Moor was very pleased, and went back to the camp. The sultan asked him where he had been and how his horse had been wounded. The Moor replied:

"Sir, I was bored here, so I went over to the bridge. I saw a Christian on horseback and rode toward him. When I was close to him, he shot an arrow at me. I spurred my horse on and caught up to him and knocked him to the ground. Then I dismounted and prepared to kill him. On his knees he begged my forgiveness. So I pardoned him and we became good friends. And he has promised to tell me everything that is happening in the Christian camp."

"This is excellent news to me!" said the sultan. "Go back tomorrow and find out if they intend to fight more, or if they are going back to the city of Constantinople."

The next day the Moor took one of the sultan's best horses and rode to the bridge, where he was taken inside the castle. Tirant soon arrived and paid reverence to Lord Malvei and his son, and then embraced Lady Malvei, and gave honor to the Moor. The Moor told him that he wanted to become a Christian and to serve him. They went to the church, and there he was baptized with the name Cipres of Paterno. Then he said:

"Sir, now that I have been baptized a true Christian, I wish to live and die in this holy faith. I will stay here if you like, or I will go back to the camp and tell you what is happening every day. No one in all our camp knows what is going on better than I, because all the council meetings are held in the sultan's tent, and I am a member of the council."

Tirant begged him to go back, and to advise Lord Malvei as often as he could about the Turk's plans. He agreed, and said:

"I beg you, captain, let me have some sort of sweetmeats so I can give them to the sultan. For he likes to eat these things, and with this as an excuse, I'll be able to come and go easily, and he won't suspect me."

The Lord of Malvei said:

"I can give them to you."

And he had dates and sweetmeats brought in a box, and gave them to Cipres de Paterno.

When he had returned, the sultan asked him for news about the Christians. He replied that his friend had told him that they did not intend to leave.

"Until Your Lordship changes your camp site. And sir, I was given these dates and sweetmeats."

The sultan was very pleased at what he had brought, and had him go often. So he went and told Lord Malvei everything he knew, and Lord Malvei kept Tirant informed. Cipres of Paterno swore never again to serve the sultan.

When the King of Egypt had the letter of battle drawn up, he ordered a messenger to take it to Tirant, the captain of the Greek army. It said the following:

"From Abenamar, by the will of God, King of Egypt, to you, Tirant lo Blanc, captain of the Greek army.

"I challenge you to battle, man to man, on foot or on horseback whichever you desire to your own advantage, before a competent judge. We will do combat until one of us is dead, so that I may present your head to my lady. If you wish to answer this letter, give your reply to Egypt, my messenger, and that will suffice to show your agreement, and to bring our battle to the end that I desire.

"Written in our camp on the eastern shore, the first day of this moon, and signed.

"King of Egypt"

After Tirant held counsel in his tent, he answered the King of Egypt's letter in the following way:

"I vow to God and my lady, and to the honor of chivalry, that twenty days into August, four days before or after, I will be on the eastern shore, before your camp, with all the power to do battle if you should wish it. Written by my hand and sealed with my coat of arms in the camp called Transimeno. The fifth of August.

"Tirant lo Blanc."

Here the book returns to the emperor who wanted very much to have news of the camp. He saw seven sailing ships approaching, and when they had docked he learned that they came from Sicily, and that they were bringing four thousand soldiers and many horses which the King of Sicily was sending. The reason for this I shall now relate.

As we have said previously, the eldest son of the King of Sicily was in France, married to the daughter of the King of France. He was virtuous and discreet, and his father-in-law would not allow him to leave the court because of his great love for him. It happened then that this son fell ill, and died. When his father, the King of Sicily, learned of his death he was very sad. The other son who had become a friar, did not want to leave the religious life to be king after the death of his father. The king was very upset when he saw that his son would not obey him, and he fell sick to his bed. Realizing that he was dying, he put his soul and his kingdom in order, and in his will he named his daughter, Philippe's wife, to be his successor.

When Philippe found himself king, remembering Tirant's help and honor, he decided to go to his aid with the greatest forces he could muster. But his wife, the queen, and everyone in his kingdom pleaded with him not to go that year, because the queen was with child. Seeing their great opposition, he decided to stay. He sent in his place, as captain, the Duke of Messina, with five thousand soldiers on foot and on horseback. Because of her dealings with Tirant, the queen sent him two thousand soldiers and made the Lord of Pantanalea their captain.

When the soldiers had been given lodging, the emperor said:

"I have decided to go to the camp to make peace between the Duke of Macedonia and our captain. If I don't, they'll kill each other some day. Since this sort of thing has happened twice already, we have to guard against a third time. If I get the Duke of Macedonia in my hands, I swear I'll cut off his head."

Then the emperor ordered all his men to prepare to leave.

"What, my lord!" said the empress. "Are you going with so few men?"

The emperor replied:

"These barons from Sicily are here, and they'll go with me."

All the emperor's servants quickly made ready.

The following night, while the princess was asleep, Stephanie came to her bed. She woke her and said:

"My lady, I dreamt that I saw Diafebus, and that he told me: 'Stephanie, my love, Tirant and I are so fortunate to have you here! Just being able to see you makes us sure we'll defeat the Turks.' So, my lady, when I woke up I came here to tell Your Highness that, if you wish, we can quickly satisfy your desires. And they'll know first-hand how great our love is: we will go to them when they can't come to us."

The princess said:

"Give me my chemise, and don't say another word."

She quickly dressed, and then she went to the emperor's chambers. He had not yet gotten up, and she told him:

"My lord, the maidens are afraid, hearing about the war, and especially about the battles. So, Your Majesty, please don't refuse me a favor. You should grant it to me for two reasons: First, Your Majesty should not go anywhere without me because of your age, for I love you more than anyone, and if Your Majesty got sick I could serve you and be at your bedside, because I know your nature better than anyone. The second reason is that it's nature's course that whoever is born first should die first, although sometimes we see the contrary. And if I go with Your Majesty I could see and know about war, and in case the need should arise in the future I would not be afraid."

At first the emperor tried to dissuade her, but when she insisted, he said:

"My daughter, since you want it so much, I'll give my consent."

On the day they left, the princess dressed in a skirt with gold braid, and armed herself in a coat of mail she had had made for her. She mounted a large white horse, and with a staff in her hand she went as captain over her people. In her company were sixty of the most beautiful and elegant maidens in the entire court. She made Stephanie the commander, while the Duke of Pera's daughter, Saladria, had the position of marshal. Comtesina was lord constable, and Plaerdemavida carried the emblem. Eliseu carried the large banner, Widow Repose was usher of the chamber, and each of the others had their own office. And this is how they rode until they reached Tirant's tent.

When the emperor was situated in the camp tents, he sent word to Lord Malvei, asking him to come talk with him. As soon as he received the request, he quickly went to pay homage to the emperor. He told him all about Tirant and the virtuous acts that he did every day, and the princess was very pleased to hear the praises of Tirant. Lord Malvei asked him if he would like to stay at his castle, because he would be very safe there. So he went, while all the Sicilian barons set up their tents near the river.

Lord Malvei covertly sent one of his men to the Valley of Espinosa to tell the captain that the emperor had come with his daughter and with the barons of Sicily. Tirant kept it secret until the following day so that no one would leave with the excuse of going to see the emperor or their relatives. He told only Diafebus in great secrecy.

When it was midnight, or very near it, everyone mounted their horses. He had the foot soldiers go first, with Diafebus as their captain, and with 400 lancers, their horses completely decorated. Tirant earnestly charged Diafebus to stay behind some rocks about a league from the enemy camp, and for him and his men not to show themselves even if they saw that the battle was lost. Even if he saw that they were killing him, they were not to come out to help. Still not satisfied, he made him swear not to move until he gave the command.

Each division put their men in order. Tirant did the following: All the horses were put in a row so that not one head was in front of another. And everyone was in order except the Duke of Macedonia who refused to obey any of the captain's orders. The emperor's flags were in the middle. The Duke of Sinòpoli was at the end of one wing, and the Duke of Pera was at the other end. Meanwhile the captain went up and down the line urging the men to keep in order, for if they did, with the help of Our Lord he would make them victorious that day.

When the sultan saw the Christians preparing for battle, he quickly put all his forces in order: All the men with lances were put in front; next came the archers and crossbowmen; then the Christians that the Grand Turk had hired to fight for him, on horses which were nicely covered and with large plumes, and they were more than fifteen paces behind the crossbowmen. The Turks were last of all, and they had more than four hundred bombards. They thought that with the bombards they would kill more than seven hundred men. When all the men were in place the King of Egypt sent a messenger to Tirant to thank him for keeping his promise, and to tell him that he would kill him or take him prisoner on that day. He said Tirant would taste the point of his lance very soon, and he would see how bitter it tasted. Tirant answered that he would be very happy to see how it tasted because he had so much sugar that he would not notice any bitter taste at all, but that that day he would engage him in battle, and he would spill his blood.

Tirant again urged his men on. He took away their fear, and gave them hopes of having a glorious victory. The Turks shot one bombard, and the blast went wide without touching anyone. Tirant had a small axe tied to his arm with a silk cord, and in his hand he held a small banner, and he signaled with it. The Duke of Pera, who commanded one wing, turned his men toward the flags in a very slow and orderly way, so that their backs were to the enemy. At the other end of the wing was the Duke of Sinòpoli, and he held his men steady. When the men under the Duke of Pera had turned and were in order again, Tirant signaled with the small banner, and the men under the Duke of Sinòpoli turned around in the same orderly way. Then they were all facing the mountain, where Diafebus was, with their backs to the enemy. They spurred their horses forward at a gallop, always in a very orderly way, with none of the horses going ahead of the others, When the Turks saw them going back, they began to shout:

"They're running away! They're running away!"

The foot soldiers threw away their shields, others their lances, and others their crossbows, to run after their Christian enemies. The men on horseback threw off the coverings so that their horses could run more swiftly. From time to time Tirant turned and saw all the men coming, wave after wave, in confusion, and so he was unconcerned about anything except for his troops to continue moving in a very orderly way. And the Moors with good horses came close enough to throw their lances at their backs.

When the emperor, who was up in the tower, saw his men fleeing, he believed that the battle was lost. All that night the maidens did not take off their clothes, and prayed earnestly, begging the Conqueror of Battles and His Holy Mother to give the Christians victory.

When Tirant saw the foot soldiers falling far behind, and that they had passed the place where Diafebus was, Tirant raised the banner he was carrying and they all stopped. Then each squadron drew a stone's throw apart from the one next to it. When the Turks saw them stop, they realized they had been tricked. Tirant ordered the Duke of Pera to attack first, and he charged into the enemy. When Tirant saw the enemy coming with reinforcements, he had the Marquis of Saint George lead an attack, then the Duke of Sinòpoli. And so many men were killed that it was an astonishing sight to see.

Tirant saw that half his men had been involved in the attacks, and they were still winning. Then, in the melee, he saw the King of Cappadocia killing many Christians (He recognized him by his coat of arms: a gold lion with a banner), and he took a lance and spurred toward him. When the king saw him coming he did not turn his back, but waited for him in anticipation. And when they met, it was with such force that both they and their horses fell to the ground. They both got up bravely, and slashed at each other with their swords. But so many men were fighting aground them that they could not fight well. Then the Turks helped their king mount again. Pyramus went in front of the king so Tirant could mount, and the others surrounded him, defending him until the squadron of Count Plegamans could attack. This squadron came to where the captain was, and they helped him mount behind Lord Agramunt who took him out of the thick of battle. Since many horses had lost their riders and were running loose, they caught one and gave it to their captain, and he quickly went back into the fray.

The captain commanded all the squadrons to attack, some on the right and some on the left. Then they saw helmets falling to the ground, and many knights from both sides were being killed or wounded. It was a startling sight to see. Tirant attacked too, first in one place, then in another. And he did not fight in only one place, but in many, helping wherever he was needed.

The King of Egypt was able to see Tirant fighting very bravely. He drew apart from the battle, and the Kings of Cappadocia and Africa came out with him. The King of Egypt asked them to leave the others and try to kill only Tirant. And with this accord they returned to the battle. While Tirant was fighting, the Duke of Macedonia came up behind Tirant, and plunged his sword into his neck, under the helmet. Hippolytus and Pyramus saw it, and cried:

"You traitor! Why are you trying to kill one of the best knights in the world?"

The three kings had lances, and they worked their way forward until they saw Tirant. They galloped toward him, but only the King of Egypt and the King of Cappadocia were able to reach him. The clash was so great that both Tirant and his horse fell to the ground. The horse had seven wounds.

The King of Africa attacked the Duke of Macedonia who was fighting near Tirant, and the king plunged his lance into the duke's chest with such force that it came out the other side, and that is how he paid for his wickedness.

Tirant was on the ground with his horse lying on his leg, and he could barely get up. But with a great effort he stood up, and the beaver fell from his helmet, for a lance hit him there, and another hit his left vambrace. If it had not been for his own soldiers then, he would have been killed. The King of Egypt saw him on the ground, and quickly tried to dismount. When his leg was on the saddlebow Lord Agramunt plunged a lance into his thigh, and it came out the other side. The wound left him in great pain, and he fell to the ground. When Tirant saw him stretched out on the ground like that he ran toward him, but with all the men fighting he could not reach him. The king stood up again and picked up a lance that he found lying on the ground, and he made his way forward until he was able to hurl his lance at Tirant. Tirant was hit in the cheek, and since he had no beaver, four of his teeth were knocked out, and he lost a great deal of blood, but that did not stop him, and he continued to fight. Hippolytus saw him on foot, wounded, and he made his way to him. Then he dismounted as quickly as he could, and said:

"My lord, take my horse, I beg you."

Tirant was fighting at one end of the wing, moving away from the thick of battle little by little. He mounted, and said to Hippolytus:

"What will you do?"

Hippolytus answered:

"Sir, save yourself. Even if they kill me, my love for you is such that I will consider it worthwhile."

Tirant turned back to the fighting, looking to see if he could find the King of Egypt, but because of his painful wound the king had left the battle. When Tirant saw that he could not find him, he fought the others. It was much later, while he was still fighting, that he encountered the King of Cappadocia. When this king saw him he went out to meet him, and with his sword he slightly cut the hand that held the axe. Then Tirant drew so near to him that he struck him on the head with his axe, and caved in his helmet, and the king fell to the ground, half dead. Tirant quickly dismounted, and cut the straps of his helmet.

A knight came up and cried out:

"My lord, do not kill the king. Since he is mortally wounded and is near death, be merciful and give him the short time he has left to live.

You have done enough by defeating him."

Tirant said:

"What moved you to want mercy on our enemy who has done everything possible to kill me? Now is the time only for cruelty."

And he removed the helmet and cut off his head. Tirant's axe stood out from all the others, for it was red, dripping blood from the men he had killed. The ground was covered with dead men, and was completely red from all the blood that had been spilled. Tirant mounted his horse again, and when the Turks saw their king killed, they fell upon him in great numbers, trying to kill him. Tirant was badly wounded, and was again knocked from his horse. He quickly stood up, not at all overcome by the fall or frightened because of his wounds. He went into the thick of the fray on foot, fighting to help his men, and he again mounted his horse.

This was a harsh and terrible battle, and by now it was nearly time for vespers.

Diafebus was cursing Tirant for putting him there, and he said:

"He always wants the honors for himself, and he won't share them with anyone else. He's left me here as though I weren't good for anything. But by God, I want part of the honor. Let's go!" he said. "Let's go into battle without being afraid of any danger."

He and his men came out from their concealment and they attacked very boldly. The Turks saw so many men coming out (when they had thought there were no more), and they became very dejected.

The sultan left the battle because he was slightly wounded, and he said to his men:

"I see that our forces are losing. I think it's better for us to flee than to die."

When Tirant saw the sultan and his men fleeing with their banners he rode after them and killed many of them. This battle lasted from daybreak until three hours after noon. There were so many Moors that the Christians grew weary from killing them.

The captain and most of his men reached the city that formerly belonged to the Marquis of Saint George. It had been lost to the King of Egypt, and he kept it well supplied. When the King of Egypt saw that the battle was lost, he had fled with the others, and he felt so much pain from the wound in his thigh that he had to leave the sultan and his men, and stop there. When Tirant arrived it was nearly dark. They stayed in camp until the following day. That evening they all had their wounds attended to, and many died during the night. But on that eastern shore there had never been such a harsh and deadly battle: many women became widows, and many young maidens lost their fathers, but they were filled with the hope of being set free from slavery.

The following day Tirant had the men take up arms, and they attacked the city, but the Turks defended themselves very well, for they had very good men inside. After four unsuccessful attacks, the Marquis of Saint George rode around the entire city and came to the Jewish quarter. There he called out to a Jew named Jacob. When the Jew heard the marquis' voice, he realized it was his lord, and he ran to open the gate for him. The marquis and his men quickly rode into the city, and they took half of it before the King of Egypt or the other Moors knew what had happened.

The marquis sent word to Tirant to stop fighting and to come in through the Jewish quarter because the city had already been taken. When Tirant and his men came in through that gate, he found that the marquis' forces had already defeated all the Turks, and that he had the King of Egypt trapped in a thicket of trees where he was continuing to fight, wounded as he was. When the marquis had captured the king, he sent word to the captain to come and behead his enemy, the King of Egypt. The captain replied that he would never kill a man who was being held prisoner. Whereupon the marquis seized the king by the hair, and slit his throat with a knife.

Even though Tirant was victorious that day, he would allow no celebrations to take place. He only said in everyone's presence:

"If Diafebus had done what I ordered him to, I would have killed the sultan and taken prisoner all the great dukes who were there, and I would be lord of the entire empire."

Getting back to the emperor, the great pain he felt when he thought Tirant had lost the battle was changed into relief because Lord Malvei sent one of his men on horseback for news of the battle. He returned with the news of what had happened, and how the captain had gone after the fleeing Turks.

A few moments later the emperor mounted his horse to go with the barons of Sicily, and the princess wanted to go with him. When they were in the Moorish camp they found all the tents with all the wealth inside, and the men wanted to loot them, but the emperor would not allow it. Instead he had the Lord of Pantanalea and Lord Malvei hold all the booty for safekeeping until the men who had conquered the camp were notified.

While the emperor was in the Moors' camp, the princess saw a little black boy at a distance. She rode toward him and quickly dismounted and went into the tent where the little black boy had gone to hide. Grabbing him by the hair, she took him out to the emperor and said:

"Now I can boast in front of our captain about how I have been a valiant lady-knight, who went boldly into the enemy camp, and took a Turk prisoner."

The emperor and all the others were very amused at his daughter's wit.

Diafebus saw that Tirant was angry with him, and so he did not dare show himself out of shame. When the emperor heard of the glorious battle from others but not from Diafebus, he told the princess:

"Since I've had no news from Diafebus, I fear that he may be dead."

When Stephanie heard this, she burst into tears. On their return to the castle of Malvei, she sent a man to find out what had happened to Diafebus, along with a letter that said:

"My love for you demands that I have news from you. For I have heard that you may be dead. So I beg you, my lord, to come here quickly. And if something has happened to you, I want to die with you."

When Diafebus saw this letter from his lady, he was overjoyed. He took the letter to Tirant's room. When Tirant had read it, he sent for the messenger and asked him about the emperor and the virtuous princess. The messenger told him everything that had happened in the camp, and how the princess had gone armed into the Moors' tents and had captured a black, and that she was holding him under guard.

"To show him to Your Lordship, as soon as she can see you."

Tirant was very pleased, and he ordered Diafebus to go to His Majesty, the emperor. And Diafebus rode off very quickly.

When he reached the castle of Malvei, he went directly to the emperor. The entire castle heard that Diafebus had come, and the maidens quickly went to see him—especially Stephanie. They found him in the emperor's chamber, talking about the battle.

The emperor asked how many men were killed, and Diafebus said:

"I don't know the number of Turks who are dead, but from here to the city of Saint George you can't travel on the main road: it's too full of corpses. But of our forces I can give you an exact account, because the captain has had all their bodies gathered and buried. We found the Duke of Macedonia dead from a lance wound, and the Duke of Babylonia, the Marquis of Ferrara, and the Marquis of Guast, Count Plegamans. These are the main ones. There are also many other knights who were killed, among them the High Constable. In all, one thousand two hundred thirty-four men died."

The emperor was very pleased with Tirant's accomplishments, and did not know how to reward him. Diafebus remained there, pretending he was ill, and the emperor had him taken care of as well as he would have his own daughter. Tirant stayed in the camp, guarding it well.

Meanwhile the sultan and all those who had escaped with him went into the city of Bellpuig. The sultan remained there, feeling safe, but for two weeks he kept to his room, crying over the battle they had lost, and lamenting the death of the King of Cappadocia. But he still knew nothing of the death of the King of Egypt and he was anxious to hear any news. Cipres of Paterno said to him:

"Sir, does Your Lordship want me to go? If I can talk to my friend, I'll know everything there is to know."

The sultan begged him very much, in front of all who were there, to go.

Under his jubbah Cipres wore a tunic of white damask that Tirant had given him with the cross of Saint George embroidered on it.

When he was on the road and the Moors couldn't see him, he took off the jubbah and sat on it while he rode. When the Christian spies along the road saw him, they thought he was one of their own, and they did not stop him. In the city, he asked where the captain's lodgings were. The captain was very glad to see him, and asked what news there was.

"Sir," said Cipres of Paterno, "they've found 103,700 men missing from their ranks, who have either been killed or taken prisoner. If you had pursued them, you would have taken them all, for their horses were too tired to go on. They had to stop halfway along the road to Bellpuig and spend the night: many were wounded, many were fatigued, and many died that night since there were no doctors to attend them: the cold entered their wounds, and there they died."

"Do you have any other news?"

"Yes, sir," said Cipres of Paterno. "Seven ships have come from Turkey, loaded with wheat, barley and other foods. And they say for a certainty that the Grand Caramany is on them with fifty thousand soldiers and horsemen, and that he's bringing his daughter to give her as a wife to the sultan, and that in his company is the King of Upper India."

"Have they unloaded those seven ships yet?" asked Tirant.

"No, sir," said Cipres. "The wind has been against them, and they haven't been able to make port."

They spoke of many other things, and after Cipres of Paterno had returned to the sultan, he told him about the death of the King of Egypt. And there was great wailing among the Moors, for he was much loved.

Tirant took a man with him who knew the land well, and which secret roads they could travel by to avoid difficulties. When they were in sight of the sea, they saw the city of Bellpuig at the top of a high mountain, and the ships, their sails turning to and fro in the wind, unable to make port. Tirant returned quickly, and learned that the emperor, along with all the barons from Sicily, had gone out to conquer the many villas and castles nearby. Then he and the Duke of Pera left with a party of soldiers, and he left the rest with the Marquis of Saint George as their captain. When Tirant was near the castle of Malvei, he learned that the princess had remained inside with her maidens, and with Diafebus as their protector. So he sent Hippolytus inside with a message. When Hippolytus was before the princess, he knelt and kissed her hand and said:

"Your Majesty, my lord sends me to beg Your Highness to give him safe- conduct so that he may come and go from here freely."

The princess replied, "Oh, new knight. Doesn't the good captain know that we are all under his captaincy and in his care?"

Then Hippolytus stood and embraced all the maidens. And don't think that Plaerdemavida was displeased to see Hippolytus. Meanwhile the princess took pen and ink, and wrote:

"With my own hand I sign this document. I will in no way limit your freedom to come and go as you wish. September 7, in the Castle of Malvei."

When he had the document in hand, Tirant quickly went up to the castle where he found the princess in a great hall. She took the Duke of Pera by one hand, and Tirant by the other, and sat between them. And they spoke of many things. They talked about how the emperor had been taking villas and castles, and they decided to go and help the emperor in the morning. And the princess said:

"If you go to where the emperor is, I'm going too." And she had them bring out her prisoner, saying: "Do you think that when I've been in hard-fought battles the way you have, I don't know how to take prisoners from among our cruel enemies?"

And saying these things, they went in to dine. But the princess ate very little, for she could not keep her eyes off Tirant. The duke began to talk to the lady of the castle and to Widow Repose, telling them about the battles they had won under Tirant's leadership. And Widow Repose's love of Tirant grew even stronger, but she was afraid to show it. While they were talking Plaerdemavida came up, and sitting at Tirant's feet, she said:

"My lord and captain, no one loves you as I do. I feel compassion for you, for none of these ladies has told you to lay down your weapons. In faith, that shirt you are wearing is well trampled. I saw it being put on and taken off, well-perfumed, and now I see it all torn and smelling of iron and steel."

The princess said:

"Give me that hand that has not had mercy on the deaths of the Moorish Kings, our enemies."

Stephanie took his hand and placed it in the princess's lap. When she saw it on her knees, she bent over and kissed it.

Tirant said:

"If Your Highness would give me leave to kiss your hands whenever I wished, oh how fortunate I'd be. And I would be even more so if I could kiss your feet and your legs."

The princess took his hands again, and said:

"From now on, Captain, I want your hands to do as they will with me: that is your right."

She quickly got up because they had spent the greater part of the night there. And so that the duke and the others would have no reason to gossip, they went with her to her room where she bid them all a good night. And the duke and Tirant slept in the same bed.

The following morning the trumpets blew, and they all armed themselves and mounted their horses. The princess wanted to go with them, and they rode until they found the emperor, who was attacking a well-fortified city. With Tirant's men helping, they entered the villa and killed and made prisoner of many.

The following day the emperor held council to decide where they should attack next. The captain spoke, and said:

"Sire, it would be better if Your Highness would go with the barons of Sicily back to the palace with all the prisoners we've taken. The Duke and I will take charge of guarding and conquering the nearby cities and villas. And Your Majesty can send us the supplies we need."

When they were back in the castle, the emperor summoned Tirant, and then had the princess and the other maidens come, and he said:

"Captain, since fortune has been so contrary to our High Constable, the Count of Bitinua, who is dead, who do you think we should choose as our next constable?"

Tirant knelt and said:

"My lord, if Your Majesty would be pleased to give the office of High Constable to Diafebus, I would consider it a great favor."

"I will do as you wish," said the emperor. "Because of my affection for you, and because of his many merits, from this moment on, I grant to Diafebus the office of High Constable. And to you I give the County of Sant Angel, which I take from my daughter and bestow upon you. Tomorrow I will have a celebration where you will take the title of count."

Tirant replied:

"Sire, I give you infinite thanks for doing me such a great honor, but I will accept it only if I can give the title in turn to Diafebus, my closest relative."

"It makes no difference to me what you do with it afterward, as long as I have offered it and you have accepted it."

Then Tirant knelt and kissed the emperor's hands and feet for his honor.

The morning of the next day the emperor wanted mass held in the middle of a meadow, and he wanted Diafebus between himself and his daughter. After mass the emperor put the ring on Diafebus' hand and kissed him on the mouth. Then all the trumpets began to peal very loudly, and a king-of-arms cried out in a loud voice: "This is the most eminent and virtuous knight, Count of Sant Angel and High Constable of the Greek Empire."

Afterward the dances and festivities began, and all day long the princess did nothing but dance with the High Constable. When it was time to eat the emperor had the High Constable sit at his right, and the duke sat on his left, while the princess sat to the right of the constable. Tirant acted as steward since he was giving the celebration. The ladies ate at other tables, and the barons and knights ate at their right. Next were all the soldiers. And that day all the prisoners ate at tables to honor the celebration. Tirant even had the horses eating barley mixed with bread.

When the dinner was half finished, Tirant summoned the kings-of-arms and heralds, and gave them a thousand ducats. And all the trumpets were pealing, and they came before the emperor's table and cried out, "Largesse, largesse!"

After the meal the repast was held with many sugared dainties. Then they all rode, armed and holding the constable's banners, jousting before the emperor. They held a beautiful display of arms without getting hurt. And they went like this up to the place where the sultan usually held camp, and came back very happily.

When they thought it was time to have the evening meal, they held the festivities in that same place, and they were very well served with many varied dishes. During the entire meal, as Tirant was serving it, he seemed very sad. The princess had him come over to her, and she whispered in his ear:

"Tell me, Tirant, why are you so sad? Your face shows that something is wrong. Tell me, what it is, please!"

"My lady, I have so many troubles that they could not be counted. My life is worth nothing. Your Highness is leaving tomorrow, and I will be left behind in great sadness, knowing that I will not see you."

"It is only right," said the princess, "that anyone who causes misfortune should suffer for it. You are the one who brought it on: You advised the emperor to go back to the city with all the prisoners. I've never seen such bad advice given by any man who was in love. But if you would like me to pretend I am sick for two or three weeks, I will do it because of my love for you, and I'm sure the emperor will wait because of his love for me."

"But what will we do," said Tirant, "with all these prisoners we have here? I can't find any way to relieve my pain. Sometimes I feel like taking poison, or dying a sudden death, to escape this anguish."

"Don't do any such thing, Tirant," said the princess. "Go talk to Stephanie, and see if she can do something to help that won't be difficult for me, and will bring you relief."

Tirant quickly went to Stephanie and told her his troubles. And they, and the constable, agreed that when everybody was resting and the maidens were asleep, the two men would come to the chamber and there they would decide what they could do to give release to their passion.

When it was night, and time for everyone in the castle to be asleep, the maidens had gone to bed. All the ladies were sleeping with Widow Repose; there were only five sleeping in the room they had to pass through.

The princess and Stephanie were in their chamber, and when Plaerdemavida saw that the princess did not want to go to sleep, and then she heard her putting perfume on, she quickly thought that there was going to be a night of merry-making.

When the time came, Stephanie picked up a lighted candlestick in one hand, and went to the bed where the five maidens were sleeping, and she looked at them all, one at a time, to see if they were asleep. Plaerdemavida wanted to see and hear everything that would happen, and she tried to stay awake. And when Stephanie came with the candlestick, she closed her eyes and pretended to be sleeping. When Stephanie saw that all the ladies were asleep, she quietly opened the door so that no one would hear her, and she found the two knights already waiting at the door more devoutly than the Jews await the Messiah. As they came in, she put out the light and took the constable's hand. She led the way, with Tirant following the constable, until they came to the door of the chamber where the princess was waiting for them, alone.

When Tirant saw how beautifully she was dressed, he bowed deeply to her, and with one knee on the ground, he kissed her hands many times, and they exchanged amorous words. Later, when they felt that it was time for them to go, they said goodnight and went back to their room. Who could sleep that night, some because of love, and others because of pain?

As soon as it was light everyone got up, because the emperor had to leave that day. When Plaerdemavida was up she went to the princess's chamber and found her dressing. Stephanie was sitting on the floor, not yet finished dressing, because her hands would not help her tie on her hat, and her eyes were half closed so that she could scarcely see.

"Holy Mary, help me!" said Plaerdemavida. "Tell me, Stephanie, what kind of behavior is this. What's wrong with you? I'll go get the doctors so they can bring you back to health."

"That's not necessary," said Stephanie. "My illness won't last long. It's only a headache. The air from the river last night made me ill."

"Be careful about what you're saying," said Plaerdemavida. "I'm afraid you may die. And if you die, your death will be criminal. Be careful about pain in your heels, I've heard doctors say about us women that pain comes to our heels first, then our feet, then it comes up to our knees, and our thighs, and sometimes it goes into our secret place. There it brings us a great deal of pain, and it goes up to our head from there. And don't think that this sickness comes often, as the great philosopher Galen says—a very wise doctor, for it only comes once in a lifetime. Even though it's an incurable illness, it is never deadly, and there are many treatments if a person wants to try them. What I'm telling you is true, and you shouldn't be astonished that I know about sickness. If you show me your tongue I'll be able to tell you what your illness is."

Stephanie stuck out her tongue. When Plaerdemavida had seen it she said to her:

"I would swear by everything my father taught me that you lost blood last night."

Stephanie quickly answered:

"You're right. I had a nosebleed."

"I don't know if it came out of your nose or your heel," said Plaerdemavida, "but you've lost blood. And my lady, if Your Majesty would like, I'll tell you a dream I had last night, as long as Your Highness will promise me that if I say something that annoys you, you'll forgive me."

The princess was delighted by what Plaerdemavida had said, and laughing, she told her to say whatever she liked, that she forgave her. And Plaerdemavida began to tell about her dream.

"I'll tell Your Majesty everything I dreamed. As I was asleep in a side chamber with four maidens, I saw Stephanie come in with a lighted candle so that it wouldn't shine too brightly, and she came up to our bed and saw us all sleeping. The truth is that I was half asleep: I don't know if I was asleep or awake. In my dream I saw how Stephanie opened the chamber door very quietly so that she wouldn't make any noise, and she found my lord Tirant and the constable there, waiting. They were dressed in their doublets, with cloaks and swords, and they wore woolen stockings on their feet so they wouldn't make any noise when they walked. When they came in, she put out the light, and went in front, holding the constable's hand. After him came your knight. She was like a blind man's guide, and she put them in your chamber. Your Highness was all perfumed, dressed and not naked. Tirant held you in his arms and carried you around the room, kissing you over and over again, and Your Highness was saying, 'Stop it, Tirant, stop it!' And he put you on a bed. And Plaerdemavida went up the bed and said, 'Oh, in the bed! If only the people who knew you before could see you now!' And it seemed to me that I got out of bed in my chemise and went up to that hole in the door, and that I watched everything you were doing."

The princess laughed, and said:
"Was there more to your dream?"
"Holy Mary, yes!" said Plaerdemavida. "Let me go on, and I'll tell you the whole thing. My lady, you said, 'Tirant, I let you come here so you could have a little rest, because of the great affection I feel for you.'

"And Tirant wasn't sure he would do what you told him. And you said: 'Don't refuse me what I'm asking of you, because my chastity that I've kept can pride itself on being free of all sin.' 'I felt sure,' said Tirant, 'that you would be in agreement with my wishes without being afraid of any future danger, but since Your Highness is displeased, I will do whatever Your Majesty desires.' And you made him swear that he would not anger you in any way: 'And even if you wanted to, the anguish you would give me would be enormous—I would curse you all the days of my life, for when virginity is lost it cannot be regained.' I dreamed that you and he said all these things to each other. Then, in my vision, I saw how he kissed you again and again and untied the cord over your bosom, and that he quickly kissed your breasts. After he had spent some time kissing you he tried to put his hands under your skirts, and you, my good lady, would not permit it. And I think that if you had allowed it his oath would have been in danger. Your Highness said to him, 'The time will come when what you want so much will be given to you, and my virginity, intact, will be yours.' Then he put his face next to yours, and with his arms around your neck, and yours around his, like vines on a tree, he received your loving kisses. Later, still dreaming, I saw how Stephanie was on that bed, and it seemed to me that her legs were turning white, and she said many times, 'Oh, my lord, you're hurting me! Have a little pity on me; don't kill me.' And Tirant was saying to her, 'Stephanie, why do you want to put your honor in jeopardy by screaming so loudly? Don't you know that walls sometimes have ears?' And she grabbed the sheet and stuffed it in her mouth and bit down on it with her teeth so she wouldn't scream. But after a short while she couldn't help giving out a loud shriek and saying, 'Poor me, what shall I do? The pain is making me scream. From what I can see you've decided to kill me.'

"Then the constable closed her mouth. When I heard that sweet moan I cursed my misfortune because I wasn't the third one with my Hippolytus. The more I thought about it, the more it grieved me, and it seems to me that I took a little water, and washed my heart, my breasts, and my stomach to take away pain. And as my soul looked through the hole I saw how, after a second, Stephanie held out her arms and gave up, in surrender. But still she said: 'Go away, you cruel, unloving man. You have no pity or mercy on maidens until you've taken away their chastity. Oh, you faithless man! If I decided not to forgive you, what punishment would you deserve? And all the while I'm complaining about you, the more I love you.'

"She called to the princess and Tirant, and showing them the shirt, she said: 'Love must make amends for this blood of mine.' She said this with tears in her eyes. After all this, when day was approaching, Your Majesty and Tirant consoled her as well as you could. Then, when the roosters started to crow again, Your Highness begged Tirant to go so that you would not be seen by anyone in the castle. And Tirant begged Your Highness to release him from his oath so that he could achieve the glorious triumph that he desired, as his cousin had done. Your Highness refused, and you were victorious in the battle. When they had gone I woke up. I didn't see a thing, not Hippolytus or anyone else, but I began to think that it might really have happened, because I found my breasts and my belly wet with water. My pain increased so much that I began to toss and turn in bed like a sick man who is about to die. So I decided to love Hippolytus with all my heart, and pass my life in pain, just as Stephanie is doing. Shall I keep my eyes closed with no one coming to give me relief? Love has disturbed my feelings so much that I'll die if Hippolytus doesn't come to my aid. If I could at least spend my life sleeping! By heaven, it's a trial to wake up when you're having a good dream."

The other maidens had gotten up, and they came into the chamber to help their lady dress. After mass the emperor left with the barons of Sicily, and the Duke of Pera, and all the prisoners. Tirant and the constable accompanied them a good league. The emperor told them to go back, and since he had told them once already, they had to do it. After Tirant had taken his leave of the emperor and the barons, he approached the princess and asked if Her Majesty wanted something. The princess lifted the veil she wore in front of her face and her eyes could not help shedding tears, and she could say nothing but:

"Perhaps..."

And she could say no more because the words would not come, and everything was sobs and sighs of farewell. She let the veil fall completely over her face so that her sadness would not reach the ears of the emperor or the rest of the people.

No one could remember anything ever having happened to any knight like what happened to Tirant who, after he had said farewell to the princess, fell off the horse he was riding. As soon as he had fallen he got up and raised his hand toward the horse, saying that it was the one that was hurt. The emperor and many others saw it and ran to him. And he pretended to be looking at the horse's hoof.

The emperor said to him:

"How did you happen to fall?"

And Tirant told him:

"My lord, I thought my horse was hurt, and I started getting down to see what was wrong with it, and the stirrup broke. But it's nothing to be surprised at, my lord, to see a man fall: a horse has four feet and it falls down: all the more reason for a man to fall since he has only two."

He quickly mounted again, and each went his way. Tirant came to the castle of the Lord of Malvei. He ordered the constable and half of the men, both those on horse and on foot, to go to the camp and guard it.

"I'll go," said Tirant, "to the port where the ships are, and have them unloaded. And if I see that there isn't enough I'll send them to the city again, or to Rhodes."

By night Tirant was in the port, and he found the ships almost unloaded. The ships' masters and the sailors were very happy at the captain's visit, and they told him that the seven Genoese ships had sailed into the port of Bellpuig.

"We have all been very cautious because we were afraid they would come here and attack us."

Tirant said:

"That shows they are afraid of you, since they haven't dared to attack. Shall we make them more afraid than they already are?"

They took a fishing boat and armed it. And they sent it out to see how many men there could be, more or less, on the ships, and how many vessels were in port. That night he had all the wheat unloaded. By morning the spy-boat returned with the news that there were seven large ships, and that they had unloaded all the horses; that all the men were on land, and that now they had begun to unload the wheat and other food.

"By the Lord who sustains the whole world," said Tirant, "I will do everything I can, since they've taken off the horses, to eat of their wheat."

He quickly had the ships prepared, and many soldiers and bowmen boarded them. Tirant struck out to sea that night. It was no more than thirty miles from one port to another. When day broke, clear and beautiful, the men on land saw Tirant's five ships, and thinking that they were part of those coming with the Grand Caramany they paid no attention to them at all. As the ships came into port each of them attacked another ship, and many men jumped aboard the others. Then they attacked the two remaining ships, and since few men were aboard they took them all with very little trouble and without anyone being killed. Then they brought back all the ships loaded with wheat and barley, salted oxen and wine from Cyprus. I can assure you that in the Christian camp it was very helpful and timely since, because of all the fighting, they had no wheat or meat unless it came to them by sea. Tirant gave the wheat to the Lord of Malvei; all the rest he had transported to the camp at the city of Saint George.

When Tirant returned from the attack he spoke to the Turks who had been made his prisoners on the ship, and asked them for news about Turkey. They told him that it was true that the Grand Caramany was coming with a great armada, along with the King of Upper India, and that the Caramany was bringing his daughter, who was a maiden of great beauty, to give to the sultan for his wife.

"And he is bringing many maidens with him, of high station, and the betrothed of the Great Turk's son is with them."

One of the Turks said:

"When we docked at the port they told us that a devil of a Frenchman was here as captain of the Greeks and that he is winning all their battles, and they say he is called Tirant. In faith, he may do all those great things they say he does, but his name is ugly and vile because Tirant means a robber of goods, or more properly, a thief. And believe me, his actions will do justice to his name. Because according to a letter that the King of Egypt wrote, he didn't dare fight him man to man, and it also said that he was in love with the emperor's daughter. When he's won the battles, he'll get the emperor's daughter pregnant, and then the wife, and then he'll kill the emperor. That's the way the French are: they're evil people! And then you'll see that, if the Turks and the Christians let him live long, he'll make himself emperor."

"Upon my word," said Tirant, "you have spoken the truth: these French are very evil people. And he'll do even worse than you've said, because he's a real thief, and he travels the roads to rob. And you'll certainly see him get the emperor's daughter pregnant, and he'll take the throne, and afterward who will stop him from raping all the maidens?"

"By heaven," said the sailor, "I see that you know him well, and you know about the treachery he's done and that he will do."

Hippolytus was standing there, and he drew his sword to cut off the man's head, but Tirant got up quickly and took the sword away from him. And Tirant, continuing to speak badly of himself, made him talk more. The sailor said:

"I swear by the water I was baptized with that if I could catch that traitor, Tirant, the way I've caught many others, I'd have him hanged from the highest mast on the entire ship."

Tirant laughed, and was very amused by what the sailor said. If it had been someone else instead of Tirant, they would have dealt severely with him, or would have hanged him. But Tirant took a silk jacket and thirty ducats and gave them to him, and as soon as they were on land, he freed him. Imagine how the poor sailor must have felt when he discovered that it was Tirant! He knelt, and begged his forgiveness. And Tirant very willingly forgave him.

The following day the barons from Sicily came to the camp. When they were at the castle of Malvei they saw many carts carrying bombards to the port. They were told that the captain was at the port, and they went there, knowing that he wanted to go to sea. They begged him to allow them to go along. The captain was glad to, precisely because they were from the islands, and they knew how to sail. He gave orders to his captains and had many men go on board the ships, both soldiers and crossbowmen. Although the ships were not very large, they were armed with good men, and they were well supplied. Other ships were loaded with wheat, horses, and as many men as they could carry.

Soon they saw a galley with sails unfurled and oars driving it on, and they quickly realized that enemy ships were approaching. The captain had all the men go on board, and they carried the bombards and everything they needed on board. When it was nearly vespers the ships could be seen from the port. Then the captain's ship moved out in front of all the others. When the Turks saw it they shouted with joy, saying that that ship would soon be theirs. The Grand Caramany had his daughter and all the other women come out on deck so they could see the ship they would capture. A few minutes later the Lord of Pantanalea's ship moved out, and then the Duke of Messina's ship. And the Turks' and Genoese's shouts of joy grew louder.

The Grand Caramany said to his daughter:

"Choose one of the ships you see. I'll give it to you; I want it to be yours."

She asked for the first one she had seen, and it was promised to her. Then Lord Agramunt's ship came out, then Hippolytus's, and they all came out, in order, one at a time. The good Prior of Saint John came out last because he was captain of the rear guard. When he came out it was nearly dark of night. When the Genoese saw the twelve large ships, they were astonished, wondering where they had come from. Afterward came all the whaling ships, and all the ship's boats; then the fishing boats. The boats that had no mast raised a long staff or an oar, and fastened it down tightly, and at the top of the staff they put a light inside a lantern. The captain's ship first raised a lamp at the stern. Then all the other vessels, large and small, did the same, following the captain's orders, and when all the lights were lit there were seventy-four. The enemy saw all the lights, and thinking every light was a large ship, they said:

"This must be the armada of the Grand Master of Rhodes, and the armada of the King of Sicily. When they heard we were here they must have gotten together this great armada to try to destroy us."

So they decided to flee and go back to Turkey.

When morning came Tirant did not see any of the vessels, except the Grand Caramany's ship. When it was nearly noon he reached the ship, and they went into battle. The Turks threw quicklime at them to blind them.

Then they hurled boiling oil with iron ladles. Both sides threw boiling pitch at each other, and they did not stop day or night. Many men on both ships died, and there were so many broken lances, shields, darts, arrows and spears that the dead bodies thrown in the sea could not sink.

Now let us leave them fighting, and see what the other barons and knights are doing. The eleven ships did not see the captain's ship because he had put out his light. But they sighted ten ships within reach of a bombard, and they pulled alongside.

Hippolytus did not want to draw close to any of them; instead he sailed windward and observed the battle. He saw that Lord Pantanalea's ship was being defeated, and that so many Turks had climbed on board that they outnumbered the Christians. Then Hippolytus attacked the enemy ship, and since most of the Turks were now on the other ship and had taken everything except the sterncastle, Hippolytus and his men went on board the Turks' ship, and all the dead and wounded Turks and Genoese they found, they threw into the sea. Then they assisted Lord Pantanalea, and their help was like a dose of medicine. Hippolytus consoled them, urging them to take heart, and he removed fear from the fearful, and gave them all courage and new hope. Soon he left, and went back to his ship to help those who most needed his aid.

When Lord Pantanalea saw that there was no one left on the Turk's ship, he divided his men between the two ships, and he set sail in pursuit of the ships that were fleeing, and was the first to reach them. He attacked one ship, and while they were in combat another ship arrived. It surrendered immediately, so that he had three ships. The eleven ships did the same to the two galleys so that they took fourteen ships, and there were two that they made beach themselves. The others escaped.

Now let us see what Tirant is doing, for I can still see them in battle. They began fighting at noon and continued all night long until the following day. They fought twenty-seven times, and Tirant, alone and without help, fearlessly attacked time after time.

"I will take you," said Tirant, "or I will die trying."

During the fighting Tirant was wounded in the arm by a spear. Then, when he tried to climb the forecastle an arrow struck him in the thigh.

The Turks well needed to wound him, for in great desperation three Turks leaped inside the forecastle, but they were no sooner inside than they were thrown into the water.

When the Grand Caramany saw that his men were losing badly, he had a case full of money, jewelry and clothing brought up. He had his daughter dressed in a jubbah with gold brocade, and he tied a golden silk rope around her neck. He had the case full of jewelry and all their riches tied to the other end of the rope, and he threw his daughter and the case into the sea. Then he threw all the other maidens on board into the waters.

Then he and the King of Upper India went into the daughter's chamber, leaving the ship entirely deserted. They lay their heads on the bed, and covering themselves, they awaited their death.

When the ship was completely taken, Tirant, wounded as he was, went on board and asked for the Grand Caramany.

"Captain," said one of the gentlemen from the captain's ship, "he's hiding below decks with his head covered, waiting to be killed. And the King of Upper India is with him."

"The king is here?" asked the captain.

"Yes, sir. Both of them are here."

"Have them come up," said the captain. "I want to talk to them."

And the gentleman carried out the captain's order. But the Grand Caramany refused to go, saying that he preferred to die in his daughter's chamber instead of on deck.

"No," said the king. "Let us go up and die like men."

But he wouldn't go until the gentleman had to use a little force with him. Tirant honored them like kings because he was such a humane knight.

He had them sit while he stood, but with the wound in his thigh he could not remain standing long, so he had to sit down.

And very kindly, he said:

"Your cruelty has been very great, and the most cruel death would not be enough for what you deserve—and especially you, Grand Caramany, for you have killed your daughter and other Moorish women so cruelly and with such inhumanity. They would have fallen into the hands of a man who would have given them their freedom. And although you are not worthy of forgiveness, the emperor is such a man that he will spare your lives."

And he said no more.

The Grand Caramany replied:

"You say I killed my daughter. I don't have to answer for that to you or to anybody. I would rather see her dead than dishonored by you or any of your men. And I don't want anyone enjoying my jewelry or my treasure. And don't think you're going to sway my heart, because I'm ready to throw my body into the bitter sea or give it up to the earth before I would do anything you told me to."

Instead of answering the Grand Caramany, Tirant politely asked them to go on board his ship, and they had to do it in spite of themselves. When the captain had them inside, he divided up the few men he had left between the two ships, and they set sail. He unplugged the ship's scuppers, and such a gush of blood came pouring out that it seemed as though the ship was full of it. On the Turk's ship there wasn't a living soul except for the two kings. And on the captain's ship, out of four hundred eight men, only fifty-four survived, and sixteen of those were wounded.

CHAPTER VI - A TRUCE

As Tirant came near the port of Transimeno they saw the whaling ships that had been with the Turkish armada quickly entering the port of Bellpuig, shouting out the bad news about the capture of the kings, and the loss of the armada and all its men. When Tirant reached port, he found many of his ships there, and many of the enemy's that had been captured. After Tirant had been there for two days, all his men had returned except Hippolytus.

Earlier, when Hippolytus had not been able to find his captain, he thought Tirant must have gone toward Turkey, so he ordered his pilot to set that course. While not finding the captain, he did see a new ship from the armada. When he followed the ship, it fled and stopped at an island that was nearly unpopulated. The wind was against it, and the men abandoned ship and made land by boat. When Hippolytus drew alongside, he captured the ship that was empty of men but full of riches, and took possession of it.

When the captain saw that everyone was there except Hippolytus, he sent out three ships to search for him. And they found him coming back with his prize. When the captain got news of it, and saw that he was returning with such great honor, he was very content.

This Hippolytus turned out to be a very valiant knight, generous and courageous. And he accomplished singular acts in his life because he tried to imitate his master and lord.

When Lord Malvei learned that Tirant had come back triumphant and victorious, he was very glad, and he rode out to meet him. But before going, he sent one messenger to the emperor and another to the camp, and then everyone rejoiced. On hearing the news, the emperor had all the bells in the city rung, and there were great celebrations.

When Lord Malvei found Tirant, he advised him to go to the emperor as soon as he could. And there was nothing Tirant wanted more, because he wanted to see the princess. He assembled all the men who had been with him, and they set sail.

When they were in sight of the city of Constantinople, the emperor was told that their captain was coming with the entire armada, and the ships were already in sight. The emperor quickly had a wooden bridge constructed that extended thirty paces out over the water, entirely covered with rich satin cloths. And he had a catafalque placed in the center of the marketplace, covered with brocade and silk, for himself, the empress, the princess and all the maidens. And from the catafalque to the end of the bridge where they would disembark, he had cloth of red velvet put down so that the captain would step on silk instead of on the ground. (And when it was over, whoever managed to take a piece of silk was able to keep it, and many hands were wounded with swords and knives as they tried to cut a piece of silk.)

As the ships came into port, the captain's ship drew alongside the wooden bridge, and he came out with the Grand Caramany on his right, the King of Upper India on his left, and all the barons in front. They were met by all the townspeople, and led in a great procession to the marketplace where the emperor and all the ladies were.

When Tirant was up on the catafalque with the emperor, he knelt and kissed his hand, and he told the Grand Caramany to kiss his hand. But the Caramany answered that he would not; then Tirant immediately dealt him such a hard blow to the head with his gauntlet that the Caramany was forced to put his head to the ground, and Tirant said to him:

"Dog, you son of a dog, now you're going to kiss his feet and his hand whether you want to or not."

"I won't do it of my own free will, or even by force," said the Grand Caramany. "And if you and I were in a different place, I'd show you what it means to come close to a king. You still don't know how far my power extends. But I swear to you by our holy prophet, Mohammed, and by this beard, that if I ever get my freedom back, I'll make you kiss the feet of one of my blacks."

And he said no more. But his companion, the other king, so that he would not be dealt the blow too, knelt on the hard ground and kissed his hand and foot. Then the emperor had them seized and placed under a stiff guard inside an iron cell.

The emperor and all the ladies came down from the catafalque, and they went to the great church of Saint Sophia. Tirant took the empress by the arm and escorted her, and she said to him:

"Captain, you are the most glorious man in the world. If only you had come to the kingdom of Germany in my time, when my father was emperor of Rome, in those days when I was wooed by a thousand suitors. If I had seen you, out of the thousand I would have chosen you. But now that I am old and belong to another, my hope comes along too late."

The princess heard all these things, and when they got to the palace, she said to Tirant:

"That old mother of mine is pitying herself, and she would like to play too. She thinks that if you had come in her day, she would be worthy of your love."

Then the emperor came out and asked the captain about his wounds. Tirant answered that they felt a little feverish:

"And I think the sea voyage has made my fever rise."

The emperor ordered the doctors to take him to his quarters. When they had treated him they told him to stay in bed so that his arm would not be permanently injured. Tirant followed the doctors' advice, and the emperor visited him every day, and told the empress and his daughter to visit him twice a day, in the morning and in the afternoon. Widow Repose, moved more by love than mercy, served him continually.

Now let us go back and see how the Turks are dealing with the Christians who stayed in the camp. After they heard of the cruel battle between the captain and the Grand Turk, they often came to the city of Saint George and killed or captured many Christians. They made many forays, engaging them in a cruel war, so that very few survived if they fell into their hands. How the Christians suffered when they thought about Tirant not being there, and that they would have to go out and fight without him. Not even wise Diafebus or Lord Agramunt could save their lives by placing themselves in the most dangerous positions during the battles. And they all cried out for Tirant as if he were a saint. They never felt safe, but were terrified of the Turks, because the great courage they had had during their victories when Tirant had been there, was lost now that he was gone. And they offered a special prayer to Our Lord to help Tirant, for they felt that all their hope lay with him.

At this time, in the palace, the doctors were coming to Tirant's room. The empress had finished her Hours, and she and the princess and other ladies went to Tirant and asked the doctors when they would allow Tirant to come to the palace.

"My lady," answered the doctors, "he'll be able to walk in three or four days."

When the princess was back in her chamber, a sweetness came into her heart because of her great love for Tirant, and she fell to the floor in a swoon. When the maidens saw her lying on the floor they raised such a cry that it reached the emperor's ears, and he came running, thinking the world was about to collapse around him.

He saw his daughter sprawled on the ground as though dead, and he threw himself over her, crying piteously. The mother had placed her daughter's head in her lap, and was crying and wailing so that the entire palace heard her, and her face and clothing were bathed in tears. Word was quickly sent to the doctors who were in Tirant's lodging. A gentleman came who told them, in secret:

"Come quickly. The princess is in such a state that you'll be lucky to find her still alive!"

The doctors hurried to the princess's chamber. Tirant sensed that something had happened to the princess because of the outcry the men and women were making. He got up quickly, sick as he was, and went to the princess's chambers, where he found her conscious and lying in bed.

He learned that the doctors had used all their efforts to bring back her health. When the emperor saw that his daughter had recovered, he went to his rooms with the empress, and the doctors went with him because they saw that he was exhausted from what had happened to his daughter. Tirant went into the chamber, nearly out of his mind, and when he saw the princess lying on the bed, he said, pitifully:

"I have never felt greater pain than now, when I thought I might lose the greatest treasure I had in the world. I heard shouts, and as soon as I thought of Your Majesty I said to myself, 'If something is wrong with her, she'll let me know.' But I've come myself to see what Your Highness' illness is.

The princess quickly replied:

"Tirant, my lord, you alone were the cause of my illness: it was brought on by the thought of your love. Love already has more power over me than I would like. I beg you to go see the emperor so that he won't know that you came to see me before you did him."

She put her head under the covers, and told Tirant to put his there too. Then she told him:

"Kiss my breasts to bring me consolation and to give you peace."

And he did it very willingly. After he had kissed her breasts, he kissed her eyes and her face. Then Tirant left, very content. When he was in the emperor's chambers, and the doctors saw him, they reprimanded him soundly because he had gotten out of bed without their consent. Tirant answered:

"Even if it cost me my life, I wouldn't refrain from coming to see His Majesty, the emperor, for anything in the world. When I saw you leaving my side so quickly, I could only suppose that he was in some great difficulty."

Meanwhile, the men in Tirant's camp were desperate because of his illness, and they had no hope for victory without him. The sultan sent ambassadors to the camp to deal with Tirant. When they arrived the captain was not there, and they were disappointed. They sent a message to the emperor, and he told them to come and see him, for they would be allowed to come and go safely.

So they went to the emperor, and he welcomed them very graciously. He honored them highly because the King of Armenia was with them as an ambassador, and he was the brother of the Grand Caramany. Abdalla Salomon, who was more knowledgeable than the others, was asked to speak, and he said:

"My lord, we are sent to Your Majesty by that feared and most excellent and great lord of the Mohammedan sect, the great Sultan of Babylonia, and also by the Grand Turk and Lord of the Indies, and the other kings in his camp. We come before Your perfect Majesty for three things (not counting the first, which is to know about your health, life, honor and condition). The first is: a three month truce will be given to you, on land and sea, if you would like it. The second: knowing that this virtuous captain of the Christians has captured that powerful lord, the Grand Caramany, with his mighty sword, and the King of Upper India who was with him, if you would like to give him to us, we will pay three times his weight in gold as ransom. And we will give you one and a half times the weight of the King of Upper India. Let us come to the third item: If Your Excellency would like a treaty of peace (with no iniquity or ill will; but only peace and love), he will think of you as a father, and you can think of him as a son. And as a token of that peace you would give him your daughter, Carmesina, as his wife—under this condition: if a son is born to them he will have to be raised in the sect of our holy prophet, Mohammed; and if a daughter is born, she will be given to the mother to live under Christian law. He will live under his law, and the princess under hers. In this way we can put an end to all our misfortunes, and as a reward for such a marriage he will give you all the cities, towns and castles that he has taken in your empire. In addition, he will make a lasting peace with you and your people. And he will defend you against anyone who tries to harm you."

The emperor held counsel, and then invited all the ambassadors in. He told them that out of love and consideration for the Moorish sultan and the Grand Turk, he would sign the three month peace treaty, but about the other things he would reserve judgment.

One day, while Tirant was in the princess's chamber, with many other maidens there, he said:

"Oh, Tirant! Why are you hesitant about dying when you see the father in alliance with his council against his daughter? To think that so much beauty, virtue and grace, along with greatness of lineage, will be subject to a Moorish enemy of God and our holy law, and it will be destroyed and fall into decay!"

The princess quickly answered:

"How could you think that I would subject myself to a Moor, or that I would stoop to be a friend of a Moorish dog? They have as many wives as they like and not one of them is really a wife, because they can leave them whenever they wish. Forget all those thoughts, virtuous knight, and trust your Carmesina. She will defend all your rights just as you have defended hers. And you can command me in everything you wish, as if you were my lord."

Another day Tirant was going to the princess's chamber and he met Plaerdemavida. He asked her what the princess was doing, and she answered:

"Oh, you saint! Why do you want to know what my lady is doing? If you had come earlier you would have found her in bed. And if you had seen her the way I've seen her, your soul would be in paradise. The more a person sees what he loves, the more he wants it. That's why I think it's more delightful to see something than to imagine it. Come in if you'd like: you'll find her dressed in her skirt. I want to talk to you about my own desire: Why doesn't my Hippolytus come with you? It's hard to think that I hurt inside when today's pleasure shouldn't be put off for later."

"Maiden," said Tirant, "I beg you to tell me in all truth if the empress or anyone else I should fear is inside."

"I wouldn't tell you one thing if it were something else," said Plaerdemavida. "It would be bad for both of us: You for going in, and me for letting you go. I know that the princess doesn't want your love for her to go unrewarded. And since I know how much you hunger for your heart's desire, I want to help you."

Then Tirant went into the chamber and found the princess combing her hair. When she turned and saw him she said:

"Who gave you the right to come in here? You shouldn't come into my room without my permission: if the emperor knew about this he could charge you with disloyalty. I beg you to leave: my breast is trembling in fear."

Tirant paid no attention to the princess's words, but took her in his arms and kissed her again and again on her breasts, her eyes and her mouth. When the maidens saw Tirant playing with their lady that way they were silent, but when they saw Tirant putting his hand under her skirt they came to her aid. While they were frolicking this way the empress was coming to her daughter's chamber to see what she was doing, and with their games they did not hear her until she was at the chamber door.

Tirant quickly lay on the floor and they spread clothes over him. Then the princess sat on top of him, and began combing her hair. The empress sat down at her side, nearly on Tirant's head. Only God knows how shamefully afraid Tirant was then! He was in anguish while they talked about the celebrations they were planning, until a maiden came with the Hours. Then the empress got up and withdrew to one side of the room to say the Hours. The princess was afraid the empress might see him, and did not dare move. When the princess had finished combing her hair, she put her hand under the clothes and combed Tirant's hair, and from time to time he kissed her hand and took the comb away. All the maidens went in front of the empress, and then Tirant got up quietly and left with the comb the princess had given him.

When he was outside the room, thinking he was safe and that no one had seen him, he saw the emperor and a chamberlain coming directly to the princess's chamber. When Tirant saw them passing through the great hall he panicked and quickly went back into the princess's chamber and said to her:

"My lady, help me. The emperor is coming."

"Oh!" said the princess. "We get out of one bad situation, and then go into one that's even worse. I told you what would happen, but you're always coming at the worst times."

She quickly had the maidens stand in front of the empress again, and they quietly led him to another chamber. There they put mattresses on top of him so that if the emperor came in, as he often did, he would not see him. When the emperor came into the chamber he found his daughter combing her hair. He stayed there until she had finished and the empress had said her Hours, and all the maidens were dressed. When the princess was at the chamber door she asked where her gloves were. Then she said:

"Oh, I put them in a place none of you knows about."

She and her maidens went back inside the chamber where Tirant was, and took off all the mattresses covering him. Then he jumped up and caught the princess in his arms, dancing around the room with her and kissing her again and again.

"Oh, how beautiful you are! I have never seen a maiden as perfect as you. Your Majesty is so superior to all women in knowledge and discretion that I'm not surprised the Moorish sultan would want to have you in his arms."

"Appearances are deceiving," said the princess. "I'm not as perfect as you say I am. That light shining in your eyes is love. Kiss me and let me go; the emperor is waiting for me."

Tirant could not answer her because the maidens were holding onto his hands so he could not muss her hair with his playing around. When he saw her leaving, and that he could not touch her with his hands, he stretched out his leg and put it under her skirt so that his shoe touched her where it should not, and he put his leg between her thighs. Then the princess ran out of his chamber to be with the emperor, and Widow Repose took Tirant out through the garden door.

When Tirant was in his own lodging he took off his shoes and stockings. Then he had the stocking and shoe that had touched the princess embroidered with pearls, diamonds and rubies worth more than twenty-five thousand ducats.

On the day of the joust he wore the shoe and stocking, and everyone who saw it was amazed at the fine jewels, for a shoe like that had never been seen before. And on that foot he wore no armor, but only on the left foot. As a crest for his helmet, he wore four golden rods, the Holy Grail. And upon that was the comb the princess had given him, with a motto that read: "There is no virtue but that which exists in her."

Every day Tirant was in the court, talking and taking his ease with the emperor and much more so with the ladies. And he changed clothes every day, but he always wore the same stocking. One day the princess said to him in a mocking tone:

"Tell me, Tirant this custom you have of wearing an embroidered stocking on one foot but not on the other, is it something they do in France or in some other place?"

This was the day the festival had ended, and they were on their way to Pera. And the princess said these words with Stephanie and Widow Repose close by.

"What, my lady! Doesn't Your Majesty know what this custom means? Doesn't Your Excellency remember that day when the empress came in and I was hidden with your maiden's clothing on top of me, and the empress nearly sat on my head? Afterward your father came in, and you hid me in the little chamber under the mattresses, and when they were gone, while I was playing with Your Highness, since I couldn't reach you with my hands, my foot had to take their place, and I put my leg between your thighs, and my foot touched higher up, where my soul wishes to find its happiness."

"Oh, Tirant!" said the princess. "I remember very well what you told me that day, and my body still bears the marks. But the day will come when, just as you have one leg embroidered today, you will be able to embroider both of them, and you may place them where you will, at your pleasure."

When Tirant heard her saying these words so full of love, he quickly dismounted from his horse, saying that his gloves had fallen, and he kissed her leg above her skirt, and said:

"The place were grace was granted should be kissed."

As soon as they reached the city of Pera, and when they were about to don their armor, they saw nine galleys approaching land. The emperor would not allow the tournament to begin until they found out where the galleys were from. The galleys put into port in less than an hour, and they turned out to be French. Their captain was a cousin of Tirant. He had been a page to the king, and the king had made him Viscount of Branches. This viscount had decided to come and help his cousin in his battles against the infidel, and he and other nobles had come, along with five thousand French archers that the King of France had given to them. And each of the archers had a page and a squire. And when the galleys had docked at Sicily, the king there had given them many horses.

The emperor postponed the tournament for the following day. Then eight hundred knights with gold spurs came out to the grounds, and no one was allowed to participate if he had not been dubbed a knight and unless he wore silk or brocade or gold trappings. The Duke of Pera was captain of half the men, and Tirant commanded the other half. So that each would know who the other was, they had small flags attached to their helmets, some green and others white. Tirant had ten knights enter the field of battle, and the duke ten others, and they began to fight very well.

Then twenty entered, then thirty, and they began to mix together. Each of them did as well as he possibly could in using his weapons. Tirant kept an eye on his men, and when he saw that they were not doing well, he entered the fray with his lance poised, and he went against another knight so ferociously that he thrust his lance completely through him and it came out the other side. Then he drew his sword and dealt terrible blows all around so that he seemed like a ravenous lion, and all the onlookers were amazed at his great strength and spirit.

The emperor was very satisfied at this singular display of arms. When it had gone on for nearly three hours, the emperor came down from the catafalque, mounted a horse and quickly rode into the fray to separate the men, because he saw that tempers were rising, and many were wounded. After all the knights had disarmed themselves, they went to the palace. There they talked about their singular display of arms, and the foreigners said they had never seen such valiant men. The sultan's ambassadors, who had seen them, were filled with wonder.

That night the emperor returned with his men and all the ladies to the city of Constantinople. The following day, after mass, they all went to the market place which was as nicely decorated as it had been the first day. When the sultan's ambassadors arrived, and everyone was present, the emperor gave them this reply:

"Nothing brings greater anguish than to have His Majesty hear abominable words that offend God and the world. I pray that His immense goodness will not permit me to do things against His holy catholic faith, like giving my daughter as wife to a man who is outside our law. For all the treasure that the Grand Caramany and the King of Upper India could pay, they cannot have their liberty unless they restore all my empire to me."

When they had heard these words the ambassadors stood up and took their leave, and went back to the sultan.

After the celebration was over and the ambassadors had gone, the emperor held war councils many times. Tirant fostered his romance, and was very insistent about staying near the princess because he saw that the end of the truce was approaching. The emperor indicated that he wanted the captain to be in camp to take charge of the men, and the captain showed that he was attending to the men going with him so that they would be ready, since he was very eager to confront the Turks.

Tirant pleaded insistently with the princess to give him the satisfaction he wanted. The princess saw how great Tirant's passion was, and she said:

"Tirant, I know full well what you want, but my reputation is spotless. Tell me, what gave you the hope of being in my bed? Just to imagine it is great infamy. If I gave in to you, I couldn't hope that it would not be known. What could I use to excuse my transgression? I beg you, Tirant, my lord, do not rob me lightly of my tender virginity."

And she would say no more. Tirant was rather stunned by the princess's words which showed how little she loved him. For he thought he had progressed in his love affair, and now he found it was entirely the opposite.

While they were talking the emperor came into the chamber, and took his daughter Carmesina by the hand. They went upstairs together to the treasure-tower to take out money and give it to Tirant so that he would go to the camp.

When they had gone Tirant was left with the maidens. He thought about what the princess had said to him, and he realized that Widow Repose had overheard his secret, and everything he had said to her. Tirant decided to see if he could win the Widow over with promises, and with warm and tender words he said:

"I believe I have been offended by my lady. I want to do great services for the princess so that she will see that I am worthy of her love. Although Stephanie already has many possessions and great wealth, I would like to give her even more. I would give Widow Repose a duke or count or marquis for a husband, and as many possessions as would make her happy. And I would like to do the same for Plaerdemavida and all the other ladies."

Stephanie thanked Tirant for herself and for all the other women. Widow Repose said to Stephanie:

"You thank him for yourself. I know how to thank him on my own."

And, smiling, she turned to Tirant and said:

"Thank you very much for your thoughtfulness. But I want no other husband, no matter how great a lord he is, except the one I adore day and night. He has not killed me yet, but he has given me reason to die. I won't say any more about that because this isn't the time or place."

When Widow Repose finished, Plaerdemavida said:

"My lord and captain, don't you know that repentance follows sin? You've come to my lady's rooms, and found them like a tomb, since you can find no mercy in them. Please don't lose hope, I beg you. Rome wasn't built in a day. Are you discouraged because of some trifle my lady said to you? When you're in a hard-fought battle, you're like a lion, and you always come out victorious, and yet are you afraid of a lone woman who, with our help, you'll conquer? Do you remember that pleasant night in the castle of Malvei when I was dreaming? You saw how mercifully you dealt with that situation. I'm only trying to tell you that we'll all help you in this affair. And I know what the solution is: you have to mix in a little force, because your fear—which comes from ignorance—stops you from using it. It's a terrible thing for maidens to have to say those awful words: 'I like it.' I'll work as hard as I can for you in this affair, I promise you. And I think that as a just reward—very inferior to my work—I deserve to have Your Grace help with the love of my Hippolytus. But I'm more than a little afraid, because I can see where his wayward steps are taking him, and I don't like the way he's going at all. I'm afraid of the danger he'll place himself in, because he is a very good swordsman, and he strikes not at the legs but at the head. And he knows much more than I have shown him."

Tirant brightened up a little at Plaerdemavida's jokes, and he stood up to tell her:

"Maiden, it looks to me as though, instead of hiding your advances toward Hippolytus, you don't care who knows about them."

"What do I care if everybody knows?" said Plaerdemavida. "You men think that just because we're maidens we won't dare to say anything. It's your nature to be good at first, and then bad afterward. You're like the ocean: when someone starts to go in the water it seems soft, and then later, when he's all the way in, it's a torrent. That's the way love begins: at first you're soft, and later on you're harsh and terrible."

While they were talking, the emperor came in. He took Tirant by the hand and led him out of the room, and they talked at great length about the war. When it was time to eat, Tirant and his men went to their quarters.

That night, when the princess wanted to go to bed, Widow Repose said to her:

"My lady, if Your Majesty knew about the things Tirant said to us ladies, you would be amazed. He took me aside and told me things about Your Excellency that I am loathe to repeat, because his words show how little he cares for you."

Widow Repose's words had a great effect on the princess. Without letting her say another word, she put her cloak back on, and they went into a tiny chamber where no one could overhear them. First the Widow told her what Tirant had said to all the ladies, and how he wanted to arrange honorable marriages for them all. Then, with great wickedness and deceit, the evil Widow gave vent to her malice:

"Tirant is a cruel man. He doesn't have the good sense of the others, but he is more shameless and daring. If Your Highness knew what he says about you, you would never be able to love him."

"Tell me at once," said the princess, "and don't make me suffer so."

"He spoke to me secretly," said Widow Repose, "and he made me swear on the Gospel that I wouldn't say a word to anyone. But since you are my mistress, and I would be going against the loyalty I owe you, any oath I've made is worthless. First, he told me that Stephanie and Plaerdemavida are in alliance with him so that, with your consent or by force, he will possess Your Majesty. And if you don't do it of your own free will, he'll plunge his sword through your neck and kill you cruelly, and then he will do the same thing to your father. He will steal all your treasure and they'll get on their ships and go back to their land. And with the treasure they carry off, the clothing and jewels, they'll find maidens there who are much more beautiful than Your Highness, for he says that you don't look any better than a serving girl and that you are completely shameless: that you'll give it to anyone who wants it. Watch out for your virtue, my lady. You can see what that mad traitor thinks of Your Highness! And that faithless man says even more: that he didn't come to this land to fight, and that he has been hurt too many times because of his misfortune of knowing you and your father. Do you think, my lady, that that way of talking is proper for knights? Look at what he thinks of the honor of Your Excellency and the emperor, who have granted him so many benefits and honors. Anyone who says things like that should burn in flames! Do you know what other things he says? That he doesn't love any woman alive, unless it's for her wealth. He says many other wicked things too. I remember he told me that if he ever had another night like that one in Malvei, even if he made you a thousand promises, he wouldn't keep any of them. With your consent or by force, he would take you, and then he would say to you, 'You evil woman, I don't thank you, now that I've had my pleasure.' Oh, my lady, my heart cries blood when I think of all the terrible things he said about Your Highness! That's why, my lady, I want to give you some advice even though you haven't asked me for it. There's no one who has more compassion for you than I have. I cradled you in my arms and fed you from my own breast, and Your Highness has hidden from me to entertain that wicked Tirant. You've had more faith in Stephanie and Plaerdemavida than in me: and they have betrayed you and sold you. Oh, poor you! How they've defamed you, and they'll do it even more from now on! Keep away from friendships like those since you know the truth, because what I tell you is the Gospel itself. You must swear that you'll never tell a soul about these things I've told Your Majesty. I'm afraid that if that traitor, Tirant, hears about it, he'll have me killed and then he'll leave. So, my lady, make pretenses, and break off your friendship with him little by little, because if Your Highness suddenly stopped seeing him, he would think that I told you. And those two ladies deserve to be whipped. Don't you see how big Stephanie's belly is? I'm astonished that the emperor hasn't noticed it. And the same will happen to Plaerdemavida."

The princess was very upset. With tears flowing from her eyes, she began to lament angrily:

"Oh, God! Where is Your justice? How is it that fire does not descend from heaven to turn that cruel, ungrateful Tirant into ashes? He was the first knight that I considered my master. I thought he would bring an end to all my troubles, and now I see everything turned around. Oh, who would ever have thought that words like these could come from the mouth of such a virtuous knight? What have I done to him, to make him want the deaths of my father and my mother and their miserable daughter? Oh, Tirant! What happened to the love we shared? What crime did I commit for you to think me vile and abominable? Did you really say that you love no lady or maiden unless it's for her wealth, and that you want to take my virginity by force? Oh, if I wanted to be cruel, before the sun came up your chamber would be full of blood; yours and the blood of all your men."

And she said no more. But hearing the call for matins, she added:

"Widow, let's go to bed, even though I'll get little sleep tonight with the great hate I have for Tirant—the one I used to love so much."

The Widow answered:

"My lady, I beg you, please. Don't say a word about this to anyone. Who knows what might happen?"

"Don't worry," said the princess. "I'll protect you."

When they were in their chamber, Stephanie saw them come in, and said:

"It looks to me, my lady, as though you've had a great deal of pleasure listening to the Widow—you've been with her so long. I'd like to know what you're thinking about."

The princess climbed into bed without answering, and began to cry bitterly. When the Widow had gone, Stephanie asked her why she was crying. The princess told her:

"Stephanie, let me be, and take care that this doesn't happen to you."

Stephanie was surprised at this, not knowing what it could mean. She did not reply, but drew close to her as she usually did. All that night the princess could not sleep a wink and cried and lamented continually.

In the morning she got up, ill, because of her lack of sleep. Nonetheless, she forced herself to go to mass.

When Tirant learned of her condition, and when Stephanie told him about her tears and crying all night long, he was very surprised, and wondered what he had done. Going up to the princess, he said:

"If Your Excellency would like to tell me what is wrong, I would be very pleased."

Tirant could say no more because of the great emotion that he felt, and the princess softly began to say the following words:

"I will spend the rest of my life hiding the cause of my grief. And don't think that it doesn't cost me a great deal of effort to keep such terrible pain hidden."

She could say no more because the doctors came, along with the empress. Tirant took his leave to go to his lodgings, immersed in thought about what the princess had told him, and he felt distressed. He could not eat, and did not want to leave his chamber until the constable went to the palace and spoke at length with Stephanie and Plaerdemavida. He told them what great anguish Tirant was in because of what the princess had said to him.

"How can we help him," said Stephanie, "if everything I mend by day the Widow tears apart at night? If it weren't for the Widow, I would have had him in her chambers, not once, but a hundred times, like it or not, the way I did that night in the castle of Malvei."

As they finished talking, they went into the princess's chamber. She was deeply involved in conversation with Widow Repose, and Stephanie could not talk to her. The emperor, knowing that the constable was there, thought that Tirant must be there too. So he had them summoned, and as they had to hold counsel, the emperor said:

"Let us go to Carmesina's chambers, and we will see how she is, because she has not felt well all day long."

The constable went first, then came the emperor and Tirant, and then everyone in the council who wished to go. They found the princess playing cards with the Widow, withdrawn to a corner of the chamber. The emperor sat at her side, asking about her illness, and she quickly answered him:

"Sire, as soon as I see Your Majesty, my illness suddenly disappears."

Then she turned her eyes on Tirant and smiled. The emperor was very happy at Carmesina's words, and much more so when he saw her in such a good mood. They spoke of many things, and the princess answered everything Tirant said to her, because Widow Repose had advised her to be nice to Tirant.

What the Widow wanted was not for Tirant to return to his country, but to lose hope of having the princess, and for him to love the Widow instead. That is why she spoke so wickedly to the princess.

When it was nearly night, the emperor and all his men went to their chambers, and the next day the emperor expressed his regret that all the men had to leave for the camp. Tirant and his men got ready as quickly as they could. While Stephanie was talking with the princess that evening, she gave her the news about Tirant, and the princess quickly said to her:

"Be quiet, Stephanie. Don't make me any angrier. All those who make appearances of love are not made exactly of gold."

Stephanie tried to talk but she would not let her.

So two or three days went by, and the princess showed a smiling face to everyone, including Tirant, because she knew that soon they would have to leave. And to the emperor she said:

"Sire, here is Tirant, your virtuous captain, who will shortly do to the sultan what he did to the Caramany and the King of Upper India, or what he did to the King of Egypt. If everyone in the world went into battle, he would certainly be the only one to win honor and lasting fame. And that is worthy of a singular prize, for he is a great warrior, and he has gone into battle with true courage."

The emperor said:

"Virtuous captain, I thank you for all the honors you have brought me, and I beg you to do the same from now on, or better, for this is the hope I place in you."

When Tirant heard so many superfluous words, and saw that the princess had brought them on, almost in mockery, he could utter only:

"Perhaps."

Tirant wanted to go to his chambers, and he went down a staircase, into a room where he found the High Constable, Stephanie and Plaerdemavida in animated conversation. Tirant went to them and said:

"My sisters, what are you talking about?"

"My lord," answered Stephanie, "about how little love the princess is showing Your Lordship when you are about to leave. Now, more than ever, she should be showering you with love. Then, my lord, we talked about what will happen to me if you go away. Because the empress said to me last night, 'Stephanie, you are in love.' I blushed and shamefully lowered my eyes. That was a sign of assent, since I was silent, because at first I didn't know what love was, except for that night at Malvei. And if you leave there will be little good fortune and a miserable gift of love for me except for all the pain I'll have for company. Oh, poor me! That's the way I will be punished—because of your wrongdoing."

"My lady," said Tirant, "didn't I tell you that the day we left I would beg the emperor, in the presence of the empress and the princess, to give his consent to this marriage? The constable will be here, and then we will hold your wedding."

"And how will I get along," said Stephanie, "when you aren't here? There won't be any celebration or dancing or festivities at all without Your Lordship here."

"Who wants festivities at a wedding if there weren't any at the engagement?" said Tirant, "Leave the partying and merrymaking for the bed."

While they were talking, the emperor came down with Carmesina. Tirant thought that this was a good time to tell the emperor. So he went over to the emperor, and in Carmesina's presence he sank to one knee, and humbly began the following plea:

"With deep humility I beg Your Majesty, and the empress, and the princess, to hold the marriage of the maiden Stephanie of Macedonia to my singular brother, the Count of Sant Angel and the High Constable of Your Highness, because marriages like these are a union of the deepest kind of love."

The emperor replied:

"I am going to delegate my power to my daughter here so that she can ask her mother's consent."

And he left without another word, while the princess stayed behind with them. When Stephanie saw that the emperor had gone so quickly, she assumed that he did not approve of the marriage, and she left the princess, Tirant, the constable and Plaerdemavida, and went into a chamber alone and began to cry.

Tirant took the princess's arm, and went with the constable and Plaerdemavida to the empress's chambers. There Tirant and the princess asked the empress to give her consent to this marriage, since the emperor had agreed, and she answered that she would be very happy to. They immediately called all the court to Stephanie's betrothal. They all gathered in the great hall, along with a cardinal who had been summoned to marry them. Then they sent word for the bride to come, and they found her still crying because she had heard no news until they came looking for her and told her that the emperor and all the others were waiting for her.

The betrothal was celebrated with dances and a sumptuous feast. The emperor wanted the wedding to take place the following day so that Tirant's departure would not be delayed, and so it was done. Great celebrations were held with jousts and dances and gaiety. And everyone was happy except poor, miserable Tirant.

The night of the wedding, Plaerdemavida caught five little kittens and put them by the window where the bride was sleeping, and they meowed all night long. After Plaerdemavida had put the cats there she went to the emperor's chambers and said to him:

"My lord, come to the bride's chamber quickly: the constable must have hurt her terribly because I heard some loud cries. I am really afraid that he may have killed your dear niece, or at least hurt her badly; and since Your Majesty is such a close relative of hers it's you who should go to her side."

Plaerdemavida's words were so amusing that the emperor dressed again and the two of them went to the door of the bridal chamber and listened. When Plaerdemavida saw that they were not talking, she quickly called out:

"My lady, my bride, how is it that you aren't crying out or talking now? It must be because in that battle your pain (That pain that reaches down to your heels, and won't let you shout that delightful 'Oh!') and your even greater haste are over. It's a great pleasure, if you listen to what the maidens say. Since you're so quiet, that's a sign that you've finished the meal, bone and all. It will be bad for you if you don't do it again. The emperor is right here, listening for you to cry out because he's afraid you might be hurt."

The emperor told her to be quiet, and not to say he was there.

"I certainly will not," said Plaerdemavida. "I want them to know that you're here."

Then the bride began to cry out and to say that he was hurting her and for him to be still, and Plaerdemavida said:

"My lord, everything the bride is saying is a lie. Her words don't come from the heart. They sound false to me, and they're not to my liking."

The emperor could not contain his laughter at Plaerdemavida's delicious remarks. Then, when the bride heard them laughing so hard she said:

"Who put those wretched cats out there? Put them somewhere else, I beg you: they won't let me sleep."

Plaerdemavida replied:

"That I certainly won't do. Didn't you know that I can get live kittens out of a dead cat?"

"Oh, what a lively young lady!" said the emperor. "How my heart is warmed by the things you say. I swear to you by the Almighty that if I didn't already have a wife I would have no other girl but you."

The empress had gone to the emperor's chamber and found the door closed, and no one was there but a page who told her that the emperor was at the door of the bridal chamber. Then she went there and found him with four maidens. Plaerdemavida saw the empress coming, and before anyone could talk she said:

"Hope to die quickly, my lady: listen to what my lord the emperor said to me—that if he didn't already have a wife he would have no one but me. And since you're in my way, fall down dead right now—as quickly as you can."

"Oh, you wicked child!" said the empress. "Is that the sort of thing you say to me?" And turning to the emperor: "And you, you blessed saint, what do you want another wife for? To give her taps instead of thrusts? Don't you know that no lady or maiden ever died from being tapped?"

And, joking, they went back to their chambers happily, and the empress and the maidens returned to theirs.

The next day, in the morning, everyone was happy, and they highly honored the constable and the bride. They took them to the main church where they heard mass with great honor. When they had read the scripture the preacher mounted the pulpit and gave a solemn sermon.

When the sermon and the mass were finished, they had the constable put on the clothing of the duchy of Macedonia, and they displayed the flags of that duchy. On his head they put a crown made entirely of fine silver, and they crowned Stephanie in the same way.

When these things were finished they left the church, riding through the city with flags flying in the wind. The emperor, with all the ladies and all the grandees, dukes, counts and marquis, and many others on horseback, rode around the entire city. Afterward they all went outside the city to a beautiful meadow where there was a shining spring called Holy Spring. After the flags were blessed, they baptized the duke and duchess of the kingdom of Macedonia by pouring perfumed water on their heads.

The duke went to the Holy Spring, and the emperor took water from the spring and baptized him again, giving him the title of Duke of Macedonia. Then the trumpets sounded, and the heralds shouted:

"This is the illustrious Duke of Macedonia, of the great lineage of Rocasalada."

At that moment three hundred knights with golden spurs came, and they all made a deep bow to the emperor, and paid great honor to the Duke of Macedonia. And from this moment on he was no longer called Constable. These three hundred knights separated into two groups, and each knight took the most beautiful lady or the one that was most to his liking. They held them with the reins of the horses they were riding on. And each of them, in order, rode forward: first those of highest station and lineage, and then those who wished to joust. And when they met, one would tell the other to give up the lady they had, or he would have to joust with him, and the one who broke the other's lance first would take his lady.

While the knights were engaged in these games, the emperor went to the city of Pera where the celebration was prepared. It was already past noon, and the knights had not yet returned, so the emperor went to the top of a high tower. He had a great horn blown that could be heard more than a league away, and when the knights heard the horn, they all set out on the road to Pera. Then three hundred other knights came out, dressed in the same color of garments, and they blocked the road. A very singular display of arms took place there which greatly pleased the emperor.

All the ladies and maidens who had been taken prisoner fled to the city and left the knights.

The combat between the knights lasted more than two hours as the emperor did not want to stop it, and when they had broken all their lances they fought with swords. The emperor called for the trumpets to sound, and they all separated, each group to a different side. When the knights were separated, each sought out his lady, and they could not find them. Then they began to say that the other knights had taken them prisoner, and each of them complained to the empress and the princess about the ladies they had lost. They answered that they knew nothing, and that they believed the other knights had them hidden. Then these knights, very furious, raised their swords and spurred toward the others, and they began to fight again.

When it had gone on for a good spell, they saw the ladies on the palace walls. A trumpet sounded, and they all gathered together and attacked the palace mightily, and the women defended it. But the men outside broke in by force of their arms. When they were inside the great patio they divided into two groups, and taking a king-of-arms, they sent him to the knights who had come most recently, demanding that they leave, for they were each there to get back their lady, along with the ones they had won. They answered that they would not leave for anything in the world. They wanted their share of what was due to them, as they had placed themselves in such grave danger of death. After this, they held combat on foot inside the palace, and it was a delicious sight to see, for some were falling here and others there. Others delivered marvelous blows with their axes, and whoever lost his axe could not fight again, nor could anyone whose body or hand touched the floor. They fought in such a way that it became a fight of ten against ten, and then it was beautiful to see. Finally the emperor had them separated, and then they were all disarmed in the great hall, and there they dined. When it was a half hour before sunset they began to dance, and they held a long and pretty dance. They took the princess and all the ladies, and dancing, they went to the city of Constantinople.

After the meal Tirant gathered all those of his lineage, thirty-five knights and gentlemen who had come with him or the Viscount of Branches. They went to kiss the foot and hand of the emperor, thanking him for the great kindness he had done them in giving his beautiful niece to Diafebus for his bride. And after they had all thanked him, the emperor smiled and said:

"Because of the great virtue I see in you, Tirant, I love you deeply. And I would not want anyone to marry a relative of mine if he were not of the lineage of Rocasalada. I would have begged you to take Stephanie, my niece, as your wife, along with the duchy of Macedonia, so that you would be more united with the crown of the Empire of Greece, and I would have given you many other things. At the time that I offered it, you did not want to be a count; instead you gave it to your relative. And now I would have given you the duchy, along with a lady who is a relative of mine, and you did not want that either. I don't know what you're waiting for! If you want me to give you my empire, don't count on it: I need it."

Tirant replied:

"The greatest glory I could have is to leave an inheritance to my relatives and friends. As an inheritance of my own I want nothing more than a horse and arms, so Your Highness will have to work a great deal to make me rich."

The old emperor was pleased by Tirant's words. Turning to his daughter, the emperor said:

"I have never known a knight with as much virtue as Tirant. If God gives me life I will see him crowned a king."

JOANOT MARTORELL

CHAPTER VII - IN THE PRINCESS'S BED

After the celebrations were over, Diafebus, the Duke of Macedonia, lived in the emperor's palace. The following day the duke invited all those of his lineage, Rocasalada, to dine. While the guests were eating, the emperor told his daughter to go to the duchess' chamber since all the foreigners from Brittany were there.

"The duke is attempting to pay them honor, and celebrations like this are useless if there are no maidens present."

The princess replied:

"My lord, I will obey Your Majesty's command."

Accompanied by many ladies and maidens she started toward the duchess' chamber. With great malice Widow Repose went up to her, and said:

"Oh, my lady! Why does Your Highness want to go where these foreigners are? Do you want to disturb their dinner? When they see Your Excellency no one will dare eat in your presence. You and your father want to honor them and give them pleasure, and yet you do them great harm. For all of them would prefer to see the wing of a partridge than all the maidens in the world. Your Highness should not act so freely, going to such a place, since you are the emperor's daughter. Think highly of yourself if you want to be well thought of by other people. It's a bad sign when I see Your Excellency always with that fool, Tirant."

"Don't I have to obey what my father, the emperor, orders me to do?" said the princess. "I don't think anyone would blame me for obeying my father's command."

But she went back to her own chamber without visiting the duchess. hen everyone had eaten, Plaerdemavida decided to see Tirant and talk to the duchess. Seeing Tirant sitting there, deep in thought, she went over to him, and to console him she said:

"Captain, my lord, my soul suffers deeply when it sees you so sad and lost in thought. Tell me, Your Grace, how I can help, for I will not fail you even if my life were in the balance."

Tirant was very grateful to her. The duchess approached them, and asked Plaerdemavida why the princess had not come. Plaerdemavida answered that Widow Repose was the cause, for she had scolded her at length.

And she would not tell what the Widow had said about Tirant so that he would not explode in anger.

"I wish," said Tirant, "that she were a man. Then I could repay her for all the wicked things she says."

"Would you like to do it properly?" asked Plaerdemavida. "Let's leave the wickedness aside and get right down to business; the remedies will come later. I'm well aware that we won't accomplish anything if we don't mix in a little force, so I'll tell you what I think. Her Highness told me to prepare a bath for her the day after tomorrow. So when everyone is eating I'll take you into the chamber where she takes her bath in such a way that no one will see you. When she comes out of the bath and goes to sleep I'll be able to place you by her side in the bed. And just as you are serious and skillful on the battlefield you must be the same way in bed. This is the quickest road for getting what you want. If you know a better one, speak up, don't hold your tongue."

The duchess said:

"Let me talk to her first, and I'll see what sort of answer she gives. Your idea will have to be the last thing we do to get what we want."

Tirant spoke:

"I wouldn't want to do anything that would offend my lady. What good would it do me to have my desire with Her Highness if it's against her will? I would rather undergo a cruel death than make Her Majesty angry in any way, or do anything against her wishes."

"In God's faith, I don't like what I'm hearing from you," said Plaerdemavida. "If the desire to love exists in you, you won't run away from the narrow path I'm offering you. My experience speaks for itself, and it desires to serve you and bring you all the good I can—even more than I can. But I see that you're going off in a strange direction. You want to go down a dead-end street. From now on you go find someone else to take care of your problem. I don't want to have anything more to do with it."

"Maiden," said Tirant, "I beg you, please, don't be angry. Let's put our minds together and do what's best. If you fail me in this, there's nothing left for me to do but go off, hopeless, like a madman."

"Not even the angels," said Plaerdemavida, "could give you better advice than I have."

They decided that the duchess should go to the princess's chamber to see if it was possible for him to talk to her. When they got there they found her in her room, combing her hair. Then the duchess thought up some youthful mischief: she went into a room that the princess would have to pass through when she came out of her chamber. She lay down at the foot of the bed and leaned on her elbow, very dejected. When the princess heard that she was there, she sent word for her to come into the chamber, but the duchess did not want to go. And Plaerdemavida, who had contrived it all this way, told her:

"Leave her alone. She can't come. She's very sick and I don't know what's wrong with her. She's very sad."

When the princess had combed her hair, she came out of the chamber and saw the duchess with a very sad face. She went over to her and said:

"Oh, my dear sister! What's wrong? Please, I beg you, tell me quickly, for I feel very bad about your illness, and if I can help you in any way, I will."

"I'll tell Your Highness what hurts me, for I am prepared to lose my life in this matter. It's impossible for me to go back on the promise I made, by your command, to Tirant in the castle of Malvei. So, my lady, I beg Your Excellency not to allow me to remain a perjurer or for you to be the cause of my downfall, for I will have to be on bad terms with the duke and with Tirant."

As the duchess said this, tears flowed from her eyes. The painful tears of the duchess moved the princess to pity, and she forgot much of the anger she felt for Tirant. With a humble voice she answered tenderly:

"Duchess, you have to realize that I am just as sad as you are. But, my lady and sister, don't grieve any longer, for you know that I love you more than anyone in the world, and I will behave from now on as God wills. Since you want me to talk to Tirant, I will, out of love for you, even though I have little desire to do anything for him. If you knew how he treats me and all the things he's said about me, you would be astonished. I'll put up with him because of the great danger we're in, and because we all need him. But I swear to you by this blessed day that if it weren't for that I would never allow him in my presence again. Who would think that such ingratitude could exist in such a virtuous knight."

The duchess replied with the following words:

"My lady, I am astonished that Your Highness could believe that a knight as noble and virtuous as Tirant could have said even one word to offend Your Majesty. If his ears had heard anything spoken against you, he would have killed everyone including himself. So don't even think, Your Highness, that Tirant is the way he's been described to you. Some miserable person has led you to believe a false story, and is trying to destroy the reputation of the best knight in all the world."

Plaerdemavida stepped in and said:

"My lady, take that vice of having bad thoughts about Tirant out of your head, for if anyone in the world deserves merit, it's Tirant. Who is the half-wit who could make Your Majesty believe that a knight exists who can even compare to him in glory, honor and virtue? There is no one (unless they wanted to lie) who could say (unless it's with great wickedness) that Tirant would say anything but good things about Your Excellency. Forget what wicked people say, and love the one you should love, for it will be to your great glory to possess such a virtuous knight. Love one who loves you, my lady, and leave the wicked talk to that devil, Widow Repose. She's the one who's causing all this trouble, and I trust God that it will all fall back on her. I have only one hope in this world: to see her whipped through the streets of the city, naked, with cow entrails hanging down her shoulders, her eyes and her face."

"Be quiet," said the princess. "You just think Widow Repose is telling me all this, but she's not. I'm the one who can see all the terrible things that could happen. But in spite of it all, I'll do whatever you tell me."

"If you listen to my advice," said Plaerdemavida, "I'll tell you to do only things that will bring you honor."

And so they left. The duchess went back to her chambers and found Tirant there, and she told him everything that had happened. Tirant, very happy, went to the great hall where the emperor, the princess and the empress were, with all the ladies, and they danced there for a good while. And the princess continually entertained Tirant.

After the dancing was over, when the princess withdrew to dine, Widow Repose approached her. With no one around to hear, she said:

"It hurts me to see how much love permits, and I curse the day you were born. For many people constantly turn their eyes to Your Majesty, and then to me, and they say to me three times: 'Oh, Widow! Oh, Widow Repose! How can you allow a man who is a foreigner to carry off Carmesina's virginity?' Just imagine if someone who hears words like those doesn't have the right to grieve and to despair of their life? How could you think, my lady, that such a thing could be done without bishops and archbishops knowing of it? I'm only telling you all this, my lady, to bring it to mind again, for I've already told you about it several times."

She decided to say no more, and waited to see what the princess would say. The princess was brimming with emotion at this moment, but she had no time to reply to the poisonous words of the wicked Widow because the emperor was at his table, waiting for the princess, and he had sent word for her to come twice already.

The princess said:

"Madam Widow, to be able to give an answer to everything you have told me would be a delicious meal for me."

She left the chamber, and when the duchess, who was waiting to find out if Tirant could go to her that night, saw her come out so agitated and flushed, she did not dare say a word to her. But when Plaerdemavida saw her in that state too, and also saw the Widow following behind, she said to her:

"Oh, my lady, I've always noticed that when the sky turns red it's the sign of a storm."

"Shut up, you madwoman," said the princess. "You're always spouting nonsense."

You can imagine how the princess must have appeared, for when the emperor saw her he asked her why she looked that way, and if anyone had made her angry. The princess answered:

"No, my lord. Since I left Your Majesty's side I've been lying down in my bed, because my heart has been in pain. But thanks to Our Heavenly Father I have found a cure for my ache."

The emperor commanded the doctors to oversee her diet, and they ordered pheasant for dinner, which is gentle meat for the heart. The duchess sat at her side, not to eat, but to be able to talk to her and to tell her that Tirant was waiting for her in his chamber with good news. When the meal was over, the duchess leaned toward her and whispered:

"What is open has the seal of truth, and what is done secretly, as the Widow does, shows evil. A vassal cannot deceive his master, and since the Widow is my vassal, I want her death, for her actions deserve great punishment."

"My duchess," said the princess, "I love you very much, and I will do as much for you as one can reasonably do for her sister—even more. Leave Widow Repose alone, because even though she's your vassal, she's not to blame for anything."

The duchess said:

"Give me an answer to that matter of Tirant: Do you want him to come tonight? I'm sure that's what he's hoping for so anxiously. Don't tell me no, upon your life."

"I'll be very happy for him to come this evening," said the princess. "I'll wait for him here and we shall dance, and if he wishes to tell me anything, I'll listen to him."

"Oh, my dear girl," said the duchess. "Now you want to change the game on me. I'm only telling you that if you want that virtuous man, Tirant (without whom you can gain neither blessings or honor) to come see you, the same way he did that pleasant night in the castle of Malvei— let's see if you can catch my meaning now!"

"I can't think at all when you mention Tirant's name to me," said the princess. "You may certainly tell Tirant that I beg him, as a knight full of faith and virtue, to stop tempting my soul which has been crying tears of blood for many days. But after he comes here it will be I who will consent, and in a greater way than he imagines."

"Oh, my lady!" said the duchess. "If Your Excellency wishes to do battle with Tirant, place yourself in his arms again with the same fear you felt that night at Malvei, with the promises and oaths you swore to him."

"Shall I tell you something, my sister and my lady?" said the princess. "I want to keep my reputation and my honor as I value my life. And this I intend to do with God's help."

The duchess left very angrily, and when she saw Tirant she told him about her lady's bad disposition. Tirant's anguish increased to an even greater degree than usual.

When the emperor had dined, knowing that Tirant was in the duke's chamber, he sent for him and said to the princess:

"Send for the minstrels so that the knights can enjoy themselves. The time for their departure has been set."

"No," said the princess. "I feel more like going to bed than dancing."

She immediately took leave of her father and withdrew to her chamber so that she would not have to talk to Tirant. Widow Repose, who had heard her say these words, was very satisfied with what she had done. Plaerdemavida went to the duchess' chamber and said to Tirant:

"Captain, put no hope in this lady as long as Widow Repose is around her. They've already withdrawn to her chamber, and are speaking together about your affairs. You'll never get your way with her unless you do what I'm going to tell you: Tomorrow she'll take her bath, and I will be so clever that at night I'll put you in her bed. You'll find her completely naked. Do what I'm telling you, for I know she'll never say a word. Where the duchess used to sleep, I've taken her place now that she's no longer there. Since this is the case, let me take care of it."

"Maiden," said Tirant, "I am extremely grateful to you for all your gentility, and for what you are telling me, but there is one thing you should know about me: I wouldn't use force against a lady or maiden for anything in the world, even if it should cost me the crown of the Empire of Greece, or of Rome, or of the entire Kingdom of Earth. I prefer to go through the pain and trial of pleading with her, for I am completely convinced that she was created in Paradise. Her gracefulness shows that she is more angelic than human."

He said no more. Plaerdemavida, showing her anger to Tirant, said:

"Tirant, Tirant, you will never be brave or feared in battle if you don't mix a little bit of force in when you love a lady or a maiden. Since you have a good and genteel hope, and you love a maiden valiantly, go into her room and throw yourself down on her bed when she's naked or in her nightshirt, and wound her boldly, because among friends no towel is necessary. And if you don't do it, I won't be your ally any longer, for I know many knights who have deserved honor, glory and fame from their ladies because they had their hands ready and valiant. Oh Lord, how wonderful to have a tender maiden, about fourteen years old and completely naked, in your arms! Oh Lord, how wonderful to be in her bed, kissing her all the while! Oh Lord, how wonderful if she's of royal blood! Oh Lord, how wonderful to have an emperor as her father! Oh Lord, how wonderful to have her rich and generous, and free of all infamy!... Now what I want most of all is for you to do what I tell you."

By this time most of the night was gone and they wanted to lock up the palace, so Tirant had to leave. When he had said goodnight to the duchess and was already going out, Plaerdemavida said:

"Captain, my lord, I wouldn't be able to find anyone who would do as much for me: Go to sleep, and don't come back from the other side."

Tirant burst out laughing and said to her:

"You have such an angelic nature, you're always giving good advice."

And so they went their separate ways.

That night Tirant thought about everything the maiden had said to him. The next morning the emperor sent for the captain, and he immediately went and found him dressing, and the princess had come to wait on him. She was wearing a brocade skirt, with no cloth covering her breasts, and her hair, loosened somewhat, almost reached to the ground. When Tirant approached the emperor he was astonished to see as much perfection in a human body as he saw in her then. The emperor said to him:

"Captain, in God's name, I beg you to do everything possible so that you can leave with your men soon."

Tirant was so impressed by the vision of this striking lady that he was stupefied and could not speak. After some time had passed he recovered and said:

"I was thinking about the Turks when I saw Your Majesty, so I didn't hear you. Your Highness, tell me what you want me to do, I beg you."

The emperor was surprised to see him so distracted, but since he had understood so little he thought that that must be the case, for he had seemed entranced for half an hour. The emperor repeated what he had said, and Tirant answered:

"My lord, Your Majesty should know that the crier is running throughout the city, telling everyone that the departure is set for Monday, and today is Friday. So we will be leaving very soon, my lord, and nearly everyone is already prepared."

Tirant stood behind the emperor so that he would not see him, and covering his face with his hands, he looked at the princess. She and the other maidens laughed out loud while Plaerdemavida stood in front of the emperor, and taking the emperor's arm, she turned him toward her and said:

"If you have done anything noteworthy it's because of Tirant, who conquered the Grand Turk and made him lose the false and terrible madness he had about ruling the entire Greek empire. He also intended to conquer the old emperor here with pretty words, and instead the Turkish kings and the sultan desperately ran for safety to the great fortress in the city of Bellpuig. And not at their leisure, but swept along by the fear that took control of their feet. He has won renown by his own virtue, and if I had the royal scepter and were lord of the Greek empire, and if Carmesina had come from my body, I know very well whose wife I would make her. But all of us girls are foolish like this: we want nothing but honor, position, and dignity, and as a result many of us come to a bad end. What good would it do for me to belong to the line of David if I lost what I had for lack of a good man? And you, my lord, try to save your soul, since you've spared your body in battles in the past, and don't even think about giving any other husband to your daughter but... Do I have to say it? I won't... I must: the virtuous Tirant. Take this consolation while you're alive, and don't expect it to be done after your blessed days are over, because the things that nature wills and that are ordered by God must be consented to. That way you'll have glory in this world and paradise in the next."

Then she turned to the princess, and said:

"You who are of such lofty blood, take a husband soon—very soon. If your father won't give you one, I will, and I'll give you none other than Tirant. For it's a wonderful thing to have both a husband and a knight, whoever can have one. This man is greater than all the others in prowess. If you don't think so, Your Majesty, look at the disorder of your empire and the point it had reached before Tirant came to this land."

"Please be quiet, girl," said Tirant, "and don't say such outlandish things about me."

"Go on out to your battles," said Plaerdemavida, "and let me be."

The emperor answered:

"By the bones of my father, the emperor Albert, you are the most extraordinary maiden in the world, but the further you go, the more I like you. And now, as a present, I'm going to give you fifty thousand ducats."

She knelt to the ground and kissed his hand. The princess was very disturbed by what she had said, and Tirant was somewhat embarrassed. When the emperor had finished dressing he went to mass. As they came out from mass Tirant had an opportunity to talk to the princess, and he said to her:

"Anyone who makes a promise puts himself in debt."

"The promise," said the princess, "was not made in the presence of a notary."

Plaerdemavida, who was standing nearby, heard the princess's reply, and quickly said to her:

"Let's have none of that: a promise to fulfill love doesn't require any witnesses, and even less a notary. What a miserable state we'd be in if we had to have it in writing every time! There wouldn't be enough paper in the world! Do you know how it's done? In the dark and without witnesses, because the lodging is never missed."

"Oh, this madwoman!" said the princess. "Do you always have to talk to me about the same thing?"

No matter how much Tirant spoke to her, no matter how he pleaded, she would do nothing for him.

When they were in the chambers, the emperor called Carmesina and said to her:

"Tell me, my daughter, those things Plaerdemavida said—where do they come from?"

"I'm sure I don't know, my lord," said the princess. "I never spoke of such a thing to her. But this madwoman is impertinent and she says anything that comes into her head."

"She's no madwoman," said the emperor. "In fact, she's the most sensible maiden in my court. She's a good girl, and she always gives good advice. Haven't you noticed when you've come to the council chambers that when you make her talk she is always very discreet? Would you like to have our captain for your husband?"

The princess blushed shamefully, and could not utter a word. After a moment, when she had recovered, she said:

"My lord, when your captain has finished conquering the Moors, then I will do whatever Your Majesty commands me."

Tirant went to the duchess' chamber, and sent for Plaerdemavida. When she was there, he said:

"Oh, genteel lady! I don't know what help you can give me: My soul is in discord with my body, and unless you can cure my illness I don't care whether I live or die."

"I'll do it tonight," said Plaerdemavida, "if you do as I say."

"Command me, maiden," said Tirant, "and may God increase your honor. The things you said when the emperor was here, about the princess and me: who told you to say them?"

"You, and my lady, and the emperor too: You're all thinking the same thing," said Plaerdemavida. "When he asked me, I gave him even better reasons why you're worthy of having the princess as a wife. To what better man could she be given than to you? And he agrees with everything that I say. I'll tell you why, in strict confidence: He's in love with me, and he would pull up my chemise if I'd let him. He's sworn to me on the Bible that if the empress was dying, he would take me as a wife in a minute. And he told me: 'As a sign of our pact, let's kiss; this kiss will be very little, but it's better to have something than nothing.' And I answered him: 'Now that you are old, you're a lecher. When you were young, were you virtuous?' Only a few hours ago he gave me this string of fat pearls, and now he's with his daughter, asking her if she wants you for a husband. Do you know why I said that to him? Because if you go to her chamber at night and it's your bad fortune to cause a commotion, and they try to charge me with something, I'll have an alibi. I'll say: 'My lord, I already told Your Majesty. The princess ordered me to let him in.' And that way no one will be able to say anything. So that you can see my good will and how much I want to help and honor Your Grace, when the emperor is dining, come to me. I promise to put you in my lady's bed, and in the refreshing night you'll see how solace comes to those who are in love."

While they were talking, the emperor, knowing that Tirant was in the duchess' chamber, sent for him, and interrupted their conversation.

When Tirant held counsel with the emperor, they spoke at length about war and what things would be needed, and at that time they were all dressed in readiness for battle. When the dark shadows of night had fallen, Tirant came to the duchess' chamber, and while the emperor was with the ladies, Plaerdemavida went into the chamber very happily, took Tirant by the hand and led him away. He was dressed in a jacket of red satin, with a cloak over his shoulders and a sword in his hand. Plaerdemavida put him in the chamber. A large box was there with a hole she had made so he could breathe. The bath had been prepared, and it stood in front of the box. After the ladies had eaten, they danced with the gallant knights. When they saw that Tirant was not there they stopped dancing, and the emperor retired to his chamber while the ladies departed, and left the princess alone with her ladies-in-waiting in her chamber where Tirant was. Plaerdemavida opened the box under the pretext of taking out a sheet of delicate linen for the bath, and she left it slightly open, putting clothing on top so that none of the other women would see him. The princess began to take off her clothes, and Plaerdemavida prepared her seat which had been placed directly in front so that Tirant could see her clearly.

When she was completely naked Plaerdemavida brought a lighted candle to give pleasure to Tirant, and looking at all of her body and everything that was in view, she said:

"In faith, my lady, if Tirant were here and could touch you with his hands the way I am, I believe he would prefer that to being made ruler of the kingdom of France."

"Don't believe it," said the princess. "He would rather be king than touch me the way you are."

"Oh, my lord Tirant! Where are you now? Why aren't you standing here, nearby, so that you can see and touch the thing you love most in this world and in the world beyond? Look, my lord Tirant, here are the locks of my princess; I kiss them in your name, for you are the best of all knights in the world. Here are her eyes and her mouth: I kiss them for you. Here are her crystalline breasts: I hold one in each hand,

and I kiss them for you. See how small, how firm, how white and smooth they are. Look Tirant, here is her belly, her thighs and her secret place. Oh, wretched me, if I were a man I would want to spend my last days here. Oh, Tirant! Where are you now? Why don't you come to me when I call you so tenderly? Only the hands of Tirant are worthy to touch where I am touching, and no one else, because this is a morsel that there is no one who would not like to choke on."

Tirant was watching all this, and could not have been more pleased by the fine wit of Plaerdemavida's comments, and he felt sorely tempted to come out of the box.

When they had been there some time, joking, the princess stepped into the bath and told Plaerdemavida to remove her clothes and join her.

"I will, under one condition."

"What's that?" asked the princess.

Plaerdemavida answered:

"That you consent to have Tirant in your bed for one hour while you're in it."

"Hush! You're mad!" said the princess.

"If you please, my lady, tell me what you would say if Tirant came here one night without any of us knowing it?"

"What else could I tell him," said the princess, "but beg him to leave, and if he wouldn't go, I would keep quiet rather than be defamed."

"In faith, my lady," said Plaerdemavida, "that's what I would do too."

While they were saying these things, Widow Repose came in, and the princess begged her to join her in the bath. The Widow removed all her clothing except her red stockings and a linen hat on her head; and although she was very pretty and well endowed, the red stockings and the hat on her head made her so ugly that she looked like a devil, and it is true that any lady or maiden you see in that sort of attire will look very ugly to you no matter how genteel she may be.

When the bath was finished they brought the repast to the princess, which was a pair of partridges, and then a dozen eggs with sugar and cinnamon. Afterward she lay down in her bed to sleep.

The Widow went to her chamber with the other ladies except for two who slept in the chamber. When they were all asleep, Plaerdemavida got up from the bed and she led Tirant from the box in her nightshirt, and made him take off all his clothing, quietly, so that no one would hear him. And Tirant's heart, hands and feet were trembling.

"What's this?" said Plaerdemavida. "There's not a man in the world who is valiant with weapons, but who isn't afraid when he's with women. In battle there's not a man alive you're afraid of, and here you tremble at the sight of one lone maiden. Don't worry, I'll be with you the whole time. I won't leave your side."

"By the faith I owe our Heavenly Father, I would be happier to joust ten knights to the death than commit an act like this."

The maiden took him by the hand, and he followed her, trembling, and said:

"Maiden, all my fear is really shame, because of the extreme good will that I desire for my lady. I would much rather go back than continue on when I think that Her Majesty knows nothing about any of this. When she sees what's happening she will be completely frightened, and I would rather die than offend Her Majesty."

Plaerdemavida was very angry with Tirant's words, and she said:

"Oh, you faint-hearted knight. Does a maiden frighten you so much that you're afraid to go near her? Oh, unlucky captain. Do you have so little courage that you dare say such words to me? Pluck up your courage.

"When the emperor comes, what story will you invent to tell him? I'll have you discovered, and God and the whole world will know that you have spoken ill, and let me remind you that this time you'll lose your honor and your fame. Do what I tell you and I'll give you a secure life and have you wearing the crown of the Greek Empire, because the time has come when I can tell you only one thing: to go quickly and take those steps that will lead you to the princess."

Seeing the frankness in Plaerdemavida's words, Tirant said:

"Let's go on without delay, I beg you, and let me see that glorified body. And since there's no light I'll see her only with the eyes of the imagination."

"I've used great ingenuity to bring you here," said Plaerdemavida, "so conduct yourself in a proper way."

And she let go his hand. Tirant discovered that Plaerdemavida had left him, and he did not know where she was because there was no light in the room. She made him wait half an hour, barefoot, and in his shirt-sleeves. He called to her as softly as he could, and she heard him perfectly well but did not answer. When Plaerdemavida saw that she had made him grow quite cold, she had pity on him, and going up to him she said:

"That's the way people who aren't in love are punished. How could you imagine that any lady or maiden of high or low station, wouldn't want to be loved? Anyone who can go in by honest or secret roads, by night or by day, through a window, a door or a roof, is thought of highly. I wouldn't be unhappy if Hippolytus would do it to me. And I wouldn't be upset if he would take me by the hair, and drag me through the room, with my consent or without it, and make me be quiet, and I would let him do anything he wanted. I would rather know that he's a man. In other things you should honor, love and serve her; but when you're alone in a room with her, that's no time to be polite."

"In faith, maiden," said Tirant, "you've pointed out my defects to me better than any confessor could, no matter how great a teacher of theology he might be. Take me to my lady's bed quickly, I beg you."

Plaerdemavida took him there, and made him lie down beside the princess. The head of the bed did not touch the wall, and when Tirant was lying down, the maiden told him to be still and not to move until she said so. Then she stood at the end of the bed, and she put her head between Tirant and the princess, facing the princess. Because the sleeves of her blouse bothered her, she rolled them up, and taking Tirant's hand, she placed it on the princess' breasts, and he touched her nipples, and her belly, and below. The princess awoke, and said:

"My heaven, what a bother you are! Can't you let me sleep?"

Plaerdemavida, with her head on the pillow, said:

"Oh! You're a very difficult lady to take. You've just come out of the bath, and your skin is so smooth and nice that it makes me feel good just to touch it."

"Touch all you like," said the princess, "but don't put your hand so far down."

"Go back to sleep," said Plaerdemavida, "and let me touch this body that's mine, because I'm here in Tirant's place. Oh, Tirant, you traitor! Where are you? If you had your hand where I have mine, wouldn't you be unhappy!"

Tirant had his hand on the princess' belly, and Plaerdemavida had her hand on Tirant's head, and when she saw that the princess was asleep, she loosened her grip, and then Tirant touched at will, and when she was about to wake up, the girl squeezed Tirant's head, and he stopped. They spent more than an hour at this play, and he did not cease touching her. When Plaerdemavida saw that she was deep in sleep she removed her hand completely from Tirant, and he carefully tried to accomplish his desire. But the princess began to wake up, and half asleep, she said:

"But what are you doing, you wretched girl? Can't you let me sleep? Have you gone mad, trying to do what's against your nature?"

It was not long until she knew that it was more than a woman, and she refused to surrender to him and began to cry out. Plaerdemavida covered her mouth and whispered in her ear so that none of the other girls would hear her:

"Hush, my lady, you don't want to be dishonored. I'm terribly afraid that the empress will hear you. Be quiet: this is your knight who is ready to die for you."

"Oh, you wicked girl!" said the princess. "You've had no fear of me or shame of the world. Without my consent you've put me in a very bad situation and defamed me."

"What's done is done, my lady," said Plaerdemavida. "It seems to me that being quiet is the only solution for you and me: it's the safest thing, and what's best in this case."

Tirant softly pleaded with her as well as he could. She found herself in a difficult situation, because love was conquering her on the one hand, and fear on the other, but since fear was stronger than love, she decided to be still and she said nothing.

When the princess first screamed, Widow Repose heard her, and she was fully aware that the cause of that scream had been Plaerdemavida, and that Tirant must be with her. And she thought that if Tirant was seducing the princess, she couldn't accomplish her own desire with him. Now everyone was silent and the princess was not saying a thing, but instead was defending herself with graceful words so that the pleasant battle would not come to an end. The Widow sat bolt upright in her bed and cried out:

"My daughter, what's wrong?"

She woke up all the girls, shrieking loudly and making so much noise that the empress heard it. They all got up, some entirely naked and others in their nightshirts, and quickly ran to the door of the bedchamber which they found closed fast, and they cried out for a light. At the very moment that they were pounding on the door and calling for light, Plaerdemavida seized Tirant by the hair, and pulled him from the place where he would have liked to end his life. She led him to a small chamber and made him jump to a rooftop there. Then she gave him a hemp rope so that he could drop down to the garden and from there could open the gate. She had it very well prepared so that when he came he could leave by another door before daybreak. But the disturbance and the cries of the Widow and the girls were so loud that she could not let him out the way she had planned, and she was forced to let him out by the roof. So, giving him the long rope, she quickly turned and closed the window and then went back to her lady.

Tirant turned around and tied the rope securely, and in his haste to leave without being seen or heard, he did not watch carefully to see whether or not the rope reached the ground. He let himself slide down the rope which hung more than thirty-five feet from the ground. He had to let go because his arms could not hold the weight of his body, and he hit the ground so hard that he broke his leg.

Let us leave Tirant stretched out on the ground, unable to move.

When Plaerdemavida returned, they brought the light, and all the women came in with the empress who immediately asked what the disturbance was and why she had cried out.

"Madam," said the princess, "a huge rat jumped up on my bed and ran over my face, and I was so frightened that I screamed. He scratched my face with his claws, and if he had gotten my eye, you can imagine what damage he would have done!"

Now that scratch had been made by Plaerdemavida when she covered her mouth so she would not scream. The emperor had gotten up, and he entered the princess's chamber with his sword in his hand, and hearing about the rat, he looked through all the rooms. But the maiden had been discreet: When the empress came in and was talking to her daughter, she jumped out onto the roof and quickly removed the rope. She heard Tirant moaning, and immediately realized that he had fallen, and she went back to the chamber without saying a word. There was so much noise throughout the palace, between the guards and the palace officials, that it was a wonder to hear and to behold; and if the Turks had entered the city the disturbance would not have been any greater. The emperor, who was a very discreet man, suspected that this had to be more than a rat, and he even looked into the coffers. Then he had all the windows opened, so that if the maiden had not been quick about removing the rope he would have found it.

When the duke and duchess, who knew what was going on, heard all the noise, they thought Tirant had been discovered. Imagine how the duke must have felt, thinking that Tirant was in such a difficult situation, and that he must have been killed or imprisoned. He quickly armed himself to help Tirant since he had his weapons there, and he said:

"Today I'll lose my entire kingdom because Tirant is in such a bad situation."

"And look at me," said the duchess. "I don't have enough strength in my hands to put on my blouse."

When the duke was armed he left his room to see what was happening, and to find out where Tirant was. And as he was going out he saw the emperor returning to his chamber. The duke asked him:

"What is it, Sire? What's the cause of this disturbance?"

The emperor answered:

"Those foolish maidens who aren't afraid of anything. According to what they say, a rat climbed over my daughter's face, and she says it left a scratch on her cheek. Go back to sleep, you're not needed here."

The duke went back to his room and told the duchess, and they were both very relieved that nothing had happened to Tirant. Then the duke said:

"For the love of Our Lady, I went out of here in such a state that if the emperor had imprisoned Tirant I would have killed him and everyone who came to his aid, and then Tirant or I would have been emperor."

"But it's best that it turned out as it did," said the duchess.

She quickly got up and went to the princess's chamber. When Plaerdemavida saw her, she said:

"My lady, please, I beg you, stay here, and don't let anyone speak badly of Tirant. I'll go and see how he is."

When she was out on the roof she did not dare speak for fear that someone would hear her, and she heard him moaning loudly, and saying:

"I can feel myself descending toward the dark and gloomy palaces. And since I cannot restore my miserable life with all my sighs, I'm content to die, because life without you, dear princess, is completely unbearable. Oh Lord and eternal God! You who are all merciful, grant me the grace of dying in the arms of that most virtuous princess, so that my soul may be more content in the next world."

At this moment Hippolytus knew nothing about Tirant's actions, but he was aware of the great uproar in the palace that was spreading throughout the city. Seeing that Tirant was inside the palace and that he had told everyone he was sleeping in the duke's chamber that night, and with the viscount and Hippolytus knowing about his love for the princess, they had all the men take up arms. Lord Agramunt said:

"I can only think that Tirant must have done some mischief in the princess's chamber, and news of it has reached the emperor, and all of us will take part in the wedding along with him. So we must prepare ourselves quickly to help him if we have to. Because in all the nights he's slept here nothing unusual has happened, and as soon as he's outside you see what a great outcry there is in the palace."

Hippolytus said:

"While you're arming yourself I'll go to the palace gate to see what's happening."

"Hurry," said the others.

When they were all outside, the viscount followed Hippolytus.

"My lord," said Hippolytus, "you go to the main gate and I'll go to the one in the garden. Whoever discovers what is really happening—what all this noise is about—will go and tell the other one."

The viscount said he thought that was a good idea. When Hippolytus was at the gate to the garden, thinking he would find it locked, he stood, listening, and he heard a mournful voice crying. It sounded like a woman's voice, and he said to himself:

"I would much rather hear Tirant than this woman's voice, whoever she is."

He stood, looking to see if he could scale the wall. When he saw that it was impossible, he went back to the gate with an easy heart, thinking it must be a woman.

"Let her wail, whoever she is—lady or maiden," said Hippolytus, "for this has nothing to do with my lord Tirant."

He left and went to the plaza where he found the viscount and others who wanted to know what had caused the disturbance. But by now the cries had subsided a great deal, and the disturbance had been quelled. Then Hippolytus explained to the viscount how he had been at the garden gate and had not been able to go in, and that he had heard what seemed to be a woman's voice moaning, and he did not know who it was, but that he thought the woman was the cause of all the outcry.

"If it please you, let's go there," said the viscount, "and if she's a lady or a maiden who needs help, let's give it to her if we can, because it's our obligation under the 'laws of chivalry.'"

They went to the garden gate, and heard the loud laments coming from inside the garden, but they could not understand what was being said or recognize the voice: with all the pain she was in, her voice was altered. The viscount said:

"Let's break down the gate. It's night, and no one will know we did it."

But the gate was unlocked, because during the night, not imagining that so much harm would be done, Plaerdemavida had left it that way so that Tirant could open it easily whenever he liked.

And they both pushed against the gate with all their might, and it flew open easily. The viscount went in first and walked toward the voice which sounded so strange.

The viscount said:

"Whoever you are, I beg you in God's name, tell me if you're an errant spirit or a mortal body who needs help."

Tirant thought it must be the emperor and his men, and so that he would not be recognized, and they would leave, he disguised his voice, even though the pain he was in had already disguised it, and he said:

"In my time I was a baptized Christian, and I am condemned to wander because of my sins. I am an invisible spirit, and if you see me, the reason will be that I am taking on form. The evil spirits here are stripping off my flesh and my bones and throwing them in the air piece by piece. Oh, what a cruel torture I am suffering. If you come any closer to me, you will share in my pain."

They were very frightened when they heard these words, and they made the sign of the cross and recited the Gospel of Saint John. The viscount spoke so loudly that Tirant heard him:

"Hippolytus, do you think we should go to our chambers and get all our armed men and some holy water, and then come back here to see what this is?"

"No," said Hippolytus, "we don't need to go back to our chambers for anything. We both have the sign of the cross on our swords: let me go there."

When Tirant heard the viscount call Hippolytus' name, he said:

"If you are Hippolytus, a native of France, come to me and have no fear."

Then Hippolytus took out his sword, and holding the handle in front of him, he made the sign of the cross and said:

"As a true Christian, I fully believe in the articles of the Catholic faith, and everything that the holy Roman church teaches: in this holy faith I want to live and die."

He went closer in great fear, but the viscount was even more afraid, and did not dare to approach. And in a soft voice Tirant called to him and said:

"Come closer. I am Tirant."

At that he became even more frightened, and was ready to go back. Tirant saw this, and raising his voice he said:

"Oh, what a cowardly knight you are!"

Hippolytus recognized him when he spoke, and ran up to him and said:

"Oh, my lord, is it you? What misfortune brought you here?"

"Don't be worried, and don't say anything," said Tirant. "But who is that with you? If he's of the lineage of Brittany, have him come here."

"Yes, my lord," said Hippolytus. "It's the viscount."

He called him, and when the viscount saw Tirant he was amazed at the adventure and at everything he had said to them during the time they had not recognized him.

"Let's not waste words," said Tirant. "Hurry and take me away from here."

Together they lifted him in their arms and took him out of the garden and closed the gate. Then they carried him to his lodging and lay him under the portico.

"I'm in more pain than I've ever felt before," said Tirant. "Of all the times I've been wounded and near death, my body has never felt so much pain. I'll need to have doctors without the emperor knowing about it."

"My lord," said Hippolytus, "may I give you some advice? You are so badly hurt that it can't be kept hidden, especially with the disturbance in the palace. Mount your horse if you can, my lord, and let's go to the palaces of Bellestar where your horses are. We'll make everyone think that your horse fell on you and broke your leg "

The viscount answered:

"It's true, my cousin and lord, Hippolytus is right. Otherwise the emperor will certainly hear about it. I would be happy if, after you're cured and we've accomplished our aims, we returned to our lands."

"My lord viscount," said Tirant, "this is no time to talk about these things, but you, Hippolytus, have them bring the animals here secretly, and bring the horse with the smoothest gait."

Let us return to the princess. Plaerdemavida stayed out on the roof until she saw them carry Tirant away. Then she went into the room where the princess was with the duchess and all the ladies. The empress was astonished that there should be such a great uproar in the palace over a rat, and sitting on her bed she said:

"Do you know the best thing for us to do, ladies? Since the palace is calmed down again, let's go back to sleep."

The princess called Plaerdemavida and whispered to her, asking where Tirant was.

"My lady, he's gone," said Plaerdemavida, "and he's in great pain."

But she did not dare tell her that he had a broken leg, or what he had said. She was very pleased that they had not seen or found him. The empress got up, and Widow Repose said:

"It would be a good idea, my lady, to tell your daughter to sleep with you, so that if the rat came back it wouldn't frighten her even more."

The empress answered:

"What the Widow says is true. Come, my child: you will sleep better with me than by yourself."

"No, my lady. Let Your Excellency go on: the duchess and I will sleep together. Don't spend a bad night on my account."

The empress said:

"Come with me. I'm getting cold standing here."

"My lady, since you insist," said the princess, "you go on, and I'll come soon."

The empress left, telling her to come right away. The princess turned to the Widow and said angrily:

"Now I know how much you're to blame. Who gave you the right to tell my mother that I should go and sleep with her, and to deprive me of my pleasure? From what I can see, you don't live by virtue, but by envy and malice."

The Widow replied

"I'll tell you what I've done wrong. I honored and loved you more than you liked: that's how I'm to blame. Do you imagine, my lady, that I have no feelings for Tirant, and that I didn't see him letting himself down by the rope, and it breaking, and him falling so hard I think he broke his legs and his ribs?..."

She began to cry miserably, and threw herself to the ground, and pulled her hair, saying:

"The best of all knights is dead!"

When the princess heard these words, she said three times:

"Jesus, Jesus, Jesus!"

And she fell to the floor in a faint. She had cried out the name of Jesus so loudly that the empress, who was in her chamber, asleep in her bed, heard it. She quickly got up and hurried to her daughter's chamber. She found her there, unconscious, and nothing helped to revive her. The emperor had to get up, and all the doctors came. But still the princess did not regain consciousness, and three hours passed before she did. The emperor asked how his daughter had come to such a state. They told him:

"My lord, she saw another tiny rat, and because her imagination was dwelling on the one she had seen on her bed, when she saw this one she suffered a terrible shock."

"Oh, old emperor, sad and embittered! In my last days must I suffer so much pain? Oh, cruel death! Why don't you come to me when I want you so?"

When he had said this he lost consciousness and fell in a faint beside his daughter. The cries and shouts were so great throughout the whole palace that it was astonishing to see and hear the laments the people were making: and this disturbance was greater than the first.

Tirant, standing before the portico waiting for the animals to be brought, heard such loud cries that he thought the sky was falling in. He quickly mounted, full of pain and anguish, and the pain grew as he became fearful that the princess might have come to some harm. Hippolytus took a cloth and wrapped his leg so that the cold would not get into it. So, as best they could, they rode to the gates of the city. The guards recognized Tirant and asked him where he was going at this hour. He answered that he was going to Bellestar to look after his horses because he would soon be leaving for the camp. The gates were quickly opened for him and Tirant went on his way. When they had ridden half a league, Tirant said:

"I am deeply afraid that the emperor has done the princess some harm because of me. I want to go back and help her in case she needs me."

The viscount said

"In faith, you're in fine condition to help her!"

"My dear viscount," said Tirant, "I feel no pain now! You know that a greater injury makes a lesser one diminish. I beg you, please, let's go back to the city so that we can help her in case she needs us."

"You've lost your mind," said the viscount. "You want to go back to the city so that the emperor will find out what you've done. We'll be doing well enough if we can keep this from the people so that they won't blame you for it. You can be certain that if you go back you won't escape injury or death if things are the way you say they are."

fear of the maidens who were nearby. The doctors left quickly without saying anything to the emperor so that he would not have a relapse, because his constitution was very delicate.

When the doctors reached Tirant they found him lying on a bed in great pain. They looked at his leg and found it completely broken, the bones protruding from the flesh. With their ministrations Tirant fainted three times, and each time they had to revive him. The doctors treated him as best they could the first time and said that under no circumstances should he be moved from his bed, because his life was in danger. Then they went back to the palace. The emperor asked them where they had been, since he had not seen them at mealtime. One of them answered:

"My lord, your captain has been injured, and we went to Bellestar to minister to him."

The emperor said;

"And how was he hurt?"

"My lord," said the doctor, "they say that early this morning he left the city to go to where his horses are so that Monday morning everyone would be ready to leave. He was riding a Sicilian horse and, galloping along the road, he fell in a trench and hurt his leg."

"Holy Virgin Mary," said the emperor. "Tirant has no lack of troubles. I want to go see him immediately."

When the doctors heard the emperor's decision—that he wanted to leave—they detained him for a day so that he would have time to recover. The emperor saw that the doctors advised against it, so he decided to stay. He went to the princess's chambers to ask about her illness and to explain what had happened to Tirant. What grief the princess felt in her heart! But she did not dare show it for fear of her father, and her own pain seemed as nothing when she thought of Tirant's suffering.

The emperor stayed with his daughter until dinnertime. The following day, seeing the doctors pass by from a window and knowing that they were going to see Tirant, he called to them to wait. Then he mounted and went with them and saw their second treatment. From what he saw he understood at once that Tirant would not be able to go to the encampment for a long time. When they had finished their treatment, the emperor said:

"I can't begin to tell you how much grief I feel. As soon as I heard about your injury I knew how great my misfortune was, because I had placed all my hope in your leadership. I had envisioned the blood of those cruel enemies of mine and of the holy Catholic faith being shed by the strength of your arm, and the blow of your sword. But now, when they hear that you are not there, they will be afraid of no one and will overrun my entire empire."

Tirant weakly said:

"My lord, you don't need my sword and my leadership. In your empire you have courageous knights who can take on the enemy right now. But it only seems right to me, since you are pressing me so much, that I should go to the camp. My lord, I will be ready to go on the day we had set."

When the emperor heard him say that, he was very happy, and he took his leave and returned to the city. When the empress saw him she said:

"My lord, tell us the truth about our captain. How is he? Is he near death, or is there hope for him?"

In the presence of the princess and the maidens the emperor said to the empress:

"My lady, I don't think he's in danger of dying, but there is no doubt that he's in a bad way. The bones in his leg are sticking out through the skin, and it's a terrible sight to see. But he says he will be ready to leave Monday."

"Holy Mother of Jesus!" said the princess. "What is Your Majesty trying to do? You want a man who is so badly hurt that he's at death's door to go to the encampment and end his days while he's on the road? How could he help the soldiers? Do you want to put his life and the entire empire in danger too? No, my lord; that's no way to fight these battles. It's better to have him alive than dead, because with him living all your enemies will be afraid, and once he's dead they won't be afraid of anything."

The emperor went into the council chamber where they were waiting for him, and they all agreed from what he had seen of Tirant that he should not be moved.

After the emperor had left Bellestar, where Tirant was, Tirant immediately ordered a box made so that he could be carried in it. When it was Sunday evening and the duke and all the others had gone back to the city, and without anyone knowing of it except Hippolytus, Tirant ordered the viscount and Lord Agramunt not to disturb him until they were ready to depart. They had not an inkling that Tirant would commit such an act of folly as to leave.

Tirant gave one doctor a large amount of money to go with him, but the other doctor ordered him not to move and would not go along. Tirant had them put him in the box, and using shafts to carry it on their shoulders, they left for the encampment. Before he left he ordered them to tell everyone who came from the city that since he had not been able to sleep at night he was resting. Some who came to see him went back, and others stayed, waiting for him to awaken. When it was noon the Duke of Macedonia who was a close relative, as was the viscount, wanted to go inside.

Saying that anyone who was wounded should not sleep so much, they forced their way in and discovered that he was gone. They quickly mounted their horses and rode after him, and they sent word to the emperor, telling how his captain had obeyed his command, and cursing the emperor and all of his kind. When the emperor heard the news, he said:

"By the living God, he carries out his promises!"

When the duke and the viscount overtook him and learned that he had passed out on the road five times, they reprimanded the doctor and Hippolytus, and said they cared nothing for him.

"And you, Hippolytus," said the duke, "of our lineage of Rocasalada and of the kindred of Brittany, to allow our master and lord to leave! The day his life ends we will all be lost and no one will ever hear of us again. You deserve the worst sort of reprimand. If I had no fear of God or felt no sense of worldly shame, I'd do worse to you with this sword than Cain did to Abel: You miserable knight! Get away from me, or upon my word of honor you'll get the punishment you deserve."

And turning to the doctor he gave vent to his anger.

"I lose all patience when I think of the outrageous act of this doctor who put the light of Rocasalada in mortal danger."

And the duke rode furiously at the doctor, his sword raised, while the doctor attempted to flee to save his miserable skin, but it gained him nothing because when he reached him he brought the sword down on his head so hard that it split in half, down to his shoulders, and his brains flew out.

When the emperor received news of the death of such a singular doctor he quickly rode to Tirant, and found him in a hermitage where the duke had put him: there he was being given everything he needed. When the emperor saw Tirant's condition he took great pity and had all his doctors come there to see how his leg was. The doctors found it much worse and they told him that if he had gone one league further, either he would have died or had to have his leg cut off.

All the barons in the empire came to see him. The emperor held council there and they decided that since Tirant could not go, all the men should leave the next day. Tirant said:

"My lord, I think Your Majesty should give two months' wages to all the men, and since they will only serve one and a half months, everyone will be happy, and they'll put up a better fight."

The emperor answered that he would do it immediately, and he said:

"This evening I've received letters from the Marquis of Saint George in our camp, telling me that great numbers of Moors have come. It says here that the King of Jerusalem, who is a cousin of the Grand Caramany has come, and with him are his wife and children and some sixty thousand soldiers from the land of Enedast, a very fertile and abundant province. As soon as a male child is born there, he is raised with great care. When he is ten years old they teach him to ride and to fence. Then they teach him to fight, and throw a lance. And last, they teach him how to butcher, so that he will get used to cutting up meat and will not be afraid of spilling blood. This makes them cruel, and when they are in battle and capture Christians, they quarter them and haven't the slightest feeling of pity about flesh or blood. The King of Lower India has come here, and they say he is the brother of the prisoner from Upper India; he is a very rich man and he's bringing forty-five thousand soldiers with him. Another king, called Menador, has come with thirty-seven thousand soldiers. The King of Damascus has come with fifty-five thousand. King Veruntament has come with forty-two thousand. And many others have come with them."

Tirant replied:

"Let them come, my lord. I have so much faith in the divine mercy of Our Lord and in His most Holy Mother, Our Lady, that, even if there were twice as many as there are, with the help of the singular knights Your Majesty has, we would be victorious over them."

When they had finished their conversation, the emperor commended Tirant to God, and ordered the doctors to leave him alone and to allow him to depart.

The princess was very upset by Tirant's injury. When it was Monday, all the soldiers were ready to leave. The Duke of Pera and the Duke of Macedonia were in charge of leading all the men. When they reached the camp of the Marquis of Saint George, the others were very happy to see them. Tirant stayed in the hermitage, waiting for the doctors to give him permission to go into the city. Lord Agramunt who never wanted to leave him alone, remained with him, for he said that he had left his country only for love of him, and that he would not leave him while he was injured. Hippolytus stayed in his company, and went to the city every day for whatever he needed, but especially to bring news about the princess to Tirant. And when they wanted to make him eat or do other things the doctors prescribed, they would say it was for the princess, and he would do it immediately.

After this had happened to Tirant, the princess often reprimanded Plaerdemavida for what she had done, and wanted to shut her up in a dark room to have her do penance there; but she defended herself with choice words, or with jokes, saying:

"What will your father say if he finds out? Do you know what I'll tell him? That it was you who told me what to do, and that Tirant has stolen your virginity. Your father wants me to be your stepmother, and I can assure you that when I am I'll punish you. When that valiant knight, Tirant, comes again, you won't cry out the way you did the last time. Instead you'll be quiet, and you won't move."

The princess became very angry, and told her to shut her mouth.

"Since you're speaking to me so harshly, my lady, I want to leave Your Highness' service, and I'm going to go back to my father, the count."

She immediately left the chambers and gathered up all her clothing and jewels. Leaving the Widow of Montsant, who was in the court, in charge, and without saying a word to anyone, she mounted a horse and with five squires she rode to where Tirant was.

When the princess discovered that Plaerdemavida had gone, she was very upset and wanted her to return. She sent men in all directions to make her come back.

Plaerdemavida rode by back roads to the hermitage where Tirant was, and when he saw her he forgot his pain. When Plaerdemavida went up to him and saw how much his appearance had changed, she would not hold back her tears. And with a weak voice she said:

"Oh, I am the most miserable person in the world! I am so sorry when I think of your injury, because I am to blame for all the harm that has come to the best knight in the world. I can only ask you for mercy."

With a sigh Tirant said:

"Virtuous maiden, there is no reason at all for you to ask my forgiveness: you're not to blame for anything, and even if you were, I would pardon you not just once but a thousand times, because I know how much affection you've always had for me. I won't say another word about this because I want to know what the princess has been doing while I've been gone. I'm sure Her Highness's love has grown weak, and she probably doesn't want to see me again."

Plaerdemavida, with a smile, told him she was very happy to do him such a service, and in a soft voice she said:

"After you left there was so much shouting and such a tumult in the palace that the emperor got out of bed. He went looking through all the rooms furiously, with a sword in his hand, saying whether it was a mouse or a man he would kill it without mercy. The empress went back to her chambers to sleep. The love-sick Widow went to the princess with her own wickedness, because she is related to the old witch who brings only harm to those who love her. With a false expression of compassion on her face she told her: 'My lady, I saw Tirant lower himself by a rope, and half-way down it broke; and he fell from such a height that he was smashed to pieces.' And she began to wail very loudly. When the princess heard the news she could say only, 'Jesus, Jesus, Jesus,' three times, and immediately her spirit left her. I don't know where it went or on what business, because she was senseless for three hours. All the doctors came, but they couldn't revive her, and at that moment the emperor thought he was losing everything that nature and fortune had given him. And the tumult and cries in the palace were even greater than they had been the first time."

Then she told him everything she and the princess had said to each other.

"All her anger is feigned. She can't make up her mind about how to behave the first time she sees you: Whether or not to show that she is bothered by your injury. Because she says that if she smiles at you, you'll want to come back every day, and if she doesn't, you will be angry with her."

Tirant replied:

"What crime does Her Highness say that I've committed besides loving her? Her Majesty would do me a great favor if she would just grant me a visit. I believe that then most of her anger would disappear."

Plaerdemavida answered:

"My lord, do me a favor. Write her a letter, and I'll work with her so that she'll give you an answer. That way you'll be able to know what she is thinking."

As they were talking, the men that the princess had sent in search of Plaerdemavida entered the chamber. When they saw her they told her what the princess had ordered them to do. Plaerdemavida answered:

"Tell my lady that she can't force me to serve her. I want to go to my parents' home."

"If I had found you someplace else," said the knight, "I would have forced you to go back. But I don't imagine the captain will be happy if the princess's will isn't carried out, and as a virtuous knight he will take care of the situation."

"Don't doubt for a minute," said Tirant, "that my lady will be served in every way. This maiden will quickly go with you."

Tirant had ink and paper brought, and with the great pain he felt in his leg he could not write as well as he wanted to, but in spite of his injury he wrote the following words of love:

"Who knows the great perfection that I see in Your Majesty, and in no one else? The fear I have of not having Your Highness' love makes me feel twice as much pain, because if I lost Your Majesty I would lose everything. You must know that in you all perfection is contained. My petition is based on that moment when you heard about my injury and said, 'Jesus, Jesus, Jesus!'—which has moved me deeply."

When Plaerdemavida had left Tirant, and the princess knew that she was coming, she ran to the landing of the stairs and said to her:

"Oh, my beloved sister! What made you so angry that you wanted to leave me?"

"Why, my lady!" said Plaerdemavida: "Your Excellency swept me from your mind and didn't want to see me again."

The princess took her by the hand, and led her to her bedchambers. She turned to the men who had brought her, and thanked them. When they were inside the chambers the princess said:

"Don't you know, Plaerdemavida, that disagreements between parents and their children often reach heights of anger, and that the same thing happens between brothers or sisters? Even if you and I had words, that's no reason for you to be angry with me. You know very well that I love you more than all the maidens in the world, and you know all my secrets as you do my heart."

"Your Majesty spins very fine words," said Plaerdemavida, "but your actions are bad. You want to believe Widow Repose and all her wickedness, and you won't listen to me or anyone else. She was the cause of all this trouble. I remember that night when my lord Tirant broke his leg and Your Highness fainted: there was nothing but tears and anguish. But the Widow was the only one who was glad. Your Excellency has many virtues, but you lack patience."

"Let's stop talking about these things now," said the princess. "Tell me about Tirant: How is he? When can I see him? The happiness he brings me makes me think about him more than I would like to."

"Since the time he left you, all the memories of Your Excellency make him sigh and grieve. You can be sure that no one deserves you as much as Tirant does. And he sends you this letter."

The princess took it very happily, and when she had read it she decided to write an answer:

"I tried to beg you several times not to steal my chastity; and if my words did not move you to pity, my tears should have. But you brought so much pain to your princess. The sound of my last words was carried to the ears of Widow Repose, and the empress came. I don't know how it was that I said, 'Jesus, Jesus, Jesus,' and I threw myself in the duchess' lap because I hated life..."

When she had finished her answer she gave it to Hippolytus. When Hippolytus returned to Tirant, he gave him the letter. Tirant was very pleased to get it. He had paper and ink brought to him, and despite his injury he wrote the following letter:

"Now is the time when all things are at rest, except I who am awake, thinking of Your Highness and how you have forgotten about all the years I have been in love with you. But I give thanks to God for allowing me to know a maiden who is so full of perfection. And I see full well that no one but myself deserves Your Majesty's beauty. If you feel that I am worthy of reply, I am prepared to obey everything Your Excellency commands me."

When Tirant had finished writing the letter he gave it to Hippolytus and begged him to give it to the princess in Plaerdemavida's presence, and to get a reply if possible. Hippolytus gave the letter to the princess as he had been commanded, and the princess took it, very pleased. As the empress came to see her daughter at that moment, she could not read it immediately. But when she saw that the empress was engaged in conversation with Hippolytus, asking him about Tirant's injury, and him answering her, the princess got up from where she had been sitting and went into her chamber with Plaerdemavida to read the letter.

After they had spoken at length about Tirant's illness, the empress said to Hippolytus:

"Your face looks quite altered, Hippolytus, thin and discolored. The illness of such a valiant knight as Tirant must bring grief to all his relatives. I have been suffering greatly too. At night I wake up, filled with anxiety. Then, after I remember his injury, I go back to sleep."

Hippolytus quickly answered:

"If I were near a lady, and found myself in her bed, I wouldn't let her have as much rest as Your Majesty gets, no matter how deeply she slept. But it doesn't surprise me in Your Majesty: you sleep alone, and no one says a word to you. That's what is making my face so thin, not Tirant's illness. Every day I ask Our Lord with all my heart to take away these painful thoughts that I keep having. Only those who know what love is have a real knowledge of what suffering means."

The empress presumed that Hippolytus must be in love and that all the sadness in his face was nothing but the passion of love. She thought also that since Plaerdemavida had said many times that she loved Hippolytus, she must be the one he was troubled about. And the empress unhesitatingly asked Hippolytus who the lady was that was causing him so much grief.

"Tell me, who is bringing you so much sadness?"

"My bitter misfortune," said Hippolytus. "And here, where I am, don't let Your Majesty think that my life is in less danger than Tirant's."

"In case you should tell me," said the empress, "I would keep it to myself always."

"Who would dare reveal his grief," said Hippolytus, "to a lady of such excellence?"

"There is no one," said the empress, "who should not listen to what another wants to say. And the loftier one's position, the more humbly they should listen."

"My lady," said Hippolytus, "since you want to know: love, it's love that I have, and it's not clothing that I can remove."

"I'm not lacking in knowledge," said the empress, "about what you're saying. You say you're in love, and I ask you: with whom?"

"I don't have my five senses," said Hippolytus, "to tell you."

"Oh, man of little understanding" said the empress. "Why don't you say what it is that's making you suffer?"

"There are four things," said Hippolytus, "that surpass all others in excellence, and the fifth is the knowledge of truth. It is Your Majesty whom the heavens have foretold that I should love all the days of my life..."

Having said this he did not dare raise his face again, and he said nothing more. As he was leaving, the empress called him, but because of his shame he did not dare turn around. Hippolytus thought to himself that if she asked him why he didn't stop he would say he did not hear her. He went to his room thinking that he had spoken wrongly and acted even worse, and he was deeply repentant of what he had said.

The empress stood there, thinking about what Hippolytus had told her.

When Hippolytus knew that the empress had gone back to her chambers, he felt both ashamed and frightened at how daring he had been. He wished he were already gone so that he would not have to face the empress again. But he had to return to the palace for the princess's reply. He went into her chambers and found her on Plaerdemavida's knees, with other maidens who felt affection for Tirant. Hippolytus begged her for a reply to the letter he had brought. The princess said to Hippolytus:

"Since the messenger is faithful, I beg you to excuse me from writing my reply. You may tell him that I will make arrangements with the emperor for us to go and see him one day this week, and if it pleases the Divine Being he will soon he well again, and we will be excused from this task."

Hippolytus answered:

"My lady, your heart shows that you have no compassion. From all the harm you have caused him you could tell him just this little bit of good news that he hopes to hear from you."

The princess replied:

"Since I don't want to show my lack of knowledge, I will keep quiet, but your over-loose tongue ought to be answered. Plaerdemavida, pull out three hairs from my head, and give them to Hippolytus so that he will give them to my master, Tirant. And tell him, since I cannot write to him, to take the hairs as his answer."

"God help me if I'll take them," said Hippolytus, "unless you tell me what they mean and why there are three of them and not four, or ten instead of twenty. For God's sake, my lady! Does Your Highness think we are following the old customs when these niceties were the rule? Back then a maiden who had a love-sick swain, and who was in love with him, would give him a bouquet of perfumed flowers or a hair or two from her head, and the poor fellow considered himself very fortunate. I know very well that my lord Tirant would like to take hold of you in bed, naked or in your nightgown, and he wouldn't care a jot if your bed wasn't perfumed. But if Your Majesty is going to give me three hairs to take to Tirant, well, I'm not used to carrying things like that: send them with someone else, and let Your Excellency tell me with what hope they've come out of your head."

"I'll be glad to tell you," said the princess. "One hair stands for the great love I've always had for him above all people in the world, and it was so much that I forgot my father and my mother, and if you press me, I nearly forgot God; and I wanted to offer him my body along with everything I own. The second one stands for all the grief he is causing me. The third one means that I know well how little he loves me. Now you know completely what the hairs mean, and with your wickedness you won't take them with you."

She took them out of his hands, and very angrily tore them apart and threw them on the ground, and tears burst from her eyes and ran down her breasts. When Hippolytus saw that the princess had become angry over such a slight matter, he said with a humble expression:

"It's true that you were held in your mother's chamber, but you were not violated. Tell me, my lady, how can you blame Tirant for having attempted such a singular act? Who could condemn him to any punishment? If he is lost, more than ten thousand soldiers will be lost, and they will be sorely needed to bring the war to a successful conclusion. Look how many men the King of Sicily has at the service of Your Highness; and the Grand-Master of Rhodes, the Viscount of Branches—how many men he's brought. Well, if Tirant weren't here, none of those men would stay. Then you'll see if Widow Repose will fight the battles for you and your father."

To help Hippolytus in Tirant's favor, Plaerdemavida said:

"It would have been better for me if I had never known of Your Majesty's existence. You don't love the person who deserves it as you should. How can I serve you with a willing spirit if I see such ingratitude in you? If Your Excellency could feel that glory that many maidens have experienced, if God would grant that I might show you the glory that lovers feel in this life, and the pleasure it brings with it, then you would be worthy of being among the privileged ones who have loved well, and you would be deserving of eternal praises in this life. But Your Excellency is like a person who smells the odor of meat but does not taste it. If Your Highness would taste its sweetness and the pleasure it brings in this instance, when you died you would rise again in glorious renown. But my lady, since I see that you don't love my lord Tirant, there's no reason for you to love any of his men. There will come a time when you will cry over him and his friends, and you'll tear your eyes from your face, and curse the day and night for the rest of your life. I know that the day Tirant can ride again, seeing Your Highness' great unhappiness he will go back to his country, and all the others will follow him because of the affection they have for him. You will be left all alone as you deserve, and the entire empire will be lost. And when you're dead and you appear before the judgment seat of your Lord, He will ask for an account of your life with words like these:

"'It was by My command that man was made in My image, and from man's rib a female companion was made. And, moreover, I said: Increase and multiply and fill the earth. Carmesina, I have taken your brother from you so that you would be at the head of the empire. Now tell me, what account do you give to me concerning that which I encharged to you? Have you left behind sons to defend the Catholic faith and increase the numbers of Christians?' What are you going to answer?" said Plaerdemavida. "Oh, my lady, you will not be able to give a good reply! I'll tell you what your reply will be: 'Oh Lord, full of mercy and pity! You Who are so merciful, forgive me!' And the guardian angel will make you say these words: 'It is true, Lord, that I loved a knight who was very virtuous in arms, whom Your Holy Majesty sent to us to rescue Your Christian people from the hands of the infidel. I loved him and I held him in great devotion, and I wanted him for a husband, as my beloved. And I had a maiden in my service whose name was Plaerdemavida, who always gave me good advice and I did not want to accept it. She put him in my bed one night and, like a fool, I cried out. And when I realized what was happening I stopped shouting, and was quiet. A widow who heard me scream began to cry out and woke up the entire palace, so a great deal of anguish and pain followed because of my fear. Later they begged me to give in to the knight, but I never would.' And they'll have to leave you in hell along with Widow Repose. And when I leave this life there will be a great celebration in paradise, and they will give me a seat in the eternal glory of the Highest, and as an obedient daughter I will be crowned with the other saints."

The emperor entered the room without anyone seeing him. He stayed near his daughter for a little while, and then he took Hippolytus by the hand, and they spoke of the war and of the captain's illness. As they were talking they passed through a room where the empress was, and at that moment Hippolytus would have liked to have been a day's journey away. When she saw him she smiled and looked at him fondly. Then she got up from where she was sitting and approached the emperor, and the three of them stood, talking of many things. They dwelt especially on the cruel misfortune in which their son departed from this miserable world in the flower of his youth, and the empress began to cry.

Many old knights who formed part of the council entered the chamber, and they consoled the empress. Then they told Hippolytus of the great valor the emperor had shown when they brought him the news that his son had died. The good man, on hearing of the death of his son, had answered the cardinal and the others who brought him the news:

"Be assured that what you are telling me is nothing new, because I bore him to die. It is the law of nature to receive life, and to relinquish it when it is asked of us."

The emperor withdrew to one side of the chamber to speak with some of his council, and Hippolytus remained with the empress. When she saw that he was silent she thought it must be because he felt embarrassed. And she said:

"Although I can't speak to you in as fine a manner as I would like, you will understand it much better than my lips could express it. I beg you to tell me who made you say what you did. Tell me if it came from your master Tirant, so that if I decided to love you he could make better use of the power that he wants. I'm dying to know."

Hippolytus quickly replied, lowering his voice:

"I'll tell you everything. I was with the emperor, and we came into these chambers, and when I saw Your Majesty I nearly fell to the ground. I was afraid the emperor would notice, because at that moment fear and shame were battling within me. Afterward I sighed, and I saw that Your Highness was laughing pleasantly at my sigh. My lady, I beg you not to make me say anything further, but command me to do anything dangerous, and Your Majesty will see how steadfast Hippolytus is. As for what Your Majesty said about Tirant, I swear to you that neither Tirant nor my confessor (which is even worse) knew any such thing about me."

"Hippolytus, you must tell me your thoughts openly. Love doesn't recognize nobility, lineage or equality; it doesn't differentiate between people in high and low positions. You can be sure that no matter how criminal your words were, I wouldn't tell them to the emperor or to anyone else on earth."

Hippolytus plucked up his courage, and in a whisper, he said:

"Because of my great attraction for you, my lady, I often wanted to reveal my deep love for Your Majesty. But fear stopped me from telling you my feelings until now, since you are the most excellent of all things excellent. But if love makes me speak indiscreetly, you must suffer it patiently, and must punish me with tender words. Tell me, I beg you, how I must behave in your honor."

The empress replied:

"You've given my heart many worries and cares. I'm wondering what has given you hope of having me since the distance between our ages is so great. If it became known, what would they say about me? That I've fallen in love with my grandson. Any maiden would be overjoyed to be loved by you. But I would rather someone else had your love, without any crime or infamy, than for me to perish because of love."

The empress could say no more since the emperor had gotten up from where he was sitting. He went over to the empress and took her by the hand, and they went in to dine.

That night Hippolytus could not talk to the princess, but he spoke with Plaerdemavida, and she said to him:

"What were you talking to the empress about for so long? You two are always together."

"It's nothing," said Hippolytus. "She was just asking about our captain."

Early the next day, Hippolytus left without a reply from the princess. When Tirant saw him, he said:

"It's been five days since I've seen you."

"My lord," said Hippolytus, "the emperor made me stay there, and so did the princess, and while we were out walking we talked about you. Everyone intends to come see you. That's why the princess decided not to give you any answer, because her visit will be so soon."

Tirant said:

"That is very good news."

He had the doctors come, and begged them to take him to the city since he was feeling so well.

"I can tell you, truly, that I'll get better in one day in the city than I could here in ten. Do you know why? I was born and raised near the sea, and sea air is very healthy for me."

All the doctors agreed, and two of them went to tell the emperor. The emperor then rode to where the captain was, and Tirant was taken to the city in four days on a bier carried on the shoulders of four men.

When he was in his chambers, the empress and all her ladies went to see him. They were very happy that he was feeling better, and all the ladies from the palace as well as the city often visited him. But the empress, who was warned by one of her maidens she trusted much more than the others, seldom left her daughter alone when she was in Tirant's room, and so they had little time to talk about their love. In the meantime Plaerdemavida came every day, trying to find a way for the battle to come to a conclusion.

Let us stop talking about Tirant now, and return to the encampment.

When the truce ended, the war began, cruel and savage, for the Turks knew about Tirant's injury. Every day they came near the city of Saint George where the camp was, and every day there were fierce battles, and many men from both sides were killed. Each day the emperor wrote to them to tell them how Tirant was, and to encourage them. He told them that Tirant was getting out of bed now to strengthen his leg and to help him recover. They all felt comforted, especially the Duke of Macedonia, who loved him dearly.

Tirant was getting better daily, and he could walk through his chambers with the aid of a staff. Almost every day the ladies came to see him and keep him company, and the princess entertained him. And do not think that Tirant wanted to be healed very soon; this was because of the lovely sight that he had daily of the princess. He had few thoughts about going to war; instead it was his wish to fulfill his desire with his lady, and as for the war—let someone go there who wanted to.

As the emperor and the empress were in Tirant's room, he could not talk to the princess without being overheard by the empress. So he called Hippolytus and quietly said to him:

"Go outside and then come back in shortly and go to the empress's side. Start talking to her about whatever you think will please her most, and I will see if I can talk to the princess about my love for her."

Hippolytus returned as he had agreed, and went to the empress, and quietly said to her:

"I always want to be near Your Excellency. This is because I love you so much, and I beg you to grant me a boon that will increase my honor and my fame. If I am loved by Your Majesty, then there will be no one more fortunate than I."

And he said no more.

The empress replied:

"Your great virtue is making me go beyond the bounds of chastity. If you swear to me by all that is holy that you will say nothing of this to the emperor or to anyone, you will have everything you like. In the still of night wait for me quietly on the roof near my chamber. And if you come, have no doubts, for I love you dearly, and I will not be late unless death itself stands in my way."

Hippolytus tried to tell her about one thing he was afraid of, and the empress told him that to think of every possible danger was a sign of weakness in spirit.

"Do what I tell you, and don't worry about another thing now."

Hippolytus answered:

"My lady, I will be happy to do everything Your Majesty commands me."

When they had finished their conversation the empress left Tirant's lodgings with all the other ladies. And when they were in the palace, the empress said:

"Let us go visit the emperor."

When they were together with him they conversed pleasantly. Afterward the empress stood up, feeling the anguish of her new love, and she said to Carmesina:

"Stay here with these maidens and keep your father company."

The empress then went to her chambers and told her maidens to have the stewards come, as she wanted to change the satin curtains and put up others fringed in silk, saying:

"The emperor told me that he would like to come here, and I want to entertain him a little since he has not come for a long time."

She quickly had the entire chamber furnished with linens of silk brocade. Then she had the chamber and the bed sprinkled with perfume.

After they had eaten, the empress retired, saying she had a headache, and in everyone's presence a maiden named Eliseu said to her:

"My lady, does Your Highness want me to call the doctors to help minister to you?"

"Do as you like," said the empress, "but summon them in such a way that the emperor does not find out, so that he will have no excuse for not coming tonight,"

The doctors came quickly and took her pulse, and they found it very rapid, because she hoped to do battle with a young knight, and she was fearful. The doctors said:

"My lady, Your Majesty should take a few sweetened hempseeds with a glass of malmsey: that will help your headache and make you sleep."

"As far as sleeping is concerned, I don't think I'll do much of that with my illness. The way I'm feeling I'll probably be tossing and turning all over the bed."

"My lady," said the doctors, "if that happens to Your Majesty, send for us right away. Or if you wish we'll stand watch at the door to your chamber or there inside so that we can look at your face from time to time. And we'll do this all night long."

"I won't accept that offer right now," said the empress. "I want the whole bed to myself, and I don't want any of you looking at my face. The illness I have won't stand for anybody to be watching."

The doctors left. When they were at the door they told her not to forget the comfits and to moisten them well with malmsey. The empress was so obedient that she ate a large box of them. Then she had her bed sprinkled with perfume, and she had civet put on the sheets and pillows. When this was done and she was perfumed, she told her maidens to go to sleep and to close the door to their chamber.

In the empress's chamber there was a sitting room where she always went to dress, and in the sitting room was a door that opened out to the roof where Hippolytus was. When she got out of bed Eliseu heard her and quickly got up, thinking something was wrong, and when she was in the chamber she said:

"Why did Your Highness get out of bed? Are you feeling worse?"

"No," said the empress. "I'm fine, but I forgot to say the devout prayer that I always pray every night."

Eliseu said:

"My lady, would you be so kind as to tell it to me?"

"I'll be happy to," said the empress. "This is it: At night, at the first star you see, you must kneel down on the ground and say three 'Our Fathers' and three 'Hail Marys' in reverence to the three Kings of the Orient, that just as they were guided and guarded while they were watching and sleeping, and when they were in the hands of King Herod, that they will give you grace to be free from infancy and so that all your affairs will be prosperous and increase in all that is good. Now don't disturb me in my devotions."

The maiden went to her bed and the empress went into the sitting room. When she saw that the maiden was in bed she put a dress of green velvet lined with sable on over her chemise. Then she opened the door to the roof and saw Hippolytus crouched down so that no one would see him. That made her very pleased as she thought that her honor would be safe. When Hippolytus saw her, he got up quickly and went to her. He knelt on the ground and kissed her hands and tried to kiss her feet. But the worthy lady would not permit it, and instead kissed him again and again on the mouth. She then took his hand and showed him great love and told him to come to her chamber. Hippolytus said:

"My lady, Your Majesty must excuse me, but I will not go to your chamber until my desire has a taste of its future glory."

And he took her in his arms, and lay her on the floor, and there they enjoyed the climax of their love.

Afterward they went into the sitting room very happily. Hippolytus, with great joy, gave her true peace, and with a happy spirit and loving expression, he said:

"If I dared to say what glory I feel at this moment with the great perfection I've found in Your Majesty, I don't believe my tongue would have enough power to express it."

The empress, smiling, replied:

"Although my mind finds itself tormented, I will not complain about you, or even less about God or myself, because I have been able to win you."

"My lady," said Hippolytus, "now is not the time for words. Let us go to bed, and there we will speak of other matters that will increase your delight, and will be of great consolation to me."

After he had said this, Hippolytus quickly stood naked. Then he went to the genteel lady and removed the clothing she had on so that she was left in her chemise. And whoever saw her in this way would recognize that she was like a maiden, and that she possessed as much beauty as can be found in this world. Her daughter, Carmesina, resembled her in many ways, but not in all, for this lady's beauty, in her time, surpassed that of her daughter. The young gallant took her by the arm and placed her on the bed, and there they remained, talking and sporting as lovers do. When half the night had passed, the lady heaved a deep sigh.

"Why is Your Majesty sighing" said Hippolytus. "Is it because I did not satisfy you?"

"It is quite the opposite," said the empress. "The feelings I have toward you have increased even more. At first I thought of you as a good man, and now I find you much better and more valiant. The reason for my sighing has been only that I am grieved because they will hold you as a heretic."

"What, my lady!" said Hippolytus. "Why should I be considered a heretic?"

"Because," said the empress, "you have fallen in love with your mother."

"'My lady,'" said Hippolytus, "no one knows how worthy you are but me."

The two lovers spoke of these things and of many others, with all the delights and sweet words that two people in love enjoy. They did not sleep the whole night through, and morning was nearly upon them. The empress had spoken the truth when she told the doctors that she would sleep very little that night. Now, tired from staying awake, they slept, for the new day had arrived. When the day was fully upon them the maiden Eliseu, who was completely dressed by now, entered the empress's chambers to ask her how she was, and if she wanted anything. When she approached the bed she saw a man lying at the side of the empress, her arm under the gallant's head, and his mouth to her breast.

"Oh, Holy Mary help me!" said Eliseo. "Who is this traitor who has deceived my lady?" She was tempted to cry out, loudly: "Kill the traitor who, by cunning and deception, has entered this chamber to possess the delights of this bed!" Then she thought that no one would be so bold as to enter there against the empress's will. She tried as hard as she could to see who it was, but it was impossible because he had his head hidden. She was afraid that the other maidens might enter the chamber to wait on the empress as they usually did, so Eliseu went in to where they were sleeping, and said to them:

"My lady bids you not to leave the room so that you will not make any noise, because sleep has not yet satisfied her eyes."

After half an hour had passed the doctors came to see how the empress was. The maiden went to the door and said the lady was resting because during the night she had been a little ill.

"We will stay here," said the doctors, "until Her Majesty awakens. That is the emperor's command."

The maiden did not know how to remedy the situation, nor whether she should awaken her or not. She was filled with indecision until the emperor knocked on the chamber door. The maiden, upset, and without sufficient patience or discretion, went anxiously to the bed and cried out, softly:

"Wake up, my lady, wake up! Death is approaching! Your poor husband is knocking at the door and he knows that you have offended him. Who is this cruel man who lies at your side and brings so much grief? Is he an unknown king? I pray to God Almighty that I will see him with a crown of fire on his head. If he is a duke I hope to see him end his days in prison. If he is a marquis, I hope to see his hands and feet eaten. If he is a count, he should die by evil weapons. If he is a viscount, may a Turk's sword slice him through from his head down to his navel. And if he is a knight, sailing at the sea's will, may he end his days in the deep."

When the empress found herself awakened by such an evil noise, which was worse than a trumpet, she lay motionless, unable to utter a word. Hippolytus did not understand the maiden's words, but he did understand her tone of voice. And so that no one would recognize him, he put his head under the blanket. When he saw what great anguish his lady was in he put his arm around her and made her duck under the blanket, asking her why she was so frightened.

"Oh, my son!" said the empress. "Get up: the emperor is at the door, and your life and mine are in God's hands at this very moment. And if I cannot speak to you, or you to me, forgive me with all your heart, as I do you, because now I see that this day has been the beginning and the end of all happiness and delight, and the final hour of your life and mine."

When Hippolytus heard the empress saying these words, he began to feel very sorry for himself, because he had never been in a situation like this before. Young as he was, he joined the empress, serving her up tears instead of advice and aid. But he begged the maiden to bring him the sword that was in the sitting room, and plucking up his courage, he said:

"Here I shall become a martyr before Your Majesty, and deliver up my spirit."

At that instant the empress heard no noise whatsoever, and she said to Hippolytus:

"Go hide in that sitting room, my son. I will delay them, and you can escape with your life."

"I wouldn't abandon Your Majesty even if they gave me the whole Greek Empire four times over. I will give my life and everything I have before I leave Your Highness, and I beg you to kiss me as a token of faith," said Hippolytus.

When the empress heard these words her pain increased, and with the increase of pain she felt her love increasing. As she heard no noise at all she went to the chamber door to see if she could hear soldiers or some other bad sign. Through a small crack in the door she saw the emperor and the doctors discussing her illness, and she realized that there was no danger. She ran back to Hippolytus and pulling his ears, she kissed him hard. Then she said:

"My son, by the great love I have for you I beg you to go into that sitting room until I can make up an excuse for the emperor and the doctors."

"My lady," said Hippolytus, "in all things I will be more obedient to you than if you had bought me as a captive, but don't ask me to leave here, because I don't know if they will harm you."

"Don't worry," said the empress. "It's not what Eliseu told me, at all. There would be a great uproar in the palace if it were."

Hippolytus quickly went into the sitting room, and the empress got back into her bed and had the doors to the chamber opened. The emperor and the doctors went to her bed and asked about her illness and how she had spent the night. The empress answered that her headache and the pain in her stomach had not let her sleep all night long, and she had not been able to rest until the stars in the sky had disappeared.

"Then, since I could no longer stay awake, I slept, and now I feel much happier than before. And I believe that if that pleasant dream had lasted longer, I would feel even better. But in this world a person cannot be completely happy: with the painful awakening this maiden has given me, my spirit is in more anguish than I can say. If I could go back to the way I was, it would be a great consolation to me. I could touch and hold in my arms the things I love and have loved most in this world."

The emperor said:

"Tell me, my lady, what was it that you held in your arms?"

The empress answered:

"My lord, the greatest blessing that I have ever had in the world. I fell asleep, and soon it seemed to me that I was up on the roof in my chemise, saying the prayer that I always pray to the three Kings of the Orient. And when I had finished the blessed prayer, I heard a voice telling me: 'Do not go, for in this place you will possess the grace you are asking for.' And soon I saw my beloved son coming toward me, accompanied by many gentlemen, all dressed in white, and they held Hippolytus by the hand. Surrounding me, the two of them caught up my hands and kissed them, and they wanted to kiss my feet, but I would not let them. And as we sat on the roof we exchanged many words which gave me great delight, and they were so many and so delicious that they will always remain in my heart. Afterward we entered the chamber, and I held him by the hand. My son and I got into bed, and I put my right arm around his shoulders, and his mouth kissed my breasts. I have never had such a pleasant sleep. And my son said to me, 'My lady, since you cannot have me in this miserable world, take my brother Hippolytus as your son, for I love him as much as I love Carmesina.' And when he said these words he was lying beside me, and Hippolytus was obediently kneeling in the middle of the chamber. I asked him where his room was, and he told me that he was among the martyred knights in paradise, because he had died in battle against the infidel. And I could not ask him more because Eliseu woke me up with a sound more strident than a trumpet."

"Didn't I say," said the emperor, "that all her talk was only about her son?"

"Oh, my lord," said the empress, "it has hurt no one more than me. I held him in this arm; his pleasant mouth was touching my breasts; and the dreams you have in the morning often come true. I think he still may not have left. I would like to try to go back to sleep to see if he will talk to me again."

"I beg you," said the emperor, "put this madness out of your head, and get up out of bed."

"I beg you, my lord," said the empress, "for my health and pleasure, let me rest a little. My eyes are clouded from lack of sleep."

"My lord," said the doctors, "it would be better if Your Majesty would leave and we let her sleep, because if we take this pleasure from her it would not be surprising if her illness got much worse."

The emperor left, and so did all the maidens in the chamber except Eliseu. When the doors were closed the empress had Hippolytus come back in, and she said to the maiden:

"Since fortune has permitted you to know about this matter, I command you to serve Hippolytus, even more than myself, with all your heart. Stay in that sitting room until we have slept a little. I shall favor you more highly than all the others, and I will marry you to a man of higher station than the others. Afterward Hippolytus will give you so many of his possessions that you will be very satisfied."

"Heaven help me," said Eliseu, "but I have no desire to serve Hippolytus, and even less to love and honor him, but since Your Majesty commands me, I'll do it. Otherwise I wouldn't stoop to the floor to pick up a needle for him. I tell you, since the time I saw him lying next to Your Majesty, I have never felt more ill will for any man in the world than I feel for him. I would like to see a lion eat up his eyes, his face, and all the rest of him!"

Hippolytus answered:

"Maiden, I never meant to make you angry. I want to love you and do more for you than for all the other maidens in the world."

"Do it for the others," said Eliseu, "but don't bother with me. I don't want anything that belongs to you."

And she quickly went into the sitting room, and began to cry. The two lovers stayed in bed so long that it was nearly time for Vespers when they got up, and they found the maiden still crying. When she saw them coming into the sitting room she stopped her wailing, and the empress consoled her and begged her not to say anything about what Hippolytus had done.

"My lady," said the maiden, "Your Majesty needn't worry about me. I would die before I'd tell anybody anything without your command. As for the second thing, have no fear: I will serve Hippolytus in every way I can, out of consideration for Your Majesty."

The empress was satisfied, and she left Hippolytus in the sitting room and went back to her bed. Then she commanded the chamber doors to be opened. Soon her daughter was there, along with all the maidens, the emperor and the doctors. And again she told them about her pleasant dream.

The meal was served, and the empress ate like someone who was tired from walking a long distance. The maiden was diligent in serving Hippolytus, and she gave him some pheasants to eat. And when he did not want to eat, she begged him on behalf of her lady. Hippolytus spoke to her and joked, but she would not answer him unless it was something to do with her service.

Here was the empress, not moving from her bed until the following day when the emperor had already eaten lunch. After she had dressed she went to chapel to hear mass, and there was a great dispute among the priests as to whether they should read the scriptures, because it was already past noon.

Hippolytus remained in the sitting room with this pleasure for a week. When the lady saw that he was quite exhausted, she asked him to leave, telling him to return to her chamber another day after he had rested, and he could take her as he pleased. And from a box where she kept her jewelry the empress took out a gold chain, and put it around his neck, saying:

"Pray God that I may live, Hippolytus, because I will be surprised if I don't put a crown on your head before many years have passed. Now, for love of me, wear this. Since it will be in view you will remember someone who loves you as much as she does her own life."

Hippolytus knelt to the ground, thanked her, and kissed her hand and her mouth and said:

"My lady, how could Your Majesty deprive yourself of such an exquisite jewel to give it to me? If it were mine I would give it to Your Highness where it would be put to better use. I beg you to keep it."

The empress answered:

"Hippolytus, never refuse what your lover gives you."

"Then, my lady, how will you command my life? What do you want me to do?"

"I beg you to leave. I am terribly afraid that tomorrow the emperor may enter this sitting room and find you here. Go now, and let this fear of mine pass. There will be other days when you can return."

Let us leave these endearments of hers for Hippolytus now, and return to Tirant to see how his love is doing. When his leg was mended he often went to the palace without anyone's help. His only obstacle was that the doctors would not let him go as often as he would have liked. The emperor often asked them how many days it would be before he would be entirely well so that he could leave for battle. They told him that he would soon be well enough to ride. When Tirant knew how much the emperor wanted him to go, he felt great anguish because he could not have his desire or at least some contact with the princess.

The passion that the Widow carried inside had not been revealed until that time. But when she learned from the emperor that Tirant would be leaving soon, she thought that she might be able to persuade him to take her along to the camp with the excuse that she would serve him there. And if this was impossible, her diabolical plans were to spread a seed throughout the court called discord. She went to the princess and said:

"Did you know, my lady, that Tirant told me as we were leaving mass that he wanted to talk to me. I told him that I would be glad to talk to him if I could have Your Majesty's permission. I think he realizes that he will be leaving soon, and he wants to see if he can commit some treachery against Your Highness. He is thinking to himself: If he can do it, well and good, and if he can't, then when he's gone he'll forget all about you. He told me the other day that that's the way he is, and he laughed as though he had said something wonderful."

"Then let's do this," said the princess. "You go talk to him, and we'll see if there is some treachery in his heart. Your advice is good: I should be careful with him."

"But, my lady," said the Widow, "if I'm to find out what's really in his heart, you must not leave this room until I come back."

The Widow went out, called a page and told him:

"Tell Tirant that the princess is here, in this chamber, and is very anxious to talk to him."

The page quickly went to tell him. When Tirant heard that his lady had asked him to come, he did not wait for anyone to go with him. The Widow was watching carefully to see when he would come, and as soon as she saw him she pretended to be coming out of the princess's chamber at that very moment, and she went up to him and said:

"Unfortunately, the empress just took the princess to her chambers, and they are talking right now. I asked her to send for you because just as Jesus Christ enlightened his disciples, so you spread light to everyone whenever you are in the palace, and as soon as you leave we feel sad. The princess told me to come and keep you company until the empress is gone. So let's sit down until Her Highness comes: I don't want you to hurt your leg on my account."

They sat in the drawing room, and Tirant said:

"Calling to mind, my lady, what you just said to me, the consolation you feel when you see me, I thank you very much for saying that. Take this chain as proof of my affection, I beg you, so that when you look at it you'll think of me, because I want to do a great deal for you."

The Widow answered:

"There's no one who doesn't know how you hurt your leg, but because of their situation they don't want to offend you or make you angry, and because of the war they hide their feelings and pretend not to know anything. If they were certain there would be peace, Carmesina would be the first to throw you into everlasting and bitter grief. Are you so blind that you can't see the dishonest things that are plotted and carried out in this palace? It all seems so vile and abominable to me that I won't agree to any of it. That's why they don't like me. I know for a fact that you're not highly regarded the way you should be. Tell me, wouldn't it be better for you to love a woman who was expert in the art of loving, and very honest, even if she weren't a virgin? She would follow you across the sea and over land, in war and in peace. She would serve you in your tents both night and day, and would never think of anything but how to please you."

"Tell me, my lady," said Tirant, "who is the woman who would perform such remarkable services for me?"

"Oh, wretched me!" said the Widow. "Why are you trying to make me suffer more than I already do? Haven't I said enough? Don't pretend that you don't understand what's so clear. I've tried to find a time when we wouldn't be interrupted by anyone to reveal my pain to you. It seems to me that I've made my intention known to you very clearly, and the knight who is so graciously offered such a gift can feel very fortunate."

Tirant did not hesitate to reply:

"To satisfy you, I'll answer your kind words. It makes me angry that I can't do what you are asking because your words are filled with so much love. But my free will is captive, and even if I wanted to, my five senses would not allow it."

"Everything I've told you was only to test your patience, and to show you, Lord Tirant, how much I want to serve you. I think you should be aware of all the things you don't know. I don't want you to be deceived by the princess's actions: she no longer has any honor, and she has none of her father's or her mother's honor either. She could have satisfied her appetites honestly with a valiant and virtuous knight like you, or with many others who are in love with her, but the sky, the earth, the sea and the sands abominate the sin she has committed (and still commits daily). Only Our Lord would permit such an abominable crime of adultery without punishing her! If you knew what I know you would spit in her face.

"But why should I try to exaggerate such an ugly crime with unnecessary words? She has become involved with Lauseta—that's his name. He's a black slave, a Moorish gardener who takes care of the orchard. And don't think, Your Grace, that all these things I've told you are simply fables, because I'll let you see it with your own eyes. She has made me live with this enormous pain for a long time. How many kinds of herbs have I gone to pick, and then placed them inside her to destroy the fetus in her infamous stomach! Oh wretch, the poor thing was punished because of my sin! And its body wasn't buried, but instead made its trip down the river. What else could I do so that the grandchild would not be seen by the emperor, its grandfather? She has the pleasure, if it can be called that, and I have the blame."

Tirant, with all the melancholy he felt, said:

"Widow, your words have gone straight to my miserable heart. They hurt me more deeply than I have ever been hurt before. I beg you, virtuous lady, show me the cause of my pain, because otherwise I couldn't believe words that sound so unreasonable. It seems impossible that such a celestial person would freely place her beauty in the hands of a black savage."

Then he was silent. Widow Repose was very worried because Tirant did not fully believe her false words. During this conversation the emperor came into the chamber, and when he saw Tirant, he took him by the hand, and they both went into a room to talk about the war. The Widow was left alone, and she began to say to herself:

"Since Tirant did not believe me, this deception I have planned won't succeed. But I'll make him give in to me, even if I have to sell my soul to the devil to do it."

Furious, she swept into the princess's chamber. Then, feigning laughter, she showed her the gold chain Tirant had given her, and she said:

"You'd be astonished, my lady, if you knew his latest whim. He wants to bring a galley here, and carry you off to his land by force."

And she continued to invent stories almost in mockery. When the princess saw that she was mocking Tirant, she became inwardly very angry, and she left and went to her sitting room. She began to think a great deal about Tirant and how deeply she loved him, and of the gifts that he gave to her ladies because of her. The thought of how much she loved him made her reflect deeply, and brought her bitter pain. After thinking for a long time, she dressed and went out to the hall to talk to Tirant, because she knew that he would soon have to leave for the field of battle.

Widow Repose waited for Tirant, and said to him:

"My captain, I would like to have your word that you will not tell the princess, even in jest, what I said to you. Before twenty-four hours have gone by I will let you see it with your own eyes."

"Widow," said Tirant, "I will be very happy if you show me. And so that you will have complete confidence in me, I promise by the blessed Saint George, in whose name I hold the honor of chivalry, not to tell a soul."

As the emperor turned he saw the Widow, and said to her:

"Go quickly and tell the empress and my daughter to go to the orchard right away. I'll be waiting for them there."

Soon all the ladies were with the emperor, and they talked about many things, including how the emperor had sent the order to the camp for two thousand lancers to come and accompany the captain. When the princess heard the news she became very agitated, and pretending that she had a headache, she said:

"I will not deprive myself just because the captain is here; I'll let my hair down even though he's present."

Then she let down all her hair, allowing it to hang loose—and it was the most beautiful hair any maiden ever had. When Tirant saw it in all its splendor he was astonished, and his love doubled in strength. The princess was dressed that day in a skirt of white damask. At that moment her hands were struggling with the cord of her skirt, and she seemed to be in great anguish as she walked alone through the orchard. The emperor tried to question her about her illness, and asked if she wanted the doctors to come. She answered no, that:

"My illness requires neither doctors nor medicine."

At this moment Widow Repose got up from where she was sitting, and taking a companion and two squires along as her escorts, she went to a painter's house and told him:

"Since the festival of Corpus Christi is near, I would like to put on a play. You're the best painter in the world: Could you make a mask of flesh color according to my instructions? It should be over a fine, black skin that would look like Lauseta, the gardener of our orchard. It should have hair on its face, some white and some black, and I'll put gloves on my hands so that I will appear entirely black."

"Madam," answered the painter, "that can be done, but I have a great deal of work right now. However, if you pay me well, I'll put aside all my other work so that I can serve you."

The Widow reached into her purse and gave him thirty ducats in gold so that he would do a good job. And he made it with the exact shape and features of Lauseta.

When the princess had strolled through the garden at length, she saw Lauseta pruning an orange tree, because it was his job to work in the garden, and she went up to him to talk to him. The Widow, who had returned by now, was watching Tirant, and she made a sign to him so that he would notice that his lady was talking to the Negro, Lauseta. Tirant turned around (for he was at the emperor's side), and saw the princess speaking animatedly with the black gardener, and he said to himself:

"Oh, that wicked Widow! She's still trying to make me believe that what she told me is the truth! No matter what she says or does, no one can tell me that the princess would do such a terrible thing, and nothing in the world will make me believe it unless I see it with my own eyes."

At that moment the emperor called a maiden and said to her:

"Come here, Praxidis,"—for that was her name. "Go over to my daughter and ask her to call the captain and tell him that she wants him to leave for the camp soon. Often young knights will do more for ladies than they will for themselves."

The princess replied that she would, since His Majesty had asked her to. After she had spent a while talking with Lauseta about the orange trees and the myrtles, she went back to strolling through the garden. When she was near the emperor she called to Tirant and told him that she was tired, and she asked him to take her arm so they could walk through the garden together. God knows how happy Tirant felt when the princess said this to him. And when they were some distance from the others, Tirant said:

"I have only you in my thoughts now, and I spend day and night thinking of you. If fortune would like to have a little pity on me, let it allow me to have only a part of my desire, because then I will become the most glorious knight who ever lived. All I need is a little hope from Your Excellency."

The virtuous lady kept her pain secret, and replied:

"Tirant, my lord, harbor no doubt whatsoever about what I tell you, because even if I have occasionally been cruel with you, I don't want you to think I have not always been with you in spirit. I have always loved you and looked on you as a god, and I can tell you that as my age increases so does my love. And now the time has come when you can know fully whether I love you, for I want to give you the prize of your love. And I beg you, please, to guard my honor as you do your own life."

Tirant's heart was filled with happiness when he saw that this lofty lady had shown her great love for him, and that he was on the path of possessing the crown of the Empire of Greece. He felt that he could conquer the entire world, and he wanted to tell his cousin Diafebus, the Duke of Macedonia, about it, because he thought everyone would feel just as delighted as he did. And as a greater pledge, he took out a reliquary he carried, and he made the princess place her hands there, asking her to declare that she would marry him, and she very happily swore it. Then Tirant said:

"My lady, I make the same oath to be faithful and true to you and never to forget you for anyone else in the world."

When all this had been done, Tirant knelt down on the ground to kiss her hands because he was more afraid of offending her than of a saint. The princess said:

"To keep my honor and my reputation I am holding back what you most desire. After your great victory, we will take that sweet, delicious fruit of love which is plucked in matrimony, and you will wear the crown of the Empire of Greece."

In a trembling voice, Tirant said:

"I am so anxious to have what I desire most in the world that every hour I wait seems like a thousand years. I would like to change that future time to the present."

The princess, with a kind face, quickly answered:

"I cannot completely resist your entreaties without offending you. But shame and fear hold me back, telling me to keep myself from losing what I will never be able to recover. I beg you, let us leave this conversation so the emperor will not begin to wonder about me. You talk to Plaerdemavida, and whatever you decide I will agree to."

They kissed many times without anyone seeing them, because the orange trees were between them and the emperor, and protected them from everyone's view. When they returned to the emperor, the princess saw him deep in thought and said to him:

"My lord, what are you thinking about?"

The emperor answered:

"My daughter, I want to hold a celebration tomorrow in Tirant's honor. For every battle he has won on land and on sea, I want that many flags placed in our Church of Santa Sofia, and for every castle, villa and city he has conquered, I want that many standards placed around the high altar with Tirant's coat of arms. For he has brought this empire so many benefits, showing himself to be truly a lover of the public good and a conqueror of the world."

The emperor sent for all those in his council and told them what he wanted, and they all praised him, saying it would be a very good thing to do. When they had made their calculations they found that in four and one half years he had conquered three hundred seventy-two villas, cities and castles.

When the emperor held his council and Tirant found out that he was discussing these things, he did not want to be present, and he went to his chambers. On leaving the orchard, Tirant said to Hippolytus:

"Tell Plaerdemavida to go out to the great hall. I have to talk to her."

Hippolytus took the message, and she quickly went there. Tirant embraced her, and smiling, he took her hand. When they had sat down by a window he said:

"I have been with Her Highness and we have exchanged many words of love, and she promised to do whatever you and I decided. I was to tell you all my concerns, and tonight I would speak with Her Majesty. We held hands and solemnly swore that as long as she and I should live I would be her servant, husband and lord, and I would have a resting place of perpetual glory and delight in her chambers, in her bed."

JOANOT MARTORELL

Plaerdemavida listened to Tirant. She thought for a moment, and then said:

"I was not born among the lower classes in Rome. My mother was born in that city, and my ancestors were noble citizens of Rome. Tirant, lord of the world, why did you speak to me so timidly? Is Your Grace unaware of what you have in me? My heart, my body, my will and all my thoughts have no other purpose in this world than to serve Your Grace. I won't say anything more to you because a knight who is waiting to go into battle shouldn't be worn out by words. But when the emperor is dining I'll go to your rooms and give you news that will please you very much."

Then Tirant kissed her eyes and her face with great joy. He left her, and Plaerdemavida went back to the garden where she found the princess with the emperor. The emperor went into the upper chambers, and Plaerdemavida and the princess entertained themselves and decided what time Tirant should come. The princess told her everything that she had said and done with Tirant, and Plaerdemavida was very glad to see how happy her lady was.

The hour arrived when the emperor was to dine, and Tirant did not forget to go to the palace quickly. He met Plaerdemavida coming down the stairs to his quarters. She told him how it was to be done, and what time he should come. Then they went back the way they had come.

After everyone in the palace had retired and was asleep, the princess got up from her bed, and the only ones with her were Plaerdemavida and another named Lady Montblanc who knew all about the affair. The princess put on a dress that the emperor had ordered made for her wedding. Neither he nor anyone else had ever seen it, and it was the most beautiful dress anyone had ever seen at that time. Her gown was of crimson satin embroidered with pearls. Her mantle was lined with ermine, and on her head she wore a stunning imperial crown. Plaerdemavida and Lady Montblanc took lighted torches in their hands, and waited for Tirant to come. When the clock struck eleven (which was the hour that he was awaiting so anxiously), he quickly went to the garden gate. Climbing the stairs to the sitting room, he found Lady Montblanc with the lighted torch, and as soon as she saw him she knelt before him and said:

"Of knights, the best, and the most beloved in the world by a beautiful lady."

And Tirant replied:

"Maiden, may your wishes be fulfilled."

They both went up to the sitting room and waited there until Plaerdemavida came in, happier and more content than Paris was when he carried off Helen. They went into one chamber while the princess was coming in from another door, and they met very happily, and Tirant knelt on the ground, and she did likewise. They remained like this for some time. Then they kissed, and their kiss was so delicious that one could have walked a mile while they had their lips pressed together. Plaerdemavida saw the danger in their dilatoriness, and went up to them and said:

"I declare you good and loyal lovers, but I will not leave this battlefield until you are lying in bed together. And I won't deem you a knight if you make peace before spilling blood."

They stood up, and the princess took the crown from her head and placed it on Tirant's head. Then she fell to her knees and said:

"Oh Lord God, Jesus Christ, all powerful and merciful, Who, having pity on mankind, came down from heaven to earth and took on human form in the virgin womb of the most Holy Virgin Mary, Your Mother and Our Lady, and Who died on the tree of the true cross to redeem the sins of mankind, and came back to life on the third day by Your own power, in a glorified body, true God and true man! May it please Your most Holy Majesty to allow my lord Tirant to possess this crown, with the title and reign over all the Empire of Greece, after the death of my father, inasmuch as Your divine goodness has granted him the grace to have retaken it and freed it from the infidel. And may this be done in honor, praise and glory of Your most Holy Majesty and of Your most Holy Mother, and for the benefit of the holy Catholic faith."

When she had finished her prayer, the princess got up and took some scales that the emperor used for weighing gold coins, and she said:

"My lord Tirant, good fortune has decided that on this day I will submit to your power of my own free will, and without my mother's and father's consent, or that of the people of Greece. Here I hold some scales of perfection: on the right side is love, honor and chastity; on the other side is shame, infamy and grief. Choose which of these pleases you most, Tirant."

As one who always wished to serve honor, Tirant took the scale on the right hand side, and said:

"Before I was given news of Your Majesty I had heard of your virtues, which as I now know would be too many to mention. For Your Highness practices virtue continually and has such great beauty that it is far greater than that of all other ladies in the world."

Then, holding up the scale on the right, he said:

"I place love and honor above the crown and the scale with all the firmness that it has. And I beg you dearly to speak no more of this. Rather, with true will, let our marriage take place."

The princess answered:

"You have embraced the scale of love and honor. Now I beg you to preserve my chastity, and for the present do not violate it. Otherwise, what will the emperor say, and my mother, and the entire country who think of me as a saint? What will they say of me? There will be no one who can trust Carmesina. And when you are gone away, if I am offended by anyone, who will I go to for help? A brother or a husband? And if I become with child, what counsel could I take?"

Tirant could no longer withstand the tears of the princess, and, smiling, he replied:

"My lady, I have been waiting so long to see you in your nightgown or completely naked on a bed. I don't want your crown or your kingdom. But give me all my rights which belong to me, as our Holy Mother Church commands with the following words: 'If a maiden gives herself in true matrimony, he who is able but does not have copulation after marriage is in mortal sin.' As for me, my lady, if you love my body you should love my soul too, and Your Majesty should not willfully cause me to sin. You know very well that if a man goes into battle while he's in mortal sin, God will not come to his aid."

And as he was saying these words Tirant was not slow about removing her clothing: he unfastened her skirt while he kissed her again and again, saying:

"Every hour that we're not in bed is like a year to me. Since God has given me such a treasure, I don't want to lose it."

Plaerdemavida exclaimed:

"Oh, my lord! Why wait until you are in bed? Do it on top of her clothes so that they can be a more certain witness. We'll close our eyes and say that we saw nothing. If you wait for Her Highness to take off her clothes you'll have to wait until morning. Afterward Our Heavenly Father could punish you as a knight unworthy of love. Heaven help you if you should fail at a time like this. Seeing that you were such a polite lover, Our Heavenly Father wouldn't want to give you a morsel like this again, nor would He have anything to give you. There's no man in the world who wouldn't swallow it, even if he knew for a certainty that he would choke to death."

The princess answered:

"Be quiet, you enemy of all goodness! I would never have thought, Plaerdemavida, that you could be so cruel. Up to today I've always thought of you as a mother or a sister, but now you are like a stepmother because of the reprehensible advice you're giving about me."

At this point Tirant had finished removing her clothing, and he took her in his arms and placed her on the bed. When the princess saw herself in such a situation, and that Tirant, who had taken off his clothes, was at her side working with the artillery to penetrate the castle, she saw that she could not defend it by the strength of her arms. She thought that perhaps with feminine arms she could resist him, and with her eyes pouring forth tears she began to lament:

"You are trying to keep me from loving you. You want to use your absolute power over me and make me very angry. Tirant, open the eyes of your understanding, and look at the misfortune that awaits you, and when you recognize it, give way to reason, and restrain your lustful appetite."

The princess made all these and other laments with her eyes pouring forth tears. Tirant saw all the tears and the discreet words of his lady, and he decided to make her content that night and to follow her will. Although all night long the two lovers slept very little, but rather played and found amusement now near the head of the bed and now near its foot, caressing each other continually, both of them very content. When it was nearly daybreak and the people in the palace were beginning to stir, the princess said:

"For my own satisfaction I would that the day had not come so quickly, and it would be my pleasure if this delight could last a year, or never end. Arise, Tirant, lord of the Empire of Greece, for tomorrow, or whenever it pleases you, you may return to the same place."

Tirant got up very reluctantly, and said:

"I shall do what you command, but I fear that my desire will never be satisfied, and my thoughts are very restless."

So that no one should see or hear him, he left full of passion and anguish, kissing her wildly at the moment of their parting. When he was gone Plaerdemavida was so distraught that she could bear no more. The princess sent for her and had Lady Montblanc summoned, and both knew what had taken place between her and Tirant.

"God help me!" said Plaerdemavida. "Your Highness had the pleasure and Tirant the delight, and I the sin. But it grieves me so much that there was no consummation that I feel I shall die from anger. Bring that skinny, spineless knight to me, and you'll see what I say to him! I shall never again do anything for him; instead I will try to stand in his way whenever I can."

"In faith," said Lady Montblanc, "he has shown great virtue as the most valiant and courteous knight he is, for he has wished to forego his pleasure rather than anger my mistress."

They spoke of this at length until it was bright daylight and the emperor sent word to the empress and to his daughter that all the ladies should dress in their finery, and then they should all come to the festivities being held for Tirant. He also sent word to all the knights and ladies of the city so that they would go to the palace. God knows well that in that instance the princess would have liked more to sleep than to leave her chambers. But for love of Tirant and so that the celebration could take place, she left her bed and dressed very beautifully, and they went out from the great hall where they found the emperor with all his retinue of nobles and knights and ladies of the city.

When the procession was ready, they went through the city with the two hundred seventy-two flags in front, until they came to the church. Tirant went up to the princess, and she received him warmly, but she could only say:

"Tirant, my lord, all that I have is yours."

Tirant did not dare answer her because the empress and the others were near. The mass was begun with great solemnity. On administering the holy water they set up one flag; after confession another was put in place; then, at psalm or scripture reading they put up another one. Finally, when the mass was over, all the flags were in place. Tirant did not want to sit in his usual place, or even next to the emperor. Instead he went into a chapel with his Hours in his hand, and from there he could see the princess very well. In truth, Tirant said very few Hours at that mass. I could not tell you about the princess, but as long as the holy service lasted she did not take her eyes from Tirant.

CHAPTER IX - WIDOW REPOSE

After the service was over and everyone had eaten, there was dancing in the square. While they were dancing the princess went to the palace, to her chamber, to change clothes, and she had them close the door. When she was in her tunic she went up to the treasure tower with two maidens. There the three of them weighed out a load of ducats. The princess gave them to Plaerdemavida to carry to Tirant's rooms. When she had dressed again she went back to where the emperor was. She went up to him and to Tirant who was nearby. She whispered in Tirant's ear so that the emperor would not hear:

"Your hands have caressed me so much that there is no part of my body that does not remember your touch."

Tirant answered:

"It is very fortunate for me that my hands have learned something new."

The emperor said:

"What are you two talking about so secretly."

"My lord," said the princess, "I was asking Tirant if there would be jousts at this celebration. He told me there would not, and that they were waiting to hold them against the Turks."

"That is the best news I could possibly hear," said the emperor. "Do you feel well enough to be able to leave?"

"Yes, by the Holy Virgin!" said Tirant. "When the celebration is over, I will take the doctors with me, and I'll be able to go."

They spoke of other things until Plaerdemavida came and signaled from a distance. When the emperor began to talk to other people Tirant quietly went to Plaerdemavida to ask her what she wanted. She answered:

"It is only logical that you've lost the prize of all your efforts so many times, my lord, with your neglect and lack of persistence. You don't deserve to be rewarded any further since you're satisfied with what you have, and you've lost it through your own fault. As far as I'm concerned, I don't want to be involved in your love affairs any longer. You don't need me—you need Widow Repose: she'll give you what you deserve. I'm not bound to do anything more for you: you are the most disloyal, unworthy knight who was ever born. And that you can't deny. If I were a knight, I would fight you. You were in bed with a maiden in your arms—the most beautiful, most pleasing, the worthiest lady who ever lived—and you shouldn't have left her just because she begged you to or because she shed tears. And if she went there a virgin, I saw her leave a virgin—to your shame and confusion. The great error you committed will hurt me all my life. There is no lady or maiden in the world who wouldn't consider you the lowest of men if she knew what you have done. I don't want to talk about this anymore: I've already said enough. I only want to tell you that when the emperor sits down to dinner, you'll have to be there. I've just now come from your chambers, and here's the key to your room. I beg you to go there quickly. I brought the keys so that no one could read what you'll find written there."

Tirant took the keys, and wanted to reply to what Plaerdemavida had told him, but it was impossible because the emperor was telling him to come right away. When he was there the emperor told him that he was to sit alone at the table. The emperor, the empress, the princess, and all the maidens waited on him. And there was no knight or lady who dared approach to serve him, because they were all in their seats waiting to hear what an old knight who was very experienced in arms would say. He was a very eloquent and great reader who began to recite all the chivalresque deeds that Tirant had performed. The men and women forgot to eat as they listened to the great honors that Tirant had achieved up to that day. When Tirant had finished eating, the knight stopped reading— and his recitation had lasted more than three hours.

When evening arrived, the dinner was as abundant as the afternoon meal had been. After the dancing there were farces and short plays, as were required at such festivities. These festivities lasted almost the whole night through, and the emperor did not want to leave until dawn. The princess was never bored at the celebration because she could see and talk to Tirant. And Tirant barely dared to talk to the princess for fear of the emperor who was very near, but he told her quietly:

"My lady, last night was certainly more enjoyable to me than tonight is."

Plaerdemavida quickly interjected:

"My lord, your words are fine, but not your actions."

Then, when the emperor saw that dawn was breaking he got up and wanted everyone to go with him to escort Tirant to his chambers. Tirant thanked him for the great honor he was paying him, and he wanted to escort the emperor to his chambers, but the worthy lord would not permit it.

When Tirant was in his chambers he thought that because Plaerdemavida was so unhappy with him she had probably written him some letter, but when he went into his room he saw a heap of gold on the floor. He was astonished at the princess's great virtue, and he thought more highly of her good will than he did of the gift. He had Hippolytus come, and ordered him to safeguard it.

When it was time for mass all the lords went, and Tirant found no way to talk to the princess, to thank her for what she had sent him, until after dinner. After eating they told the emperor that since he had slept so little the night before he should go and rest, and that when it was time for the festivities they would all return. As the ladies went back to the palace Tirant drew near to the princess and told her:

"I haven't the spirit to talk, nor can my tongue express all the words of love that befit the works of honor that Your Majesty bestows on me every day."

She quickly replied, although she did not dare to speak much because the emperor was passing by. She only said to him:

"You are my lord; I am in your power. Decide what you will do with me: make war or peace. If I don't help you, who are my lord, whom would I help? What I do now is little, if you consider what I plan to do. But if you want more, the doors to the treasure are open for you, and closed for anyone else."

With Tirant again thanking her, they reached the emperor's chambers, and the emperor went inside with the ladies. Only Widow Repose remained outside. She stood at the head of the stairs, waiting for Tirant. With her feminine malice she was prepared to commit an unspeakable crime. When she saw Tirant she put on a sympathetic face, and with graceful gestures designed to make him love her, she said:

"I'm not surprised that you want to conquer the world: you've already captivated me. With the pity I have for Your Grace, I want to help you. So, my lord Tirant, if you'd like to be in a certain secret place after two o'clock, you'll be able to see everything I've told you about."

Tirant said that was agreeable to him, and that he would be ready. The Widow left Tirant at once. Behind the garden she and a very old woman had a house already prepared, and she had her furnish it nicely with a bed, as would befit Tirant. When the raging Widow saw that the time had come, she went looking for Tirant secretly, and she made him swear at length, and then disguise himself. Then they went to the old lady's chambers. In the chamber was a small window overlooking the garden, and through it a person could see everything that went on in the garden; but the window was very high, and only by climbing a ladder could you see out. The Widow brought two large mirrors, and put one at the window and the other one lower, in front of Tirant, facing the first mirror. And everything that appeared in the top one was reflected in the lower one.

When the Widow had done this and had left Tirant in the room, she went quickly to the palace, and found the princess sleeping in her bed. The Widow said to her:

"Get up, my lady. My lord, the emperor, sent me to tell you that the doctors want you to get out of your bed and not to sleep so long. After you stayed up so late last night, and having eaten lunch, if you sleep now with this warm weather it could endanger your health."

She opened the windows of the chamber so that she would not sleep, and the princess permitted her to because of her father's tender words.

When she was up she put on a brocade tunic with the top completely unbuttoned, no kerchief over her breast, and her hair hanging loose over her shoulders. Then the Widow said to her:

"The doctors think it would be good for you to go down to the garden and see all the greenery, and we'll entertain ourselves there with some games so that your drowsiness will pass. I have a costume for the festival of Corpus Christi that looks like your gardener. Plaerdemavida likes these things very much and she will put it on, and will tell you her usual witty things."

The princess went down to the garden with the Widow and two maidens while Tirant was watching the mirror carefully. He saw the princess coming with the maidens, and watched as they sat down near a small stream. The Widow had foreseen everything, and she had sent the black gardener to the city of Pera so that he would not be in the garden.

The Widow helped dress Plaerdemavida, and put the mask on her that had been made to look exactly like the black gardener; and she went into the garden wearing his clothing. When Tirant saw her coming he thought that it was in fact the Moorish gardener, carrying a spade over his shoulder. He began to dig, and soon approached the princess. He sat at her side, and took her hands and kissed them. Then he put his hands on her breasts and touched her nipples, and made overtures of love. The princess broke into great peals of laughter, and all her weariness left her. Then he drew her even closer and put his hands under her skirts, while all the maidens laughed, as they listened to Plaerdemavida's amusing words. The Widow turned toward Tirant and twisted her hands as she spat on the ground, indicating the loathing and pain she felt for what the princess was doing.

Imagine poor, miserable Tirant, who the day before had been so pleased at having won a lady of such high rank as his betrothed, the thing he desired most in the world, and then to see his misery, his affliction and his pain with his own eyes. And when he began to think, he wondered if the mirrors were reflecting a false image, and he broke them and looked inside to see if they contained something evil made by the art of necromancy, but he found nothing of the sort. He wanted to get up to the window to find out if he could see more, and to discover how those games would end, and he saw that there was no ladder, because the Widow had been afraid that he might do this and she had hidden it. Tirant, finding no other recourse, took the bench from in front of the bed and stood it up. Then, taking a cord that he cut from the curtains, he passed it over a beam and pulled himself up by it. He saw how the black gardener had taken the princess by the hand, and was leading her to a hut in the garden where he kept his gardening tools and a bed to sleep on. Plaerdemavida led her into that room, where they looked through everything, including the clothing which the black man kept in a chest. After a time the princess came out, as the Widow and a maiden were walking near the hut. When they saw her, the Widow went over to the maiden and gave her a scarf. To go ahead with the game and make everyone laugh, she said to her:

"Put it under the princess's skirts."

When she was in front of Her Highness, the maiden knelt on the ground as the Widow had instructed her, and put the rag under her skirts. And the princess' naiveté played into the hands of the Widow's malice. When Tirant saw such a heinous thing, he was completely aghast, and with a voice full of anguish, he began to lament:

"Oh, fortune, enemy of all who want to live upright in this world: Now, when I had achieved such a marriage, you have let me be dishonored by a man of the most vile condition and nature that could be found. Oh, princess, my lady! I would never have believed that in a maiden of such tender years there could be so little shame and boldness that you would commit such an abominable sin."

At this moment Widow Repose came in. She had waited a short time at the door, and when she heard Tirant's lament, she said:

"Now all the things I have begun are coming to pass."

When she entered the room she saw that Tirant was in great anguish, his pillow full of tears, continuing his lamentations. She sat down near him to see if Tirant wanted to say anything to her, and ready to do whatever he said. When the Widow saw that Tirant was not changing his tone, she said to him:

"That lover of all dishonesty won't leave her abominable life, no matter how much you beg or threaten her. Her only desire is to satisfy her lust. What can I do, poor me? With these breasts," and she pulled them out so that Tirant would see them, "I nursed that lady."

She let them hang out like this for a good while, pretending that with her lamentations she had forgotten to cover them. Then she added:

"Lord Tirant, take comfort from me. Oh, Almighty God, Holy Trinity! With great anguish in my soul, with great anger and many tears, I revealed those thoughts that ran through my mind almost every day. But at night, alone in my room, I would find myself drying my tearful eyes—with sackcloth so that I would feel the pain even more."

Tirant quickly replied:

"Your love, Widow Repose, can't be compared to mine, because yours is diminishing: It grows smaller and smaller, while mine is increasing. But I have more reason to grieve than any lover because in one day's time I have reached the highest peak of love that fortune could grant me, and the next day I have been the most confused and downtrodden lover in the entire world. My eyes have seen a black Moor easily possess what I have not been able to have by supplications or by all the dangers and hardships I have endured. A man as unlucky as I should not go on living, so that he will not have to trust any maid or maiden."

He got up from the bed as though to leave, and the Widow said to him:

"My lord, rest a while. There are many people outside, and I value my life so much that I would not want anyone to see you leaving. I'll go to the window and tell Your Grace when it is safe to go."

Tirant went slowly back to the bed, never ceasing to ponder his grief. The Widow went into the room of the old mistress of the house and quickly took off her clothing and dressed in a perfumed blouse, and a skirt of black velvet. With her blouse completely unfastened she went into the bedchamber and lay down beside Tirant very boldly and shamelessly, and said:

"If you knew the hardships my soul endures for love, you could not help but have pity on me. Where will you find greater affection than mine in any woman? It would be more to your glory to have me always in your chambers or in your tents, serving you in every way that I can, than to love a false maiden who is given over to a black captive Moor. Take me as a servant and as one who loves you more than her own life."

"My lady," said Tirant, "please don't torment my sad soul. I can't give an answer to anything you've said. I can only tell you that I could not forget Her Majesty any more than I could renounce my faith."

The Widow said:

"Since you don't want to love me, at least let me lie next to you a while, completely naked."

She quickly removed her tunic, which was already unfastened. When Tirant saw her in her chemise, he leapt out of bed, flung open the door, and went back to his quarters with great pain. And the Widow was left with no less.

When Tirant was in his room his emotion was so great that he did not know what to do, and as he walked back and forth tears flowed from his eyes. And so he did nothing for three hours but pace, lie down and get up again. Then he left the room full of anger. As secretly as he could he went in disguise to the garden gate, and in the orchard he found the black gardener who had arrived only shortly before. He saw him in the doorway of his room, putting on a pair of red pants. When Tirant saw him, he looked around, and no one else was in sight. Then he seized him by the hair, pushed him into the room and cut off his head. He returned to his room without anyone seeing him, because everyone was in the square where the celebration was taking place. Tirant then said:

"Oh, just and true God! You who correct our faults, I ask of you vengeance and not justice for this lady. Tell me, pitiless maiden, was my disposition less agreeable to your desires than this black gardener? If you had loved as I thought you did, you would still be mine. But you never did love me."

Let us leave Tirant in his lament now, and return to the emperor who, with all the ladies, was getting ready for the celebration. At this moment a message arrived, telling him about an unfortunate event that had happened in the camp three days previously.

The Duke of Macedonia and the Duke of Pera were captains of the camp, and they often went out to do battle against the Turks. But the Turks were afraid of all the water that the Christians released. They often fought, and many men from both sides died. But for every ten Christians who died, three hundred Turks died. The reason for this was that when the Turks came into the city of Saint George, the Christians released all the river waters, and from the canals the ground was like clay so that the horses could not get out of it, and the men on foot could not escape.

But one day the Turks decided to come four thousand strong, armed with spades and baskets, and picks, vinegar and fire to cut through the mountain so that the water would spread down the dry river bed, and would leave them free. Further on, a league from where the Turks were, was a large section of a toppled wall where there was no one. All the Moorish soldiers went there at night. The foot soldiers stayed in that deserted place while those on horseback went into a forest half a league away so they would not be seen. In the morning the spies came and told the captains that the Turks had arrived. They held council, and they all agreed to mount and ride against the Turks.

First they sent out scouts, who came back with the news that the enemy was going to try to cut through the mountain to control the water. The Christians went there. As soon as they arrived the foot soldiers began skirmishes that lasted a long time, so that many men from both sides died. Finally, when it was nearly noon, the Turks found themselves too tightly pressed, and they abandoned their tools and took flight. The Christians quickly went to the pass half a league away, and there was so much water there that they could not cross it except at great effort and danger. Then, when they did make their way across, the others were at a great advantage. At a gallop the Moors left all the foot soldiers behind, with about five thousand men following them until they took refuge in the unpopulated village. But it was too heavily populated for the Christians! When the Turks regrouped at the broken wall, the Duke of Macedonia said:

"Gentlemen, I don't think we should go any further. We don't know what kind of an ambush may be in store for us: the enemy is always thinking of how they can do us the most harm."

The Duke of Pera, who was the other captain, was very envious, and he said maliciously:

"Duke of Macedonia, you have very little experience in arms, and here you are telling us about the danger we could run into. Turn back and flee: you would be better off with women in the city than here!"

The Duke of Macedonia did not want to create discord among the men, and have them start fighting among themselves. So he tried to hold his tongue, but he could not restrain himself, and he answered:

"Duke of Pera, you would be better off if you kept quiet. Who has been honored in battle? I, the Duke of Macedonia, am known as a conqueror, while the Duke of Pera is held in low esteem because of the battles he has engaged in."

The other knights and grandees interrupted the argument, and made them stop. Some wanted to advance and others to retreat. But in the end they had to go on, because the Duke of Pera said:

"Whoever wants to come with me or go back is free to do so."

And he started out, so all the others felt they had to follow him. When they reached the deserted village, the Turks on top of the wall defended it bravely. There was a ditch there, and they had to dismount and fight with lances, because they had no other arms. While they were doing this, the forces of the sultan and the Turk came out, some through one gate and some through another, and they caught them in the middle. There was a great slaughter, and they captured many of them. I can say about this sad adventure that everyone who dismounted was killed or taken prisoner, and only one knight was able to escape. With this victory the Turks returned to the city of Bellpuig and put their captives in strong prisons.

This news reached the emperor while he was in the hall waiting for the ladies to come so they could go to the square for the celebrations.

The emperor, in the presence of all who were there, cried:

"Oh, disconsolate widows, lament, tear out your hair, scratch your faces, dress in mourning! For the flower of chivalry has died, and it will never be recovered."

The crying, the wailing, was so great in the palace that it soon spread throughout the city. And the festivities turned into mourning and lamentations.

Then the emperor sent for Tirant to give him the sad news and show him the letters he had received. When the chamberlain came to Tirant's door, he heard him crying out:

"Oh, poor me! Oh, cruel fortune! Why have you done these things to me? To think that that excellent lady would give herself to a black Moor, the enemy of our faith. Would that I had never seen such a thing—the woman I loved most in the world and hoped to serve. Oh, you wicked Widow! I wish I had never known you, for you will be the cause of my death and destruction!"

The emperor's chamberlain heard him talking and crying, but he could not make out the words because the door was closed. But to do the emperor's bidding, he called out:

"Oh, captain! The emperor is calling you and wishes to see you."

When the chamberlain returned to the emperor, he said:

"Sire, your captain already knows about the terrible things that have happened. I heard him grieving piteously!"

The captain came to the chamber and saw the princess lying on the ground with the doctors gathered around her. When he saw her like this, he could not help but exclaim, "Why are you allowing this lady to die without helping her? Even though her guilt cannot be excused, I still pray God that she will live longer than I."

The doctors didn't understand him, and thought he was bewailing the bad news. And Tirant thought everyone was crying because of the princess. Then he turned and saw the empress who had torn all the veils from her head. At another side he saw the emperor sitting on the floor, still as a statue. He had the letters in his hand, and motioned Tirant over and gave them to him. When Tirant read them, he said:

"It's worse than I thought."

Then he began to console the emperor. At this moment the princess regained consciousness. She opened her eyes, and begged Tirant to come to her. The princess made him sit next to her and said:

"Oh, my last hope! If you truly love me, don't let your life and mine be taken from this world until the day that all the dukes, counts and marquis are recovered who have been killed or placed in cruel prisons."

While she was speaking, two men who had fled the camp came in, and she could say no more, nor could Tirant answer. They told them in detail about the destruction, and about the terrible argument between the Duke of Macedonia and the Duke of Pera, and how five thousand knights had been killed or taken prisoner. The emperor, his eyes brimming with tears and barely able to speak, began to lament:

"Oh, unlucky captains! You, more willful than wise, have ignored my counsel. Find comfort in a cruel prison, thinking that you will never again see your emperor, for your actions have not been well thought out."

The emperor got up from his seat, and went into a chamber, tears springing from his eyes, his head in his hands. When the princess saw how he was grieving, she lost consciousness. The wisest doctor of them all said:

"I have little hope for this lady's life. She has fainted three times and now I cannot feel her pulse."

When Tirant heard the doctor say these words, he quickly said:

"Oh, cruel death! Wouldn't it be better and more just for you to come to me first, instead of letting me see her die? Even though she has deeply hurt me, I want to keep her company."

And with extreme grief he fell to the ground and all the weight of his body fell on the leg which had been broken, and it broke again, and was even worse than before. Blood came out of his nose and his ears, and especially from his leg, and it was a wonder that he did not lose his life. They quickly went to tell the emperor, and he said:

"It is not at all surprising, for of all his relatives there is not one left who is not dead or being held prisoner. But this is my consolation, because to get his relatives and friends out of prison he will perform admirable feats."

The emperor began to go to Tirant when he saw his daughter lying half dead. And he said:

"God help me, I don't know which of them to help first."

But he had his daughter lifted up and placed in her bed, and then Tirant was put in a beautiful room. They quickly removed his clothing and treated his leg, straightening it a little. And he was completely unaware of everything they did for him, because he was unconscious for thirty-six hours. When he regained consciousness, he asked who had brought him there, and Hippolytus told him:

"What, my lord! Don't you know what a great fright you brought us?

You've been unconscious for two days, and haven't had anything to eat. Your body can't hold up that way, so please take what the doctors order you to have."

"I don't want anything that will bring my health back," said Tirant. "I want only death."

They quickly went to tell the emperor, and the princess overheard, for she had now regained consciousness. Then Tirant said:

"Tell me how the princess is."

Hippolytus answered:

"Very well, my lord. She's recovered now."

"I'm sure she is," said Tirant. "Her illness could not be great. A few days ago she had things she wanted a great deal, but now I don't think she will brag much about them. She's not the first to do this, nor will she be the last. I know very well that she's not made of iron. Oh, how painful it is for a man not to be able to share his grief."

At this moment the emperor came in, followed by all the ladies with the empress, and they all asked him how he was. But he did not want to answer anyone. They were all astonished that he had not answered the greetings of the emperor or the ladies, and continuing to show his grief he began to lament:

"Oh, Son of God, all powerful Jesus. I am dying of love, and You wished to die for love, to free mankind. You suffered so much pain, lashings, wounds and torments, and my pain was the sight of a black Moor. Outside of You, Lord, who can compare with my love? Lord, Your Holy Mother, and Our Lady, suffered great pain at the foot of the cross, and I stood with a cord in my hand, with two mirrors that represented, Lord, the greatest pain that any Christian has ever endured."

The emperor and all the ladies were in the room, along with the cardinal and many other clergymen, and they were all astonished at the pious words they heard Tirant saying.

Then Tirant lowered his head, and began to lament again, because death was calling him. The doctors ordered many things for him, but they did not help. Hearing of his illness, an old Jewess came to the emperor, and very boldly said:

"Your Majesty sees that Tirant's life is near its end, all the doctors have given up hope, and I am the only one who can help him. Call the soldiers together, and have them start shouting and go into his chambers and beat their swords against their shields. When he wakes up and sees so many armed men and hears them shouting, and he asks what is happening, you can tell him the Turks are at the gates of the city. Then all those thoughts of his will disappear, and with that virtue he has and out of fear of being shamed, he will get up."

The emperor sent for his doctors and his wise men and explained what the Jewess had advised. They all agreed that it would be worth trying.

The shouting and the uproar were so loud in the city that Tirant heard it even before they came into his chamber. The Jewess, who stood at the head of the bed, told him:

"Get up, my captain. Don't be afraid of death. Here are your enemies, the Turks, at the gates to the city, and they're coming to take revenge on you."

When Tirant heard the old lady saying this, he said:

"Is it true that the Turks are so close?"

"They're even closer than you think," said the Jewess. "Get up. Go to the window, and you'll see what they plan to do to you."

Tirant immediately called for his clothes, and he had his leg bound with towels. Then he put his armor on as best he could and mounted his horse, along with many other men. He was so ready and willing to fight that his illness went almost entirely away. The emperor and the doctor who were there told him to take some restoratives, and that would make him better able to do battle. He did everything they advised him, and then he realized that it had all been contrived to help him get over his illness. Tirant said:

"Praise be to God: a woman has delivered me from the arms of death, for another woman had killed me."

With all the noise the soldiers raised, the princess ran to her mother's chamber. They saw the emperor coming back with Tirant, and all the ladies looked out the windows to see what had happened. When Tirant was in front of the princess's window he lifted his head and put both hands over his face. The empress asked her daughter why Tirant had covered his face, because the only reason that was ever done was when a love affair had gone wrong. The princess answered that she didn't have any idea.

After they had gone by and were at the palace door, the emperor dismounted, and Tirant begged his leave to go to his lodging. The emperor did everything he could to make Tirant dismount, telling him he would be given everything he needed in the palace, but Tirant insisted on leaving. The princess wondered why Tirant did not want to stay in the palace despite all the emperor's pleas, for he had wanted to many times before. She also wondered why he had covered his face.

When Tirant reached his lodging, he immediately went to his room and called Lord Agramunt and Hippolytus. He begged them to arm and provision ten galley ships. They said they would, and leaving Tirant, they stocked the galleys.

After Tirant had eaten, he arranged everything for his departure. He ordered all his men to go by land to the castle of Malvei, and said he would go by sea and they would meet there. When it was evening and the doctors had left, they told the emperor that Tirant was all right. When it was nearly the hour for prayer, the princess, upset that she did not see Tirant, asked Plaerdemavida and Lady Montblanc to go to Tirant's lodging to find out what was wrong. As the maidens were coming, one of Tirant's pages saw them and quickly went into Tirant's chambers and said:

"Cheer up, my lord, two gallant ladies are coming with a message from the princess."

"Go right away," said Tirant, "and tell them I am all right but that I'm sleeping."

The page did what he was told, for Tirant did not want to see them.

When the maidens returned to the palace with the reply, the princess insisted so much that her mother and the emperor went to Tirant's lodging, and when Tirant heard that the emperor was coming he gave two pages instructions about what to do. When the emperor was at the door to his chamber, the more clever of the pages said:

"Your Majesty should not come into the chamber because of the captain's sickness. He has not rested for so many days that he is catching up on all the rest he needs now. He is nearly drenched with sweat, and it would be good for a doctor to come in without awakening him."

Tirant quickly got into bed, and he moistened his face with a wet cloth and pretended to be asleep. The doctor came in, and when he left again he told the emperor:

"My lord, it would be very harmful for us to awaken him now. Why doesn't Your Highness go now. Tomorrow morning you can come back and visit him."

The princess could not take it calmly when she was not able to see Tirant, but she had to return with the emperor. When Tirant knew that they had all gone, he quickly got up and had all his clothing gathered and taken to the galley. At midnight he secretly went on board, and he would have liked to cast anchor then, but the ship was not ready.

In the morning, when the sun came up, the emperor heard the galley trumpets giving the signal for the men to go on board. Tirant sent Lord Agramunt to the emperor as his courier, and when he was before him he gave him the following message:

"Your captain has gone on board one of the galleys, and has ordered the ships to go to the port of Transimeno. He will go by ship to the castle of Malvei while the soldiers go there by land. I have been sent here to tell Your Highness about his decision to leave."

The emperor answered:

"Knight, I am very happy to have this good news, and I give many thanks to Divine Goodness for bringing health to our captain so that he can leave. This is what I wanted most in the world after the salvation of my soul."

Lord Agramunt kissed his hand and begged his leave. Then he went to the empress's chamber and bade her farewell, and did the same to the princess. When the empress saw that Hippolytus would have to go, and the princess saw that Tirant was leaving, they shed bitter tears, especially the princess because Tirant was going without a word to her. They quickly went to the emperor's chamber to see if it was true that they were leaving, and the emperor told them everything. The princess urged the emperor to go to the water's edge so that she could go along, and the empress did not dally. The emperor reached the sea before they did, and he went on board the ship, begging Tirant to do everything he could for the empire. Tirant spoke to him very kindly, and said he would do everything he could, and the emperor felt very relieved.

All the soldiers advised the emperor to go back on land quickly because a black cloud with thunder and lightning was coming their way. So the emperor went on land. The princess was sorry that she had not been there when her father went on the galley so that she could have gone too and talked with Tirant. By now the sea was so choppy that the women were not allowed on board, nor would her father have given his permission. The princess, sighing deeply, and with tears streaming from her eyes, had no recourse other than to beg Plaerdemavida to go on board the galley and find out why Tirant had left so secretly, without saying anything to her, and why he had placed his hands over his face as he passed by, and also why he had not wanted to stay in the palace—which he had wanted to do so many times before.

Plaerdemavida understood exactly what her lady wanted, and she got on a boat with Hippolytus and some others who were with him. The pain that the empress felt as she saw Hippolytus going on board the galley cannot be described. When Plaerdemavida was on board, Tirant paid no attention to her. But she insisted, and said to him:

"Oh, cruel knight! Who has turned your thoughts? To leave such a virtuous lady, who has more dignity and virtue than anyone in the world, without so much as telling her goodbye! If you want her life to be sad and to hasten her death, don't go back on land, and don't look at her. But if you want to restore her bitter life, let her see Your Lordship for a short time."

When she had said this she could no longer hold back her tears, and she wrapped her cloak around herself, and moaned softly but would say no more. Tirant wanted to reply to what Plaerdemavida had told him, and very softly so that no one could hear him he said:

"Her beauty and discretion so far surpasses all the others that only a madman could compare anyone else with her. But I saw this lady with the black gardener, Lauseta, and she was not thinking of me at all. First I saw them kissing, and I was offended by the sight. Then I was even more shocked when I saw them embracing like lovers and going into a chamber. When they came back out Widow Repose knelt down at her feet and put a silk scarf high under her skirt. Painful thoughts attacked my mind when I saw how he treated her. I don't know why I didn't kill someone right then, but the wall was in my way. But I could not take the terrible jealousy of the black gardener out of my mind, and I cut through his neck with my sword. Still the pain kept increasing so much that I was beside myself, and I went into my chamber, pretending to be terribly tired so I would be left alone. And now I want to be in the sea; I want my body to float, unburied, on the waves until it reaches the princess, so that she can dress me in my shroud with her delicate hands."

Then he would say no more. When Plaerdemavida heard what was bothering Tirant and that the black gardener had been killed, and no one would know who did it unless she told them, she was very agitated. Still she forced herself to smile, and with Hippolytus there, she said:

"Even if you did see it, it was all a game to cheer up the princess. Widow Repose got some costumes from the plays for the Corpus Christi festivals, and I dressed up like our gardener."

And she told him everything that had happened.

Tirant was astonished by it all, and said he could not believe it. The maiden laughed, and said:

"My lord, the best thing would be for me to stay here while Hippolytus goes to my room. Under my bed he will find all the clothing of the black gardener. And if I'm not telling the truth, you can throw me into the ocean."

Tirant told Hippolytus to take the keys and go, and to come back quickly because the sea was very choppy. Hippolytus did what Tirant commanded. When he came back with the clothing, the ocean swells were so high that Hippolytus could not board the galley, and Plaerdemavida could not go back on land. They threw a rope to the ship and tied the clothing of the black gardener to it so that it could be pulled up to the galley. When Tirant saw the mask and the clothing, he saw all the wickedness of Widow Repose. He then swore in everyone's presence that if he could go on land just then, he would have her burned before the emperor, or he would do to her what he had done with the black man. Then Tirant begged Plaerdemavida to forgive the bad thoughts he had had about the princess, and about her, and when she was with Her Highness to beg her forgiveness. Plaerdemavida agreed, very graciously.

    Suddenly the sea became so stormy that the people who saw the boat Hippolytus was on, began to pray that it would not sink. It headed back to land, and the men on it were drenched while the boat was half-filled with water. The wind and rain were so strong and the waves were so high that the galley's ropes broke, and they were swept out to sea. Two of the galleys remained there; the people on them were saved, but the ships were lost. The three galleys that found themselves in the middle of the tempestuous sea had their masts broken and their sails torn apart. A gust of wind threw one of the galleys into a small island, and its men took refuge there. Tirant's galley and the other one were leeward. They could not make it to the island, and Tirant's galley found itself with its rudder smashed. The other galley was nearby, and it split apart. The men on board fell into the bitter sea, and all of them drown.

    Tirant's galley continued toward Barbary, and the sailors lost their bearings and did not know what seas they were in, and they lamented loudly. Tirant heard the great cries the sailors were making, and he saw the galley's boatswain, who was the best of all the sailors, commending his soul to God because a tackle-block had fallen on his head. A galley slave got up and went to Tirant, and with a great effort he said:

"My lord, order the men to bail out the water in the galley. Here is your staff of authority. Hold it in your hand and run through the galley: the boatswain is dead, and all the men see that they are very near death, and are fainting. Do everything you can to make them bale, because if we can get beyond the cape, we can save our lives. It is better for us to be captives of the Moors than to die."

    Tirant lifted his head, and said:
"What seas are we in?"
"My lord," said the galley-slave, as he pointed, "those are the seas of Sicily, and these are the seas of Tunis. And because you are a virtuous man I'm sorrier for you than I am for myself. It is Fortune's

will that we shall perish on this Barbary Coast, and in a case like this every man should beg forgiveness of the others."

Tirant quickly got up, although the dreadful sea was crashing about him so that he was barely able to stand. Then he brought out the best clothing he had, and he dressed in it. He took a sack containing a thousand ducats, and put a note inside that said: "I beg whomsoever should find my body to give it an honorable burial. I am Tirant lo Blanc from Brittany, and of that singular lineage of Roca Salada, High Captain of the Greek Empire."

By now it was already past noon, and the further the galley went the more water it took on. The cries increased and death drew near. As they were near land the Moors saw the galley approaching, and they realized that it would run aground just where they wanted it, while the Christians knew that they could not escape death or being captured.

The galley came close to land, and all the men threw themselves into the sea to save their lives. By this time it was nearly dark of night. When Tirant saw the sailors jumping overboard he decided not to leave the ship, no matter what might happen. And by then there was no boat, rope or oar that had not been lost. Tirant begged two sailors, faithful friends of his who had come on the ship with him when it was stocked in Brittany, to take care of the maiden. They took off all her clothes, and by this time nearly all the galley was underwater. Taking up a corkwood plank, the sailor tied it across her breasts while the other man helped her stand up. The sea sent a wave crashing into Plaerdemavida and the sailors, and hurled them about. The man carrying the plank drowned in order to save her. The other sailor helped the maiden as long as he could, and finally was forced to abandon her. It was her good fortune to find herself near land at night, and she could hear the loud noise the Moors were making as they captured the Christians. The maiden's feet touched bottom, and since she was all alone she stopped and decided not to go ashore. Instead she went closer to land so that she would not be in such deep water, but waves sometimes came crashing over her head. As she walked through the water close to shore, she moved away from the shouts, afraid that she would be killed. For she saw that the Moors were killing each other as each one tried to capture the most prisoners. And when lightning flashed, she could see the reflection of swords near the sea. She continued to walk in the water, completely naked, following the shoreline, and whenever she heard anyone she would duck underwater, and stay there until they were gone.

CHAPTER X - THE BARBARY COAST

Poor Plaerdemavida, raw naked, continually called on Our Lady, the Mother of God, imploring her to bring her some good person who would help her. She continued to walk nearly half a league until she came upon some fishing boats. She went into a hut and found two sheepskins, and she tied them together with a thin string and put them on, one in front and one in back, and in this way she found some protection from the cold. Then she lay down to sleep a little while, for she was completely fatigued by her travails in the ocean.

When she awoke, finding herself alone, she began to weep and lament, tears streaming from her eyes, which did harm to her eyes and her voice, making her so hoarse that she could barely speak. Then, with timorous steps, she began to search out the roads of cruel fortune. Dawn began to break and she heard a Moor coming along, singing. She hid near the road so that he would not see her, and when he had passed she saw his pure white beard and thought that perhaps this old Moor would give her counsel. So she approached the old Moor and told him all about her misfortune. The Moor was moved to compassion when he saw the maiden who was young and nice looking, and he said to her:

"Maiden, I want you to know that long ago I was a captive of Christians in Spain, in a place called Cadiz. The lady who held me captive was pleased with the services I performed for her. It happened that she had a son whose enemies came to kill him. And if it had not been for me, they would have done it, because I lifted my lady's son from the ground, and with a sword in my hand I wounded two of them and made the others flee. Because of this, my lady gave me liberty. She provided me with new clothing, and gave me money for my journey, and as I wished, she had me taken to Granada. And because of the kindness that lady showed me, you will have a place at my side. I have a daughter who is widowed, and she will take you in with all the tenderness of a sister."

Plaerdemavida immediately knelt on the ground and gave him many thanks. The Moor removed his cloak and gave it to

Plaerdemavida, and the two of them went to a place near Tunis, called Rafal.

When the Moor's daughter saw the maiden, so young and helpless, she felt great compassion. Her father begged her to be the best companion to her that she could, and he told her:

"I want you to know, my daughter, that this girl is the daughter of that lady who gave me my freedom, and I want to repay my debt with this maiden."

Because of the great love she had for him, his daughter took in the poor maiden with deep affection. She gave her a blouse and a Moorish garment with a head-dress. And anyone seeing her would think she was Moorish.

Let us return now to Tirant who, shortly after Plaerdemavida was swept overboard with the two sailors in whose care Tirant had placed her, stayed with a sailor until the galley was completely filled with water and was going down. Then Tirant decided to jump into the sea with the sailor, and with the sailor's help he would be able to reach shore. Nevertheless, Tirant never thought he would be able to avoid death, because when the Moors learned that he was Tirant, the captain of the Greeks, who had done so much damage to the Turks, they would not leave him alive for all the treasure in the world. But with the aid of Divine Providence and the sailor, they made it to shore, for it was now night, and completely dark. Crawling quietly on their hands and knees, they drew away from the sounds of the Moors. When they had gone some distance, they no longer heard any people, and they went inland, away from the sea, and they came upon a vineyard that at that time was full of grapes. The sailor said:

"My lord, for God's sake, let's stop here in this delicious vineyard, and we can take a look at the land, and tomorrow we can stay here all day long. Then tomorrow night, we can go wherever Your Lordship commands, for I will not leave you in death or in life."

Tirant gave in to his entreaties. When their stomachs were full of grapes they saw a cave and went inside to sleep, naked as they were. When they awoke they felt very cold. They got up, and to get warm they carried rocks from one place to another. When the sun came out, Tirant's legs ached terribly.

It happened then that the King of Tremicén was sending as his ambassador to the King of Tunis his best and most trusted knight. He was the captain-general of all his land, and everyone called him the commander of commanders. This ambassador had been there more than three months, and he and his men had been given lodging in a place that was lovely and abundant with animals to hunt. It so happened that that morning he went out for sport with falcons and greyhounds. While hunting, they pursued a hare which was very tired of running after being chased by dogs and falcons, and since it could find no other place to run, it went inside the cave where Tirant was. One of the hunters saw it go in, and he dismounted at the entrance to the cave and saw Tirant stretched out on the ground inside, with no desire to budge. The sailor helped him catch the hare. Then the hunter went directly out to the captain, and told him:

"Sir, come with me. Inside a small cave there is a man whose body must be the most perfect nature has every formed. But, unless my eyes deceive me, he has been hurt badly, and he seems more dead than alive."

The ambassador went toward the cave, When the sailor saw so many men coming, he left Tirant without saying a word, and fled very quietly, and the Moors did not see him.

When the ambassador reached the cave, he stood looking at Tirant for a long while, and feeling pity for him, he said:

"By our holy prophet, Mohammed, who has plucked you from such grave danger and has brought you into my hands: since nature has formed your body with such singularity, I am sure that He has given you many virtues. I have three sons, and you will be the fourth." He called his second son and told him: "Look on this man as your brother." Then he said to Tirant: "If you want to please me, tell me what brought you here. At the moment I am engaged in an undertaking for my eldest son. They are trying to take his betrothed from him, and I will not allow it, for she is a very virtuous maiden, and the daughter of King Tremicén. If Mohammed gives me success in this dangerous undertaking, do not worry about your loss, no matter how great it may be, for I will make you wealthy as soon as I return to my home."

Tirant stood and replied:

"Your Lordship, I am a gentleman, although I am not a prince or lord. As a young man I went to seek my fortune in the Levant. There I heard and believed the false and diabolical words of a widow. She had me enter an orchard at mid-day, and there she made me witness the most evil sight I would ever behold. I felt such unbearable suffering that with my own hands I took vengeance on the greatest enemy of my life. Then I boarded a ship and went to the Holy Land of Jerusalem to make amends for my sins. Sailing on a galley from there, you can see my misfortune. Saved by Divine Mercy from the stormy sea, I now beg Your Lordship's help."

The ambassador said:

"Take comfort. I have a great deal of land and am very wealthy. As soon as we get to my home, you will have everything you wish."

His son then took off his jubbah and gave it to him. And they had him sit behind the son on the horse, and took him to their village, where he was dressed in fine clothing of the Moorish style. When Tirant found himself dressed so finely, and he had heard the kind words of the commander, he felt very comforted. They wanted to travel by night, and the sky was blue and the moon full and it lit up everything very clearly; so when the wind died down they started off. But the first step Tirant took as he left the house, he fell flat on the ground, his arms outstretched. Then all the Moors said:

"This is a very bad sign. Since this Christian has fallen with his arms out to the sides, his life will not last long."

Tirant got up quickly, and hearing what the Moors were saying, he said:

"Your interpretation of this is wrong. I am called Blanc or White. And the moon is clear, white and beautiful at this moment when I fell. And the moon was straight over my head and arms, and it was pointing to the road that I have to take, while my hands were open and stretching out to the moon. And this shows that I, with Divine Power, must conquer all of Barbary."

Then all the Moors burst out laughing, and they took it as a joke and proceeded on their way, and finally they came to a castle. Now the ambassador's son (the one betrothed to the King of Tremicén's daughter) was away; hearing that his father had sent him a very good Christian prisoner, he ordered them to put Tirant in chains.

After two months the ambassador received the reply from the King of Tunis and returned to the King of Tremicén whom he found disconsolate. It happened that King Escariano's land was on the border of the kingdom of Tremicén, and he wanted the King of Tremicén to give him his daughter as a wife along with all his wealth, and after his death he wanted his kingdom. King Escariano was a very strong figure: He was completely black, and a giant compared to other men. A very powerful king, he had many men and a great deal of wealth. King Tremicén was weak in spirit, and he had sent word to King Escariano that his daughter was already betrothed to the son of his head commander. Furthermore, she was with child, and he felt that he would not want to raise another man's child in his house. However, if he was doing this only for his treasure, he was prepared to divide that with him if he would leave him and his sons in peace. Finally, they could not come to an agreement, and King Escariano had marched against him with all his forces: fifty-five thousand strong, on horseback and on foot.

Now this King of Tremicén had only about twenty thousand warriors. Knowing that the other king was near and was coming still closer, he took up position in the mountains and waited for him. King Escariano came to a river, and as they forded it he lost many men. But once across, they went up the mountains and found the King of Tremicén at the highest part, and they besieged him in a beautiful valley. In this valley were three castles with large villas and very strong fortresses. This was where the King of Tremicén lived with his wife and sons.

Two castles were on one side of the river, and one was on the other side, linked together by a huge stone bridge. King Escariano attacked one castle repeatedly, and finally took it. The King of Tremicén was in another castle that was much stronger, but he felt that all was lost. The commander had fled from the battle and came to his own castle where Tirant was. There he told his son:

"You would be better off dying than to see your beloved who is of royal blood taken from you. Go to your lord and serve him as a good knight."

The son agreed, and rode off to the castle where he heard and saw the battle. Then, very happily, he and fifteen of his horsemen, went into the castle where the king was.

The commander of commanders had fled out of fear, and he went into the castle where Tirant was being held. After he had dismounted, he asked his son about the Christian prisoner. When he was told that Tirant was in a prison cell and being carefully guarded, the commander became very angry. He remembered what Tirant had said as he left and fell on the ground: that he would conquer all of Barbary. He had thought about those words many times, and he also considered that since Tirant was a Christian he must be skillful at arms. He went in to see him. Realizing that Tirant had more than enough reason to be angry with him, he smiled and said:

"I beg you, valiant Christian, not to be angry if my son has treated you badly. I swear to you by the prophet Mohammed that it was not done by my command or consent. Instead, it was my intention to look on you as a son. I am hopeful that you will be able to help me. And don't be surprised if I make a request of you on behalf of my lord, even though you are a fugitive from battle. From your scars, I am sure that you, Christian, must know a great deal about weapons, and you must have been in many wars."

Tirant replied:

"I won't hide my past from you. In Spain I practiced the noble tradition of arms, and I can advise you and help you as much as anyone, and I will be one of the first to go into combat. Forgive me for praising myself, but my works will be their own best witness. If this king has your king under siege you should not be surprised, for that is the way with kings. If you are afraid that the bombards will demolish the castle, I will destroy every one they have."

The commander was very pleased with what Tirant told him, and helped him get ready to leave. He insisted that Tirant take whatever materials he needed to destroy the bombards, and he also gave Tirant the best horse he had, and weapons, and plenty of money.

Tirant bought some very old whale bile, and then he took quicksilver, saltpeter, Roman sulfate and other materials, and mixed them together to make an unguent, and he put it in a box. Then they left the castle as secretly as they could, crossed the river, and at night took refuge in the other castle. Now this castle was about one fourth a league from the one where the king was. When Tirant reconnoitered the land, he saw a stone bridge going across the river, and the enemy was positioned in the middle of the large orchard, so that no one dared cross over the bridge for fear of falling into the hands of the enemy. Then Tirant told the commander to give him a Moor who would not be recognized and who could be trusted, and to deliver two hundred sheep to the Moor, and they were brought immediately. Tirant then dressed in a shepherd's cloak, as though he were the Moor's servant.

King Escariano knew that none of his adversaries could hurt him, and he had thirty-seven bombards, large and small, firing continually, three times a day; and they had already knocked down half the castle.

The Moor and Tirant went up a good league toward the bridge with their sheep, and they came right into the encampment. They asked a great deal more for each sheep than it was worth so that they would not sell them quickly. They stayed there three days, leading the sheep close to the bombards. Tirant, under the pretext that he was simply looking, went near them, and spreading some of the unguent he had prepared over his hand, he put it on every one of the bombards. The unguent was made up of such ingredients that whatever metal it came into contact with would, in the space of three hours, turn to rust. So as soon as it was fired, any bombard or crossbow would break apart.

The following day, when they fired on the castle, all the bombards broke apart, and not one of them was left intact. King Escariano was very surprised at this, and he took it as a bad sign. Tirant and the Moor went back to the castle where the commander was.

Then Tirant ordered them to destroy one of the arches on the bridge, and there they put up a wooden drawbridge, with iron chains to raise and lower it. When that was done huge beams were placed on that part of the bridge and there they put up a palisade. When that was ready, Tirant armed himself well and mounted a good steed, and with a good lance in his hand he rode right into the enemy's camp, and he found five Moors enjoying the sun. Tirant rode toward them. The Moors were unconcerned, seeing that he was coming alone, and they thought it was someone from their own camp. And Tirant killed all five of them with his lance. There was a great outcry, and the entire camp rushed into action: they armed themselves and mounted their horses. Tirant concerned himself only with killing anyone in his path. When he saw that the men were armed and on horseback, and that they were coming against him, he retreated to the palisade while using his weapons continuously. Once he was in the palisade, he quickly dismounted, and the Moors came up to him. The men in the castle came down to help Tirant, and there was a great skirmish where many men died. The men from the enemy camp pressed on so forcefully that Tirant had to retreat, and they lifted the drawbridge for fear of the Moors. Then the Moors broke apart the palisade, and Tirant had it built again during the night. And so, every day, at all hours, they fought and many men from both sides were dying continually.

One day Tirant said to the commander:

"My lord, would you like me to rescue your king from the castle and bring him here to you, or to some other place where he will be safe?"

The commander answered:

"If you could do that for me, and bring my Moorish maiden and her betrothed to me, I would make you the lord of everything I own. And even if you forgot about the king, that would not matter a great deal to me."

"Then, my lord," said Tirant, "have two horses prepared, and bring a page whose face is well known. Have them go under that pine tree a half league from here with someone who can guide them."

It was quickly done. When day broke bright and clear, Tirant mounted his horse and with one hundred armed men he rode out of their stockade.

The other camp saw them and rode toward them. The battle between the two forces was fierce, and that day almost no one was left behind in the enemy camp. Then Tirant said to the commander:

"My lord, you stay here and show your face while I go where I have to."

He dug in his spurs and galloped to where the page was waiting for him. When he got there his horse was spent. He dismounted, gave it to the Moor, and took the fresh one that he had. Then he and the page left, going through the orchard as cautiously as they could so that no one would see them. And he made the page go first because the people in the castle did not know Tirant. Finally they came so close that the betrothed recognized the page, his younger brother, and told the men not to fire. When they were inside the castle the king came out to the hall to see him and to pay him honor.

"My lord," said Tirant, "you and your daughter mount our horses immediately. I'll take you to safety."

The king took the page's horse, and had the betrothed climb on its back; Tirant had the maiden climb on the back of his own horse. Then they raced out of the castle, galloping all the way, until they were a league from camp. When night fell on them, they rode more quickly. The king knew the terrain very well, and he went directly toward his strongest city: Tremicén.

When they reached the city of Tremicén there was great rejoicing because the people had recovered their king. The king had a fine room arranged for Tirant where he was well served. While he stayed there the king presented him with many gifts, and all the Moorish knights and others came to see him, and everyone was impressed with his agreeable manner.

One day Tirant came to the palace to ask the king's permission to go back to his lord, the commander, because he had given his word that he would return. The king answered:

"Virtuous Christian, do not leave me, I beg you. I've sent for your lord, the commander, and he will be here in ten days. Help me prepare the city, and I promise to ransom you and give you your freedom."

Tirant kissed the king's hands and feet, and said:

"My lord, I give you my word as a Christian that I will not leave you until I have killed King Escariano, or taken him prisoner, or until I've made him flee from your kingdom."

The king's daughter, seeing the beautiful disposition of Tirant and the virtuous acts he had done for the king, her father, and for her, and the praises that were bestowed upon him in everyone's presence, wished that God would do her the favor of having her betrothed die so that she could take Tirant for her husband.

After a few days had gone by, the commander of commanders came, and he was very happy when he learned that his son, and the king and his daughter, were out of that very grave danger. After bowing to the king, he praised Tirant highly. The king spoke to the commander, asking him to give Tirant his freedom. When it was done, Tirant kissed the king's hands and feet, and said:

"Sir, I swear to you as a Christian that I will not leave Your Grace until I have killed King Escariano or taken him prisoner, or made him leave all your lands."

The king and the others were very content.

When King Escariano learned that the King of Tremicén had escaped, his surprise turned to anger, and he set out to conquer the entire kingdom. And with his great power there were no cities, villas or castles that did not fall to him.

Hearing of this, the King of Tremicén often called his council together, and they reinforced the city, and gathered enough food to last them five years. One day, during the council, Tirant said to the king:

"Sir, do this for me: let me go as an ambassador to see King Escariano, and I'll find out what sort of situation his men are in, and if we can somehow rout them."

They all praised his advice, but most of the council were afraid he would cross over to the enemy camp, as many others had done.

Tirant got things ready, and with many men he went directly to King Escariano. When he was in the king's presence, he explained his mission:

"The King of Tremicén has sent me here because on several occasions he has heard people speak very highly of you, and he is certain that you are one of the wisest kings in the world. For that reason he is very astonished, and he wonders what has moved you to take up arms against him."

The king immediately replied:

"I want your lord to know that I have attacked him for a just reason. For no one, not your lord or anyone else, is unaware that long ago a marriage pact was drawn up between his daughter and me, signed and with the marriage date agreed upon. And now your king has treated the matter lightly, and tried to shame me. I have told you this so you will know that this maiden, whom I love and adore, is the cause for this war. And it will end with her and for no other reason. This is my reply to you."

And he turned his back, wanting to hear no more from Tirant. So Tirant left and went back to his lord, the King of Tremicén, and told him of their entire conversation. Then the king asked Tirant if the enemy had many men.

"In faith," said Tirant, "there are many, and more come to their aid every day. I wasn't able to see them all, but I would say more than eighty thousand."

They held council, and decided that Tirant and the commander would take ten thousand soldiers to another city called Asinac. Because if that city fell, the entire kingdom would be lost. So Tirant went there and fortified that city well.

The king stayed on in the city of Tremicén which was well supplied with everything he needed. And in this way they waited for the enemy to come.

It happened one day that a Jew who lived in the city of Tremicén, and was the wealthiest man in the city, left secretly and went to King Escariano. Very cunningly he told him:

"My lord, why are you plowing the sand? Everything you are doing is useless unless you capture King Tremicén first. Once he has fallen you will have power over the entire kingdom in two days. You would not have to travel the dangerous roads in fear; instead you and your men would be completely safe. If Your Lordship will reach an agreement with me I will give you a victory over your enemies, and I will also put the king and his daughter in your hands."

When King Escariano heard him say that, he took it as a joke, and he answered:

"How could you possibly do all that? But I'll tell you this: If you do arrange it, I give you my word as king to make you the most powerful man in my kingdom. But I can't believe that you could do what you said. It would be better for you to go back: instead of hurting them, you might bring me harm."

The Jew quickly replied:

"If Your Majesty will closely examine what I say, you'll understand that it's not a dream, but an infallible plan. If it will make you feel more secure, I will put my three sons in your power, and if I fail you are free to put them to a horrible death. I will do this for Your Majesty under the following conditions: I have a daughter, and I want her to have an honorable marriage (and I will give twelve thousand ducats as her dowry) with a Jew who sells oil in your camp. If you will arrange this for me, I promise to have you gain entry into the city of Tremicén. In my house there's a door that's next to the wall of the city, and it's under my care. I can put one hundred thousand soldiers into the city through there."

So they agreed, and the king arranged with the Jew that they would be in front of the city of Tremicén on the seventeenth of the month, and at midnight they would go inside under the cover of darkness.

At the proper time the king and all his captains were in front of the city of Tremicén, and the Jew did not forget the promise that was made concerning his daughter's marriage. He carefully opened the door of the Jewry, and the king rushed in with all his men. They went to the palace and fought, and finally they were able to get inside. They killed the King of Tremicén, his sons, and all the others. They took no prisoners except for the genteel lady. Then they attacked the castle, but they were not able to take it. King Escariano did not feel very safe there, so he left most of his men inside the city to guard it, while he left with the King of Tremicén's daughter who was crying over the deaths of her father, her brothers, and her betrothed. Then he put her in an impregnable castle.

The cruel news reached the commander and Tirant, and the Moors cried bitterly. They felt that they were lost, and they began to say that they should surrender to King Escariano.

Tirant told the commander:

"Sir, that is not the thing to do. You have ten thousand soldiers here, and you still have some castles and towns under your command. We can defend ourselves well here."

The commander agreed with Tirant's advice, but he still mourned the death of his king, and that of his sons even more. They wondered how the great destruction had happened, with the city being so well guarded. And they learned the truth from a man who had had his house looted, seven of his sons killed, while his wife and other children were being held under guard. He told them how the Jew had betrayed the city, and how King Escariano had then ordered all the Jew's possessions taken. Then this Jewish traitor was placed in prison and tied up. They removed all his clothing, cudgeled him, poured honey over him, and the next day had him quartered and left for the dogs to eat. For the king had said: Who can protect himself from a traitor? The treachery he had committed to his own lord, he could just as well do to him and to the entire city if need be.

Tirant then learned that King Escariano had taken the King of Tremicén's daughter to the very strong castle of Mont Tuber. The new queen was now being held in this castle with seventy men to guard her.

On a day following these cruel events, Tirant went to the city gate, worn with care. He was thinking about what had happened to his princess, and wondering what danger had befallen Plaerdemavida, and about how all his relatives were captives of the Moors. He did not know whether to leave, or even if the Moors would allow him to go. While he was thinking of all this, a Christian captive from Albania came out the gate, crying and lamenting because his master had cruelly whipped him, and was making him dig in an orchard of his near the city. Tirant knew the captive because he had talked to him several times, and considered him a discreet man. He felt pity for him, and thinking that there was no one else he could trust, he called the slave over, and said to him:

"If you will do something for me, you will be given your freedom to leave, or to stay here if you wish. However, you will have to let yourself be whipped in our camp with a strap that will not hurt you very much, and you will have to have your ears cut a little. With your help, we'll be able to take the castle of Mont Tuber where the king is. If it turns out as I think it will, you'll be able to become a great lord. And if it does not turn out well, I will still make sure you are given your liberty, and that you have a good life."

The Christian captive answered:

"I want very much to have my freedom again, so I'll do what you're asking."

Tirant thanked him, and said:

"I give you my word as a knight that I will not eat until you have your freedom."

Tirant immediately left the captive and went to talk to the commander. With the money he had, he ransomed the captive for one hundred ducats.

One day it happened that the king sent two men who told Tirant's forces that if they would come to terms with him he would be very generous to them. The commander and Tirant told them that they were not interested in any proposition; instead they wanted to avenge the deaths of the King of Tremicén and his sons. After they had this discussion, Tirant had a meal brought out for them while the Albanian prepared to carry out the plan they had made.

When the meal was over the Albanian went over to where the silver was, and stole a large, gilded urn made of silver. The guard began to shout so that Tirant, as he was talking with the men from the town, asked what all the uproar was about. Then everyone saw the Albanian running with many men behind him, and they saw them catch him and take him to the captain. The guard had hold of him by the hair, and he said:

"My lord, I would like you to pass judgment on this thief. He stole this silver urn."

Tirant wanted the commander to speak first, and he said:

"My sentence is for him to be hanged."

Tirant then said:

"Commander, this is no time for us to be killing people unless it's in battle. I beg you to change the sentence, and have him whipped and his ears cut."

So they did what he said in the presence of the men from the town. After they cut his ears they tied the urn to his neck and whipped him around the camp. The third time around, when he was in front of the town, he pulled away violently, untied his hands and began running toward the town.

The guard who was running after him fell down purposefully so that the Albanian had time to go inside the town. The men on the walls defended him with their crossbows so that no one could catch him. The townspeople took him up to the castle where the king was, and when they saw him naked and whipped, with his ears cut and bleeding, they felt sorry for him. They gave him a shirt and other clothes, and the king had so much pity on him that he let him keep the urn, and received him into his household.

Tirant pretended to be very angry at the Albanian's escape. He told the men there to ask the king to give the man back, and he said that if he would not do it, that he would cut off the hands and feet, nose and ears of every man they caught, and then he would kill them. The king answered that in no way would he give him back, and that if he could catch Tirant he would do worse to him than they had done to the captive. Tirant would listen to no more, and he left with all his men for the city they had come from. The Albanian then told King Escariano:

"When I think of the cruel things they've done to me, and the infamy that could come to me if it becomes known, my heart cries out for revenge on that treacherous, mad captain who was starving us to death. If I committed a crime it was because I needed the money. But, my lord, if Your Excellency will give me permission to come and go, I will bring you news every day about what your enemies are doing, what they are planning and where they go. That way Your Highness can do the same thing to them that you did to that famous and illustrious King of Tremicén."

The king said:

"I will agree to that: You can come and go whenever you like."

He ordered all the guards to let him pass by at will. The king asked some of his knights for advice concerning this matter, and they all told him:

"My lord, this man has been hurt very badly by his own people, and he'll do anything to bring about their total destruction. But still, it would be a good idea to keep an eye on him."

The Albanian left the castle by a back door so that no one would see him, and went directly to Tirant and told him everything that was said. Tirant gave him seven doubloons, three and one half reals, and some loose change, a sword and a basket of peaches, because there were none in that town since Tirant had had all the trees cut down to level the orchard around the villa. And Tirant told him:

"Tell the king, in secret so that he'll be more inclined to believe you, that I am having a great deal of bread kneaded because I plan to be there in three or four days."

The Albanian left Tirant, and when he was in the castle, King Escariano welcomed him. The Albanian gave the peaches to the queen, and the king was more pleased with them than if he had given her a villa, because he knew that the queen liked them, and he had not seen her laugh or smile since she had been with him. After the Albanian had given her the gift he showed the king the money he had, and said to him:

"My lord, look at this money that I took from one of the men in the enemy camp. If I go there often I can bring many things, because a relative of mine is in the service of this wicked captain, and he secretly tells me everything he does. My lord, he told me that he is having a great deal of bread made and a large supply of food stored up in order to come here. You have time to get ready to attack and defeat him."

The Albanian's words pleased the king a great deal, and he said:

"Now I will see if your relative told you the truth."

On the third day Tirant came and stayed in the same place that he had the other times. The king placed great faith in the Albanian's words and he decided to appoint him as one of the main guards of the castle. As companions, he gave him six very loyal men who had been in his service a long time. When it was this Albanian's turn to stand guard, he bought some sweetmeats and invited all the men who were with him to eat and drink. And he stood guard-duty every five days.

Tirant returned after having been away for three days, and they continually discussed peace with the king, but Tirant drew out finalizing a treaty as long as he could. This lasted two months, and Tirant was always coming and going, and he seldom attacked anyone. The king often made the Albanian go to Tirant's camp so that he would bring back fruits and sweet-meats for the queen. One day he brought a mule loaded with wine, and a bloody sword. When he was before the king he said to him:

"My lord, I learned that the captain was having a great deal of wine brought to the city, and when I heard of it I went out to the road. There, one muleteer fell behind the others. I hit him in the side with a stone, and he fell to the ground. Then I struck him so many times that I left him for dead. I took the sword and the mule from him, and it was loaded with the finest wine I have seen in many days. So I beg you, my lord, please give me permission to set up a tavern here, and when this supply has run out, I will steal or buy more, and I'll do all the harm, evil and dishonor to them that I can."

The king was well pleased, and many Moors came to drink every day. And every night that the Moor stood guard he took a large cask of wine up to the tower, and gave his companions a good deal to drink, and all the Moors were very happy to have him there.

Tirant talked with King Escariano and his men many times, going back and forth often with an escort of soldiers. When he saw with his own eyes how much King Escariano trusted the Albanian, Tirant had a round container made of iron and put some holes in it. When the night for the treachery arrived, and it was the Albanian's turn to stand watch, the Albanian put hot coals inside the container. The wind came in through the holes which were so small that the fire did not go out. Then he wrapped the container in a piece of leather and held it to his chest. When they were in the tower, standing guard, and his companions began drinking, the Albanian hid the container in a hole so that the fire would not go out. They had some large drums, and they stayed there drinking and beating them until it was nearly midnight. There were special liqueurs in the wine to bring on sleep. And with the pleasure of drink the guards slept so soundly that they never awoke. When the Albanian saw that the counter-round had gone by and the guards were sleeping, he took out the fire-box, and hid its light with his cape. Then he lit a straw, and put it in a niche in the wall that faced the camp. He did this three times. Tirant soon saw this signal which they had planned in advance, and he quickly left the camp with only a few men. All the other men stayed behind, ready and armed, waiting to be called, and the commander stayed with them as their captain. Because of all the water there, Tirant and his men had to pass near a tall tower, but the Albanian was making a great deal of noise with the drums, and when Tirant passed close to the tower they were not heard. When they were near and the guards called out, "All clear, all clear," they quickly ran ten or twelve steps, and when the guards were silent, they stopped. They kept this up until they had passed by the first tower and reached the other tower. Tirant made his men stop, and he went to the foot of the tower alone and found a cord that the Albanian had thrown down. He had tied the other end to his leg in case he fell asleep, so that when the cord was pulled he would wake up. But he never stopped beating on the drums, and when he felt the cord moving he quickly went near the tower and pulled up a rope ladder that he tied very tightly to the wall, and then he tied another. Tirant climbed the first one, and when he saw the guards sleeping he said to the Albanians:

"What shall we do with these men?"

"My lord," he answered, "leave them there. They're in no condition to do any harm."

However, Tirant wanted to see for himself, and he found the six of them with their heads cut off, covered with blood. When he saw this he had his men come up, and he put one of them in charge of the drums. There were one hundred sixty men, and they spread out over the tower. Then, with the Albanian going first, they went down to the warden's chamber. When the warden saw all these men coming he got up, completely naked, took a sword in his hand and tried to defend himself. Tirant swung an axe down on his head and split it in half, and his brains fell out onto the ground. His wife began to scream, and the Albanian, who was nearest did the same thing to her that Tirant had done to her husband. Afterward they went through the castle, and shot the bolts on the doors to the chambers, and the noise of the drums was so loud that no one heard a sound.

They went up to the towers and the guards there thought they were the watch, and said nothing to them. And when they came near they threw them off the castle through the merlons. One of them fell onto the barbican and into the moat, and was saved. Soon he got up and went shouting through the villa and everyone woke up. The news spread through the villa, but in the castle they still did not know, except for one man who was fishing. He heard the noise and opened the windows of his chamber, and he heard many people inside the castle.

Then he began to cry out, and his shouts were heard by those in the castle, but when they tried to leave their chambers they found the doors bolted. The king, who had been sleeping in the main tower, barricaded himself there with the queen and a chamber-maid.

When day broke they put many flags on the castle towers, and held great celebrations. All the outsiders in the villa fled. When the commander saw that the castle had been taken and saw the others fleeing, he attacked them and took many prisoners. When he returned, they stationed many men in the villa and others on the barbicans and in the orchards near the villa. When the commander went up to the castle he saw that none of his men had been killed or wounded, and he was the most astonished man in the world: he thought Tirant must be more angel than human, because nothing that he tried turned out to be impossible.

They searched the entire castle and found it full of many kinds of food: millet and wheat, sorghum and panic-grass—enough to last seven years, with a sparkling spring of water that came out of a rock. That night the king took pity on the queen, and calling down from a window in the tower, he said:

"Which of you is the knight I can surrender to?"

"Sir," said Tirant, "here is the commander, and a very virtuous knight."

The king realized that this was the ambassador he had talked with so many times, and he said to him:

"Since you have been sent to me as an ambassador, give me your pledge of safety so that I can do my duty as a knight and a crowned king."

Tirant answered:

"I will guarantee your safety for a month after you surrender to me. I give you my word."

The king felt as good about that as if he had been given absolute freedom. He came down from the tower, opened the door, and stood in the entryway, his sword in his hand. And he said:

"Have them bring me that little child." (This was a boy of no more than five years of age, the son of a woman who baked bread.)

When the boy was near him, he knighted the boy and kissed him on the mouth. Then, handing his sword to the boy, he placed himself in his power.

The commander then seized the king and took him to a room where he had him put in chains. This made Tirant very angry, but he said nothing so that he would not offend the commander. When the king was in chains, they went into the main tower where they found the queen in tears.

Tirant had one hundred thousand doubloons sent to Tunis to the commander's cousin who was magistrate of the king of that region. He begged him to release Lord Agramunt and all the others who were on his galley. The governor took them all out of captivity and sent them to Tirant. When they were taken on land they lost all hope of ever being freed—until they saw their captain. And don't think they felt only a small amount of relief when they saw him. Tirant immediately asked his cousin, Lord Agramunt, if he had seen Plaerdemavida. He answered:

"Since that day we lost sight of the galley, I never heard anything about her again. I'm afraid she died in the stormy sea."

It happened one day that the queen called Tirant to her chamber. Not knowing what she might want, Tirant went quickly. When he was there, the queen smiled and had him sit at her side. Then she said softly:

"My eyes have found their lost light, and when I raise my head I see you as lord of the world, for heaven and earth and all things that God has created obey you. That night when you brought us out of the terrible prison, I found such pleasure in your virtuous appearance, so handsomely formed, that I detested my betrothed and could not continue to look at him. I beg you, sir, do me the honor of ruling this land at my side."

Tirant was astonished, and he immediately replied:

"It fills me with great love to serve you, but I must confess my sin: I have been in love with a maiden of high esteem for a long while, as she has been with me. If I should betray her love, it would be worse than death to me. And there is one more reason that I must not forget: you are a Moor and I am a Christian, and our marriage would not be lawful."

With tears in her eyes, the queen replied:

"You say that I am a Moor and you are a Christian, and that such a marriage is impossible. Let me tell you how it can be done: you can easily become a Moor, and then the marriage can take place. As for the maiden you say you are in love with, I believe that is simply an excuse, and the real reason is that I do not please you."

Tirant reflected for a moment, and he saw a way by which Christianity would be exalted. He decided to show the queen great love so that she would decide to become a Christian. And smiling, he said:

"My reason obliges me to keep the faith I have sworn. But I beg of you, my lady, to receive baptism in the holy and true Christian faith, and with my help you will regain your kingdom. And for a husband I will give you a young and virtuous crowned king. Although I cannot take you as a wife, since I already have one, you would always be my friend."

The queen dried her tears and sighed:

"Your wise words have led me to this decision: give me baptism quickly, for you are the flower of all those who are baptized."

When Tirant saw that the queen wanted to become a Christian, he quickly had a gold basin and a pitcher brought from the booty they had taken from King Escariano. Tirant had the queen's head uncovered, letting her hair fall loose, and it was so beautiful that her face seemed more angelic than human. Tirant had her kneel down, and he poured water over her head from the pitcher, and said:

"Maragdina, I baptize you in the name of the Father, the Son, and the Holy Spirit."

Then she declared herself to be a good Christian, and there, in the presence of everyone, four ladies who served the queen received holy baptism. And they led very saintly lives.

When King Escariano heard that the queen had become a Christian, he sent for Tirant and told him:

"I tell you, Captain, since I see that my lady, the queen, has become a Christian, I want to follow her virtuous works. So I beg you to give me holy baptism, and to be my brother in arms for as long as we live, being friends of our friends and enemies of our enemies."

After the queen had been baptized, and the king had been instructed about Christianity, Tirant took the king out of prison and had him go down to the city. There was a lovely square in that villa, and Tirant had ordered them to make a pretty catafalque there, nicely decorated with brocade and satin cloths. The king sat on a beautiful chair covered with brocade on the catafalque, and a large silver bowl filled with water was placed at one end of the catafalque. Tirant had a very wide ladder constructed so that everyone who wanted to be baptized could go up and down.

King Escariano's captains and all his men, peacefully and unarmed, left the camp on foot because they were very near the villa. When they came to the entrance, the captains and knights went in first, then the others followed them. When they were in the square before the king's catafalque, they all bowed deeply to him, and asked what his lordship wanted of them. With a strong voice he said:

"My faithful vassals, relatives and brothers: Divine Mercy has had pity on me and on all of you—if you wish it—for He has enlightened my soul and my understanding. I have received many favors from this captain: First, he has taken me out of prison and given me freedom. Second, he has instructed me about the holy Catholic faith so that I know for a certainty that the sect of Mohammed is false and wicked, and all those who believe in it are going to total destruction and condemnation. So I beg you and command you, as good vassals and brothers, to join me and receive baptism. Trust me: you will be receiving baptism for the salvation of your souls. Those who want baptism should not move; those who do not want baptism, empty the square and leave room for the others."

After he had said this the king took off his outer garments in everyone's presence, remaining in his shirt. Tirant led him to the bowl, and pouring water from the pitcher over his head, he baptized him, saying:

"King Escariano, I baptize you in the name of the Father, and the Son, and the Holy Spirit."

Then Tirant baptized almost all the prisoners, for most of them were close relatives of the king. Afterward two captains and all their lineage were baptized: one of their people was called Bencarag and the other Capcani. On that day more than six thousand Moors were baptized by Tirant. The others stayed there the next day and the following days until they were all made Christians. Few of them left, and the most vile were those who did not receive baptism.

The news of all this was soon spread throughout Barbary, so that it reached the ears of the kings who were coming to King Escariano's aid. Very angry, they advanced as quickly as they could and took away his entire kingdom. They gave it to the King of Persia, and immediately crowned him king.

While these kings were conquering King Escariano's lands, messengers came to him daily with the bad news that they were taking his entire kingdom from him, and that he had only three castles that were defending themselves and refusing to surrender.

After King Escariano became a Christian, Tirant begged him to give all the villas and cities he had taken from the King of Tremicén back to the queen, to whom they belonged. The king very generously did this, but then he begged Tirant, as a brother in arms, to give the queen to him for his wife. So one day Tirant approached the queen, and said:

"I beg you to take this king for your husband. He loves you very much. You already know him, and you would be much better off with him than with someone who may not love you."

The queen listened to Tirant, and replied:

"I have complete trust in you, so I am putting myself and my possessions in your power. I will do whatever you command me."

Tirant knelt on the ground and gave her many thanks. He immediately sent for the king and the friar, and in everyone's presence they were betrothed. The following day they heard mass, because they were Catholic Christians. After the wedding, which took place with great solemnity—as corresponds to royalty—King Escariano took possession of the entire kingdom of Tremicén, as husband of the queen, and she was happy because it was at Tirant's command. The king loved Tirant above all others, and there was nothing that he would not do for him. And Tirant likewise loved the king and queen.

While the king and Tirant were celebrating this new marriage, news reached the king daily that the Moorish kings would soon take the three castles, and that they would fall on him and on all the Christians, and would give them all cruel deaths.

When Tirant heard of this, he said:

"Sir, we need to think of how we can save our lives. Let's gather all our men and see how many are prepared to go into battle."

"What?" said the commander. "Do you think you're the lord of the whole world? You ought to be satisfied with imprisoning this magnanimous king, and go on back to the land you came from. Let us live according to our own law, and let the new Christians forget about this so-called holy baptism. If these kings are coming with so many troops, and they find us adhering to their law, they'll have mercy on us."

King Escariano turned to the commander in a rage, and he brought his bare sword down on the commander's head so hard that his brains spilled out onto the chamber floor, and he said:

"Oh, you dog, you son of a dog, born into a wicked sect! This is the payment such a vile person deserves!"

Tirant was very displeased at the commander's death, and he felt very angry. But he held himself back and did not reprimand the king because he was afraid of causing more trouble. Some people were glad the commander was dead, and others were not. But his death served to restrain many.

Tirant mustered all the men to see how many there were, and they counted 18,230 horsemen and forty-five thousand foot soldiers. Tirant paid them all. Then they enlisted twenty-five thousand more. At the same time, four hundred forty horses and many arms arrived from Tunis where they had disembarked after arriving from Sicily. And now Tirant was unafraid of attacking three thousand enemy horsemen.

The king and Tirant left the city with all their men to meet the enemy and see if they could resist them. When they were three leagues away from them, at the top of a mountain, the Christians could see all the Moorish forces that were coming. They set up their tents in view of each other, and many embassies were sent back and forth. The Moors sent word to King Escariano, telling him and Tirant and all the other Christians to convert to Mohammedanism, because if they did not, they would all die a cruel death. When Tirant heard this, he mocked them and would not give them a reply. Then the ambassadors became very angry with Tirant.

They had conquered all of King Escariano's realm, and now they were going to attack him. Tirant said:

"Sir, they've raised camp, so they'll be here tomorrow. Your Lordship can stay here in the city with half the men while I take the other half, and we'll see how well organized they are."

"Oh, Tirant! I would much rather go with you, and we can leave Lord Agramunt here as the captain."

Tirant agreed, and made Lord Agramunt captain, telling him:

"Keep your horses saddled, and your men armed. When you see a red flag with my arms painted on it, have all your men attack on the right, and we'll destroy our enemy."

To reach the Christians, the Moors had to cross over a tall mountain that had many springs. During that night and the following day, Tirant went around the mountain and he could see all the Moors coming from a great distance. Tirant rode into a dense thicket, and he had all the men dismount and take their ease while he climbed a tall pine tree and watched the enemy come up the mountain. They set up their tents near the springs, and they were still a league away from the city. The ones who followed behind set up camp at the foot of the mountain where there were beautiful meadows and a canal. The men here had about four thousand horses.

When Tirant saw that nearly half the enemy had dismounted, he and the king attacked their camp and killed so many Moors that the number of corpses stretched out on the ground were a wonder to behold. And there would have been even more if night had not fallen. The Moors up on the mountain heard the cries, but they did not think the Christians would dare come so close to their camp.

The morning of the following day, as soon as the sun came out, King Meneador came down from the mountain, not suspecting that King Escariano and Tirant would be there. He thought, instead, that these must be thieving marauders. So he sent a messenger to them, telling them to convert back to the Mohammedan faith or he would hang as many of them as he found.

Tirant told the messenger:

"You tell your lord that I don't intend to answer his madness. But if he's a crowned king, and brave enough to come down the mountain with his men, I'll let him feel the strength of the one he wants to hang."

The messenger went back to his lord with the reply, and the king was so enraged that he dug his spurs into his horse, and all his men followed. The battle was harsh and cruel. After they had fought for a time, and there were many deaths on both sides, King Meneador retreated toward the mountain, and he sent for his brother, the King of Lower India, to come to his aid. When he was there, King Meneador told him:

"Brother, these baptized Christians are fighting so hard that I've lost most of my men, and I'm slightly wounded too. I won't hold myself as a knight unless I kill with my own hands a great traitor who is their captain. His armor and the vest he wears are damask green with three stars on each side. On one side they're gold and on the other side silver. Around his neck he wears a gold Mohammed with a long beard. And this Mohammed carries a small child holding onto his neck as he crosses a river. And that must be the one who helps him in his battles."

The King of Lower India haughtily replied:

"Show him to me. I will avenge you even if he has ten Mohammeds in his belly."

His men quickly mounted their horses and bore down upon the Christians. Shouting wildly, like madmen, they went into battle, and soon you could see horses running around without riders. When Tirant broke his lance, he made use of his ax, and he wounded or gave death with every blow. The two kings drew up to Tirant and wounded him with the point of a sword. Finding himself wounded, Tirant cried out:

"Oh, king, you who have dealt me a deadly wound according to the great pain I feel, before I enter hell, you will go before me as a messenger to open the gates, for I will send you there quickly!"

He brought his ax down on the king's head, splitting it into two parts, and the king fell at the feet of his horses. When the Moors saw his body on the ground, they struggled to pick it up. This was the King of Lower India who had spoken so boastfully. When the other king saw his brother dead, he fought desperately.

The other kings were told of his death, the King of Bogia in particular, for he had brought them together. Then they raised camp and set up their tents at the foot of the mountain.

The Christians, seeing how many men they had and that Tirant was wounded and in great pain, decided to leave during the night. The following morning the Moors prepared to give battle, but they found no one. They followed the Christians' tracks and came to the city where they had taken refuge.

Tirant had Lord Agramunt take his men out and do battle with them, and many men died on both sides. Then the Christians retreated back into the city while the Moors pounded on the gates with their lances.

The following day Lord Agramunt led his men into battle, and many died on both sides, and again they retreated into the city. Tirant was troubled that he could not take part, and that they were losing men, and he told the king:

"Sir, I don't think we should go out and do battle so often. We're only losing men."

And so they waited until Tirant was healthy again. Then, when he was nearly cured, he put on his armor and mounted his horse, and with most of the men he attacked one side of the camp. The Moors, in a tumult, came out to fight the Christians. And that day, and many others that followed, Tirant came out the worst. When Tirant saw his men fleeing that day, and that he could not keep them in order, he went to the river. He saw the King of Africa riding toward him wearing a helmet with a crown of gold and many precious stones. His saddle was silver, and his stirrups gold, while his jubbah was crimson and embroidered with large oriental pearls.

When the king saw Tirant's troubled face, he approached him and said:

"Are you the captain of the Christians?"

Tirant did not reply, but instead looked at his men who had left him, and all the dead bodies and banners scattered over the ground. That day, they had scarcely defended themselves against the Moors.

In a loud voice that the Moors and the wounded could hear, he cried out:

"Oh, poor men! Why do you bear arms? Oh, sad, vile men: you will be rightly condemned for this day on which you die so miserably, and your reputation will suffer greatly!"

When the King of Africa heard him crying this way, he called out to his men:

"I'm going to cross the river, and I'll put this Christian dog in chains or I'll kill him. If I need any assistance, come and help me."

When the king had crossed over, he rode swiftly at Tirant, and struck him so hard with his lance that Tirant's horse sank to its knees. The lance passed through his brassard and his breast-plate, and slightly pierced his chest. Tirant was feeling such great pain for the dead men, and was thinking of the princess, and he didn't notice the king until he had been wounded. He drew his sword, since his lance had been broken at the outset. And they fought for a long space of time. The king fought valiantly, and when it had lasted a long while, Tirant thrust hard at the king, but he could not reach him because the king's horse suddenly turned. However, he caught the horse's head and cut it off, so that the horse and the king tumbled to the ground. The king's men came to his aid, and mounted him on another horse, even though Tirant tried to stop them.

When Tirant realized that he could not hold out any longer, he seized a Moor and took away his lance. Then he wounded the first, the second and the third men he encountered, and knocked them to the ground; then he wounded the fourth, fifth and sixth and also knocked them down.

The Moors were astonished at the way one lone man bore arms.

Lord Agramunt was at a window in the castle, and he recognized Tirant by his coat of arms and saw that he was fighting alone. And he cried out:

"Men, go quickly and help our captain. He's about to lose his life."

Then the king went out with the few men he had. Tirant was wounded in three places, and his horse had been struck many times. For this reason Tirant was forced to retreat, but he did so against his will, and they pursued him right up to the gates.

The doctors arrived and had Tirant's armor removed, and they found many wounds including three that were very dangerous.

When the Moors saw that the Christians had withdrawn inside the city, they tightened the siege and crossed over the river. They brought so many oxen and camels that they could not be counted. They used these as an obstacle to the Christians in battle, for their horses could not run, and no one could enter or leave the city.

Tirant was afraid they might mine under the castle. He ordered the men to make a countermine, and in all the lower rooms they were to place brass basins. This was done so that if a pickaxe was about to come through a wall in that room, all the brass basins would clang together and make a great noise. After the brass basins were set up, they began to work on the countermine.

After a few days, when Tirant was well and ready to bear arms, a serving girl inside the castle was kneading flour, and she heard the basins moving around, making noise. She ran quickly to tell her mistress:

"I don't know what it is, but I've heard folks say that when basins make a noise it's the sign of a storm or of bloodshed."

The lady was the wife of the captain of the castle, and she quickly went to tell her husband, and he told the king and Tirant.

Secretly, without making a sound, they went to the room, and saw that what the girl had said was true. They quickly armed themselves and went into a chamber, and not even an hour went by before they saw light in the room. The Moors who were digging thought no one in the castle had heard them, and they made the hole much bigger. Then they began to come out of the mine. When there were more than seventy Moors in the room, the men from the castle went in and slew and quartered everyone they found. The ones who could escape back through the mine certainly didn't stand around waiting for each other, but Tirant had many bombards fired into the mine, and everyone inside died.

Tirant saw that his men were nearly faint from hunger, and he decided to do battle. He told the king:

"Sir, I'll take half the men we have left, and you can take the other half. I'll go into the little forest there, and as soon as the sun comes up, you go out through the gate of Tremicén and go all around the city, and you attack the center of their camp while I attack from the other side, and we'll see if we can't confuse them. If we do, we can take over their camp. But what disturbs me most are the cattle: we'll have to go right through them, and every time we do, they'll kill many of our horses."

A Genoese who had been a slave on Tirant's galley when the ship went down spoke up. His name was Almedixer, and he was a very discreet man and was knowledgeable about many things. He said:

"Captain, do you want me to make all the cattle run off so that there won't even be a sign of one around? The Moors will go running after them to get them back, and that will be the time to attack their camp and fall upon them."

"If you can do that," said Tirant, "upon Carmesina's name I promise to make you a great lord and give you villas and castles and a great inheritance."

The king said to Tirant:

"Brother, if that's what you're going to do, I beg you to let me go into the forest. And when I see the banner flying from the highest tower I'll attack the center of the camp."

Tirant agreed, and ordered everyone to shoe their horses and repair their saddles.

The Genoese took the hair of many goats, and mutton fat, and he crushed it all together and put it in shallow pans, and he filled more than seventy of them.

Right at the hour of midnight the king went into the forest without any of the Moors seeing him. Almedixer took the pans of grease he had made and went out of the castle at dawn, and put them one next to the other.

Then he set them on fire. When the flames were going well, the wind blew the smoke toward the cattle. And when they smelled the odor they stampeded through the middle of the camp, bringing down tents and injuring men and horses so that it seemed like all the devils in hell were after them. They even ran into each other so that hardly an ox or camel was left uninjured. Many Moors on foot and on horseback pursued them to make them turn back, and all the Moors were astonished, not understanding what had caused the stampede.

When the oxen were gone, Tirant had the white and green flag raised. The king saw the flag and rode out of the forest, crying:

"Long live the Christians!"

As they had planned, Tirant also attacked from the other side. Then the terrible, cruel battle unrolled. Whoever saw it could tell the goings on of it all, for you could see thrusts of lance and sword being given and taken that brought awful grief, and in a few hours excellent knights were lying dead on the ground. All the battles came together and made such a noise that it sounded like the earth would fall in. You could see Tirant here and there, tearing helmets from men's heads and shields from their bodies, killing and wounding and doing the most astonishing things in the world in his ever-burning fury. King Escariano was doing very well, for he was a very good knight, young and courageous. As for the Moors, there were some very good and valiant knights, the King of Africa in particular who, because of the death of his brother, threw himself against the Christians most cruelly. The King of Bogia was also a very courageous knight.

The battle was long and hard fought, and mercy was shown by no one. Everyone was using their weapons, and it was a wonder to behold. We mustn't forget about Lord Agramunt, for he fought so well that the enemy feared him.

It happened that the King of Africa recognized Tirant by his armor and rode toward him, and they ran at each other, and both the king and Tirant were knocked to the ground. But Tirant feared death and was the more spirited, and he got up first, while the king was still lying on the ground. He reached down to cut the straps of his helmet, but before he could do so the Moors saw their king on the ground, and it was a wonder that they did not kill Tirant. They pulled him off the king's body two times and threw him on the ground. When Lord Agramunt saw Tirant in such great danger, he rode over to him and saw that the camp commander was doing everything he could to kill Tirant. Lord Agramunt turned to the commander, and they engaged in such a hard fought battle that every blow intended to bring death—one of them to defend Tirant and the other to try to attack him—and both of them were badly wounded.

Almedixer was near and cried out in alarm. King Escariano raced into the tumult and saw the King of Bogia standing over Tirant, about to cut off his head. These two kings were brothers, and King Escariano recognized his brother, but still, when he saw Tirant in that situation, he immediately thrust his lance into his brother's back so powerfully that it went right through his armor and came out the other side, piercing his heart, and the King of Bogia fell to the ground, dead. Then the battle grew more cruel than it had ever been, and on that day many men from both sides died.

The battle went on very cruelly, throughout the day, but when night fell, they broke apart. The Christians went back into the city very happily, because they had been victorious on the field. They knew for a certainty that three kings had died in the battle: the King of Bogia, King Geber, and the King of Granada. Among the wounded, mention is made only of the King of Damascus and the King of Tana.

That night the men and horses rested, and before dawn the Christians were armed and ready, and the Moors were surprised that they were eager to fight, because the Moors had not been able to bury their dead. The battle took place on the second day, and it was very cruel and bloody. Large numbers of Moors died, but not very many Christians: for every Christian, one hundred Moors died. The reason so many Moors were killed was because they weren't as well armed as the Christians, and their horses and trappings weren't as good. The battle lasted five days, and the Moors couldn't endure it any longer because of the stench from the corpses, so they sent messengers to the Christians, asking for a truce. King Escariano and Tirant felt very pleased, and they agreed willingly.

The Moors then took their dead and threw them into the river, each with a note of identification attached so that downriver their relatives could bury them. But there were so many dead bodies that the river was stopped up, and the water had to change course.

Then the Moors went up the mountain while the Christians went back to the city. During this truce the Marquis of Luzana arrived; he was a servant to the King of France. In Tunis he heard of Tirant's great victories, and he decided to go to him.

The Moors decided to leave one night before the truce was over, and go to the mountains of Fez where they could defend themselves against the Christians. So, very unexpectedly, nearly at the hour of midnight, they broke camp and went on their way. Early the next morning the guards came running to the city gates to warn the captain that the Moors were leaving. When Tirant saw that they had gone beyond the pass, he set himself to conquering all the kingdoms and lands this side of the pass. After many days had gone by, Lord Agramunt said to the captain:

"My lord, it seems to me that if we want to end this conquest quickly, I should go beyond the pass to conquer the villas, castles and cities there. After Your Lordship has taken over these kingdoms, you can go over to that land, and you will easily be the master of all Barbary."

Tirant was pleased with what Lord Agramunt told him. He consulted King Escariano, and they agreed that he should leave soon. Lord Agramunt departed with ten thousand men on horseback, and eighteen thousand foot soldiers. When he had gone beyond the pass he learned that the kings had left, and each had gone back to his own land. Seeing that there were so few armed men in that land, Lord Agramunt began to conquer it, and he took over many cities, villas and castles, some willingly and others by force.

They came near a city called Montagata which belonged to the daughter of the King of Belamerin (This king had died at the beginning of the war) and to her betrothed. When the people in the city learned that the Christians were so nearby, they held a council and decided to send the keys of the city to Lord Agramunt, and, very kindly, he took them and granted them everything they requested. But when they were near the city, the rulers changed their minds and decided that they would die before they would surrender.

When Lord Agramunt saw that he had been mocked, he decided to go into battle, for he was as bold and hard as he could be. As he came close to a wall, they shot at him with a crossbow. The arrow hit him in the mouth and came out the other side. When his men saw him stretched out on the ground, badly wounded, they thought he was dead. They put him on a shield and carried him to his tent, and they fought no more that day. Then Lord Agramunt made a vow to God and to the holy apostles that because of the way they had deceived him and because of the great pain his wound was causing him, he would not leave until the city was taken and his sword had slain everyone: men and women, large and small, old and young. And he quickly sent word to Tirant.

When Tirant received the news that his cousin had been so badly wounded, he and all his men went to the city. Before they could dismount he ordered them to attack the city, and the battle was so fierce and so harsh that they took a large tower—a mosque—attached to the city walls. When night fell Tirant ordered a halt to the fighting. In the morning the Moors sent word to the captain that they would surrender on condition that they be allowed to live by their own laws, and they would give them thirty thousand gold crowns every year, and free all the prisoners they held. Tirant answered that because of the act they had committed against his cousin they would have to go to Lord Agramunt, and whatever he decided would be done.

When the Moors stood before Lord Agramunt, he would consent to nothing, no matter how much they pleaded with him. Then the town decided to send their lady and several maidens to see if they could reach an agreement with him, since many times a maiden's pleas are successful. At this point the book presents an incident to relate the deeds of Plaerdemavida.

CHAPTER XI - PLAERDEMAVIDA

By the great mercy of God, Plaerdemavida was saved from the shipwreck and taken to the city of Tunis, to the house of a fisherman's daughter, as was related previously. Then, after two years had passed the fisherman's daughter took a husband near that city. And while they held Plaerdemavida captive there, she always lived very honestly, working gold and silk as the maidens of Greece are accustomed to doing. It happened one day that her mistress went to the city of Montagata, and left Plaerdemavida to watch the house. She had gone to the city to make some purchases, and while she was there she went to talk to the king's daughter, and she told her:

"My lady, I've been told that you are planning to marry, and that you are supplying yourself with blouses embroidered with gold and silk and other things proper for maidens. I have a young slave who is able to do what I have taught her from the time she was an infant: to embroider all manner of things as befits young women. Here are some samples of what she can do. If you want her, I will give her to you for one hundred doubloons, even though I will be losing all the training I have given her."

The princess, seeing the samples, wanted her very much, and she said that she would be happy to give her the one hundred doubloons. The Moor said:

"I'll be glad to give her to you for that price, on one condition: you must tell her that I have loaned her to you for two months, because if she guessed that I had sold her, she would be so sad that she would fall into despair."

Plaerdemavida was placed in her hands and she came to love the princess very much. It happened a short time later that the city was attacked, and the Moors took many Christians prisoner. Among the men they captured was a soldier who had been an oarsman on Tirant's galley when it was lost. Plaerdemavida recognized him, and she said:

"Aren't you one of the Christians who were on Tirant's galley when it went down at sea?"

"My lady," said the man "it's true: I was there, and I nearly drowned. I reached the shore half dead, and afterward I was beaten, and bought and sold. I went through great trials in those days."

"What can you tell me about Tirant?" said Plaerdemavida. "Where did he die?"

"By the Virgin Mary!" said the prisoner. "He is very much alive. He's right here. He's the commander, and he's using all his might to conquer this land."

He also told her that Lord Agramunt was wounded, and then she asked him:

"What became of Plaerdemavida?"

"That maiden you're asking about," said the prisoner, "it's believed that she died in the sea, and our captain has grieved deeply over her."

When she heard the news she ordered all the prisoners to flee. Hearing that Tirant was alive and so near, she also wanted very much to escape, but considering how Tirant had conquered so much of the Barbary Coast, and thinking of the victories that were told about the Christian captain, she was very happy. For she had known nothing about him and believed that he had drowned in the sea. She fell to her knees, raised her clasped hands to heaven and gave thanks and praise to God Our Lord for the great success He had given to Tirant and to the new Christianity, for he was making war on the enemies of Jesus Christ so bravely. She became very hopeful that soon she would be out of captivity, and all the suffering she had gone through up to then seemed to be nothing to her: the thought that she would see Tirant consoled her that much.

On the day her mistress had to go and talk to the captains, she disguised herself so well that no one would recognize her. When the lady was before the captain, she was accompanied by fifty maidens, but Tirant would not listen to her and he sent her to his cousin, Lord Agramunt. And if he had replied badly to the ambassadors, he gave an even worse reply to the lady. Hopeless, they went back, crying and lamenting loudly. All that night, men as well as women did not cease their wailing and sighing.

In the morning Plaerdemavida told her mistress and the honorable men of the city that if they would give her liberty to go out, she would talk to the captain, and would tell him such things that he would do anything she wished. They agreed that she should go, because they had lost all hope and had only that one day left. That day Plaerdemavida dressed as a Moor, and painted her eyes so that she would not be recognized. She took thirty well-dressed maidens with her. At noon they left the city and went to the camp, and there they saw Tirant at the door of his tent. When he saw them coming he sent word that they should go to Lord Agramunt, and that he could do nothing since he had turned all his power over to him. Plaerdemavida answered:

"Tell the captain that he should not refuse to see us, and even less to speak to us, because if that captain did such a thing he would be cruel and unjust. Since he is a knight and we are maidens, in accordance with the order of chivalry he must aid us, and give us his advice and his support."

The chamberlain immediately took the reply back to the captain:

"Upon my word, my lord, there is a maiden with those Moors who is very gracious. She speaks the Christian tongue most beautifully. And if Your Grace would like to do me a very great favor for the services I have performed for you, when we take the city I beg you to make her a Christian and to give her to me for a wife."

"Have them all come here," said the captain.

When they stood before him, they made a deep bow to him. Plaerdemavida, smiling, said:

"My captain, your generous heart cannot fail to act according to its custom. Your nobility is full of mercy, and you must forget the great crime of the ignorant inhabitants of this city, who will fold their hands and kneel down and kiss your feet, begging you for mercy. Look, virtuous captain, I speak with the spirit of prophecy. Do you remember that fortunate day when you were given the honor of chivalry in that prosperous court of the King of England? And the singular battles you fought at that time and won with great honor, with no trickery? What should I say of Philippe, son of the King of France? In your great wisdom you made him King of Sicily, and now he possesses the daughter, the kingdom, and the crown. And when that blessed lord, who is of greater excellence than anyone in the world, the Emperor of Constantinople, heard of your fame, he had you come to the city of Constantinople. His high Majesty made you his captain, and you showed the Turkish enemies your strength and power, conquering them time and time again. I am a Moor who speaks by prophecy, and my heart cries tears of blood for those worthy knights, because now they are as good as dead. Cry, miserable people and lament the fact that Tirant lo Blanc has forgotten you! And it does not surprise me that he does not remember you, for he has forgotten a lady (I won't say who she is, but I can call her the greatest and best in all Christendom) in order to conquer this cursed land."

Tirant was quite astonished when he heard these words, and he begged her to tell how she knew so much.

"Oh Tirant, how little mercy you are showing. Go on pursuing those fleeing kings so that you can have all of Barbary in your lap, and let us live in blessed peace. Aren't you that prince of the line of Roca Salada who went into battle that pleasant night in the castle of Malvei with that most serene princess, the beautiful Carmesina? And if my heart hasn't gone mad or I haven't lost all my senses, it seems to me that I heard tell that Her Highness let you into her chambers at a very late hour. She put her father's crown—that of the Greek Empire—on your head, and accepted you as her universal lord, with the help of a sad maiden named Plaerdemavida. You have given so little thought to either of them, it's as if you'd never known them. Her Highness, with you forgetting about her, is more dead than alive in the Monastery of Santa Clara, always calling out the name of Tirant in whom she has placed all her hope. Oh, Tirant! How you have shed all kindness. You know full well that the Turks have overrun all of Greece, that all they have left to do is take the city of Constantinople and seize the emperor, his wife and the grieving princess."

When Tirant heard the maiden say these things, he heaved a sigh from the depths of his heart as he remembered the lady he loved more than anyone in the world. He was so stricken that he fell to the ground, senseless. When everyone saw their captain lying there, his eyes filled with tears, they thought he had delivered up his spirit to God and his body to the ground.

The doctors came and said:

"Our captain must be very ill. He looks as though he is near death."

King Escariano quickly had the maiden seized and her hands tightly bound. When Plaerdemavida saw herself treated so badly, she angrily said:

"Let me go to the captain. I nourished him from my breast before you ever heard of him. Let me use the remedies I know, because I can see that these ignorant doctors don't know how to help him."

The maiden quickly sat on the ground, unfastened her robes and the blouse she was wearing down past her bosom, uncovering her breasts.

She took Tirant's body, placed it in her lap, and lay his head on her breasts. When the maiden saw Tirant open his eyes and sigh deeply, she was very happy, and she said:

"Captain, my lord, for a long time you have been fighting us night and day. I don't want Your Grace to suffer such terrible hardships when I can free you from them. Begin with me. I am right here, a defenseless maiden, and your sword is very sharp. Now you can use your strong hand and bathe your sword with the blood of someone who, after God, wants to serve only you."

Tirant answered as well as he could:

"Maiden, it seems to me that you are like the bee that carries honey in its mouth and a stinger in its tail. I have heard things from you that have left me astonished. I want very much to know how news about that most serene princess has reached you. Tell me, I beg you, and you can count on this: In consideration of Her Majesty, I will do such things for you that you will all leave here highly satisfied."

Plaerdemavida was very happy at the captain's reply. While they were talking, Lord Agramunt came into the tent in a rage, with a bare sword in his hand. He had been misinformed by King Escariano about how Tirant had fallen into a faint in the maiden's arms. When he saw Tirant in her lap and without noticing his captain's condition, with a fierce face and a terrible voice, he cried:

"What is this poisonous woman doing here, this devil-worshipper? How can you all stand by, seeing how she's killed him, and not behead her? Since the rest of you won't do it, I will."

He grabbed her by the hair and jerked back her head. And he put his sword by her neck to take away her life. When Tirant saw the sword so close to the maiden, and heard her cry, he seized the sword with his hands. Lord Agramunt, feeling the sword against something hard, thought it was the maiden's neck. So he slashed as hard as he could, and put a large gash in Tirant's hands. And according to the doctors Tirant was very fortunate that he was not badly injured.

When Tirant saw that his cousin had shown him so little honor, he became very angry. King Escariano made Lord Agramunt leave, and Lord Agramunt lowered his eyes and became very ashamed. Then he bowed deeply to the king and to Tirant, and left the tent. And his humility and shame went a long way toward cooling Tirant's anger and making him feel pity instead.

Then Tirant turned toward the maiden and asked her very kindly if she had been a captive in Constantinople, and he asked who had told her so many things about the princess. She quickly got up, and falling to her knees, she said:

"What is this, captain! Have you lost your memory entirely? There is a great deal of truth in the fact that where there is no love there can be no remembrance. What! Aren't I poor, miserable Plaerdemavida who, for Your Lordship, endured so much pain and misery, and finally captivity?"

Tirant's eyes flew open with recognition at once, and he would not allow her to say another word, realizing full well at this moment that she was Plaerdemavida. He knelt to the ground before her, and embraced her and kissed her many times over.

After they had embraced for a good while, Tirant ordered a beautiful platform placed at the door of the tent, covered entirely with brocade cloth above, and with satin on the sides and floor. Plaerdemavida was seated at the top step of the platform, and covered with a mantle of crimson brocade lined with ermine—one belonging to Tirant that he had ordered put on her since she had completely torn her robes. The lady of the city was made to sit on the top step, and her maidens below, on the satin cloths. In this situation it seemed that Plaerdemavida was indeed a queen.

Tirant had taken the head-dress off her head, and now her hair hung loose over her shoulders. He paid her such great honor that everyone thought Tirant was going to take her as his wife. He had a proclamation read throughout the entire camp that everyone should come and kiss Plaerdemavida's hand, under penalty of death. Then he had another proclamation made that everyone in the city, men and women, were pardoned, and that each of them could live under any law they wished, and that no one in the camp should dare harm anyone from the city. Afterward he had many dishes prepared, and held a general banquet so that everyone could come who wished. And the most singular celebration ever held in a camp took place there, lasting eight days.

Plaerdemavida begged the lady of the city to be baptized, and she answered that she would do it. Then Tirant asked her if she would marry Melquisedic. Plaerdemavida also pleaded with her, and the others insisted so much that she consented. And the wedding was held with great celebrations.

Tirant often spent his time talking to Plaerdemavida. One day, while they were talking about the princess and the emperor, Plaerdemavida scolded him, and asked him why he did not forget about conquering Barbary and help the emperor and his daughter. Tirant answered that he wanted to know for certain what the situation was in the empire before he moved. He begged Plaerdemavida to tell him what had happened to her after she was swept over the side of the galley. With tears in her eyes, Plaerdemavida said:

"I beg you, lord Tirant, don't make me talk about it. Whenever I think about it I would rather die a hundred deaths than go on living."

When Tirant heard her speaking so painfully, he said:

"Rejoice, valiant maiden. I promise you, by the lady who has been the cause of your misfortune, that I will repay you. I will mix your blood with that of Roca Salada, and you will be reckoned among the women of Brittany, among whom you are certain to have the title of queen."

There was a long argument between Tirant and this maiden about the marriage he had decided upon, which was between her and Lord Agramunt. He gave her many different reasons, citing very holy authorities, so that Plaerdemavida finally submitted to Tirant's will, and replied in a few words:

"Your servant is here, Lord Tirant. Do with me according to your will."

Tirant took a beautiful chain from his neck and placed it around Plaerdemavida's neck as a sign of her future marriage. He had brocade brought, and dressed her like a queen. Then Tirant sent for Lord Agramunt, and he begged him at length not to refuse what he would tell him, since he had already made a promise. Lord Agramunt answered him:

"Lord Tirant, I am astonished that you would plead with me about anything. Just by commanding me you are doing me a great favor."

Tirant said:

"Cousin, I have decided to make you King of Fez and Bogia, and to give Plaerdemavida to you as your wife. You know how indebted all of us are to her for the work she has done for us. She is a maiden of great discretion who has lead a virtuous life, and it will be very good for both of you."

Lord Agramunt answered:

"Cousin and lord, I had no thought of taking a wife, but it is too much grace and honor for Your Lordship to entreat me to do a thing that I should beg you for. I kiss your hand and your feet."

Tirant would not allow it. Instead he took him by the arm, lifted him up, and kissed him on the mouth. Afterward he thanked him, both for the kingdoms and for the new wife.

Tirant felt more satisfied at having arranged this marriage than by all of his conquests in Barbary. He quickly had Lady Montagata's palace decorated with beautiful gold and silk cloth, and he had all the musicians from that area come, with every kind of instrument that could be found. Then he had many dainties and special wines brought to insure the success of the celebration. Plaerdemavida was very richly dressed, and her presence and appearance showed that she was a queen. She was taken to the great hall where King Escariano and Tirant were, with many other barons and knights, along with the wife of King Escariano and many other ladies of rank. After the wedding vows were exchanged there was a great celebration with dances of different types and very singular foods.

    While the celebrations lasted, Tirant had the table prepared for everyone who wished to eat, and for a week there was a great abundance of everything.

CHAPTER XII - CONQUEST

When the celebrations were over Tirant had a large ship armed, and he had it loaded with wheat to send to Constantinople to help the emperor.

He had Melquisedic, Lord of Montagata, brought to him, and he told him to go on that ship as a messenger to the emperor. He told him to become well informed about the emperor's condition, and how the empire was, and about the princess. He gave him instructions and letters of credence, and he had him embark, well outfitted and better escorted.

Then Tirant ordered his men to break camp, and to get all the cavalry and foot soldiers ready. They filled the carts with food and all the supplies and weaponry necessary to fight the cities, villas, and castles.

They went toward the city of Caramen, at the edge of Barbary and bordering on the black Kingdom of Borno. Because three kings who fled from the battle scene had taken refuge in that city, while the others had gone back to their own lands. So the great numbers of cavalry and foot soldiers went through the land, conquering castles, villas and cities. Some were taken by force, and others surrendered willingly. Many became Christian, while others remained in their sect, and they were not harmed or wronged in any way. Finally they reached the city where the kings had taken shelter. There, Tirant's forces set up their tents and encircled the city at a distance of about two crossbow shots.

Tirant held council with King Escariano, Lord Agramunt, the Marquis of Luzana, the Viscount of Branches, and many other barons and knights in the camp. They chose a Spaniard from the town of Oriola to be their envoy. His name was Lord Rocafort, and he had been a captive on a Moorish galley until Tirant had freed him. They told him to observe how many men might be in the city, and what condition they were in, and they give him detailed instructions about everything he should do and say.

After receiving assurances of safe-conduct, the envoy went to the castle where the kings were. These were the King of Fez, King Menador of Persia, and the King of Tremicén. This last king was nephew to the other King of Tremicén, and had been chosen king when his uncle had been killed by King Escariano. The other kings had died in the battles they had been waging.

The envoy stood before the kings who had gathered to listen to his embassy, and without greeting them or showing them any reverence, he said:

"I have come to you who were powerful kings on behalf of the most Christian King Escariano and the magnanimous captain, Tirant lo Blanc, to notify you of the will of their lordships. They say that you and your forces must leave the city of Caramen and all of Barbary within three days."

King Menador of Persia gave the reply for the other kings:

"You can tell that traitor and renegade, King Escariano, Mohammed's enemy and ours, and his friend Tirant lo Blanc, that we won't leave the city, much less Barbary, for them. And so that they'll know how great our power is, let them be ready for battle tomorrow because we'll come out of the city and give them terrible destruction."

As soon as King Menador had finished, Tirant's ambassador turned his back and left without another word, and he went back to his camp. When he was with King Escariano and Tirant, he told them all about King Menador of Persia's reply. Tirant immediately called together all the barons, knights and captains of both cavalry and foot soldiers. When they were together, he told them to get ready because the Moors were going to do battle with them.

The following morning the Moors put their forces together in a beautiful plain outside the city, and they began to move toward Tirant's camp. The Christians' spy saw the Moors coming, and ran to warn Tirant. Tirant had all his cavalry ready and his foot soldiers in order, and they went toward the Moors.

When the battalions drew near each other, the trumpets and pipes began to sound, and the screams and shouts of both armies were so great that it seemed as though heaven and earth would come together. Tirant ordered his first battalion to attack, and the good captain Lord Rocafort went into battle so fiercely that it was a wonder to behold.

The King of Tremicén, who was captain of the first battalion of Moors also attacked so powerfully that the best knight in the world could have done no better, and they fought so fiercely against the

Christians that the Christians were beaten back. Then the second squadron of Moors attacked very savagely, and one could see lances breaking, and knights and horses falling, and many men lying dead on the ground, both Christians and Moors.

Tirant saw that the battle was going badly, and that his men were being beaten. So he had four squadrons attack together, his being the only one that held back. They attacked so powerfully that in a few hours, before the enemy realized what had happened, they had killed a great number of Moors.

King Escariano came face to face with the King of Fez, and their horses clashed so mightily that they broke their lances. They both fell to the ground, and got up, fighting with their swords, like lions. When the two sides saw their king on the ground, they rushed in to help them, and in the harsh battle that followed, many men died.

Then Tirant attacked too, with his men, and you would have had to see the great tumult and the terrible cries of the Moors who were not able to resist the Christians. King Menador of Persia, who had gone into battle like a raging dog, came against Tirant, and hit his head with his sword so hard that he nearly knocked Tirant from his horse.

Tirant then raised his sword and brought it down so hard that he cut the king's arm completely off at the shoulder, and the king soon fell to the ground, dead.

During the battle it happened that Tirant came upon the King of Tremicén, and gave him such a blow to the head with his sword, that he knocked the king to the ground. And if it had not been for the king's good helmet, he would have been dead. Tirant went on ahead, and the Moors picked up their king and lay him over a horse, taking him quickly back to the city.

When the battle had gone on for a long while, the Moors could not stand up against the Christians, and they had to turn and flee. When Tirant saw the Moors running away, he cried:

"The time has come, good knights, the day is ours! Kill them all!"

They rushed after the Moors who were trying to take refuge inside the city. But with all their efforts, the Moors could not avoid the deaths of more than forty thousand of their men that day.

With the battle won, Tirant immediately had a galley armed in the port of One, and he entrusted a knight named Espèrcius as its captain. This man was a native of Tremicén, and a good Christian. Tirant charged him to go to Genoa, Venice, Pisa and Majorca (which at this time was a great trading center), and to enlist as many ships, galleys, caravels, and all kinds of vessels, as could carry many men. He was to promise them a year's wages, and take them to the port of Constantine in the kingdom of Tunis. When Espèrcius was informed about everything he was to do, he embarked on his journey.

When Ambassador Melquisedic left Barbary he had such favorable weather that he reached Constantinople in a few days. When the emperor was informed that a ship was in port, he immediately sent a knight to find out what ship it was, and what its purpose was in coming. The knight went to the port, boarded the ship and spoke with the ambassador. Then he returned to the palace and told the emperor that the ship had come from Barbary, that Tirant had sent it, stocked with wheat, to His Majesty, and that a knight was on it whom Tirant had sent as his ambassador.

When the emperor heard this news he felt very relieved because of the straits they were in, and he gave thanks and praise to God, Our Lord, that he had not been forgotten. The emperor immediately commanded all the knights of the city to go and escort the ambassador that Tirant had sent, and they all went to the port, and had them disembark.

The ambassador, accompanied by the people with him, came out, very finely dressed. When they were on land, they were received by the emperor's knights, who paid the ambassador high honors because of their great desire for Tirant to come. They took him to the emperor and the empress who were in the emperor's chamber. The ambassador bowed to the emperor, and kissed his foot and hand, and also the empress's hand.

They received them, smiling, and showing great pleasure at their arrival.

The ambassador explained his mission to the emperor and his council, and they were all astonished and comforted by Tirant's great prosperity in conquering Barbary. Then the ambassador asked permission to go see the princess. Hippolytus escorted him to the convent where she was staying, and he presented her with a letter from Tirant. She felt very comforted by his words, convinced that he would be coming to her soon. Then she asked the ambassador what news he had of Plaerdemavida: if she was dead or alive. He told about her adventure in detail, and how she had married Lord Agramunt, and how Tirant had promised to make her a queen. Then he took his leave of the princess and went to the lodging.

A few days later the emperor had a letter composed to Tirant, explaining in detail the situation his empire was in: that the empire had been overrun by the Turks, and now all that remained was the city of Constantinople, the city of Pera, and a few castles. He had the ambassador come before him, and gave him the letter. Then he begged him earnestly to press Tirant to remember him and to have compassion on his old age, and on all the people who were in danger of renouncing the faith of Jesus Christ, and on the women and maidens who lived in fear of being dishonored unless they had divine aid and his aid as well. The ambassador took his leave, kissing his feet and hand, and likewise the empress's.

Afterward the ambassador went to the convent where the princess was, and he told her that he had come to see Her Highness in case she wished to command anything of him. The princess told him she was very pleased that he would be returning so soon, for she trusted his goodness and gentility that he would do everything possible to make Tirant come quickly to free them from the great danger they were in. And she earnestly begged him to do this. Then she gave him a letter she was sending to Tirant.

When their talk was over, the ambassador kissed the princess's hand, and took his leave of her. As the ambassador had carried out all the things Tirant had entrusted to him, he boarded the ship, and had the sails raised so they could be on their way. In a few days he reached the city where Tirant was, who received him very happily. Bowing, he gave him the emperor's letter.

When Tirant had read the emperor's letter, he felt great compassion for him. His eyes filled with tears when he thought of his anguish, and he remembered the Duke of Macedonia and his other relatives and friends who were being held captive in the hands of the infidels because of him, and that they had no hope of escaping without him. He also thought about all he had conquered in the Empire of Greece while he had been there, and that it and much more had been lost in such a brief span of time.

He asked the ambassador about all that he had seen, and he told him everything. He also asked him about the princess and how she was. He answered that he had found her in the convent of Santa Clara (for with his absence she had given herself over to the service of God) and about how she also wore a veil over her face and led a very holy life, and how she had received him very happily.

"She asked me how you were and what had happened to you, and she begged me at length to plead with you not to forget her, especially now that they were in danger of becoming prisoners of the Moors. And that if she had ever angered Your Lordship, she begged you not to make her grieve for it. That, as you were merciful toward your enemies, you would treat her, who was your own, as well. That you should think of her as your own flesh, and not forget her."

And he told him many other things that the book does not relate.

The ambassador gave him the princess's letter, and it said the following:

"After I read your letter, I was filled with infinite joy, and great happiness softened my sad heart. The greatest peace, calm and joy I have felt after I lost your presence is this outpouring of my words, as I feel myself coming back to you. For I have been, I am and will be your secret captive. I thank you with all my heart, for I know all that you have suffered because of me. And I forgive you for the false opinions you held about me, on the sole condition that the African soil find itself abandoned by you so that you will return to me and my deserted people. Let me bring to your memory the crown of the Empire of Greece that awaits you; and my virginity which you so desired, and that is now in danger of being stolen by some infidel; and I, your wife, who am in danger of being taken captive. I don't know what to say, I don't know what to show you! Until now my thoughts have been able to hold these deceptions: gazing at, kissing, adoring some jewels and things that were yours, and finding my consolation in them. Then, going to the doors of my room, saying: 'Here is where my Tirant sat, here he caught me, here he kissed me, here in this bed he held me naked.' And so, rambling most of the night and day, I ease my troubled mind. Let these thoughts cease, then, for they avail me very little, and let Tirant come, for he will be my true consolation, my end, the remedy and peace for my ills, and the redemption of the Christian people."

When Tirant had finished reading the princess's letter, he felt great agony from the pain and compassion he had for the emperor and for the princess, and in thinking of the Duke of Macedonia, his cousin, being held prisoner, and of all his other relatives and friends.

Tirant then told King Escariano that they would leave and go to Tunis. Before they left, he gave the kingdoms of Fez and Bogia to Lord Agramunt. Then all the men set out for Tunis.

When the kingdom of Tunis learned that King Escariano and Captain Tirant were coming with such a mighty force, they sent word to them, begging them not to harm them. Since their lord had died, they would be happy to obey them and to do whatever they commanded. They willingly accepted, and entered the city of Tunis very peacefully.

Tirant had them swear to accept King Escariano as their lord, and all the cities, villas and castles surrendered to him.

While Tirant was feeling very content, the news reached him that six large ships had docked at the port of Constantine. He immediately sent Melquisedic, giving him many doubloons, and ordered him to load the six ships with wheat, and send them to Constantinople.

Melquisedic departed and quickly carried out Tirant's orders, and in a few days they were stocked, and they set sail. Then Tirant had King Escariano take possession of the kingdom of Tunis, and they swore their allegiance to him as their king and lord.

When all these things had been done, he felt like the happiest man in the world. He begged King Escariano to go with him to Constantinople, with all his forces, to recover the Empire of Greece that the Moorish sultan and the Grand Turk had seized. And King Escariano told him that he would be very happy to carry out everything that he commanded.

He also told Lord Agramunt, King of Fez and Bogia, to go to his kingdoms and to enlist as many men as could go with him. Lord Agramunt was very happy, and he left immediately. Then King Escariano wrote letters to the entire kingdom of Tunis, to all the captains and knights, telling them to be in the city of Constantine on a certain day with all their arms and everything they needed for battle. And in three months they were in the city of Constantine. There were forty-four thousand men on horseback and one hundred thousand on foot from the kingdom of Tremicén and from Tunis. Then came the King of Fez and Bogia, Lord Agramunt, with twenty thousand men on horseback and fifty thousand foot soldiers.

While these men were coming, the galley of Knight Espèrcius arrived with many ships, galleys and other vessels, from Genoa, Spain, Venice and Pisa, and there were even more. When Espèrcius disembarked from the galley, he told Tirant that he had carried out everything he had been charged with. Tirant was very satisfied at all this. He quickly had the galley loaded, and he told Espèrcius that he wanted him to go as his ambassador to the King of Sicily, and he replied that he would do it gladly. Tirant gave him instructions about what to say to the King of Sicily, and Knight Espèrcius went aboard his galley and set out for Sicily.

A few days after the ambassador had left, all the ships were together in the port of Constantine, and when Tirant saw that he had enough vessels, and that he would need no more, he paid for the fleet for one year. Then he immediately had thirty ships stocked with wheat and supplies from the Barbary Coast. When the ships were loaded, a day was set for all the armed men to meet. Those on horseback and those on foot, and all the people in the city and many others came to a beautiful spot in front of the city of Constantine. Tirant had a very tall catafalque made there so that all the people could be around it. Then Tirant, King Escariano, the King of Fez and many other barons and knights went onto the catafalque until it was completely filled. The others stayed down below, and when the people were silent, Tirant spoke briefly, and a friar gave a sermon.

When the sermon was over, all the Moors who were not baptized cried out, asking for baptism. Tirant immediately had large basins filled with water, as well as conches, casks and tubs, and all the friars and clerics came, for Tirant had had many monasteries and even more churches built in the cities he had taken, and many clerics and friars had come from the Christian realms. Everyone was baptized—those who were leaving as well as those who were staying behind—and in three days three hundred thirty-four thousand Moors—men, women and children—were baptized.

Afterward, Tirant went to talk to King Escariano, and he said to him:

"I have been thinking, my lord and brother, that if it is to your liking, instead of going with us by sea you could return to your kingdom of Ethiopia, and enlist as many men as possible, foot soldiers and cavalry, and I will go by sea with these men. And with you on one side and me on the other, we will catch the sultan and the Turk in the middle, and we will destroy them."

King Escariano said he would prefer to go with him, but that he understood how much aid he could give him with all his men, and he was content to do so. The book explains that this King Escariano was a very strong and valiant knight, and that he was totally black. For he was lord of the Negritos of Ethiopia, and was called King Jamjam. He was very powerful, owning many horses as well as great treasures, and he was well loved by his vassals. His kingdom was so large that it extended to Barbary, and the kingdom of Tremicén, and on the other side to the Indies and Abyssinia through which the River Tigris passes.

Then King Escariano prepared to depart with five hundred knights, and he and the queen took their leave of Tirant, and the King and Queen of Fez, and all the other barons. Tirant accompanied him more than a league, and then he returned to the city of Constantine to give the order for the men to ready themselves with their horses and their entire army. Here the history ceases to speak of Tirant, and it returns to Ambassador Espèrcius who was going to the island of Sicily.

After Ambassador Espèrcius left the port of Constantine, he had such favorable weather that in a few days he reached the island of Sicily. He learned that the king was in the city of Messina, and he went there. When he was near the port he dressed very well and had all his men put on their finery. Then he disembarked and went to the king's palace.

When he was before the king, he bowed, and the king honored him and asked the reason for his coming. The ambassador answered:

"Most excellent sir, Tirant lo Blanc sends me to Your Majesty as his ambassador."

He immediately gave the ambassador a very fine room, and he had everything he needed brought to him. He also sent beef of an ox and pork and fresh bread to the galley for the men.

On the morning of the following day, after the king had heard mass, he summoned his council, and when they were seated in a great hall he told the ambassador to explain his mission. The ambassador said:

"Most excellent sir, Your Excellency is aware that Tirant lo Blanc was carrying on a war for the Emperor of Constantinople against the Moorish sultan and the Grand Turk. It happened that they took from the emperor all the lands Tirant had conquered, and so he has decided to take the mightiest force he can to Constantinople. He begs Your Highness to go with him personally with all your forces, to help carry out the conquest of the Empire of Greece. And since he has so much confidence in Your Lordship he will be here very soon."

The ambassador said no more. The king quickly replied:

"Knight, it makes me very happy to know of the good fortune of my brother Tirant, and I am very pleased to be able to help him."

The ambassador stood and thanked the king. When they left the parley, the king had letters drawn up to all the barons and knights of Sicily, and to all the cities and royal villas, that on a certain day they should send all their magistrates to the city of Palermo, because he had decided to hold a general parliament there.

On the appointed day the king and all those who were invited were in Palermo, and when the parliament opened the king asked the entire kingdom for aid. They were all happy to give their assistance, and those who could decided to go with him. When the parliament was over, all who had decided to go quickly made ready, and in a short time the king gathered four thousand horses, and he had at his disposal a large fleet of ships and many provisions.

Here the book ceases to speak of the King of Sicily, who is putting all his ships in order, and gathering all the provisions and the horses and arms, and it returns to the six ships Tirant had sent to Constantinople, loaded with wheat.

After the six ships had left the port of Constantine they had such a favorable wind that in a few days they reached the Port of Valona, which is in Greece. There they received news that the sultan and the Turk had passed the Bosphorus with many ships and galleys that they had sent for from Alexandria and Turkey, and that they had laid siege to the city of Constantinople. The emperor was extremely concerned, and all those in the city prayed continually to Jesus Christ to send Tirant so that they could be freed from their captivity. At the same time they felt very confident because they were sure that Tirant was coming with all his forces. The princess returned to the emperor's palace to console her father, and she told him to gather courage, for Our Lord would help them. The emperor had made Hippolytus his captain-major, and every day he performed great acts of chivalry. If it had not been for him, the sultan would have taken the city before Tirant arrived.

When the captains of the six ships learned that the sultan's forces were about to fall on Constantinople they sent a courier by land to the emperor, informing him that they were there, in the port of Valona, but that they did not dare go on to aid His Majesty out of fear of the Moorish army that was facing the city. However, they notified His Majesty that Tirant had already left the city of Constantine and that he was coming with great haste to assist him. In addition, they armed a brigantine and sent it to Tirant to warn him that the Turk and the sultan had laid siege to the city of Constantinople. The brigantine left very secretly and steered for Sicily, and it had such favorable weather that in a few days it reached the port of Palermo.

As soon as King Escariano had left Constantine, Tirant ordered all the horses, the food supplies and the people brought together. The thirty ships stocked with wheat arrived, and he had them filled with men. When they were all on board, Tirant, the King of Fez and Plaerdemavida went on the ship, along with all the knights who had been on land with Tirant. When everything was ready, they sailed toward Sicily.

When the brigantine that had come from the port of Valona saw Tirant's fleet, it sailed out of the port and steered toward them, asking for the captain's ship, and it was pointed out to them. When the brigantine was next to Tirant's ship they told him that the six ships were in the port of Valona and that they had not been able to pass by the sultan's fleet, and of the siege that had been laid against the city. This made Tirant very angry, and he sailed to the port of Palermo where he saw the ships of the King of Sicily that began to celebrate with trumpets and bombards. Those of Tirant answered them, and they raised such a din that it seemed as though the world was going to cave in.

As soon as Tirant's armada was in port and had laid anchor, the King of Sicily came on board Tirant's ship and there they embraced and kissed. The King of Sicily honored all the barons and knights who were on Tirant's ship, and he kissed and embraced the King of Fez, and they all went on land together. Tirant ordered that no one on the ships was to go on land, since he wanted to leave the following day. The King of Sicily had his queen come to the sea, and she honored Tirant and the King of Fez and the queen, especially when she heard that she had been the servant of so virtuous a lady as the princess. They all went to the palace together, with a great multitude of ladies and maidens, and other people who followed them. When they were in the palace a splendid meal was prepared for them, and they ate their fill with great pleasure from all sorts of victuals.

When they left their tables, Tirant and the King of Sicily went into a chamber. The Queen of Sicily and the King of Fez, along with his wife, remained in the hall with many ladies and gentlemen, and they began to dance and entertain themselves. Tirant told the King of Sicily about all the misfortunes he had suffered, and how afterward Our Lord had protected him and had given him a great victory, and how he had conquered all of Barbary. Then he told him of the condition the emperor was in, and that he needed their aid immediately. The King of Sicily answered him:

"My brother and my lord, the horses and arms have been prepared, along with most of the men."

Tirant answered:

"My brother and lord, I beg you to have a proclamation sent out through the city that everyone shall gather, as you wish to depart this evening."

The King of Sicily immediately sent one of his chamberlains, and the trumpeters went through the city commanding all those who were to leave to gather together, and it was quickly done. Tirant and the king went back to the hall with the queen, and there they found a little diversion. The Queen of Sicily drew apart with the Queen of Fez, and embraced her, asking her many questions about the princess, about her beauty and about the love between Tirant and the princess. The Queen of Fez praised the princess, saying she would never be able to tell of all her wonderful qualities. She passed lightly over the love affair with great discretion. Then she began to flatter the queen—an art at which she was a master—telling her that after Her Highness, the princess, she was without equal in the world; that she had never seen or heard of a lady with such a genteel mind or so much beauty as Her Majesty, and that she was very much in love with her and her singular qualities; and she told her many other things, all of which gave the Queen of Sicily great pleasure.

After the party and celebrations had ended it was time to dine, and they ate with great satisfaction. When they had left the table, Tirant begged the King of Sicily to make ready quickly, and the king told him he would. They took their leave of the Queen of Sicily and of all those who were staying with her. The King of Sicily entrusted the regency of the kingdom to a cousin-german of the queen, who was Duke of Messina, a good and virtuous knight. He made him viceroy, and put the queen and his entire household in his charge.

When everything was done that was necessary, the king and Tirant and all their company gathered together, and the entire fleet, Tirant's as well as that of the King of Sicily, set sail. At the port of Valona the six ships loaded with wheat were waiting, and they were very pleased when they saw Tirant's fleet.

Here the book ceases talking about Tirant and continues with the story of King Escariano. As soon as King Escariano left Tirant, he and his wife, the queen, rode until they came to his land—the Kingdom of Ethiopia. After he had rested a few days, he called all the barons and knights of his kingdom to the city of Trogodita, and he told them:

"It must have come to your knowledge that I was the prisoner of the captain of the Christians: Tirant lo Blanc. He is the best knight in the world, for he gave us our liberty and made us his companion in arms. Furthermore, he has given me as my wife the daughter of the King of Tremicén, along with that kingdom, and he has also given to me the Kingdom of Tunis. Now he must carry out the conquest of the Greek Empire for the Emperor of Constantinople—because the sultan and the Grand Turk have taken away his entire empire. So he has called on me, as his brother and servant, to help him with all my power. Thus, I beg all of you who are willing, to come with me to Constantinople."

One by one, they each responded that they loved him with a great love, and that they would follow him and die for him, not only in Constantinople but to the ends of the world.

King Escariano thanked them all. Then he sent messages to all the cities and towns of his kingdom that all who wished to put themselves at his service—both cavalry and foot soldiers, citizens and foreigners—should come to the city of Trogodita. When they had all gathered there, King Escariano found that as part of his army he had at his command twenty thousand horsemen, strong and able with weapons. The queen also made ready, and they left the city of Trogodita with their entire army.

Here the book returns to Tirant lo Blanc's armada as they are going to Constantinople.

When Tirant was at the port of Valona he sent a galley into the port and commanded the captains of the six ships to come out of the port and follow the armada. So they set sail and came out of the port and followed the fleet. When the armada was in the canal of Romania it set its course for the port of Gigeo, which is the port of Troy, and there they waited for the rest of the armada to join them.

Tirant held counsel with the King of Sicily and the King of Fez and all the other barons and knights, for he knew that the sultan's entire armada was in the port of Constantinople, and that they had more than three hundred vessels. It was decided to send a man overland who knew the Moorish language, and who would go into Constantinople at night to inform the emperor that Tirant and his entire armada were in the port of Troy, a little more than one hundred miles from Constantinople. They did not want to give him any sort of letter, so that if he were taken prisoner by the Moors they would not have any warning. So they would tell him everything he should say to the emperor.

When the council was over Tirant called a knight from Tunis who had been a Moor of the royal house. His name was Sinegerus, and he was a very ingenious and eloquent man, and a valiant knight. He had been a captive in Constantinople, and knew the area well. Tirant told him everything he was to say to the emperor and the princess, and he gave him his seal so the emperor would have faith in him.

This knight dressed himself in Moorish fashion as a lackey. A brigantine picked him up, and at night they put him ashore a league from the Moorish camp that was laying siege to the city of Constantinople. The knight carefully turned away from the encampment and set out for the city, but before he could escape he fell into the hands of spies from the Moorish camp. He spoke to them very discreetly in their language, and told them he was one of them, and they let him pass. When he reached the city, the men who were guarding the gate seized him, thinking he was from the Moorish encampment. He told them not to harm him because he was Tirant's ambassador, and that he was coming to talk to the emperor. The guards immediately took him to the emperor who, at that moment, was getting up from the dinner table.

When Sinegerus was before the emperor, he knelt and kissed his hand and foot, and gave him Tirant's seal. The emperor looked at it and recognized Tirant's coat of arms. Then the emperor embraced him, telling him he was very welcome. Sinegerus said:

"Most excellent Sire, I was sent here by that great captain Tirant lo Blanc who commends himself in grace and mercy to Your Majesty, for soon, with the help of God our Lord, he will free you from all your enemies. In addition, he begs you to put all your cavalry in order, and have the city well-guarded, for tomorrow morning he will attack the Moorish armada, and he fears that when the Moors see their squadron lost they will mount a powerful attack against the city. Tirant is coming with enough might to take them and kill them all, and of this Your Majesty should not have the slightest doubt."

"Friend," said the emperor, "we feel very relieved by what you have told us. May our Lord grant us the grace that it will be as you have said, for we have so much trust in the great virtue and chivalry of Tirant, that with the help of God he will fulfill our good desire and his own."

The emperor immediately summoned Hippolytus, his high captain, and when he was before him he said:

"Our captain, you know that Tirant is in the port of Troy with a great squadron. He has decided to attack the Moorish army tomorrow morning, and so it is very important that you quickly call all the cavalry in the city and all the constables and captains of the foot soldiers, and that you have your men ready in case the Moors decide to attack the city."

After the ambassador, Sinegerus, had explained his mission, he asked the emperor's permission to go pay reverence to the empress and the princess, and the emperor gave his consent. When he had received permission he went to the empress' chambers where he found her daughter with all the ladies. The knight bowed to the empress and kissed her hand, and then the princess's hand. Then, kneeling, he said:

"Ladies, my captain and lord Tirant lo Blanc sends me to kiss your hands. And he offers to come here very soon to pay his respects to you."

When the princess heard that Tirant was coming and that he was so close, she became so happy that she nearly fainted. For some time she seemed delirious with happiness. When she had recovered, the empress and the princess rejoiced with the ambassador. They asked him about many things, especially what men were coming in Tirant's company.

The ambassador answered that the King of Sicily was coming with him with all his forces, and the King of Fez with all his forces and with his wife, the queen, whose name was Plaerdemavida. And all the barons of the kingdoms of Tunis and Tremicén were coming. Many other knights who had accepted payment for their services were coming from Spain, France and Italy because of the great fame and renown of Tirant. And also that magnanimous King Escariano, the lord of Ethiopia, was coming overland.

"He is coming with a mighty army of men on foot and on horseback, and he is bringing his wife, the queen, with him. She is very desirous of seeing Your Excellency, Princess, because of the great beauty she has heard attributed to you. For this queen is one of the most beautiful women in the world, and possesses all virtues."

He also told them how Plaerdemavida had married Lord Agramunt, and that she was coming so His Majesty the emperor and the ladies would honor her for the wedding. He explained to them at length how Tirant had carried out the conquest of Barbary, and how he had given away all that he had conquered and won, and had kept nothing. And that everyone who saw him or heard of him adored him. He told them many other virtuous and praiseworthy things about Tirant, which neither ink nor words would suffice to describe.

When the empress and the princess heard about all Tirant's virtues and singular acts, they were astonished at the great grace that God, our Lord, had given him so that he was loved by everyone. And they wept with happiness when they thought that he would be the restorer and defender of the crown of the Empire of Greece. For they were already beyond hope, and each of the women thought they would be made captives and dishonored by the enemies of the faith. And they were very pleased when he told them about the coming of the Queen of Ethiopia, especially the princess, because they had told her she was very beautiful and virtuous, and she wanted very much to have her friendship. And they talked late into the night.

The empress remained in her chamber and the princess went to her own. The ambassador took her by the arm and accompanied her, and she asked him why he had kissed her hand three times. He answered that it was by his lord Tirant's command, who begged her to please pardon him, for he would never dare come to her because of the great error he had committed.

The princess answered:

"Knight, tell my lord Tirant that where there is no error, there is no need for forgiveness. But if he feels he has wronged me, I beg him to correct it by coming here quickly, for it is the thing I desire most in this world."

The ambassador took his leave of the princess and went to the lodging that the emperor had prepared for him. That night Captain Hippolytus had a careful watch set up throughout the city, and no one slept at all with their great fear of the Moors, and because they were looking forward to the battle Tirant would give the Moorish army.

Here the book stops talking of the emperor who is having the city well-guarded, and goes back to tell about Widow Repose, alias the Devil.

When Widow Repose heard that Tirant was coming and that he was already so nearby, she was stricken with such fear that she thought she was going to die, and she said that her heart felt terribly ill. She went into her chamber, and there she lamented loudly, crying and striking her head and face, for at that moment she felt she was dead, and she truly believed that Tirant would deal a cruel sentence against her. Since she knew that he had been informed by Plaerdemavida, she thought that if the princess knew of the heinous crime she had accused her of, how could she possibly face her? On the other hand, she was still terribly in love with Tirant, and thus she was driven mad.

She spent the entire night this way, fantasizing and struggling within herself, for she did not know what to do. And it was not something she dared tell to anyone, nor could she ask for advice, because if she did they would all be her enemies.

Finally she decided to poison herself in such a way that her wickedness would not be known, so that her body would not be burned or given to the dogs to eat.

She immediately took some arsenic that she had for making a depilatory, and she put it in a glass of water and drank it. She left the door to her chamber open, undressed and lay down on the bed. Then she began to cry loudly, saying that she was dying. The maidens who were sleeping nearby heard the loud cries and quickly got up and went to the Widow's chamber, and there they found her screaming continuously.

The empress and the princess got out of bed, and there was a great uproar in the palace. The emperor got up quickly, thinking the Moors had broken into the city with their weapons, or that his daughter might have unexpectedly fallen ill. He fainted, and the doctors were summoned. When the empress and the princess heard that the emperor had fainted, they left Widow Repose and went running to the emperor's chamber where they found him more dead than alive. Then the princess began to wail loudly, and it was terrible to see her anguish. The doctors came quickly and immediately tended to him. As soon as he regained consciousness he asked what had caused all the disturbance, and if the Moors had entered the city. They told him no, but that Widow Repose was having great dizzy spells, and that she was crying terribly and was very close to death. The emperor ordered the doctors to go, and to do whatever they could to save her. The doctors went immediately, and at the very minute they reached her chambers, she surrendered her soul to Pluto's realm.

When the princess learned that Widow Repose had died, she wailed loudly, because of her great love for her, for she had been nursed by her. She had them place her in a beautiful coffin, because she wanted her to be given a very honorable burial. In the morning the emperor and all his court, the empress and the princess and all the magistrates and honorable men of the city, escorted the body of the Widow to the great church of Santa Sofia, and there they held a very solemn funeral. Then the emperor and all the people went back to the palace.

Here the book leaves off speaking of Widow Repose and returns to Tirant. After Tirant had put the knight Sinegerus ashore so that he could warn the emperor, he had his entire fleet make ready. He commanded his vessels to attack the ships, and the galleys to attack the galleys. At the same time he ordered all the captains, when they attacked the Moors, to create a tremendous noise with trumpets, pipes and horns, and the others with bombards and terrible cries to frighten them to death.

When everything was ready he gave the order to set sail. All the ships very quietly left the port of Troy at daybreak and sailed all day and the following night. Our Lord favored them so much that the entire day was foggy and misty and neither the Moors nor the people in the city could see them. They came upon the Moorish fleet two hours before daybreak while the Moorish armada was completely unsuspecting. Then they attacked the Moorish fleet mightily, with a great explosion of trumpets, pipes and horns and loud cries, and many bombards that they shot simultaneously. And the noise they made was so loud that it seemed as though the earth and the sky would cave in. They built great bonfires on each ship that lit up the heavens. When the Moors heard such a loud noise and saw the light and the ships bearing down on them, they were so frightened that they did not know what they were doing, for they had been caught sleeping and unarmed. All the ships were taken with little difficulty since they were so alarmed that they gave no resistance. And there was such a slaughter that it was a sight to see, for they beheaded every man they found on the ships and spared no one.

Those who threw themselves into the sea and swam ashore carried the bad news to the sultan and the Turk. When the Moors in the camp learned that all the ships had been seized and all the men were dead, and they had heard the noise and seen the fires, they did not know who had done it and they were frightened. They all armed and mounted their horses and prepared for battle, because they were afraid they would be tricked as the ships were. They went down to the water's edge so that no one would come ashore.

When Tirant saw that all the Moorish ships had been taken, he was the happiest man in the world, and he knelt down, and with great devotion he said:

"Great Lord, full of infinite mercy and grace, I give thanks to Your immense goodness for all the help You have given me. Without losing one of my soldiers You have let me take three hundred ships."

This victory was won so quickly that when they had finished taking the ships it had barely turned daylight. When those on the city wall heard the loud noise of the bombards and the trumpets and shouting near the port, and saw so many lights, they were astonished, for it seemed that all the might in the world was there. They realized that it was Tirant's armada that had attacked the Moorish fleet, and they were surprised that at that moment the Moorish camp had not attacked the city. And everyone in the city became excited when they realized that Tirant was attacking the Moorish ships.

The emperor heard the noise, got up quickly and mounted his horse, along with the few who were in the palace at that time. He went through the streets asking all the people to be ready to defend the city if necessary. The Moors were so upset by the lost ships and afraid of a landing that they paid little attention to the city. They were trapped and could not turn back, and they thought they would all be dead or taken captive. They carefully watched the shoreline so that no one from Tirant's armada could come ashore.

When the day was bright and clear, Tirant had his men board all the ships that he had taken from the Moors, then they raised their sails and the entire armada left the port of Constantinople and made for the Black Sea along the Bosphorus. Tirant thought that if he cut off their way by land he could do whatever he wanted with them. So he pretended to be leaving with the booty, taking all the Moorish ships.

That day Tirant sailed toward the Black Sea until, in the evening, the Moors lost sight of the ships. Tirant did this so that the Moors would think he was leaving and would not try to stop them when they went ashore. When the night was dark, Tirant had his entire squadron turn back toward land. He touched land four leagues from the Moorish camp, and the men disembarked with all the horses and artillery they needed, and enough food for their encampment. The Moors were completely unaware that they were there and they left their ships well supplied.

When all the men were ready and on horseback, they took several mules and went at least half a league from their ships along the basin of a river, until they reached a large stone bridge. Here Tirant had all the men set up camp at the head of the bridge next to the river. They had the river between them and the enemy so that the Moors would not fall upon them during the night. Tirant had his tent set up on the bridge so that no one could go past, and he had many bombards installed on the bridge so that if the enemy came they would be well met. He also sent his spies toward the Moors' camp so that he would be forewarned if anyone came.

As soon as they were settled, Tirant took a foot soldier and dressed him like a Moor to deliver a letter to the emperor in Constantinople. The letter told about his victories over the ships of the Moorish sultan and the Grand Turk. It said they had captured three hundred ships filled with food, and that he wanted to send the food to the emperor. And finally it asked the emperor how much food the city had.

When Tirant had finished the letter he gave it to the man he had chosen to go to Constantinople. His name was Carillo, and he was Greek, a native of Constantinople, so he knew very well how to get there. By night he took back roads to the city so that the Moors in the camp did not see him. When he was at the gate the guards seized him and took him to the emperor. He bowed, and kissed his hand and foot, and gave him Tirant's letter. The emperor was very happy to get it, and he read it immediately, and then praised God for His mercy. He called the empress and his daughter, the princess, and showed them Tirant's letter, and they were very pleased that Tirant had captured the Moors' ships.

The emperor summoned his captain, Hippolytus, and showed him Tirant's letter. Hippolytus immediately left the emperor and with other men a search was made, and they found that they still had provisions for three months. Hippolytus returned to the emperor and told him:

"Sire, we have enough supplies in the city to last three months, or even four, if necessary. So, my lord, before we use up these supplies, Tirant will have lifted the siege of the city."

The emperor called his secretary, and had him write a letter to Tirant, explaining in detail what he had decided. Then he called Sinegerus, and said:

"Knight, I want you to take this letter to Tirant, and also to tell him everything you have seen."

He replied that he would. When the ambassador Sinegerus had taken the emperor's letter, he kissed his hand and foot and took his leave. Then he went to say goodbye to the empress and the princess, and he found her in her chamber. She begged him to tell Tirant about her, and she hoped he would think of her. She wanted him to think of how many hardships they had suffered since she had seen him. In any case, she wanted to see him as soon as possible, and if she couldn't, she was sure she would die. The knight answered that he would do everything she commanded, and he kissed her hand. The princess embraced him, and he bowed and left the palace. He dressed as a Moor and took Carillo, who had brought the letter to the emperor, as his companion. They left the city at twelve o'clock midnight, and took the same roads by which Carillo had come secretly, and no one in the Moorish camp saw them. At dawn they reached the bridge where Tirant had his camp. When the guards recognized them they let them pass, and they went directly to Tirant's tent and found him already up.

Tirant was very happy to see them, and he asked Sinegerus for news about the emperor and the empress, and his heart, the princess. He told him about everything he had seen, and what the emperor told him. He also told him what the princess had said.

When the sultan and the Turk discovered that Tirant had disembarked and that he had set up camp on the stone bridge, they were sure they were lost, for they saw that they could not escape by sea or by land without falling into Tirant's hands. At the same time, if they stayed there long they would die of hunger, because they did not even have enough food to last two months since their ships had not been able to unload their cargo. When they saw the fate that was to befall them, like bold knights and without showing the least faintness of heart they held council to see what could be done.

In this council there were terrible arguments. Some advised them to attack the city: if they could take it they could hold fast there until they received aid, for they could not imagine that the city would not be well supplied. Others said they should set up battle stations in front of Tirant's camp, because he was such a valiant knight that he would be certain to do battle. And they had so many excellent cavalry that they could not help but defeat them. And even if they did not, it was better to die as knights than to let themselves be trapped like sheep. And if fortune smiled on them and allowed them to be the victors in battle they could go past safely and stay there until they had taken the city.

Others were of the opinion that it would be better to send an embassy to Tirant so he would grant them a truce and let them go past. They would all go to their land and leave the Empire of Greece behind, and they would also give back all the fortresses they had taken, and all the prisoners and captives. At the end of the council they decided to send an embassy to Tirant, and if he would not let them go by, then they could take other measures: First they could attack the city, and if they could not take it then their last recourse would be to die like knights with their swords in their hands.

So the council ended, and they chose as their ambassadors the son of the Grand Caramany and the Prince of Scythia, who were very knowledgeable about war. They told them to estimate how many men Tirant had and how many were ready and armed, and they gave them instructions about everything they were to say and do.

With the ambassadors went two hundred unarmed men on horses. Before they left they sent a messenger to Tirant's camp to ask for safe passage, and it was granted to them. The ambassadors then set out on the road to the camp.

Meanwhile, Tirant called the Marquis of Lizana, his admiral, and told him to pay what was due to the hired ships. And he was to divide their provisions into three parts, taking some to the castle of Sinòpoli, and others to the castle of Pera, and the last to the city of Pera, along with five hundred soldiers. Then the ships could return to their home ports. He also commanded him to arm the ships that had been taken from the Moors and his remaining ships, and to supply them well, and that were to go to the city of Constantinople.

"And after they have unloaded their cargo, let them appear constantly in view of the Moors' encampment and bombarded them and cause them as much harm as they can."

The admiral did this, and also ordered two well-armed galleys to remain in the river, near Tirant's camp, in case he needed to send them somewhere. Then Tirant went to the tent of the Queen of Fez, and told her:

"My sister, I beg you to go with these ships to Constantinople, so that you can console the lady who holds my soul captive. I am afraid that during this time, while I'm not able to go to her, some harm may befall her, and that would be worse than death for me."

The gracious queen would not allow Tirant to speak. Instead, with a kindly face and soft voice, she said:

"My brother, to me your requests are commands. I am deeply in your debt because of the great benefits and honors I've received from you."

Then Tirant embraced her and kissed her on the cheek, and said to her:

"My sister, I cannot thank you enough for the great love I see in you."

The queen tried to kiss his hands, and Tirant would not allow it.

Later, the morning of the following day, the queen went to depart with all her maidens; and the King of Sicily, along with Tirant and five hundred armed men, accompanied her to the sea. When the queen had boarded a ship they took their leave of her and returned to camp. The admiral had all the ships set sail, and they started on their way to Constantinople.

Then the Moorish ambassadors reached Tirant's camp, and were astonished at all the horses and men there. In Tirant's tent the son of the Grand Caramany explained his mission:

"You know, great captain, how many people are lost in battles of this sort. And many more would be lost in this one where graves are prepared for so many soldiers. So, to avoid all that inhumanity we, ambassadors of our lord the sultan, and the Grand Turk, have come to learn what Your Lordship's intention is in this matter. If it please you, we would ask for a truce of three or more months, and if your generous person should wish it, a lasting peace for one hundred and one years. They will be very happy to be friends of your friends and enemies of your enemies, in brotherhood. If this is done they will leave the empire of Greece, restoring to your dominion all cities, castles, towns and lands within the boundaries of Greece. In addition, they will free all Christian prisoners held in our power, and they will comply with any other reasonable demand. But if you do not wish to come to an agreement with them, you may be certain that they will very quickly give you a terrible lesson with cruel weapons."

And that was the end of his speech.

Tirant saw immediately that he had finally achieved the glory he desired so much. But with great discretion he did not agree at once; he told them to rest, and that he would soon give them a reply. So they took their leave, and Tirant's knights took them back to their tents with honor.

Like a virtuous captain, Tirant sent word for his illustrious kings and dukes and noble chivalry to come to his tent the next day, for after mass he wanted to hold counsel concerning the embassy. And as they all loved Tirant deeply, they quickly went to his tent. After they had heard mass they each sat down according to their rank, and when there was silence in the council, Tirant said:

"Most illustrious and magnificent lords, Your Lordships are aware of the embassy sent by the Moorish sultan and the Grand Turk, asking us for a truce. In the first place we must consider that they are in bad straits. We know that we have them in a position where they need food and other things necessary to survive. My opinion is that we could not give greater service to His Majesty the emperor than if we did not grant them a truce or any agreement at all. Instead we should have them place themselves in our power with no assurances concerning their property or their lives. And if they do not agree to this, let them do all the harm they can, for we are certain we can make them perish from hunger. Furthermore, if we want to do battle with them it is in our power, because we are much more powerful than they. However, I believe it would be great madness for us to battle them, for they are desperate, and we could lose many of our own men and put the entire country in danger. My lords and brothers, my opinion is this: we should give them no reply at all without consulting His Majesty, the emperor, so that if anything of the sort should happen, we would not be blamed. So I beg all Your Lordships, my brothers, to advise me about the reply that should be given."

And he finished his speech.

***

In the meantime the fleet left Tirant's camp to go to the illustrious city of Constantinople, and the wind and weather were so favorable that on that same day, two hours before Phoebus ended its journey, they reached the city. The noble citizens and the townspeople, hearing the cries of happiness, ran to the wall to see the help they wanted so much. The fleet came in, flying the flags of His imperial Majesty and the valiant captain, Tirant. There was no less happiness inside the city, as they rang the bells and praised divine Providence.

When the princess saw Plaerdemavida, her servant, coming so triumphantly as a queen, she dismounted in order to pay her honor. The queen threw herself at her feet to honor her, but the lady would not allow that, and instead kissed her many times on the mouth as a sign of her great love. The night the virtuous Queen of Fez arrived at Constantinople the princess wanted her to sleep with her so they could talk at their leisure. When they were in bed the princess said:

"My virtuous sister and lady, my heart has been very anxious all the time you were gone. I couldn't write down all the reasons for this, for I loved you more than all the ladies and maidens in the world. I found it impossible to live without you, especially when I thought that because of me you had died a frightening death at the terrible hands of the sea. I beg you, my sister and lady, please tell me how I offended virtuous Tirant who so cruelly left the one who loved him more than her own life. And don't think that I am the way I was when you left me, because love has won over me so that I am beside myself. And I'm afraid that if I don't see my Tirant soon my life will not last long."

The lady ended her pitiful words, weeping uncontrollably. The virtuous queen comforted her with tender words, and when the princess had recovered, the queen said:

"My lady, Your Highness should rejoice at one thing: you are not at all to blame. I told Tirant everything. When he knew the truth he was very confused and ashamed, and through me he asks Your Majesty to pardon him. My lady, Your Highness should forgive him because he was deceived by someone who was deeply trusted, and Your Majesty is unaware of her cruelty. Trust me, my lady, I have never failed you when you needed me. I will soon have him come here to pay you homage, for I know that he truly has no other desire than to honor you and offer his services to Your Majesty."

"My sister," said the princess, "I can see now that in the past when you were in my service, you gave me good advice and I didn't realize it. From now on I will do what you advise me."

When the princess had finished, the queen said:

"My lady, if Your Highness will do this I promise to fulfill your desire very quickly—even more than you wish."

And with these words and others like them, they spent most of the night. The princess took great pleasure in the queen's words, for it had been a long time since they had seen each other and they had a great deal to talk about. The queen said:

"My lady, let us give ourselves up to the night so that Your Highness will not grow tired."

And they did.

***

When virtuous Tirant held council with the great kings, dukes, counts and barons about the reply they would give to the ambassadors of the sultan and the Turk, the council decided unanimously that His Majesty the emperor should be consulted. Tirant thought he had reached the end he so much desired to have a justifiable reason for going and paying homage to the lady who held his heart captive.

Thinking that this business was of great importance, and that it affected his honor more than it did the others', he decided to go alone, secretly, to the noble, beloved city to talk with His Majesty, the emperor, and to know his decision. In that way peace could be brought to the Empire of Greece, and he could enjoy restful tranquility in the arms of his lady.

When darkness of night fell, he spoke to the King of Sicily and the King of Fez, and left the camp in their hands. Then he went on board a galley and sailed to Constantinople, which was some twenty miles from Tirant's camp. When Tirant reached the port and the galley was anchored, it was ten o'clock at night. He ordered the ship's commander not to leave. Then he disguised himself, and disembarked, and when he was at the city gates, he told the guards to open them, that he was a servant of Tirant who had come to speak to His Majesty, the emperor. The guards let him pass, and he went to the emperor's palace. When he was inside they told him that the emperor had gone to bed. Tirant went to the Queen of Fez's chamber and found her praying. When the queen saw him she quickly recognized him and ran to embrace him and kiss him, and she said:

"Lord Tirant, I can't tell you how happy I am that you are here, and now I have even more reason to thank God for hearing my prayers. Come, my lord, so worthy of glory. It is time now for you to receive the payment for your honorable deeds in the arms of the lady who is your real happiness. And if you don't do what I tell you to this time, I swear that you'll never have my help again. Instead I'll go back to my land as quickly as I can."

Tirant did not let the queen go on. He said:

"My lady and sister, if I have disobeyed you in the past, I beg you to forgive me. I promise and swear to you, on the order of chivalry that I hold, that there will be nothing in the world that you will command of me that I will not obey, even if I am certain it will bring me death. For I am very sure that you always gave me good advice, if only I had taken advantage of it."

"Now then," said the queen, "we shall see what you are able to do. You will have to go into a list in a closed field of battle, because I won't consider you a knight if I don't see you as the victor in a delicious battle. Wait here, and I will go talk to the princess. I'll ask her to come here tonight to sleep with me."

The queen quickly left Tirant and went to the princess's chamber, and found her ready to go to bed. When the princess saw the queen, she said:

"What has happened, sister, to bring you here in such a hurry?"

The queen pretended to be very happy, and she put her head close to the princess's and said:

"My lady, please come sleep with me in my bed tonight. I have many things to tell Your Majesty. A galley has come from Tirant's camp, and a man came ashore and talked to me."

The princess very happily told her she would do it, because she had slept with her other times, and the queen had also slept in her bed. They did this when they wanted to talk freely without awakening the suspicion of the empress and the maidens. The princess took the queen's hand, and they went to her chamber. They found it in good order and well perfumed, as the queen had prepared it. The princess quickly got into bed because of her great desire to have news about Tirant, and her maidens helped her undress. When the princess was in bed, they bade her a good night—which they did not know was already prepared for her.

When the maidens had left the bedroom the queen bolted the door herself and told her maidens to go to sleep because she was going to pray a little while, and she would go to bed later and did not want anyone there.

All the maidens went into another chamber where they slept. When the queen had dismissed them all she went into the sitting room and said to Tirant:

"Glorious knight, strip yourself to your nightshirt, and go lie beside the lady who loves you more than her own life. Apply the spurs strongly and without mercy, as befits a knight. And don't come to me with any squeamishness, because I swear to you on my word as a queen that if you don't do it now you'll never get another chance to have this much glory for the rest of your life."

When Tirant heard such beautiful words from the queen he knelt down on the floor and kissed her hands and feet. Then he said:

"My lady and my sister, you've bound my liberty with strong chains. What you are doing for me is so great that, even if I were your captive for the rest of my life, I don't believe I could repay what I owe you."

"My lord, Tirant," said the queen, "don't waste time. Take your clothes off right now."

The virtuous Tirant flung his clothes into the air, and in a trice he was naked and barefoot. The queen took him by the hand and led him to the bed where the princess was. The queen said to the princess:

"My lady, here is your adventurous knight whom Your Majesty loves so much. Be a good companion to him, Your Grace, as one would expect from Your Excellency. You're not unaware of how many trials and hardships he has gone through to win your love. Make wise use of him, for you are the discretion of the world, and he is your husband. And Your Majesty should think of nothing but the present, because one never knows what the future will bring."

The princess answered:

"False sister, I never thought you would betray me like this. But I have confidence in the virtue of my lord, Tirant, who will make up for your great lack."

And don't imagine that during this conversation Tirant was idle; instead he applied himself to his labor. The queen left them and went to a bed in the chamber, to sleep. When the queen had gone, the princess turned to Tirant who was pushing forward in his battle, and she said:

"Calm yourself, my lord, and don't try to use your bellicose strength, because the strength of a delicate maiden is not so great that she can resist such a knight. Upon your mercy, don't treat me like this. The struggle of love doesn't require great force; it is not won by strength, but by ingenious flattery and sweet deception. Stop your insistence, my lord; don't be cruel: don't think that this is a camp or list of infidels; don't try to conquer someone who is already conquered by your goodness. Let me have part of your manliness so that I may resist you. Oh, my lord!

"How can something which is forced give you pleasure? Oh! Can love allow you to harm the thing that is loved? Restrain yourself, my lord, upon your virtue and nobility. Wait, poor thing! The arms of love should not cut, nor should the enamored lance break or wound! Have pity, have compassion on this solitary maiden. Oh, false and cruel knight! I will cry out! Wait, for I want to scream. Lord Tirant, will you have no compassion on me? You are not Tirant. Wretched me! Is this what I desired so? Oh, hope of my life, here is your dead princess!"

And do not think that Tirant refrained from doing his work because of the pitiful words of the princess, for in a short time Tirant was the conqueror in the delicious battle, and the princess gave up her arms and swooned. Tirant jumped out of bed, thinking he had killed her, and he went to call the queen so that she would come and help him. The queen got up quickly and took a jar of water and sprinkled it on the princess's face, and rubbed her temples. She recovered her senses, and giving a deep sigh, she said:

"Even if these are the signs of love, they should not be used with so much force and cruelty. Now, lord Tirant, I must believe that you did not love me with a virtuous love. If only you had waited for the day of solemnity and the ceremonial festivities to lawfully enter the doors of my chastity."

The queen did not wait for the princess to say any more, and with a smiling face she said:

"Oh, my blessed lady! How well you know how to act like you're hurt! A knight's arms do no harm to a maiden. May God give me a death like the one you pretend he's giving you! May I be attacked by the illness you're talking about if by morning you don't feel completely cured."

The princess was not entirely consoled at the loss of her virginity, and since she did not want to answer the queen's insane words, she kept quiet. The two lovers spent the entire night playing that happy sport that lovers play.

CHAPTER XIII - THE WEDDING

During the night Tirant told the princess about all the misfortunes he had suffered because of her love. Then he took great pleasure in telling her about his prosperity and victory, but finally he told her that he felt less glory in any of it than he did in conquering her illustrious person. When she had gathered her strength and her sweet anger was over, she told Tirant about the life she had led while he was gone, and how during this time she had never seen anyone laugh or take joy in anything. Withdrawn from all delights, alone in continual prayer, deep in religion because of her love, she had been able to survive until they brought her the happy news of his arrival. And they exchanged many other delicious words, full of loving sighs.

The queen, who was responsible for this affair, saw that daylight was near, and she realized that when people in love have some pleasure, they do not think of anything that would disturb them. She got up from her bed, anxiously, and went to where the lovers were. She told them that since their night had been good she hoped God would give them a good morning. They returned her good wishes very graciously, and she found them very happy, taking joy in one another. The queen said to Tirant:

"Lord of the Empire of Greece: Get up, it's already day. You must leave as secretly as you can so that no one will see you."

Tirant would have liked that night to last a year. Many times, while kissing the princess, he begged her to forgive him. The princess answered:

"My lord Tirant, love obliges me to forgive you, on the condition that you come back soon, for I cannot live without you. Now I know what love is, and before I did not know."

The lady had barely uttered the last syllable of her loving words when Tirant said:

"Your Highness will see how short the war will become so that I, your captive, can wait on you with loving service."

And with a kiss of deepest love they parted. The queen took him by the hand and led him through a back door into the orchard.

Saying very courteous words, they each went their way. Tirant went to Hippolytus' quarters, and the queen went back to the princess, and took Tirant's place in the bed. And there they slept peacefully until well into the day.

Hippolytus' happiness was by no means slight when he saw his master and lord Tirant. With the great love he had for him, he threw himself at his feet, attempting to kiss them. Tirant would not allow it, and lifted him from the floor, and embraced and kissed him. They greeted each other at length, for they had not seen each other since fate had carried off Tirant. Tirant told Hippolytus to go to the palace and tell the emperor that he had come and wished to speak with him secretly.

Hippolytus quickly went to the emperor and told him of Tirant's arrival. The emperor thought Tirant must have come because of very important matters, and he told Hippolytus to have him come immediately. Hippolytus went to his quarters and told Tirant what the emperor had said. The two relatives left Hippolytus' lodging in disguise and went to the palace. They found the emperor in his chamber as he was finishing dressing.

When Tirant was before His Majesty he threw himself at his feet, to kiss them. The great lord would not permit it, and instead took Tirant by the hand, lifted him from the floor and kissed him on the mouth. Tirant kissed his hand, and the emperor took his hand and led him to another chamber where he made him sit at his side. Tears ran down the emperor's cheeks because of his great happiness, and because of all the losses he had suffered—which he knew well would not have happened if Tirant had been there. Tirant said:

"Most excellent Sire, the Moorish sultan and the Grand Turk have sent me on this mission which has many conditions that affect Your Majesty.

"Since it would be very presumptuous of me to give a reply without the express license of Your Majesty, I entreat Your Grace that it be examined carefully in the council and a decision be reached about what is to be done, so that if it should be brought up in the future, I would not be held to blame. The Moorish sultan and the Grand Turk are asking Your Majesty for a truce of three months, or for longer if Your Majesty wishes. And if you want a lasting peace for one hundred one years, they will be happy to form an alliance with Your Majesty to be friends of your friends and enemies of your enemies."

The emperor answered:

"Our virtuous captain and son: We hold you in such high esteem and trust that we would have accepted whatever you decided. But to please you, I will hold counsel on the matter."

The great emperor ordered the council to meet quickly so that Tirant could return to camp. Taking his leave of the emperor, Tirant went to pay his respects to the empress and the princess. He found them together in the princess's chamber because she was pretending to be sick, and the empress had come to be with her. The empress was very glad to see Tirant. The princess pretended to greet him coldly so as not to arouse suspicions about what had happened the night before. They spoke of many things, and the princess especially asked Tirant if he had any news about the arrival of the Queen of Ethiopia. Tirant answered:

"My lady, three days ago I received a letter, by messenger, from King Escariano. He asked me not to do battle with the Moors until he arrived. And he assured me that he would be here in two weeks."

The princess answered:

"Captain, there is nothing I desire more than to see this queen. I hear that her beauty is greater than that of anyone in the world."

Tirant answered:

"My lady, they told you the truth. After Your Majesty I don't think a more beautiful or more virtuous woman can be found anywhere. She has the same desire you do: her only reason for coming here is because of all the perfection she has heard about Your Majesty."

While Tirant, the empress and the princess were speaking, Stephanie, Duchess of Macedonia, came into the chamber. With the absence of her husband, she had entered religion and did not want to leave it until that fortunate day when she hoped all her troubles would end. She threw herself at Tirant's feet and cried aloud, tears flowing down her cheeks. Tirant would not allow the duchess to kneel. He took her arm and raised her from the floor. Then he embraced her and kissed her, and said:

"I promise you, on my order of chivalry, that before a month has gone by the Duke of Macedonia and all the others will be out of prison and they will be here. That is the sole reason I came."

When the Duchess of Macedonia heard Tirant's words, she threw herself at his feet, wanting to kiss them. Tirant would not allow it, and lifting her from the floor he kissed her again. Then, taking her hands, they sat down and told each other about their past difficulties.

While the captain was entertaining the ladies and consoling the Duchess of Macedonia, the emperor called for a council meeting and explained the mission that the sultan and the Turk had sent Tirant on, just as Tirant had told it to him. When all the council members learned the good news there were arguments and disagreements among them. Finally, after much deliberation, they sent for the emperor and said to him:

"Your Majesty, we advise you to make a lasting peace with the sultan and with the Turk and with all the other great lords in their company, with the stipulation that they put themselves in Your Excellency's power as your prisoners. And they must not be released until they have carried out all their promises, and the other Moors have left, unarmed and on foot."

The emperor was very happy with this decision since it was such good advice. He went to the princess's chamber where he found Tirant, and taking him by the hand, he had him sit by his side in great friendship, and told him what he wanted.

"Tirant, my captain and son, our council has come to the decision we mentioned. So, I beg you to depart as quickly as you can to give reply to the embassy."

Tirant said he would do as he was ordered, and he took his leave of the emperor. He went to the empress and the princess and bade them farewell, and they begged him to do everything he could to liberate the Empire of Greece. Tirant replied:

"My ladies, may Our Lord grant that it be done as quickly as Your Excellencies wish."

He took his leave of the princess, and the queen accompanied him to the door of his chamber to tell him that as soon as it was dark he should go through the orchard door and come to her room where he could talk to the princess. Tirant said he would do as she commanded.

After Tirant had left the ladies he went to Hippolytus' room to wait for the dark of night so he could have his heart's desire. Alone and in disguise, when the time was right he crept softly through the familiar orchard toward the queen's chamber, and there he found the princess, with the queen, waiting for him. The princess greeted him with great happiness, and the three of them went into the chamber.

Tirant gamboled with the princess and they passed the time in amorous solace and delicious chatter until it was time for bed. The princess got into bed first, and the queen dismissed all the ladies and put valiant Tirant at the side of his lady, who treated him with more love than she had the night before. After the queen had placed them in the list and they were in delicious battle, she left to go to sleep, trusting that they would be in such agreement that the battle would never come to an end.

Tirant did not sleep the entire night, like a brave knight who understands that one who is valiant in battle must be valiant in bed. As day drew near Tirant said to the princess:

"My lady and my life, I must go. I promised His Majesty the emperor that tomorrow, at break of day, I would be in my camp."

The princess answered:

"My lord and my love, your departure grieves me deeply. If it were possible I would never let you out of my sight. If I felt pain before, now it will be a thousand times worse. Do me the grace, my lord, not to delay your return unless you want to cut short my life, for I cannot live without you."

When Tirant had her permission he got up from the bed and dressed, and with kisses of deep-felt love along with tears he left the princess. Going out the back gate of the orchard, he went to Hippolytus' lodging. Hippolytus got up, and quickly escorted Tirant to the city gates so they would be opened for him. Tirant went to the ocean and boarded the galley that left the port secretly and rowed to the encampment.

The sun had been up scarcely an hour when the galley was in sight of the camp. The entire camp knew the captain had returned, and the King of Sicily and the King of Fez rode with their men to escort Tirant, and they took him to his triumphal tent with great honor. Tirant explained to them everything His Majesty the emperor had decided, and they were all very content.

The morning of the following day the captain asked the kings and grandees to come to mass. They all quickly went to his tent with many knights. After mass he sent word to the ambassadors of the sultan and the Turk to come, as he wanted to give them an answer. The ambassadors were very glad to receive the news. Dressed in Moorish fashion, and accompanied by many noble knights from Tirant's camp, the great lords went with great pomp and gravity to the tent of the valiant captain. Before they left their tent the ambassadors put their mounts and servants in readiness so that when they had the reply from Tirant they could return to their camp.

When the ambassadors were in the presence of the valiant captain they bowed deeply to him and Tirant paid them as much honor as he thought they deserved. When they were seated before him, Tirant gave the following reply:

"Do not be astonished that the answer has been so long in coming, for I wanted to consult His Majesty, the emperor, about your embassy. He, with great benignity and clemency, has had compassion on you. As you well know, your life or death is in our hands. So that you may know how great is the humanity and clemency of the emperor, he is content to spare your lives and grant you mercy in this fashion: The sultan and Turk, with all the kings and lords in your camp, will place themselves in the emperor's power as prisoners. There you will stay until such a time as you have restored all the lands you have taken from the empire. At the same time you will bring to him all the prisoners and captives in the lands of the sultan as well as the Turk. And His Majesty the emperor is willing to let all the Moors leave who are in your camp, but on foot and unarmed. And if you are not satisfied with the emperor's mercy, you can all prepare to die, for I promise you that not one of you will be spared."

On the morning of the following day the Moors held council regarding the reply they should give to Tirant, and the council decided to acquiesce to everything Tirant asked for. The ambassadors delivered the reply to Tirant, saying that the sultan and the Turk, with the counsel and will of all the rest, were content to do everything his lordship had asked.

Soon all those who were to be hostages rode in, and there were twenty-two in all, all titled and of high nobility. I will not give their names here so that I will not take up too much space, but I can tell you that because of their great hunger they were hardly slow in coming down the road. They all presented themselves to Tirant, and bowed deeply. Tirant welcomed them, paying them great honor, and gave them a magnificent banquet.

After the banquet, Tirant put all the prisoners on two galleys, and then he went on board himself to go with them.

The two galleys sailed away from the camp, and quickly reached Constantinople. When the captain was near the port of Constantinople, and the people in the town heard that Tirant was coming in triumph, bringing the highest lords of the Moorish people as prisoners, they were the happiest people in the world. Everyone ran to the ocean to see the prisoners. An immense crowd gathered, both men and women, shouting:

"Long live our blessed captain! May God protect and prolong his life, for he has freed us from so much misery!"

Tirant refused to leave the galleys until the emperor sent Hippolytus along with other knights. When Hippolytus was on the galley with Tirant, he told him:

"My lord, His Majesty, the emperor, has sent me to Your Lordship, and he begs you to come on land."

Tirant said he would be happy to do what he commanded. The captain quickly had the galleys draw near to land and they lowered the ladders. Then Tirant had all the prisoners disembark with him. When they were on land they met all the officials and magistrates of the city who received them with great honor, and Tirant with great reverence. They all left the shore together and went to the emperor's palace, and the populace followed them.

When they were in the palace square they saw the emperor up above on the catafalque, seated in the imperial chair, with the empress to his left, and the princess to the right of the emperor, but a little lower, as a sign that she would be the successor to the empire. When Tirant and the prisoners were in view of the emperor, they all knelt to the ground; then they went up to the catafalque where the emperor was. They made another deep bow, and Tirant moved to the front.

When he stood before the emperor he threw himself at his feet to kiss them, but the emperor would not allow it. Instead he took him by the arm, lifted him from the ground and kissed him on the mouth, and Tirant kissed his hand. The Turk and the other great lords did the same. The emperor received them with great humanity, and ordered them taken to the other catafalque.

The tables were prepared immediately, and each was seated according to his station. The emperor wanted Tirant to eat at his table, and the five of them ate there: the emperor, the empress, the princess and Tirant, and the Queen of Fez. The emperor ordered the prisoners to be served with great honor and reverence, for even though they were infidels they were still men of great dignity and station. And it was all done well, with a great abundance of precious foods and wines of different kinds. They were astonished, and they said that the Christians were more experienced than the Moors in eating.

When they had eaten, Tirant asked the emperor's permission to go to the Moorish camp and have the Moors sent to Turkey. The emperor agreed. Tirant took his leave of the empress and the princess, and he withdrew to the galleys, and sailed to the fleet in front of the Moorish camp. When the admiral saw Tirant approaching he commanded the trumpets, pipes and horns to be blown, and they greeted the captain with loud cries. The admiral went on board the captain's ship and said to him:

"Sir, what does Your Lordship require?"

Tirant answered:

"Have all the ships come near shore, and all the Moors will go to Turkey."

The admiral said he would carry out the order. He returned to his ship and gave the signal for all the ships to draw in to shore. And it was done very quickly. Tirant had a man that he had brought from the sultan put ashore, and he told the Moors to go aboard the ships without fear, and that they would go to Turkey. The Moors, who wanted nothing else in the world because of their great hunger, quickly gathered and left behind their horses and arms, with their tents still standing, containing all their booty. When the ships were loaded with Moors, they carried them over to their land: It was very near as they only had to cross the Bosphorus; then they returned for more. You can imagine how many men there were, for four hundred vessels, including ships and galleys and other vessels made ten crossings.

When the men of Tirant's camp learned that all the Moors were gone, they all ran as fast as they could to take a share of the booty. After the men on the vessels had taken the Moors across, they went ashore and they still had time to take part of the booty. It could truly be said that that camp was the richest one there had ever been, for they had captured and robbed the entire Empire of Greece, and they had it all right there, and a lot of good it did them! And the men who found themselves with that booty were rich for the rest of their lives.

When the entire Moorish camp had been sacked, Tirant ordered all the men back to their camp. He kept only the King of Sicily and the King of Fez with him, along with some other barons who wanted to pay homage to the emperor. They left the Moors' camp and went overland to the illustrious city of Constantinople, while the ships sailed into the port of the city.

After the emperor had left the table and the prisoners had eaten their fill, he ordered Hippolytus to take all the prisoners to the top of the palace towers which were prepared for them. Hippolytus went to the catafalque where the prisoners were and told them to go with him. They came down from the catafalque and followed Hippolytus as he led them up to the towers. Hippolytus put the Moorish sultan and the Grand Turk in a beautiful chamber. Then he told them:

"Sirs, His Majesty the emperor commands Your Lordships to rest here, and to be a little patient if you are not being treated as befits your worthiness."

The sultan replied:

"Virtuous knight, we are grateful to His Majesty the emperor for the great honor he is doing us, because he is not treating or regarding us as prisoners, but as brothers. We are deeply obligated to him for this, and when we are given our liberty and our power again, we shall serve him in everything he commands."

Afterward Hippolytus ordered the four pages never to leave the chamber, and to serve them with all respect in everything they commanded. Then he ordered guards to keep watch over the tower. Hippolytus took the rest of the prisoners and placed them in the other towers where they were given very nice chambers and servants to serve them, and they were very content. And he gave them good guards so that they would be well served and well-guarded.

The emperor went to the palace with all the ladies and gave orders that nothing on the square should be touched, because he had been advised by Tirant that the King of Sicily and the King of Fez would be coming to pay him their respects. He ordered Hippolytus to arrange for good lodgings in the city, and Hippolytus, who was virtuous and discreet, carried out everything the emperor commanded him.

A few days later the emperor was told that Tirant was coming with the King of Sicily and other lords, and that they were a league away from the city. The emperor had Hippolytus and all the officials from the city, along with the nobles and knights who were there, go out to receive them. When they were at the palace, Tirant, the King of Sicily and the others dismounted. The new guests were astonished at the great beauty of the ladies, especially of the princess.

After they had entertained the ladies, the emperor was told that the dinner was ready. Later they cleared the tables, and the dances began. The square was full of people from the city who were looking at such a beautiful celebration. Others were dancing, and it was lovely to see such a victory celebration. In the city there were also other kinds of dances and games, for the emperor had ordered celebrations held for a week.

Tirant would not leave the side of the King of Sicily during all these festivities. Instead they slept and ate together continuously— the better to cover up what had taken place between him and the princess. The others spent the eight days celebrating. Every day Tirant told the princess of his love, and begged Her Highness to arrange the marriage so that they could enjoy its delights without fear.

The princess answered:

"Oh, most virtuous of all men! Don't beg me for the one thing I want most in the whole world, and don't think me so ungrateful that I've forgotten what your great nobility has brought us. Please, my lord, do not become angry because you have to wait for the culmination of our happiness, for you have already won a glorious victory over me. Just think how it has been to your glory and that of your men that you have recovered the entire empire, and conquered and killed so many Moorish kings and lords. Now the only thing Your Lordship lacks is to have dominion over all the empire as part of your matrimony. Since you have returned to me, and you are the mainstay of my life, I promise to renounce the crown in your favor, and to complete our wedding vows with you as emperor since my father, being advanced in years, wants me to rule in his stead."

Tirant would not allow the lady to continue, and with a loving heart he said:

"Even if I could, I find it difficult to accept your gracious and generous offer. May the Divine Power not permit me to commit such great folly as to take the crown of the empire during the emperor's lifetime. I only ask His Majesty to keep me as a son and servant, and the captive of his daughter. I want nothing else in this world."

When Tirant finished these words of love, tears sprang from his lady's eyes. Throwing herself into his arms, and clinging from his neck, she kissed him many times. After a moment she said:

"My lord and my life, no tongue could express the perfection and virtues of your noble person, and now I truly understand that you are unique in all the world. May you long possess the crown of the Greek Empire, and may I be able to serve you all your life."

And they departed with many words of mutual love.

Tirant spent the night in amorous thoughts, waiting for Phoebus to arrive in the east, spreading its luminous rays over our horizon. At the proper time the captain went before the emperor, and said:

"Your Majesty remembers the promise given by the sultan and the Turk to Your Excellency, of restoring to your power all the lands they occupy in the Greek Empire. So, great lord, if Your Majesty will grant me permission, I will leave to take possession of them for Your Majesty. If fortune favors us, Sire, Your Excellency will command all the land that your predecessor, the emperor Justine, commanded."

The emperor answered:

"We are well aware of the many services and honors you have done for us and for the entire empire, and we are greatly indebted to you. We would therefore like to give you and your people the entire empire while we are still alive, and furthermore we wish to give you our daughter Carmesina as your wife, if you will accept her. For we are at such an age that we are no longer able to rule, much less to defend the empire."

When Tirant heard the emperor's kind words he threw himself at his feet and kissed them with great humility and love, and he said:

"My lord, may heaven never permit Tirant lo Blanc, Your Majesty's humble servant, to commit such an error as to allow Your Highness to lose the command of your empire during your lifetime; before that should happen I would rather die. But Sire, if you would do me the grace of giving me something that is worth much more, as Your Majesty has offered, I would value it more than if you gave me ten empires."

Seeing his great gentility, the emperor took him by the arm, lifted him from the floor and kissed him on the mouth, and Tirant kissed his hand. The emperor took Tirant's hand and led him to the chambers of the princess, who was with all her ladies, entertaining the King of Sicily. When the great emperor came into the room everyone stood up and bowed to him. As the emperor sat down he made the princess sit at his right, Tirant at his left, and the King of Sicily in front of them. The emperor then turned to his daughter, and said:

"My daughter, you're aware of the great service and high honors Tirant here has bestowed on us. And that he has liberated the entire empire from all the hardships that the Moors have inflicted on us. As we realize that we do not have enough to offer him for all he has done for us, we have decided that we have nothing dearer or of greater value or that we love more than you yourself. So we have offered you to him, and I beg and command you, my dear daughter, to take him as your husband and lord: that will be the way you can best serve me."

The lady answered with a gracious and modest continence:

"Most merciful and kind lord, it is to my glory that Your Majesty has placed me in such high esteem that I am a worthy reward for all the services and honors which valiant Tirant has done for Your Majesty and for everyone in the empire. Even though I am not worthy to remove his shoe, when one thinks of all the unique qualities and virtues he possesses, I hope he will accept me as his servant and his captive, for I am ready to do whatever Your Majesty or he commands me."

The emperor sent for the archbishop of the city to betroth them immediately. And this gracious union was a matter of no slight happiness, for during a long while Tirant and the princess could not speak, so inflamed with true love were they. As soon as the archbishop arrived, the emperor ordered him to betroth his daughter and Tirant, and he did so.

When the betrothal was completed, there was much celebrating and great happiness throughout the city. A marvelous feast was prepared as suited such a betrothal, and music was performed by many groups from the towers and through windows of the great halls. The foreigners and everyone in general took great pleasure in this betrothal, for they had faith that the bold spirit of Tirant would allow them to live in peace. And the celebrations, both in the palace and in the city, lasted a week.

The emperor sent a proclamation throughout the city, with many trumpets and drums, that they should all consider Tirant his successor and the Caesar of the empire. And he made them swear that after his death they would hold him as their emperor and lord. And from that time forward the new Prince Tirant was named Caesar of the Greek Empire.

CHAPTER XIV - DEATH

Tirant decided to leave as soon as he could in order to recover all of the Greek Empire, and put it in the emperor's power. At the same time it hurt him to think of being away from the princess, for life without her was impossible. He was tired of war now, and he wanted peace and tranquility. When he received news that the magnanimous King Escariano was coming with many men, and that he was in Pinxenais which borders on Greece, and is ten days journey from Constantinople, he decided to go out to meet him.

After he had taken his leave of the emperor, the empress, and of his princess and wife, he left the city of Constantinople, and went to his camp with grandees and other nobles. When the Caesar reached his camp he had the trumpets blow for the camp to be raised. Everyone got ready, and the following morning they left the bridge and went toward the place where King Escariano was.

As the powerful army was going along, many castles and villas delivered themselves over to the Caesar (We omit their names to avoid being prolix.). Finally they reached the city of Strenes where King Escariano's army was resting.

When King Escariano knew that his dear friend and brother at arms was coming, he rode out with his grandees and met him on the road. They dismounted quickly, embraced and kissed very warmly. Tirant told King Escariano that the King of Sicily and the King of Fez were with him. King Escariano went to the other kings, and embraced and kissed them very courteously. Then they mounted their horses again and went toward the city. When they reached King Escariano's tents, Prince Tirant and the kings dismounted in front of the tent of the illustrious Queen of Ethiopia who welcomed them, and embraced and kissed them all.

They decided to send the beautiful queen to the city of Constantinople, and five hundred soldiers made ready to go, accompanied by many nobles and knights. The illustrious queen took leave of her lord, King Escariano, Tirant, and the other kings and lords who escorted her for a league. Then Tirant and the others bade the queen farewell, and she continued on to Constantinople while Tirant and the others returned to the city.

Tirant and King Escariano immediately commanded their camps to be raised and each of them put their men in order. They left the city and went toward the province of Thrace. They reached a city called Stagira, which is surrounded by walls adorned with beautiful towers. The city immediately opened all the gates to them. After all the renegade Greeks had been made good Christians again, they swore fidelity to the emperor. And all the Moors who did not want to be baptized were thrown out of the city. It was in this same city that the great philosopher Aristotle had been born, and he was considered a saint.

While Prince Tirant had his tents set up in this city and was resting, he sent two Moorish ambassadors through the outlying territories, and to all the cities, castles and villas of the neighboring provinces. They delivered up their keys and rendered homage to Prince Tirant, and he replaced the captain of every city, villa and castle.

They then left the city of Stagira and headed for Macedonia, stopping at a city called Olympus. This city takes its name from a nearby mountain, one of the highest in the world. Here they were better received than in any of the places they had been, because they knew that the Caesar was the cousin of Diafebus, their duke and lord.

The prince left the duchy of Macedonia, and they went to the city of Trebizond which delivered itself over immediately. They brought all the knights who were held prisoner here, and with them was Captain Diafebus, Duke of Macedonia. Prince Tirant asked for the Duke of Macedonia, and he was brought to him. But he was so changed that Tirant would never have recognized him: His beard had grown down to his waist, and the hair on his head reached past his shoulders; he was thin and discolored, and his appearance was very different; he wore a yellow cloak, with a blue turban around his head. All the other knights were dressed the same way. When the Duke of Macedonia was before the Caesar, he threw himself at his feet, wanting to kiss them. The Caesar lifted him up, and with tears running from his eyes, he kissed him on the mouth.

Soon the Marquis of Saint George presented himself before Tirant, and kneeling, he thanked him for freeing them. Prince Tirant, with great affection, lifted him from the ground and kissed him on the mouth. After the marquis, came the Duke of Pera, his brother, and the prior of Saint John, and all the other knights. The Caesar received them with great love, and honored them as they deserved.

After the illustrious Queen of Ethiopia left the city of Strenes, she journeyed quickly to the renowned city of Constantinople. When the queen stood before the princess, she began to kneel, but the princess caught her by the arm, raised her up, and kissed her warmly three times. Then she took her hand and made her sit at her side.

The princess was astonished at the queen's great beauty. At the same time the Queen of Ethiopia was startled by the beauty of the princess. Everyone in the court was impressed by the queen's beauty, and they whispered about Tirant's great virtue in turning down such a beautiful lady, for they were sure that she had asked him to be her husband and lord of the kingdom of Tunis and of all Barbary, and he had left it all for love of the princess.

After the Caesar had held celebrations for the Duke of Macedonia and his companions, he gave them their leave. They left the city of Trebizond and went to the illustrious city of Constantinople. There they were welcomed with honor by His Majesty the emperor, by the empress and all the ladies. And the Duke of Macedonia was especially welcomed by the duchess, his wife, who loved him more than her life. With the arrival of the prisoners, great celebrations were held in the court.

After the Duke of Macedonia had left the city of Trebizond with all his companions, Tirant quickly had all the others break camp, and he had King Escariano and all his men, and each captain with his squadron, depart. So one squadron left after another, in an orderly fashion, and they went to the land of Bendin, six days journey away, and when the Caesar arrived there with his entire army, they surrendered to him by order of the sultan and the Turk.

When the captains had been placed in the city and in the fortress, they advanced and recovered the entire province of Blagay and all the land of Brina and all the land of Foxa and all the land of Bocina, for each of these is a large province with many cities, castles and villas, and they all surrendered willingly to the Caesar. They were accustomed to being subject to the Greek Empire, and they wanted to be so again because of the bad treatment they had received from the Moors.

The Caesar left these provinces and recovered many other cities. From here he went to the Kingdom of Persia, and he took it by force of arms, for it did not belong to the sultan or the Turk and it had its own king. The virtuous Prince Tirant conquered many other provinces and lands, and joined them under the dominion and power of the empire with such great triumph and victory that it would be tiring to tell it all. He recovered all of Greece, Asia Minor, all of Persia, all

Selonich (which is Galipoli), Morea, Arca, the Cape of Arca, Valona. And by sea he sent the fleet he had in Constantinople to take the islands, with his admiral, the Marquis of Lizana, as its captain. And he took all the islands which had belonged to the empire: Calistres, Colcos, Oritige, Tesbrie, Nimocha, Flaxen, Meclotapace, and many other islands the book does not mention to avoid prolixity.

After the admiral had conquered all the islands that once formed part of the empire, he had his entire fleet return to Constantinople, and they entered the city firing their bombards and shouting their greetings to the illustrious city. The townspeople ran to the sea wall to greet the fleet with joy. The admiral disembarked, accompanied by many well-dressed knights and noblemen, and they went to bow to His Majesty the emperor who received them very cordially, and they all kissed his foot and his hand.

Wanting to reward many nobles and knights who had been released from their imprisonment, he gave them over in matrimony to maidens of high station, all of them servants of the empress and the princess, and he also gave them large estates so they could live out their lives honorably. When the engagements had been made, their weddings were postponed until the day Prince Tirant would be wed to the princess.

But Fortune would not permit a mortal body to have so much delight and glory in this world. For God did not create human nature to reach bliss and glory in this world, but instead to enjoy the glory of paradise. No one ponders this: everyday virtuous men perform illustrious acts worthy of immortal memory, as did this magnanimous and virtuous prince and valiant knight, Tirant lo Blanc. For with his great skill at arms and high degree of intelligence, he conquered so many kingdoms and brought uncountable numbers of people in Barbary and in Greece into the Holy Catholic faith. And yet, he was unable to see the finality of all that he had so desired and labored for.

Among so many other sorrows, I find it impossible to free my weary hands from setting down on white paper how fortune lets man go unrewarded. This, despite the fact of the glorious actions of Tirant, gives me renewed anguish, for they did not bring him the prize he so richly deserved.

So then, after the Caesar had defeated and recovered the entire empire, and subjugated many other nearby provinces, he started back in great triumph to the city of Constantinople. In his company went the magnanimous King of Fez and many other kings, dukes, counts, and marquis, and innumerable knights (who came with him to share in the enormous celebration that would take place upon his return, and out of love for King Escariano, and to celebrate Tirant's wedding), and no one would leave his side. When the emperor received word that he was coming, he prepared an enormous celebration.

When Tirant was one day's journey from Constantinople, in a city called Andrinopol, he stopped because the emperor had sent word to him not to come to the city until he should tell him. While the virtuous Caesar was enjoying himself in that city, finding sport and pleasure, and strolling with King Escariano and the King of Sicily at a river's edge which ran alongside the walls of the city, he felt such a great and powerful pain in his side that they had to take him in their arms and carry him back into the city.

When Tirant was in his bed the six doctors who accompanied him came to him—the best in the world—and four of King Escariano's. They gave him many kinds of medicine, but these brought no relief to his pain. Then Tirant realized he was dying, and he asked for confession. They had the confessor who accompanied him come quickly. He was a good priest of the Order of Saint Francis, a teacher of holy theology, and a man of great knowledge. While the Caesar was making confession the King of Fez sent an urgent message to the emperor, giving His Majesty to know that the Caesar was very ill, and that his doctors could not help him. He begged his grace to send his own doctors very quickly, as he had great doubts that they would arrive in time.

After the Caesar had confessed, he had the precious body of Jesus Christ brought to him. He looked at it with great devotion, and with tears in his eyes he prayed:

"Almighty Lord, humble, sweet and benign! How can I thank You for all the love You have shown to me, a weak creature? I give You infinite thanks, Lord, for all Your gifts. And I humbly beseech You, Lord, since You have saved me so many times from danger (and You are now giving me death, which I accept most obediently, since it is Your holy will, in remission and penance for my weaknesses), that You will grant me, Lord, forgiveness of my sins in order to have Your absolution and mercy."

After he had said these words, he received the holy body of Jesus Christ. And the people in the room with him whispered that he did not seem to be a knight, but rather a holy man. When he had given restitution to his soul, he had his secretary come, and he gave his last will and testament in the presence of all those who were with him.

"I, Tirant lo Blanc, of the lineage of Rocasalada and the House of Brittany, knight of the Garter, and Prince and Caesar of the Greek Empire, with an illness from which I fear I will die, but with full knowledge, and firm and manifest word: with my lords and brothers at arms present, King Escariano, the King of Sicily, and my cousin-german, the King of Fez, and many other kings, dukes, counts and marquis, in the name of my Lord Jesus Christ, I do make and leave the following final will and testament.

"I name as executors of this testament the virtuous and most excellent Carmesina, Princess of the Greek Empire and my wife, and my dear cousin-german Diafebus, the Duke of Macedonia.

"I wish that one hundred thousand ducats be taken from my estate, and be distributed according to the wishes of my executors. Moreover, I encharge the said executors to take my body to Brittany, to the Church of Our Lady, where lie all those of my lineage of Rocasalada.

"I also desire and command that from my estate one hundred thousand ducats be given to each of the men of my lineage who are here. And of all my other property and rights which I have gained with Divine help, and which have been given to me by His Majesty, the emperor, I make as my beneficiary my servant and nephew Hippolytus of Rocasalada. It is my wish that he take my place, and be my successor."

After Tirant had made his testament, he told the secretary to write a note to the princess with these words:

"Since death is so near to me, I want to write to you, dear lady, my last, sad farewell.

"Fortune has not allowed me to have you—the prize for my deeds. And death would not be so painful to me if I could have ended my life in your arms.

"But I beg Your Highness to go on living, so that you will keep the great love that I have had for you.

"And since fortune has not allowed me to speak to you or to see you—for I believe you would have cured me and saved my life—I have decided to write you this letter, because death will not grant me more time, so that at least you will be certain of my great love. I cannot tell you more, for the great pain I am suffering will not allow it. I only beg of you to take in your charge my relatives and servants.

"Your Tirant, who kisses your feet and hands, commends to you his soul."

After Prince Tirant had made his testament, he begged King Escariano, the King of Sicily and the King of Fez to carry him to

Constantinople before his life ended. For the greatest pain he felt was that he might die without seeing the princess. And he was of the belief that if he saw her she would give him health and life.

The doctors gave their approval because, since they considered him as good as dead, they thought that with the great consolation he would feel if he saw the princess, whom he loved deeply, nature could have a more beneficial effect than all the medicines in the world. They quickly put him on a litter, and he was carried on men's shoulders very comfortably. He was accompanied by all the kings and grandees, with only five hundred soldiers. All the others remained in the city.

When the emperor received the King of Fez's letter, he fell into deep anguish and concern. As secretly as he could he sent for his doctors and the Duke of Macedonia and Hippolytus. He showed them the King of Fez's letter, and begged them to ride there quickly. The Duke of Macedonia and Hippolytus left the imperial palace without a word to anyone, and went off with the doctors, for the emperor feared that if the princess heard of it she would faint and it could be very dangerous for her.

When the Duke of Macedonia and Hippolytus, along with the doctors, were half a day's journey from Constantinople, they met Tirant on the road. They dismounted, and the litter was laid on the ground. The Duke of Macedonia went up to Tirant and said:

"Cousin, my lord, how is Your Lordship?"

Tirant answered:

"Cousin, I am most pleased that I have seen you before I died, for my life is ending. I beg you to kiss me, you and Hippolytus, for this will be the last farewell I shall have from you."

The duke and Hippolytus kissed him, crying openly. Then Tirant told them that he commended his soul to them, and that he wished them to hold more love for the princess, his wife, than they did for himself. The duke answered:

"My lord and cousin, is a knight as valiant as Your Lordship growing weak hearted? Have faith in Our Lord, that He, in His mercy, will help you and bring you back to health."

As he was saying these words, Tirant cried out, loudly:

"Jesus, Son of David, have pity on me! Virgin Mary, guardian angel, angel Michael, defend me! Jesus, into Your hands, Lord, I commend my spirit."

And with these words, he delivered up his noble soul, while his beautiful body lay in the arms of the Duke of Macedonia. The tears and wailing were so great from all who were there, that it was a pity to hear them. For Prince Tirant was loved by all.

After they had cried for some time, King Escariano called the King of Sicily, the King of Fez, the Duke of Macedonia, Hippolytus, and some of the others, and they held counsel about what they had to do. They all agreed that King Escariano, along with the others in his company, should accompany Tirant's body to the city, but that they should not go in, for as King Escariano had not yet seen the emperor, it was not the time or place for them to meet. In addition, they decided to embalm Tirant's body, for they had to take it to Brittany.

They departed with Tirant's body from the place where he had died, and made their way toward the city of Constantinople. By the time they arrived it was well into the night. They gathered at the city gate, and King Escariano took his leave of the King of Sicily, the King of Fez, the Duke of Macedonia and Hippolytus, and he returned with his men to the city he had come from, lamenting loudly, for King Escariano loved Tirant deeply. The others placed Tirant's body in a house within the city, where it was embalmed by the doctors.

After they had embalmed it, they dressed it and took it to the main church of the city: Saint Sofia. There a very large and tall cenotaph was prepared for him, covered entirely with brocade, and on the cenotaph was a large bed. There they placed Tirant's body, stretched out on the bed, with his sword at his side.

When the emperor learned that Tirant was dead, he rent his royal garments. Coming down from his imperial seat and lamenting over Tirant's death, he said:

"Today is the day when our scepter is lost, and I see the crown taken from my head and dashed to the ground. Let everyone dress in deep black mourning, let all the bells ring at once, and let everyone wail over this loss, which is so terrible that my voice is scarcely able to speak of it."

The emperor spent the greater part of the night lamenting, and when day came he went to the church to pay him honor, and to make a large tomb for him with the funeral rites that are normally given to great lords. When the princess saw everyone crying she was very surprised. She wondered what the people in the palace and her maidens were crying about. She thought her father, the emperor, might have died, and she got up quickly, dressed in her chemise, and looked out the window. She saw the Duke of Macedonia, crying and tearing at his hair, and Hippolytus and many others clawing at their faces, and hitting their heads against the walls.

"By the one God," said the princess, "I beg you to tell me the truth. What is the cause of all this uproar and sadness?"

The Widow of Montsant said:

"My lady, it is inevitable that you will hear of it at any moment. Tirant has passed from this life to the other. At midnight they took him to the church to give him a holy funeral as he deserves. The emperor is there, crying and bemoaning his death, and is inconsolable."

The princess was left numb: She did not cry, she could not speak. She could only moan softly and sigh, and after a moment she said:

"Give me the clothes my father had made for my wedding."

They were quickly brought. When she had them on, the Widow of Montsant said:

"But my lady! At the death of such an admirable knight who died in the service of His Majesty, the emperor, and of yours, are you going to dress that way, as if you were going to your wedding? Everyone else is dressed in mourning and sadness, because they cannot stop crying, and Your Highness, who should be the saddest and for whom it should mean the most, has dressed yourself in an unheard-of way."

"Don't worry yourself, Widow," said the princess. "You will know the meaning of this when it is time."

When she had dressed, the sad lady of the imperial palace came down with all the ladies and maidens, and with steps hastened by the anguish she felt, she went to the church where Tirant's body lay. She stepped to the top of the great cenotaph, and when she saw Tirant's body she felt her heart would break, and yet passion lifted her spirit and she went over to his bed with warm tears flowing from her eyes, and threw herself upon Tirant's body. The suffering woman kissed his cold body. Everyone who heard her weep shed great tears of grief. Then she said:

"I want to go looking for the soul of the one who was my Tirant in the blessed places where it rests. And I do so want to keep you company in death since in life, where I loved you so much, I have not been able to serve you. Oh, you ladies and maidens, do not cry! Save your tears for a more opportune time. It's enough for me to cry and lament, since these are my sorrows."

When she had said these words, she fell upon the body in a faint. She was quickly lifted away from the body, and the doctors helped her regain consciousness. When she had recovered her senses, the lady again threw herself upon the body, kissing Tirant's cold mouth.

She tore at her hair and clothing, along with the skin of her breasts and her face, this sad lady, more grievous than any other. Stretched out on his body, she kissed his cold mouth, mixing her warm tears with Tirant's cold ones. She wanted to talk, but could not, and she knew no words sad enough to express her grief. With trembling hands she opened Tirant's eyes which she kissed first with her mouth, and then filled with all the tears flowing from her own eyes. And it seemed as though Tirant, while dead, was crying for the grief of the living Carmesina. And she was crying blood, for she had exhausted all her tears. So she cried over his body— she who had lost everything to him who lost his life for her— and with words that would be enough to break precious stones, diamonds and steel itself, she cried grievously:

"Don't think, my soul, that I will keep you from Tirant for long. I will give burial to your body and to mine. The dead bodies will be embraced in one grave, and together we will share the same glory in heaven."

The emperor, distressed by his daughter's words, said:

"My daughter's sorrow and tears will never end. My good knights, pick her up, and take her to my palace, and leave her in her chambers, either with her consent or by force."

And so it was done. Her father, desperate, went with her, saying:

"My daughter, you are the lady of all I possess. Do not go to such an extreme, for your grief is death to me. Stop your crying and put on a happy face for the people to see."

The princess answered:

"Oh emperor, my lord, life-giver of this miserable daughter! Your Majesty truly wants to console my grief! Oh, poor me, I cannot hold back my tears!"

When the poor father saw his daughter and the other women crying, he could not bear to remain in her chambers, and with his terrible anguish he left. Then the princess sat on the bed and said:

"Come, my faithful maidens, and help me undress, for there will be time enough to cry."

And she prepared her body in the most comely way she could, and said:

"I am the infanta who hoped to rule over the entire empire of Greece. It is my duty to move everyone here to grief and compassion for the death of the virtuous and blessed knight, Tirant lo Blanc. Oh, my Tirant, out of grief for your death let our right hands wound our breasts and tear at our faces so that our misery will be so much greater, for you were our shield and the shield of the whole empire. Oh sword of virtue, great was the sorrow that was prepared for us! And don't think, Tirant, that I have wiped you from my memory: As long as I am alive I will weep for your death. Now, my dear maidens, help me to cry this short time that is left of my life, for I cannot remain with you long."

The crying and wailing was so great that it made the entire city resound. When they saw the princess nearly more dead than alive, they cursed fortune which had brought them such anguish. The doctors came and said she had all the signs of a dying woman: She felt such grief for Tirant's death that blood was coming from her mouth.

The grieving empress came into the chamber, knowing that her daughter was not well. When she saw her in that state she suffered such a shock that she could not speak. When she had recovered, she said:

"Oh, my daughter! Is this the joy and happiness I hoped to have from you? Is this the wedding your father and I and all the people hoped to be consoled by? Everywhere I turn I see nothing but grief and sorrow!

"I see the poor emperor, lying on the floor; I see the ladies and maidens, their hair unkempt, their skin covered with blood, their breasts uncovered and scratched, crying throughout the palace, revealing their grief to everyone. I see the knights and grandees, all in mourning, all lamenting, twisting their hands, tearing the hair from their head. What a bitter day, so filled with sadness! I see all the orders of friars coming with pain in their voices, and not one of them can sing. Tell me, what kind of celebration is this for everyone to run from it? Scarcely anyone can talk without a grieving face. Oh, sad is the mother who bears such a daughter! I beg you, my daughter, be happy and put an end to all this sadness. This way you will give consolation to your old and grieving father, and your sad, unfortunate mother who has raised you so delicately."

And she could say no more, such was the grief that held her.

"How can Your Excellency tell me, my lady, to find consolation and rejoice if I have lost such a knight who was my husband and lord, and had no equal in the world? Have my protector, my father and lord, come so that he can see my death and my end, and so that part of his daughter will be left for him."

When the sad father was there, she begged him kindly to sit at one side and the empress at the other. With herself between them, she said these words:

"I beg you all to have my father confessor come quickly."

When he was there the princess told him:

"Father, I wish to make a general confession in the presence of all who are here."

Then the confessor had her make a general confession, and afterward he absolved her of all punishment and guilt. When absolution had been granted the princess asked that the precious body of Jesus Christ be brought to her, and with great devotion and contrition she received it. And all those in the chamber were astonished at the great constancy and firmness of spirit the princess had, and at the many prayers she said before the Corpus. There was no heart of steel in the world who, hearing her words, would not burst into tears.

When the princess had given restitution to her soul she had the emperor's secretary come, and turning to her father, she said:

"Father and lord, if it please Your Majesty, I would like to dispose of my possessions and my soul."

The emperor answered:

"My daughter, I give you my leave to do whatever pleases you. For if I lose you I lose my life and all good things on this earth."

The princess thanked him, and turning to the secretary, she dictated her will:

"I make, as executors of my will, Diafebus, Duke of Macedonia and Stephanie, his wife. And I beg and command them to place my body together with Tirant's in the place he will be buried. For, as we were not able to remain together in life, at least in death our bodies will be united until the end of the world.

"In addition, all my clothing and jewelry shall be sold, and the proceeds will be given to my maidens for their weddings. As for all the other rights I have in the Greek Empire, I make the empress, my mother, the successor in my place."

When the princess had put her possessions and her soul in order, she said farewell to her father, the emperor, kissing his hands and his mouth again and again, and she did the same to her mother, the empress, asking their forgiveness and their blessing with great humility.

"Oh unfortunate and miserable me!" said the princess. "I see the emperor more dead than alive because of me. On the one hand the death of Tirant pulls me, and on the other my father's death pulls me: Each of them is winning me over."

Her miserable father, his face wet with tears, saw that his daughter was ready to die and could barely speak. He heard her say such painful words, and saw all the wailing that was going on in the chamber and throughout the palace. He felt greatly disturbed and was beside himself. He tried to get up from the bed to go out, but he fell to the ground, senseless. They picked him up, unconscious, and put him on a bed in another chamber, and there he ended his days before his daughter, the princess.

Because of the emperor's death there was loud wailing, and the news reached the empress and the princess. The empress ran as quickly as she could, but the emperor had already passed from this life. Imagine how the poor lady must have felt: to see her husband, her daughter, and her son-in-law all dead! And don't ask me what grief there was in the palace. So much tribulation—all in one day!

The princess said:

"Help me sit down on my bed, and you will hear my words. You all know that with the death of the emperor, my father, I am the successor to the Greek Empire. And so my knights, I command you, by the allegiance you owe to His Majesty, the emperor, and now to me, to bring my father's and Tirant's body here to me."

And they had to do it. The emperor was put on the right, and Tirant on the left, while she was in between them. She kissed her father many times, and Tirant many times more, and she cried in a miserable voice:

"Look, knights, you who suffer from love. Take note of me and see if I am not fortunate! On one side I have an emperor, and on the other the best knight in the world. Look and see if I should not go into the next world happy, for I will have such good company. Come to me, my loyal sisters and companions, and kiss me, one by one. Then you will feel a part of my misery."

And they did. First came the Queen of Ethiopia, then the Queen of Fez, then the Duchess of Macedonia, and then all her other maidens and her mother's maidens. They kissed her hand and her mouth, and they sadly bade the princess farewell, shedding many tears. She had them bring her the cross, and looking at it steadfastly, she said these words with great devotion:

"Receive the soul of Your servant, oh Lord, and free me from infernal bonds and pains. May I feel, oh Lord, the blessed rest of heaven and of eternal light, and may I deserve to have, among Your chosen saints, everlasting life and glory. Oh God, full of pure love and goodness. You Who know only how to forgive. Grant me, oh Lord, that my soul, drawn apart and stripped of earthly vices, may be placed in the company of those redeemed by You. I give myself to God Who created me."

Saying these words, the princess gave up her spirit to her creator.

CHAPTER XV - AFTERMATH

The destruction of the very last of the lineage of the royal house of Greece was complete. After going through so much past misery with all its trials and hardships, they would have obtained a happy peace—if fortune had allowed it. And so, no one should depend on worldly prosperity, for it fails when it is most unexpected.

When the princess had passed on from this life, the wailing and crying in the palace was so loud that it echoed throughout the entire city. And the heartache felt for Tirant and the emperor was renewed and redoubled. The poor empress fell into such a deep faint that the doctors could not revive her, and Hippolytus beat his head and face, believing that she was dead. Finally, with all the remedies they tried, after more than an hour, she seemed to awaken slightly. Hippolytus remained steadfast at her side in great anguish, rubbing her wrists and wetting her face with rose water. When she regained consciousness, they picked her up in their arms and carried her to her chamber, putting her on a bed.

Hippolytus was always at her side, comforting her, and kissing her often to bring to mind the love they had continually had for each other. The empress loved him more than her daughter and herself because of the great kindness and genteelness she had found in Hippolytus who had always obeyed her every wish. And don't think that at that moment Hippolytus was feeling great pain, for as soon as Tirant was dead he realized that he would be emperor, especially after the death of the emperor and his daughter, for he had great confidence in the love the empress had for him. Putting aside all shame, she would take him as her husband.

After the empress had spoken a short while with Hippolytus, and their pain had been somewhat alleviated with kisses, she said to him:

"My son and my lord, I beg you, as lord here, to order funerals held for the emperor, my daughter, and Tirant, so that afterward your desire and mine can be carried out."

When Hippolytus heard such loving words he kissed her hand and her mouth, and said he would do everything Her Majesty commanded. Hippolytus went to the princess's chamber where the three bodies were lying, and on behalf of the empress he ordered them to take Tirant to his cenotaph in the church immediately. And it was quickly done.

Then he ordered the surgeons to embalm the bodies of the emperor and the princess. Hippolytus had another cenotaph put up in the Church of Saint Sofia, much more beautiful and higher than Tirant's, and he had the emperor's body brought to the cenotaph. He had the princess put in Tirant's bed, on his right hand side.

He ordered a proclamation read throughout the city that all those who wished to dress in mourning should go to a certain house in the city, and there mourning cloth would be given to men as well as to women. In the space of one day everyone in the palace and the city, and all the foreigners were dressed in mourning. In addition, Hippolytus decreed that all the clergy—friars, chaplains and nuns—within two days journey from Constantinople should come to participate in the funerals of the dead, and one thousand two hundred were counted.

They decided that the burial should take place two weeks after the emperor's death, and all the barons of Greece were summoned, so that they could be present for the emperor's funeral rites. Then he sent a message to King Escariano on behalf of himself and the empress, inviting him to come and honor the burial of the emperor and his daughter, and his dear friend and brother Tirant. For, since he had not been able to honor their wedding he would be able to honor his burial. King Escariano sent word to him that he would do so, but that he had hoped to enter Constantinople with happier news. And he left for Constantinople with one hundred knights.

While the people were arriving, Hippolytus had the King of Sicily, the King of Fez, the Duke of Macedonia, the Marquis of Lizana, and the Viscount of Branches and some others gather in a chamber. Then he said to them:

"My lords and brothers, Your Lordships are not unaware of the great danger that has befallen us with the death of our father and lord, Tirant. He expected to be emperor, and he would have ennobled and enriched all those of our lineage. Now that there is no hope of that, we must take counsel about what should be done. Your Lordships realize that the entire empire is in the empress's power. Although she is advanced in years, some great lord will be very pleased to marry her, and he will find it very agreeable to be emperor. After her death, he will be the ruler, and he may treat foreigners (which is what we are) badly. I am of the opinion that we should make one of us emperor, and all of us should help him; and the one who is elected will enrich the others very well. Now, I beg you, let each of you give your opinion."

Then the King of Sicily said he felt it was a good idea that one of them should be made emperor, and that they should select whoever was willing. The King of Fez spoke, because he was the eldest of their line, and he said:

"My lords and brothers, it seems to me good advice that one of us should be chosen emperor. But it is my opinion that we should follow the dictates of Tirant's will, then the princess's, and with these two wills we shall see who among us is indicated."

Everyone agreed with what the King of Fez had said. They sent for the secretaries of Tirant and the emperor, and had the wills read. When they had read them, they made the secretaries leave the room, and the Duke of Macedonia spoke:

"My lords and brothers, as I see it, our selection is very clear and cannot be disputed. I see that our good relative and lord leaves as recipient of all the rights he has earned in the Greek Empire, Hippolytus here. Further, I see that the princess has bestowed the entire empire on her mother.

"So from what I see there is no other action we can take, considering the friendship we all know Hippolytus has with the empress, than for him to take her as his wife. In that way he will become emperor, and he will keep each of us in our station, for he is our relative."

Then the Marquis of Lizana spoke:

"Lords, I find the Duke of Macedonia's advice to be good, and praise it, for we all have wives, and furthermore it is Tirant's command."

All the rest praised him and agreed that Hippolytus should be chosen emperor and husband of the empress. When Hippolytus saw the gentility of his relatives, he praised them, and gave them many thanks for their great love. And he made a vow before God and Our Lady that if God granted that he become emperor, he would repay them in such a way that they would all be very happy. And they decided that after the funeral rites were held for the dead, they would raise him to the status of emperor, and would hold the wedding for him and the empress.

Tirant's relatives agreed, and the following night King Escariano entered Constantinople, dressed in mourning, with all his men. He was received with great honor by Hippolytus, and by his wife, the queen, who was very happy to see him. Hippolytus placed him in the emperor's palace, in a beautiful apartment. The King of Sicily, the King of Fez, the Duke of Macedonia, and many other knights came to see him, and a great celebration was held.

After this, King Escariano took his leave of them, and taking the queen, his wife, by the hand, he went with Hippolytus to pay honor to the empress. When they were in her chamber, King Escariano bowed before the empress, and she warmly embraced him. She took him by the hand, and had him sit at her side. Then King Escariano said:

"I left my land in order to help Tirant lo Blanc recover the empire, and the queen, my wife, came only to attend the wedding of my brother Tirant and the virtuous princess. Their deaths have made me both sad and angry. Now that they are gone, I am ready to serve you for the rest of my life."

The empress hesitated, and then said softly:

"It is great glory for me that so magnanimous a king should say such words to me. I thank you very much for coming, and even more for helping us put an end to this conquest. But with it I have lost three of the best people in the world, and because of this the rest of my life will be filled with sadness."

The empress could speak no more, and tears sprang from her eyes. King Escariano also began to cry.

That night Hippolytus went to sleep with the empress, and he told her about his conversation with his relatives, and what they had all decided:

"That I should take you as my wife. My lady, I know that I am not worthy of being your husband, or even your servant. But I trust in Your Highness' love and virtue, and I hope that you will accept me as Your Majesty's captive. And trust me, my lady, to do well. I will be so obedient to you that you can command me more than ever before, for I never wanted anything but to serve you."

The empress answered:

"Hippolytus, my son, you know how much I love you, and I will be very pleased if you will take me as your wife. But remember, my son and lord, even though I'm old you will never find anyone who loves you as much as I do."

Then Hippolytus knelt to kiss her hands and feet, but she lifted him up and embraced him and kissed him. And they spent that delicious night with little thought about those who were lying on the cenotaphs for burial.

In the morning, before Phoebus had spread its shiny rays over the earth, the knight got up, full of new joy, for that night Hippolytus had entertained his lady very well. He arranged everything that was necessary for the burial.

On the appointed day all the barons and knights who were invited went to the city of Constantinople. On the first day they buried the emperor with the most beautiful sacramental lights ever given to a prince. To exalt the occasion there were many kings, dukes, counts and marquis, and many noble knights. All the people from the city were there, lamenting over their good lord, and the clergy performed the ceremony, singing so that all were weeping. And on that day the emperor's body solely was buried. The second day was reserved for the princess's burial, and the third for Tirant's.

There was so much wailing and lamenting during those three days that no one felt like crying for the rest of the year. When the funeral rites for the emperor were over, the emperor's body was placed in a beautiful tomb which the emperor had ordered made some time before. The bodies of Tirant and the princess were placed in a wooden coffin, for they had to be taken to Brittany.

When this was done, the King of Sicily, the King of Fez, and the Duke of Macedonia went to King Escariano and told him all about the council they had held with Tirant's relatives, and how they had decided to raise Hippolytus to the status of emperor. King Escariano said:

"I am very pleased by your decision. I think Hippolytus is a good and virtuous knight, and he deserves to be emperor."

Then they asked him to go with them and carry the news to the empress, and he was glad to do so. The three kings left with the Duke of Macedonia, and it was the noblest embassy that had ever been made to a man or a woman. They entered the empress's chamber, and she welcomed them with great honor. She took the hand of King Escariano and the King of Sicily, and they sat down in the imperial throne room, with the empress between the two kings. They had agreed that King Escariano should explain their mission, and he began:

"As we deeply appreciate the honor of your illustrious person, we hope it will be agreeable to you to take a husband. And we beg Your Majesty not to be angry at what I am going to tell you. Your Majesty knows what good condition the Greek Empire is in because of that singular knight, Tirant. You know the rights that His Majesty, the emperor, granted to him, and you know that he left those rights to his nephew, Hippolytus. And so we beg and advise Your Majesty to take Hippolytus as your husband and lord. He is such a virtuous knight that Your Majesty will be greatly loved and revered by him, and he is such a knight that he will be able to rule and defend the empire, which has been reconquered through so much effort."

The empress then said very graciously:

"Great lords, I realize that you are my brothers, and I trust that you would never advise me to do anything that would be harmful to me or my honor. So I freely place myself in Your Lordships' hands to deal with me and my empire as though it were your own."

They all bowed deeply to the empress and gave her many thanks. And they left, very satisfied with the empress' reply. The three kings went with the Duke of Macedonia to Hippolytus' chamber, and he received them very warmly. They told him about the entire conversation they had had with the empress, and how she had agreed to do everything they wanted.

Hippolytus knelt, and thanked them, and he was very happy. They quickly took him to the empress's chamber, and then had the bishop come from the city and marry them. In attendance were the Queen of Ethiopia, the Queen of Fez, the Duchess of Macedonia, and all the ladies of the court. They were all very pleased because of all the hard times they had had, and which they were afraid would continue.

The news that the empress had married Hippolytus ran through the city, and everyone was glad. They all gave thanks to God for giving them such a good lord. Everyone in the city liked Hippolytus because in times of need he had been their captain, and he had treated them very well.

Soon afterward the King of Sicily departed, and the emperor entreated the King of Fez and the Viscount of Branches to carry the bodies of Tirant and the princess to Brittany. They said they would do it very willingly out of love for His Majesty and Tirant. The emperor commanded the admiral to put forty galleys in order so they would go in his honor. And they were quickly armed and put in order.

The emperor had ordered a very beautiful wooden coffin made, all covered with gold, and decorated so that it looked like the sepulcher of a great lord. And he had the bodies of Tirant and the princess placed inside, all dressed in brocade, with their faces uncovered so that they seemed to be sleeping.

He had the coffin put on board a galley with all of Tirant's weapons and flags on it so that they could be placed upon the sepulcher where Tirant would lie, to serve as a perpetual memorial. And the emperor gave the King of Fez two hundred thousand ducats so that the sepulcher of Tirant and the princess could be made in Brittany in accord with their great merit. When everything was in order the King of Fez and the Queen set sail, and they had such good weather that in a few short days they reached Brittany very safely.

    The King of Fez, the queen, and the Viscount of Branches, along with many noblemen and knights, made port in a city called Nantes, and here they were well received and entertained by the Duke of Brittany, and the Duchess. They took the coffin with Tirant and the princess, and with a great procession of many clerics, friars and monks they carried it to the high church of the city, and it was placed in a tomb held up by four lions. This tomb was worked in a very clear alabaster, and molded in fine gold were these words:

> The knight who in arms was phoenix
> And the lady most beautiful of all,
> Lie dead in this tomb,
> While their living fame resounds throughout the world:
> Tirant lo Blanc and noble Carmesina.

And above the tomb these three verses were sculpted in gold:

> Cruel love that united them in life
> And has taken their life in great pain,
> After their death, encloses them in the sepulcher.

    Words could not express the mourning that took place in Brittany. There was great mourning over his death by the Duke of Brittany and the Duchess and all Tirant's relatives when they learned of the actions of everlasting renown he had performed and the great prosperity he had achieved. The King of Fez had large amounts of money given in charity for the souls of Tirant and the princess. He spent the two thousand ducats the emperor had given him very well. And he decided to return to his homeland, for he had stayed in Brittany six months to carry out everything the emperor had encharged to him.

    The King and Queen of Fez took their leave of the duke and duchess and all the relatives who were very sad to see them leave. And the Viscount of Branches also took his leave of everyone. They embarked on the galleys and set their course toward the lands of the King of Fez. Our Heavenly Father gave them such good weather that in a few days they reached the port of Tangier. And the King of Fez and the Queen disembarked with all their people. The Viscount of Branches returned to Constantinople with the forty galleys, and was well received by the emperor who was greatly desirous of knowing what had happened in Brittany.

The Viscount of Branches very discreetly told the emperor about everything that had been done, just as it had been directed by his majesty. The emperor was highly pleased, and immediately bought the county of Benaixi, which belonged to the princess, for three hundred thousand ducats, and gave it to the Viscount of Branches as a reward for his works, Then he gave a large inheritance to all those who had married servants of the empress and the princess so that they could live well and honorably, each according to his station, and all were very happy. Then he arranged marriages for all his other knights.

Fortune favored Emperor Hippolytus so much, and he was such a virtuous knight that he greatly increased the Empire of Greece, and he added to it many provinces that he conquered, and due to his great diligence he amassed a very large treasure. He was deeply loved and feared by his subjects and also by the neighboring lords who lived near the empire.

A few days after he was made emperor he had the Moorish sultan and the Grand Turk released from prison, along with all the other kings and lords who had been imprisoned with them. They made peace and a truce for one hundred one years, and they were so content that they said they would come to his aid against the entire world. Afterward the emperor had them go to Turkey aboard two galleys.

This Emperor Hippolytus had a long life. But after the death of her daughter, the empress lived only three years. After a short time the emperor took another wife, who was the daughter of the King of England. This empress was extremely beautiful, humble, and a very virtuous and devout Christian. The genteel lady bore Emperor Hippolytus three sons and two daughters, and the sons were exceptional and valiant knights. The eldest son was named Hippolytus, like his father, and he lived his entire life a magnanimous man and performed singular acts of chivalry which this book does not relate, but defers to the books that were written about him. But the emperor, his father, left all his relatives and servants well provided for before he died.

And when the emperor and the empress passed from this life they were very old. They both died on the same day, and were placed in a very luxurious tomb which the emperor had ordered made. And you may be sure that because of their excellent rule and their good and virtuous life they are in the glory of paradise.

JOANOT MARTORELL

DEO GRATIAS

Here ends the book of the valiant and singular knight, Tirant lo Blanc, Prince and Caesar of the Greek Empire of Constantinople, which was translated from English into the Portuguese language, and afterward into the Valencian tongue by the magnificent and virtuous knight, Johanot Martorell who, because of his death, was able to finish the translation of only the first three parts. The fourth part, which is the end of the book, was translated at the behest of the noble Isabel de Loris by the magnificent knight Marti Johan d' Galba. If any defect should be found he wishes it to be attributed to his ignorance, and may Our Lord Jesus Christ, in His great goodness, grant him the glory of paradise as a reward for his works. And he protests that if he has put some things in this book that are not Catholic, he retracts them and submits them to the correction of the Holy Catholic Church.

This work was printed in the city of Valencia, the 20th day of the month of November in the year of the Birth of Our Lord Jesus Christ 1490.

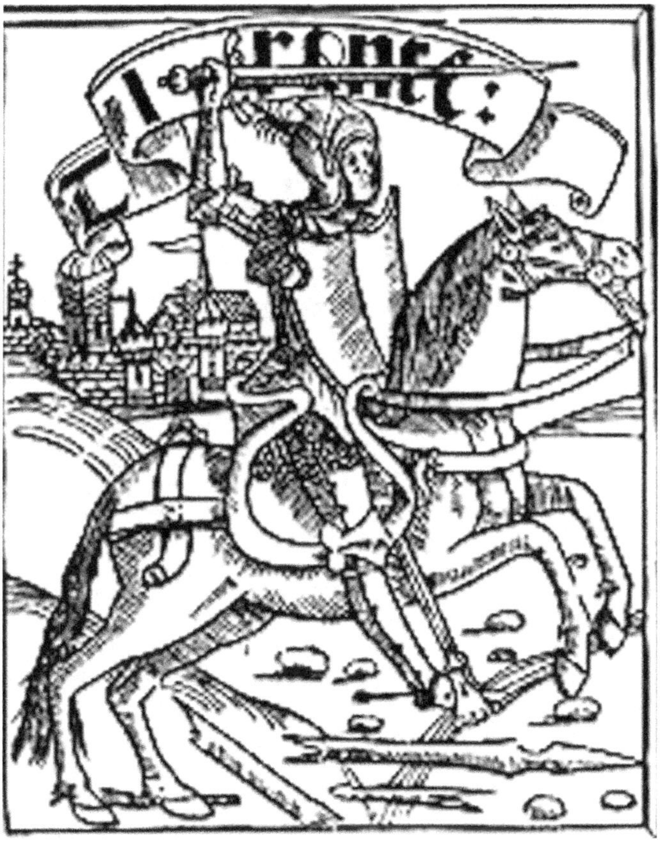

Other books by Robert S. Rudder:

Magic Realism in Cervantes (Translation of work by Arturo Serrano Plaja): Univ. of California Pr.

The Life of Lazarillo de Tormes (Edition and translation): Frederick Ungar Publishing Co.

The Orgy (Edition and translation of Latin American drama): Univ. of California Pr.

The Literature of Spain in English Translation: a Bibliography: Frederick Ungar Publishing Co.

City of Kings (Translation of work by Rosario Castellanos): Latin American Literary Review Pr.

Nazarin (Translation of work by Benito Pérez Galdós): Latin American Literary Review Pr.

The Medicine Man (Translation of work by Francisco Rojas González): Latin American Literary Review Pr.

Solitaire of Love (Translation of work by Cristina Peri Rossi): Duke University Pr.

The Forbidden (Translation of work by Benito Pérez Galdós): Cambridge Scholars Pub.

The Paradox of Saint Teresa of Ávila: A Study in Will and Humility: Edwin Mellen Pr.

Intimate Disasters (Translation of work by Cristina Peri Rossi): Latin American Literary Review Pr.: (Forthcoming).

Ebooks by Robert S. Rudder:

The Life of Lazarillo de Tormes (Edition and translation).

Tales of the White Knight: Tirant lo Blanc (Edition and translation of work by Joanot Martorell).

La Celestina (Edition in Spanish, with glossary and notes).

Afternoon of the Dinosaur (Translation of work by Cristina Peri Rossi).

The Celestina (Annotated English translation of work by Fernando de Rojas).

A Dozen Orgies: Latin American Plays of the Twentieth Century (Anthology of one-act dramas in English translation).

Printed in Great Britain
by Amazon